To Dream of the Dead

To Dream of the Dead

Phil Rickman

Quercus

First published in Great Britain in 2008 by

Quercus
21 Bloomsbury Square
London
WC1A 2NS

A CIP catalogue record for this book is available
from the British Library

ISBN 978 1 84724 578 6 (HB)
ISBN 978 1 84724 579 3 (TPB)

10 9 8 7 6 5 4 3 2 1

Printed and bound in Great Britain by
Clays Ltd, St Ives plc.

www.getalife/welshborder.co.uk

The relocation bible

LEDWARDINE

Once known as The Village in the Orchard, this community may have begun as simply that. The old centre of the village is still partly enclosed by the remains of an apple orchard dating back at least to medieval times, as do some of its black and white timber-framed houses. Earlier settlement is suggested by recent archaeological discoveries at the foot of Cole Hill, whose Iron Age fortifications are a reminder of a turbulent past. Today, Ledwardine (Jewel of The New Cotswolds – *Daily Telegraph*) is serene and inviting. The cobbled village square, with its small, open market-hall supported by oak pillars, is enlivened by a variety of retail outlets, including bookshop, gallery and delicatessen, as well as the 15th century Black Swan Inn, noted for its fine food.

FACILITIES: the village, although largely self-sufficient, is a mere ten-minute drive from the nearest town of Leominster and no more than twenty-five minutes from the progressive cathedral city of Hereford, now undergoing extensive commercial renewal. Several highly reputable private schools are within easy reach.

STAR-RATING **** and rising!

WE SAY: buy now, while prices are competitive and this area is still relatively obscure.

WEDNESDAY

Betty said she prayed today
For the sky to blow away

Nick Drake
'River Man'

1

The Grotto

WATCHING THE WOODEN horses bobbing on their golden carousel, Bliss had become aware of darkness like a hole behind the spinning lights.

High Town on a damp midwinter evening, fogged faces around the fast-food outlets. Bliss was waving cheerfully to his kids on the painted horses. Doing the dad thing. His kids not exactly waving back, just minimally hingeing their fingers, sarcastic little sods.

Kirsty's kids. Hereford kids, somehow fathered by Francis Bliss from Knowsley, Merseyside. His kids had Hereford accents. His kids' little mates thought he talked weird, laughing at him behind their hands, trying to imitate him, this joke Scouser.

Joke Scouser in Hereford. On two or three Wednesday evenings before Christmas – a tradition now in the city – shops would open until nine p.m. Bliss and Kirsty and the kids had been three years running; must be a tradition for them, too.

So why were the festive lights ice-blue? Why no carol singers, no buskers, no exotic folkies in hairy blankets playing 'Silent Night' on the Andean pipes?

Maybe the council's Ethnic Advisory Directorate had advised against, in deference to Hereford's handful of Muslims.

'They're coming round again,' Kirsty said. 'Wave.'

Bliss waved at the carousel. It was like a birthday cake at a frigging funeral tea. Beyond it, too many shopfronts dulled by low-powered security lighting. Car-friendly superstores coining it on the perimeter while the old town-centre family firms starved to death. Now the council was creating this massive new retail mall on the northern fringe, swallowing the old cattle market, answering no obvious need except to turn Old Hereford into something indistinguishable from the rest of the shit cities in landfill Britain.

Watching the random seepage of shoppers – going nowhere, buying not much – Bliss felt lonely. Kirsty had moved away from the carousel, gloved hands turning up the collar of her new sheepskin jacket.

'All right, Frank, what's the matter with you?'

He sighed, never able to tell her just how much he hated that. Growing up, it was always Frannie, Francis on Sundays, but Kirsty had to call him *Frank*.

'I don't understand you any more,' Kirsty said. '*One night* for me and the children. Just one night …'

'*For the children*?' Bliss staring at his wife. '*Kairsty*, they're only doing it for our sake. They'd rather be at home, plugged into their frigging computers.'

'Yes,' Kirsty said grimly. 'You would say that, wouldn't you?'

'Don't think it gives me any pleasure.'

'What *does* give you pleasure, Frank?'

Kirsty turning away – not an answer she could face. Bliss breathing in hard and shutting his eyes, the carousel crooning through its speakers about letting it snow, when it so obviously wasn't going to snow, not tonight and definitely not for Christmas; what it was going to do was rain and rain, and nobody ever sang let it frigging rain.

Bliss spun round instinctively at the sound of a ricocheting tin.

Lager can. It rolled out in front of the Ann Summers store, which seemed to be closed. It had bounced off a bloke wearing an ape suit and an ape mask and a sandwich board pleading DON'T LET DRINK MAKE A MONKEY OUT OF YOU.

Three young lads, early teens, were jetting fizzy beer at the feller in the ape suit. Two community support officers moseying over, a young woman and a stocky man with a delta of cheek veins.

'Fuck me,' one of the kids said. 'Who sent for the traffic warden?'

'… your language, boy.' The senior plastic plod visibly clenching up – you had to feel sorry for them. 'How old are you?'

The boy went right up to him, thin head on an exaggerated tilt, teeth like a shark's, embryo of a moustache.

'And how old are *you*, grandad?'

'You throw that tin?'

'What you gonner do, run me over with your Zimmer, is it?'

Bliss purred like a cat, deep in his throat, Kirsty muttering, 'You're off duty, Frank.'

The three kids had formed a rough semicircle now, in front of a blacked-out shopfront with a poster on the door: SAVE THE SERPENT.

'You can't arrest us,' another of them said to the support guy. 'You got no powers of arrest. You can't fucking touch us, ole man, you're just—'

'However …' In this crazy blaze of … well, it might not be actual pleasure but it was certainly relief, Bliss had found himself at the centre of the action '… *I* can.'

As if he was frigging Spiderman just landed from the roof. Or a magician, his ID appearing like the ace of spades in his left hand. He could hear Kirsty backing off, heels clacking like a skidding horse.

'What's more …' Committed now, Bliss advanced on the biggest kid, the old accent kicking in like nicotine '… I *also* happen to have a key to the notoriously vomit-stained cell we fascist cops like to call Santa's Grotto.'

Bliss smiling fondly at the kid, and the kid sneering but saying nothing.

'Fancy a few hours in the Grotto, do we, sonny? Sniffing icky sicky, while we wait for our old fellers to drag their arses out the pub and come and fetch us? Or maybe they won't bother till morning. *I* wouldn't.'

A movement then, from one of the others in the shadow of a darkened doorway – hand dipping into a pocket down his leg. *Knife?*

Jesus … careful.

Kids. Frigging little scallies. Grown men were easier these days, these three too young and maybe too pissed to understand that sticking a cop bought you zero sanctuary.

Difficult. Bliss didn't move, snatching a quick glance at the plastic plod who'd got his arms spread like a goalie, which meant that if knifeboy went for him now the old feller would catch it full in the chest. Mother of God, who trained these buggers?

The hand came out of the pocket, the fear-switch in Bliss's trip-box giving a little tremble. Best to stay friendly.

'Up to you, son. B-and-B in the grotto, is it?'

Boy's hand still in shadow. Instant of crackling tension. Wafting stench of hot meat from a fast-food van.

Nah. Empty.

Pretty sure. Most likely the pocket was empty, too. This was still Hereford. Just. Feed him a get-out.

'Yeh, thought not. Now piss off home, yer gobby little twats.'

Watching them go, one looking back, about to raise a finger, and Bliss taking a step towards him—

'You do that again, sunshine, and I will frigging *burst* you!'

—as the mobile started shuddering silently in his hip pocket and the carousel invited them all to have a merry little Christmas.

'Good of you, sir,' the community-support woman said. 'It's, um, DI Bliss, isn't it?'

'No way,' Bliss said. 'Not here, luv. Got enough paperwork on me desk.'

Realising he was sweating, and it wasn't warm sweat. This sharp-end stuff … strictly for the baby bobbies and the rugby boys. Ten years out of uniform, you wondered how anybody over twenty-five could keep this up, night after night.

He dragged out his still-quivering phone, flipped it open, feeling not that bad now, all the same, and not considering the possible consequences until he looked up and saw those familiar female features gargoyling in the swirl of light from the carousel and remembered that he wasn't here on his own.

'You *bastard.*'

Gloved hands curling into claws.

'Kirsty, tell me what else I—'

'You *swore* to me you'd left that bloody thing at home.'

Bliss squeezed the phone tight.

'Never gonner change, are you, Frank?'

Kirsty's face glowing white-gold as the little screen printed out *KAREN*. Bliss slammed the phone to an ear.

'Karen.'

'Thought you'd want to know about this, boss. Where exactly are you?'

'Pricing vibrators in Ann Summers.' Bliss was feeling totally manic now. 'Complete waste of money nowadays, Karen, what's a mobile for? Pop it in, get yer boyfriend to give you a ring. Magic.'

Stepping blindly into the extreme danger zone; no way he could share that one with Kirsty.

Like, indirectly, he just had.

'You could be there in a few minutes, then,' Karen said.

Bliss looked up at the clock on the market hall. Eight minutes to nine.

'You shit, Frank!'

'Kirst—'

'You stupid, thoughtless, irresponsible piece of *shit*! Suppose one of them youths'd had a knife? Or even a gun, for Christ's sake? *What about your children?*'

'Jesus, Kirsty, it's not frigging Birmingham!'

Kirsty spinning away in blind fury, Karen saying, 'Um, if you've got a domestic issue there, boss, I can probably reach Superintendent Howe—'

'*Acting* Superintendent.' Bliss saw the carousel stopping, his kids getting down. 'Let's not make it any worse. What is this, exactly? Go on, tell me.'

'It's a murder, boss.'

'We're sure about that, are we?'

'You know the Blackfriars Monastery? Widemarsh Street?'

'That's the bit of a ruin behind the old wassname—?'

'Coningsby Hospital. Look, really, if there's a problem …'

'*No* problem, Karen.'

Bliss pulled out his car keys, shrugged in a *sorry, out-of-my-hands* kind of way, and held them out to Kirsty. It was like pushing a ham sandwich into the cage of the lioness with cubs, but they'd need transport.

'Five minutes, then, Karen. You're there now?'

'Yeah.'

'You all right, Karen?'

Something in her voice he hadn't heard before. Other people's, yes, coppers' even, but not hers.

'Yeah, it's just … I mean, you think you've seen it all, don't you?'

'Doc 'n' soc on the way?'

'Sure.'

'Don't bother coming home tonight, Frank.' Kirsty ripping the bunch of keys from Bliss's fingers, the two kids looking pitiful. 'You can go home with *Karen*. Spend the other five per cent of your time with the bitch.'

Bliss covered the bottom of the phone, the plastics looking on; how embarrassing was this?

Karen said, 'Before somebody else tells you, boss, I've contaminated the crime scene. Threw up. Only a bit. I'm sorry.'

'It happens, Karen.'

Not to her, though. Bliss was remembering how once, end of a long, long night, he'd watched Karen Dowell eat a whole bag of chips in the mortuary. With a kebab? Yeh, it *was* a kebab.

Kirsty was walking away, holding Naomi's hand in one of hers, Naomi holding one of Daniel's. Of course, the kids were both a bit too old for that; Kirsty was blatantly making a point, the kids playing along, the way kids did.

It was six days from Christmas.

And yeh, he felt like a complete shit.

But not really *lonely* any more. What could that mean?

'So don't say I never warned you, Frannie,' Karen Dowell said.

2

Moon Sat Up

COMING UP TO seven p.m., it stopped raining and Jane went to get some sense out of the river.

Slopping in her red wellies across the square, where the electric gaslamps were pooled in mist, and down to the bottom of Church Street, glossy and slippery. On the bridge, she looked over the peeling parapet, watching him licking his lips.

'You're not actually going to *do* this …?'

Zipping up her parka to seal in a serious shiver, because she didn't recognise him any more. In this county, the Wye was always the big hitter, lesser rivers staying out of the action. In old pictures of the village, this one was barely visible, a bit-player not often even named. Slow and sullen, this guy, and – yeah – probably resentful.

Tonight, though, for the first time Jane could remember, he was roaring and spitting and slavering at his banks. All those centuries of low-level brooding, and then … hey, climate change, *now* who's a loser?

'Only, I thought we had an understanding,' Jane said, desolate.

Because if this guy came out, there was no way the dig would start before Christmas.

Wasn't fair. All the times she'd leaned over here, talking to him – influenced, naturally, by Nick Drake's mysterious song, where the singer goes to tell the riverman all he can about some kind of plan. Nobody would ever know what the plan was because, within a short time, Nick Drake was dead from an overdose of antidepressants, long years before Jane was born, with only Lol left to carry his lamp.

Above a flank of Cole Hill, the moon was floating in a pale lagoon inside a reef of rain clouds. Jane's hands and face felt cold. She looked away, up towards the haloed village centre and the grey finger of the church steeple. She'd seen the news pictures of Tewkesbury and Upton: canoes on the lanes, homes evacuated. It had never happened here to that extent, *never* – people kept insisting that.

But these were, like, strange days.

The main roads around Letton – always the first place north of Hereford to go – had been closed just after lunch, due to flash floods, and the school buses had been sent for early. Nobody wanted to spend a night in the school, least of all the teaching staff, and there was nothing lost, anyway, in the last week before Christmas.

Fitting each hand inside the opposite cuff, Jane hugged her arms together, leaning over the stonework, sensing the extreme violence down there, everything swollen and turbulent.

Across the bridge, a puddle the size of a duck pond had appeared in the village-hall car park, reflecting strips of flickering mauve light from the low-energy tubes inside. The lights were on for tonight's public meeting – which wasn't going to be as well attended as it ought to be. It had somehow coincided with late-night Christmas shopping in Hereford. No accident, Mum thought, and she was probably right. A devious bastard, Councillor Pierce.

'Janey?'

Lamplight came zigzagging up the bank, bouncing off familiar bottle glasses, and Jane dredged up a grin.

'You been snorkelling or something, Gomer?'

Up he came from the riverside footpath, over the broken-down wooden stile, the old lambing-light swinging from a hand in a sawn-off mitten. Patting at his chest for his ciggy tin. Still quite nimble for his age, which was reassuring.

'What do you reckon, then?' Jane said. 'Seriously.'

'Oh, he'll be out, Janey, sure to.'

'Really?'

'Count on him.'

'When?'

'Tonight, mabbe tomorrow.'

Gomer set the lamp on the wall, its beam pointing down at the water.

His specs were speckled with spray and his white hair looked like broken glass.

'You mean if it rains again?' Jane said.

'No ifs about it, girl.' Gomer mouthed a roll-up. 'Ole moon sat up in his chair, see?'

'Chair?'

Jane peered at him. This was a new one. Gomer brought out his matches.

'Ole moon's on his back, he'll collect the water. Moon's sat up, it d' run off him, see, and down on us. You never yeard that?'

'Erm … no.'

'Yeard it first from my ole mam, sixty year ago, sure t' be. Weather don't change, see.'

'It does, Gomer.'

She must've sounded unusually sober against the snarling of the water because he tilted his head under the flat cap, peering at her.

'Global warmin'? Load of ole wallop, Janey. Anythin' to put the wind up ordinary folk.'

'You seen those pictures of the big ice-cliffs cracking up in the Antarctic?'

Gomer's match went out and he struck another.

'All I'm sayin', girl, science, he en't got all the answers, do he?'

'Yeah, but *something* has to be going on, because this hasn't happened before, has it?' Jane feeling her voice going shrill; it wasn't a joke any more – up in the Midlands people had *died*. 'I mean, have *you* seen this before? Like, here? We ever come this close to a real flood?'

'Not in my time, 'cept for the lanes getting blocked, but what's that in the life of a river?' Gomer looked up towards the square, where the Christmas tree was lit up like a shaky beacon of hope. 'You'll be all right, Janey. En't gonner reach the ole vicarage in a good while.'

'What about your bungalow?'

She didn't think Gomer's bungalow was on the flood plain, but it had to be close. Always said it wasn't where he'd've chosen to live but Minnie had liked the views.

Gomer said he'd brought one of his diggers down. Took real deep water to stop a JCB getting through.

'En't sure about them poor buggers on the hestate, mind.'

Nodding across the bridge at the new houses, one defiantly done out with flashing festive bling – Santa's sleigh, orange and white, in perpetual, rippling motion. The estate had been built a couple of years ago, and most of it was definitely on the flood plain – which, of course, nobody could remember ever being actually flooded, although that wouldn't matter a toss anyway, when the council needed to sanction more houses. Government targets to meet, boxes to tick.

This was possibly the most terrifying thing about growing up: you could no longer rely on adults in authority operating from any foundation of common sense. They just played it for short-term gain, lining their nests and covering their backs. How long, if Gomer was right, before the Christmas Bling house became like some kind of garish riverboat?

'What about Coleman's Meadow, Gomer? If the river comes out, could the flood water get that far?'

Twice they'd abandoned the dig – Jane really losing hope, now, that anything significant would be uncovered before the end of the school holidays, never mind the start.

'Could it, Gomer?'

'You still plannin' to be a harchaeologist, Janey?'

'Absolutely. Two university interviews in the New Year. Fingers crossed.'

Be fantastic if she could someday work around here. The Ledwardine stones could all be in place again by the summer, but there were probably years of excavation to come on the Dinedor Serpent, the other side of Hereford, and who knew what else was waiting to be found? Suddenly, this county had become a hot spot for prehistoric archaeology – two really major discoveries within a year. As though the landscape itself was throwing off centuries like superfluous bedclothes, an old light pulsing to the surface, and Jane could feel the urgency of it in her spine.

'Gomer, *is* the meadow likely to get flooded?'

'Mabbe.' Gomer took out his ciggy, fingers sprouting from the woollen mittens. 'Lowish ground, ennit?'

'The thing is, if they think it could ruin the excavation, they might not even start it till there's no danger of it all getting drowned.'

Meanwhile, Councillor sodding Pierce, who didn't give a toss what lay under Coleman's Meadow, would keep on trying to screw it, like his council had done with the Serpent. Playing for time, and Jane would be back at school before they got to sink the first trowel.

'You going to the parish meeting, Gomer?'

'Mabbe look in, mabbe not. Nobody gonner listen to an ole gravedigger. You still banned, is it, Janey?'

'Well, not *banned* exactly. Mum's just …'

… politely requested that she stay away.

It's not going to help, flower. It's reached the stage where we need a degree of subtlety, or they're going to win.

Mum thinking the mad kid wouldn't be able to hold back, would make a scene, heckling Pierce, making the good guys look like loonies.

The brown water flung itself at the old sandstone bridge, and Jane, officially adult now and able to vote against the bastard, bit her lip and felt helpless. Even the riverman was on the point of betraying her.

'Dreamed about my Min last night,' Gomer said.

Jane looked at him. His ciggy drooped and his glasses were as grey as stone.

'Dreamed her was still alive. Us sittin' together, by the light o' the fire. Pot of tea on the hob.'

'But you—'

'En't got no hob n' more. True enough. That was how I knowed it was a dream.' Gomer steadied his roll-up. 'Was a good dream, mind. En't often you gets a good dream, is it?'

Nearly a couple of years now since Minnie's death. Close to the actual anniversary. Gomer had put new batteries in both their watches and buried them in the churchyard with Minnie. Maybe – Jane shivered lightly – one of the watches had finally stopped and something inside him had felt that sudden empty stillness, the final parting.

'You know what they says, Janey.'

'Who?'

'Sign of rain,' Gomer said.

'Sorry?'

'What they used to say. My ole mam and her sisters. *To dream of the dead …*'

'What?'

'*To dream of the dead is a sign of rain.*'

'That's …' She stared hard at him. 'What kind of sense does that make?'

'Don't gotter make no partic'lar *sense*,' Gomer said. 'Not direc'ly, like, do it?'

'I don't know.'

'These ole sayings, they comes at the truth sideways, kind of thing.'

'Right,' Jane said.

It seemed to have gone darker. The clouds had closed down the moon, and the village lights shone brighter as if in a kind of panic. New rain slanted into Jane's cheeks, sudden, sharp and arrogant, and she thought about her own troubled nights, worrying about the dig, the future, her own future, Eirion …

'So, like, what's supposed to happen,' she said, 'if you dream about the rain?'

3

See the Rabbit

ONE OF HEREFORD'S little secrets, this ruin. In daylight, at the bottom of a secret garden surrounded by depots, offices and a school, you could easily miss it; most people, tourists and locals, didn't even know it existed.

But with night screening the surroundings, Bliss thought, it was a sawn-off Castle Dracula.

'So where is it?'

Looking around in case he'd been scammed; wouldn't be the first time these bastards had done it to him, especially around Christmas, but he wouldn't have expected it of Karen Dowell.

'The *body*, Karen?'

Bending his head on the edge of the blurry lamplight to peer into her fresh, farmer's-wife face.

'The body … we don't exactly know, boss,' Karen said.

'*What?*'

Had to be eight of them in the rose garden in front of the monastery. Bliss had registered DC Terry Stagg, several uniforms and two techies, clammy ghosts in their Durex suits.

On balance, too many for a scam. And there was this little trickle of unholy excitement, which would often accompany shared knowledge of something exquisitely repellent.

Bliss looked around, recalling being here once before. One of the kids had been involved in some choir thing at the Coningsby Hospital which fronted the site on lower Widemarsh Street. Coningsby was only a hospital in some old-time sense of the word, more of a medieval chapel with almshouses and an alleyway leading to the rose garden, where there was also a stone cross set into a little tower with steps up to it.

''Scuse, please, Francis. Let the dog see the rabbit.'

Crime-scene veteran Slim Fiddler, seventeen stone plus, squelching across the grass, messing with his Nikon. A strong wire-mesh fence separated the ruins from the St Thomas Cantilupe primary school next door. Slim Fiddler stopped a bit short of it, turned round, and the other techie, Joanna Priddy, moved aside as his flash went off.

Which was when Bliss also saw, momentarily, the rabbit.

Saw why Karen had chucked her supper.

The body ... we don't exactly know, boss.

The cross ... its base seemed to be hexagonal. About four steps went up to the next tier, which was like a squat church tower with Gothic window holes, stone balcony rails above them, and the actual cross sprouting from a spire rising out of the centre.

Thought it was a gargoyle, at first. When the flash faded, it had this stone look, the channels of blood like black mould.

'Fuck me,' Bliss said quietly.

The face was looking out from one of the Gothic windows.

'If you're going up there, best to get kitted up, Mr Bliss.'

Joanna Priddy handed him a Durex suit and Bliss clutched it numbly, as the rain blew in from Wales.

'Who found it?'

'Bloke came in for a smoke,' Karen said. 'Nobody knows where it's legal to light up, any more, do they?'

'Like we're supposed to care.'

'Comes round the back of the cross to get out of the wind, flicks his lighter and ...'

'Swallows his cig?' Bliss said. 'We looking at gangland here, Karen, or what?'

'I'd like to think we could rule out a domestic, boss.'

Bliss thought for a moment about two baddish faces he'd eyeballed walking over from High Town. After dark, away from the city centre, the people you passed became predominantly male and increasingly iffy. The whole atmosphere of this Division had changed a good deal in the past few years.

'Just the head, Karen? No other bits?'

'Not that we've found. There's a brick behind it, stood on end to prop it up. And a piece of tinsel – you can't see it now from the ground. It was round the neck, but it's slipped down.'

'Like people put round the turkey on the dish?'

'Probably.'

'Very festive,' Bliss said. 'I presume someone's checked it's, you know, real?'

'Why do you think I threw up? Not much, mind, but it was the shock, you know? Not like anything I've …'

Bliss nodded. In no great hurry, frankly, to put on the Durex suit and take a closer look. He clapped his hands together.

'Right, then. Let us summon foot soldiers. If the rest of this feller's bits are anywhere in the vicinity, I want them found before morning. I want this whole compound sealed and that school closed tomorrow. Where's Billy Grace?'

'Might not actually be Dr Grace,' Karen said. 'Somebody's on the way.'

'This cross – it's got a name?'

'I'm not sure, boss. There's some kind of information board at the back.'

Karen led Bliss towards the wire fence, the school building on the other side. She held up a torch; Bliss scanned the sign.

> Built in the 14th century and considerably
> restored in the 19th century, this is the only
> surviving example in the county of a preaching cross …
> … built in conjunction with the Blackfriars Monastery …
> … given the order by Sir John Daniel …
> … beheaded for interference in baronial
> wars in the reign of Edward III

'And when they'd topped him, did they by any chance display this Sir John's head on his own cross?'

'I wouldn't know, boss.'

'I mean, it's not some old Hereford tradition?'

'Not in my time,' Karen said.

'Somebody's looking for maximum impact here, Karen. Kind of *Look what* I've *done.*'

'Maybe more impact than you actually ... Here.' Karen handing him the rubber-covered torch. 'Might not've shown up with the flash. Try that. From where you are.'

Bliss switched on the flashlight, tracked the beam up from the base of the cross. The light finding what remained of the neck, black blood, gristle.

'Boss ...'

'What?'

'Back off. Move the light up a bit.'

Karen came alongside him and lifted his arm slightly, steadying it when the beam found the ...

'Bugger me,' Bliss said.

'Yeah, if you back right off it's all you can see at first.'

Bliss switched off the torch, took a few steps back, snapped it on again.

'What've they *done*? It's like it's ...'

'Still alive,' Karen said. 'Sorry about the smell of sick.'

'You're excused,' Bliss said.

The black hole behind the spinning lights.

How black did you want?

4

Or Die

It was a question of which century you wanted to live in, sleek, thir-tyish Lyndon Pierce was telling them. Which millennium, even.

'Comes down to that, people. All comes down to *that*.'

Punching the table. *People?* Pierce had been watching American politicians on TV?

There was silence.

Pierce stopped talking and Merrily noticed the way he patted his gelled black hair, his eyes swivelling around the 1960s pink-brick community hall, as if suddenly unsure of his ground. She leaned over, whispering in Lol's ear.

'Misjudged his audience, do you think?'

'Maybe not quite the audience he was expecting,' Lol said. 'Fixing it to coincide with shopping night in Hereford ... bad move? Your night shoppers are the local working people. He's just realising what he's got here are mainly white settlers.'

'Mmm.'

Merrily guessing that the house lights would come up at the end of the meeting on too many faces she wasn't going to recognise. At one time, as parish priest, you'd try to connect with all the newcomers. But turning up on doorsteps in a dog collar these days would cause a few to feel pressurised, patronised or – worst of all – evangelised. The incomers from Off, this was. The ones who were not Lyndon Pierce's people. The ones who really *wanted* to be living at least a century ago, as long they didn't have to go to church.

Almost a majority now in Ledwardine, the weekenders and the white settlers. Many of them coming here to retire, but that didn't mean what it used to – business people were quitting at forty-five, flogging the London terraced for a million-plus and downsizing to a farmhouse with four acres and outbuildings you could turn into holiday cottages. County Councillor Pierce pressed his palms into the table, leaning forward.

'Even when I was a boy, look, this was a very different place. Run-down, bad roads, no facilities. Not exactly sawdust on the floor of the Black Swan, but you get the idea.' He straightened up, shaking his gleaming head. 'Drunkenness? Violence? Goodness me, people, they talk about binge drinking nowadays, but my grandfather could tell you stories would make your hair curl. Stories of hard times, brutal times. Low-pay, poverty, disease …'

Pierce was still shaking his head sadly, Lol shaking his in incredulity, leaning into Merrily.

'He's talking bollocks, right? Just tell me he's talking bollocks.'

'He's talking bollocks,' Merrily said. 'But it's clever bollocks.'

Well, sure, times *had* changed for the better, in many ways. But also for the worse. Herefordshire, never a wealthy county – low wages, far more poverty than showed – was becoming increasingly unbalanced. This village wasn't the best place to live any more if you weren't loaded. No mains gas out here, only crippling oil bills. Local kids needed a fork-lift truck to reach the foot of the housing ladder.

'Councillor Pierce.' James Bull-Davies, chairing the meeting, had been fairly quiet so far; now he leaned forward in his high-backed chair, the caged lights purpling his bald patch. 'For what it's worth, my family's been here since the fifteenth century at least. We all realise how deprived the place was in former times, but frankly … don't see the relevance.'

Probably knowing he was on shaky ground, all the same. Too many of James's ancestors had grown fat on the backs of deprived peasantry. Pierce didn't look at him.

'Give me a moment, Colonel. Even fifteen years ago, this community was dying. Some of you'll remember how, after a long and bitter fight, we lost our primary school – didn't have the population to support it.'

James Bull-Davies glared at Pierce. *Colonel* never went down well.

Forced to leave the Army when his father died, to take over the failing family estate, James had shouldered his fate, stiffened his spine and shut the door on that room of his life. *Colonel this, Colonel that … meaningless affectation.*

Merrily saw the way Pierce was ignoring him. He had people out there to reach. His main advantage being that most of them wouldn't have been here long enough to know about his agenda.

'They say that when a village loses its school, it loses its life-force. But Ledwardine survived. Why? Because we learned our lesson. We learned that survival requires growth. *Not* standing still. *Not* preserving what we've got, like a museum, but carefully planned, considered expansion. Either you makes progress or you falls behind. You grows or you dies. Am I right?'

His eyes panning the dim room for support, passing over Merrily, who'd gone new-native tonight in the black velvet skirt, her cashmere sweater, the lovely terracotta silk scarf Lol had brought back from London.

Pierce had paused. It was clear that he was building up to something. 'Any second now,' Lol said, 'he's going to call us *My Fellow Ledwardinians.*'

Merrily smothered a smile behind her woollen glove. The smell of fresh wax wafted from the glistening coat folded on her knees. Lol had bought her that, too, her first actual non-fake Barbour, reproofed in the bathroom this morning with the rain oozing through the cracked putty around the window. She was wishing she'd kept it on now; the heating was, at best, sporadic in the village hall, circa 1964.

Was the heating functioning at all, in fact? Or had Pierce contrived to have it turned off to make the place seem even less, as he would put it, *fit for purpose*? Give him time and he'd be talking about a new leisure centre, part-funded by a National Lottery grant. Squash courts, pool, sunbeds.

'So we grew,' he was saying, 'and we survived. But government criteria for what constitutes a viable community change all the time. Government get strapped for cash, they looks at what they can close. Think about that. Think what we got to lose.'

A rumble in the audience.

'Think about the post offices,' Pierce said. 'You've seen how many of them've gone from other villages. And you've seen ours put out of its own building into a little cubicle, back of the Eight Till Late.'

Two rows in front, Shirley West sat up. Shirley was running the PO cubicle. Shirley who, as they came in, had peered at Merrily with disapproval – thought a priest should be wearing a cassock and dog collar for hanging washing on the line, mowing the lawn, putting out the bin sacks.

'So how would you feel,' Pierce said, 'if even that was to be axed?'

'Speaking as chairman of the Parish Council,' James Bull-Davies said, 'it's the first I've heard of it.'

'Colonel, with all respect to the Parish Council, it would hardly be the first body on the consultation list.'

James stood up. *We have a role,* he'd told Merrily once. *That role is to defend.* But he looked worn suddenly. Stooping over the table as if the ancestral weight, the centuries of squirearchy, were finally becoming too much for his spine.

'I ... suggest we stop sidetracking, cut to the main issue.'

'This *is* the main issue, Colonel.' Pierce folded his arms. 'Grow or die, like I say. *Grow or die.*'

Repeating it like he expected everyone to stand up and start chanting *Grow or die, grow or die, grow or die!*

And then, while he had the momentum, hitting them with the big one: what if the *doctor's surgery* were to go, cosy Kent Asprey replaced by whoever was on duty at the time in some soulless community clinic maybe twelve miles away? Twelve miles to travel when you were sick. How about that, *people?*

Merrily detected a needle squeal from Edna Huws, sometimes church organist and last headmistress of Ledwardine Primary School, afflicted with a long-term blood-pressure problem.

It had started. Rising flames consuming Pierce's kindling.

And it was raining again, which wouldn't help. They didn't have rain on *GetaLife/welshborder*, the relocation website all about convincing city-based would-be migrants that they could have a greener, saner way of life out here in the west. So appealing this time of year, when Ledwardine uncovered its sensory time-capsule: cobbles flushed amber, cold evenings softened by carols and woodsmoke, mulled wine from the Black Swan.

Lyndon Pierce looked up at the windows.

'That's another thing, look. When I was a boy, the fields all around here would flood regular, and the ditches couldn't hold it and the lanes would be impassable. Now we got the bypass linking us to the main Leominster road – a lifeline.'

He paused, spread his arms wide.

'It was *growth* done that for us. Everything we got now we owe to *steady growth*. That stops, people, we're in trouble.'

The rain was driving at the windows now, pools swelling on the sills where the putty had rotted away. Pierce clenched his fists, brought them both down at once like mallets on the table.

'And that's why we must *not* throw out the wrong signals by opposing the development of Coleman's Meadow. Why we can't afford to listen to the ramblings of cranks from Off. *They* don't care if you got nowhere to collect your pension, send off a parcel, get your prescription signed and dispensed when the village is snowbound. *They* don't give a toss if this village lives or dies. They only care about what's already dead. *Dead and buried.*'

'I don't normally want to kill people,' Lol said to Merrily, 'as you know.'

5

Serpent

THE SUNRISE SPRAYED out from behind Cole Hill like a firework, with shivering shards of orange and gold. Jane was standing in the gateway with her bare arms raised, and she looked free and sexy as hell, like her hands were cupping the sun.

An instant of connection.

Probably her all-time favourite picture of herself. Eirion had taken it on his digital SLR, on that last September weekend, the day before he'd left for university. For a long time it had been her screensaver, until she'd realised it was only making her sad.

Now it was stashed in the *Sacred* folder on the laptop, along with the membership list of the Coleman's Meadow Preservation Society. Jane didn't know why she'd brought it out tonight, unless it was as a kind of prayer to God or the Goddess or whatever unimaginable force might be represented by the bursting of the light over the holy hill.

Long ago, the way to watch the Cole Hill sunrise would have been between the standing stones in Coleman's Meadow. The stones toppled and buried centuries ago by some pious or fearful farmer but which next year could be back, ancient silhouettes against the red dawn in awesome testament to the sacred status of this place. *A ritual reconnecting of the hidden wires.* This was what she'd written in an essay. And like, to *be* here when that came about. Oh God ... *If* it came about. If they could prevent Lyndon bastard Pierce fixing it so that future dawns would be rising instead over the fake-slate on the roofs of ranks of crappy, post-modern, flat-pack *luxury executive homes.*

That wouldn't happen. It couldn't. With a few thousand members now, worldwide, the Coleman's Meadow Preservation Society was a powerful lobby.

OK, maybe not *powerful* exactly; councils were rarely influenced by people whose strategies involved subtle threats on the lines of *If we cannot stop it by any other means, we are prepared to invoke the Site Guardian*. But the word was spreading.

Jane had built up the fire in the vicarage parlour. She was sitting on the sofa with Ethel, a mug of chocolate and the laptop on the coffee table, listening to an accelerating wind driving the rain into the 17th-century timbers. At least you could rely on Mum not to take any shit from Pierce tonight. Mum finally understood.

In fact, things were good with Mum right now, had been for a while. Spiritual differences, if not exactly resolved, were acknowledged as being not insurmountable. You couldn't, after all, operate as a vicar for very long around here without becoming at least *half* pagan.

Anyway, no open confrontation any more. These days Jane was kind of wincing at the memory of herself a couple of years ago, doing her cobbled-together ritual to the Lady Moon in the vicarage garden. A little girl, back then. A virgin. Pre-Eirion.

Abruptly, she killed the picture and switched off the laptop. Ethel had nosed under her arm and onto her knee, lay there purring, and Jane stroked her slowly, staring into the reddening log fire.

She picked up the mobile, almost cracked and called Eirion in Cardiff, then pulled herself together and tried Neil Cooper again. Thinking she'd leave a message on his machine so that both he and his wife would know that she definitely wasn't—

'Cooper.'

'Oh—'

'Jane,' he said, and if she was honest she'd have to admit he didn't sound over-excited.

'Sorry, I thought I'd get the machine. Coops, listen, I'm not stalking you or anything. You gave me your home number, in case anything came up?'

'And what's come up, Jane?'

'Erm … well, like … nothing. I mean, that's the point. Nothing's happening. It's all stopped. Why's it all stopped, Coops?'

She felt stupid, but he must surely understand how important this was to her. She was carrying the blazing torch lit by Lucy Devenish, folklorist of this parish, now dead, and if she let it go out …

'Weather's not helping, obviously,' Neil Cooper said.

'You've got those tent things you can put over the trenches.'

'Yeah, but it's not satisfactory. And there's no desperate hurry, is there? And anyway, I keep telling you, it's not my—'

'There is for me, Coops, I'll be back at school in the New Year.'

'Jane, they can't time the whole project to fit your personal schedule.'

'I just want— Don't want to interfere or anything, I just want to *be* there. On the fringe, quiet as a mouse. Just like want to be there when the stones are raised again.'

'Well, yeah,' he said. 'I can understand that.'

There was something Neil Cooper wasn't telling her. Or maybe he was just pissed off because the dig had been taken out of the hands of the county archaeology department: too big, too important, needed specialists in prehistory.

'And let's not forget,' Jane said, 'that if it wasn't for me you might never've discovered it in the first place. I mean, I don't like to keep throwing this at y—'

'Jane—'

'Sorry.'

'None of us will miss anything, OK? It'll be on TV. All the best bits, anyway.'

'Huh?'

His voice had sounded damp and sick in a way that didn't make sense. 'What would you expect,' he said, 'with Blore in the driving seat?'

'Sorry …' Jane was on the edge of the sofa. 'Did you say— *what* did you say?'

Coops said nothing.

'Did you say *Blore*? As in, like, *Bill* Blore, of *Trench One*?'

'I'd hate to think there was another one out there,' Coops said.

'Holy shit,' Jane said.

'Look, don't get—'

'But like, I thought the contract had gone to this … Dore Valley Archaeology?'

He was silent again.

'Come on, Coops, who am *I* going to tell?'

'Dore Valley Archaeology,' Coops said, 'no longer exists as an independent contractor. In mid-October it was acquired by Blore's company, Capstone.'

'*Wow*. I didn't know that. I mean, I didn't know he had a company.'

'They all do. Archaeology's a business. Like everything else. And Capstone have swallowed Dore Valley. More people, more resources, more prestige digs, plus TV documentaries on the side. Blore's got it sewn up, money at both ends.'

'Bill Blore,' Jane said slowly. 'Wow.'

'Oh, for God's sake, Jane …'

'Hey, I'm sorry, but *Bill*—'

'You're missing the point, Jane, and maybe I shouldn't expect you to see the significance, but you're thinking about the so-called glamorous TV presenter, while I'm seeing the man who is *not* Herefordshire Council's favourite archaeologist.'

Jane thought about this for a moment, and then she started to understand.

'The Dinedor Serpent.'

'We still prefer to call it the Rotherwas Ribbon,' Coops said primly. Well, he would. The council stuck to the original name, *Ribbon*, because that sounded less sexy than Serpent or Dragon. Easier to ignore.

But it *was* sexy. Unique, probably. Coleman's Meadow, with real standing stones to uncover, might turn out to be more immediately spectacular, but the Dinedor Serpent was the only one of its kind in Europe. Seriously significant.

So significant that the philistine bastards on Herefordshire Council were shoving a new road across it.

Jane knew all about this. She'd pasted up the news cuttings as part of her A-level project, with a picture of Prof. William Blore next to the partly uncovered Serpent.

'Coops, come on, what he said … the council were asking for it. You know that.'

'Let's not forget that if it hadn't been for the work on the road, we wouldn't have found the Ribbon in the first place.'

'*Serpent.* Yeah, but—'

'Same with Coleman's Meadow and the housing plan. Same with most finds. Most archaeology today is rescue archaeology, you grow to accept that.'

'Especially in this bloody county,' Jane said. 'But that's what's so good about Bill Blore. He doesn't accept bureaucratic bullshit.'

In her picture, big Bill Blore was stripped to the waist, deeply tanned, hard hat at an angle. Thickset, maybe, but not fat. He'd said that Herefordshire, having been neglected for decades, was now yielding stuff that could change our whole perception of Neolithic, Bronze and Iron Age societies.

And, because she'd quoted it in an essay, Jane knew exactly what he'd said about the council's decision to go ahead with the new road, regardless.

'He said local authorities shouldn't be allowed to make decisions affecting major national heritage sites. Especially councils as short-sighted, pig-headed and ignorant as Hereford's.'

'Words to that effect,' Coops said stiffly.

'Those *actual* words … actually.' Excitement began to ripple through Jane. 'Coops, this is just so *totally cool.*'

'Jane, it's *not.* Blore's got into Coleman's Meadow through the back door, now he's running this prestigious dig right under the nose of an authority he's publicly trashed. That is not cool. That is a very uncomfortable situation for all of us.'

'Only if you work for the council.'

'They're blaming my department, naturally. Lucky I still have a job. OK, unless Dore Valley had told us themselves, there was no *way* we could've known that Blore was quietly moving in while we were negotiating with them, but that's not how some people see it.'

'You wanted to leave the council anyway, didn't you?'

'Yeah,' Coops said. 'I *did.*'

Another silence. Jane held her breath. She was picking up stuff she could really use – like at the university interviews? To show how seriously au fait she was with trench gossip.

She'd also be able to tell them she'd worked with Bill Blore.

Wow.

'Just that when I was asked to join Dore Valley as a field archaeologist,' Coops said, 'nobody told me it'd be part of the Blore empire.'

'But isn't that, like … good?'

'Goodnight, Jane,' Neil Cooper said.

6

Bury them Deeper

SHIRLEY WEST WAS, arguably, the most sinister person here. Shirley did foreboding in a way that was supposed to have gone out with the Witchcraft Act.

Impressive in a born-again Christian.

A couple in front of Merrily and Lol had slid away, leaving a clear view of Shirley in that grey, tubular, quilted coat. A lagged cistern with no thermostat, and sooner or later – you just knew – she was going to overheat.

Directly ahead of her, at the front of the stage, two pictures were pinned to a display stand. One was a photo showing an empty field with a five-barred gate, the conical hill rising behind it under an overcast sky.

'Coleman's Meadow.' James Bull-Davies tapped his pen on the photo. 'Earmarked for development of what are described as executive dwellings – like these.'

Tapping the picture below it: an architect's sketch of a detached house with a double garage, token timber-framing, landscaped suburban gardens, under a blue-washed summer sky.

'Field being within the village boundaries, therefore seen by county planners as acceptable infill.'

Merrily swapped a glance with Lol. Especially acceptable to Lyndon Pierce, local councillor and chartered accountant. One of whose clients was, as it happened, the owner of Coleman's Meadow.

It was blatant, really. And because this was a small county, so much interconnected, so many business and family links, sometimes it seemed almost normal, no big deal.

Pierce had sat down now, was examining his nails, like his part was

30

over. Rain smacked at the windows, making the frames shiver and rattle, smearing the reflections in the glass.

'Complication, of course,' James said, 'being the recent discovery in Coleman's Meadow, of significant archaeological remains. Now, I don't want to pre-empt the results of the excavation, but—'

'Old stones.' A drawly male voice uncurling from halfway down the hall. Merrily didn't recognise it. 'Just a few old stones, long buried.'

'Megaliths,' James said. 'The remains of a Bronze Age monument four thousand years old which people interested in such relics would, understandably, like to have unearthed and conserved.'

'Not a problem, Colonel,' Pierce murmured. 'As I keep saying.'

'*In situ.*'

'Ah.' Pierce sat back, arms folded. '*That*'s the problem, yes. Should a prime site be sacrificed in its entirety for a few stones that wouldn't've been discovered if it hadn't been for this project – I think that's right, isn't it, Colonel?'

'Don't think anyone's ever denied that. However, we now know about them, and we appear to have two options: re-erecting them as a heritage site or—'

'Three options, in fact,' Pierce said mildly. 'The stones could be dug out and taken away for erection on another site – in a park or somewhere.'

'Somewhere well away from this village,' Shirley West said.

She hadn't moved. All you could see was stiffly permed dark brown hair sitting on the funnel collar of the grey coat.

Merrily held her breath.

'Because, see, we have to ask ourselves,' Shirley said, 'why they were buried in the first place.'

'Not our place,' James said, 'to pre-empt the results of the official excavation. Just to remind you all, the Parish Council will be discussing Coleman's Meadow early in the New Year. We have no planning powers at this level, as you realise, but we *can* make our voice heard in Hereford. In theory. So that leaves you two or three weeks to make your individual views known to *us*. In writing, if you—'

'But I can *tell* you why, Mr Davies,' Shirley said. 'We don't need no excavation to tell us they were *heathen* stones in a Christian country. Heathen stones in the very shadow of our church.'

Our church? Merrily knew for a fact that Shirley West was also a member of some born-again, pentecostal-type group in Leominster.

James said, 'Mrs West—'

'Bury them again! Bury them deeper! Or, if you have to dig them up, do as Mr Pierce says, put them in a city park or a museum where none of us have to see them.'

Merrily glanced from side to side. Was nobody going to point out – Jane would go crazy – that the stones erected elsewhere would be meaningless? That they were probably part of a prehistoric landscape pattern, aligned to the summit of Cole Hill?

'Put iron railings around them. *Confine* them and—'

'Yes, Mrs West,' James said, 'we take your point—'

'—and the evil they represent. There's a deep evil in that place and evil returns to it.'

Someone chuckled. A *would you believe this crazy woman?* kind of chuckle. Shirley whirled round.

'Don't you dare laugh at me! You come yere with your fancy talk and your unbelief. You who deny the Lord.'

'Well ...' Lyndon Pierce opened his hands. 'Anyone who knows me knows I'd be the last to make a religious issue out of this. But some of you might be surprised at how many folk've expressed similar sentiments to Mrs West's.'

Opportunist bastard. Right ...

Merrily was halfway to her feet when James Bull-Davies flicked her a warning with a slight turn of his head and a discreet one-handed wiping motion. She sat down, a tightness in her chest.

'You may also,' James said, 'wish to examine the situation from the tourism angle – for better or worse, a vital part of our economy. Herefordshire has comparatively few Neolithic monuments, none of them, it might be argued, as potentially spectacular as this one. We could expect a substantial number of visitors.'

'But what kind, sir? What *kind*?'

The drawly voice again, from somewhere in the middle of the hall.

'Mr Savitch,' James said.

Ward Savitch. Entrepreneur who'd bought up the old Kibble farm on the Dilwyn road, a mile out of the village. Turning it into a pleasure park for city slickers – paintballing weekends and corporate pheasant shoots. Jane wanted him dead.

'I think,' Savitch said, 'that we all know the kind of tourism such places attract, and it's the kind more likely to steal the milk off your step.'

Merrily watched Lol shaking his bowed head, profoundly glad that Jane had seen sense and stayed away.

'Pseudo-Druids,' Savitch said. 'Witches in robes, or ... not in robes. Or not in anything. That the kind of tourism you had in mind, Colonel?'

Nervous laughter, James lifting his hands for quiet.

'Obviously, I'm being facetious,' Savitch said. 'Don't get me wrong, I believe we can embrace the future *and* still hold on to the past. And in Ledwardine we've already got some of the finest period buildings in the county. That's the kind of heritage we should be looking to conserve, not some lumps of rock.'

'And the evil they bring yere,' Shirley West muttered. 'I *know* this.'

James Bull-Davies looked tired. 'Anyone else?'

'I haven't *quite* finished,' Savitch said. 'Let's not pretend, any of us, that we wouldn't appreciate the improved facilities that would come with growth – supermarket, restaurants ...'

'Places for the nouveau riche to unwind in the evening,' Lol whispered, 'when they've finished blasting a few hundred tame birds out of the hedge.'

'And, I believe, a fully equipped leisure-centre,' Savitch said.

There was an explosion of hard rain on the big windows. The strip lights stuttered.

Lol said. 'He's got to be a plant.'

As all the lights came up and the first few people began to leave, collecting umbrellas from the rail by the main door, Merrily saw the man in the three-piece suit.

A *young* man in a three-piece suit. One of the first out. Black umbrella.

'Nobody here with a Coleman's Meadow Preservation Society placard,' Lol was saying. 'No *Save the Stones* sweatshirts.'

'Perhaps that's no bad thing,' Merrily said. 'Some of them might well have pentacles tattooed on their foreheads. Lol, you see that guy who just went out?'

'Bloke helping Alice Meek?'

'No, on his own. Suit with a waistcoat. *You* once saw Jonathan Long, didn't you?'

'Don't think so.'

'No.' She thought about it. 'Maybe you didn't. He came to the vic, just once, with Frannie Bliss.'

'A cop?'

'Doesn't matter. Probably wasn't him at all.'

Although it *was*.

'Um ...' Lol looked at her closely. 'You *did* have something to eat before you came out?'

'I ... Yes, I did. Swear to God.'

Merrily stood up, shook out her coat. Yes, she was trying to get regular meals. Yes, she was trying to pull herself together, not get run down again, cut down on the cigs, have reflexology every couple of weeks from, God help her, Mrs Morningwood of Garway Hill. Yes, yes, yes.

'Ah, vicar ...' James Bull-Davies was stooping between her and Lol, like some long-billed wading bird. 'Wasn't really the time, seemed to me, for clerical intervention. West woman's unlikely to attract much support for Pierce. Unhinged, basically.'

'In which case, you don't think it's worth me putting a bit of distance between us? Pointing out that the Church of England itself doesn't actually have a problem with megalithic remains, which, of course, it *doesn't* ... And you're looking unconvinced.'

'Might be as well not to appear compromised by your daughter's demonstrable *enthusiasm*, if that's the best word ...?'

'She's excited. It's like they're *her* stones, and it's given her a direction at just the right time. James ... is there anything in your family records about standing stones in Coleman's Meadow?'

'Should there be?'

'If we *could* find out why they were buried, just to keep Shirley quiet?'

'If it was done in secret, wouldn't be any record. Look, if this site's as significant as your daughter and her friends appear to think then English Heritage will step in to conserve it and neither that woman nor Pierce will be able to do a bloody thing about it.'

'He won't give up. Development of Coleman's Meadow opens the way for a whole swathe of housing and before you know it ... Ledwardine New Town? That's not conspiracy-theorist talk, James, any more than Lyndon's plans for *this* site ...'

'What've you heard?'

Merrily said nothing. What she'd heard was that Stu Twigg, another of Pierce's clients, owned the ground that the village hall was built on. Ground now being eyed by an unnamed supermarket company. So that if the population of Ledwardine grew to a level which made a superstore not only viable but desirable, and the hall was to be replaced by a new leisure centre on a greenfield site elsewhere, the client – and, arguably, his accountant – would be quids in.

'Forgot you were a close friend of Gomer Parry,' James said. 'Man with little understanding of the word *slander*.'

'No, you didn't. Look, nobody's averse to immigration, all populations change ... but surely, in a village, it should be a trickle. And it should be balanced. Right now, virtually the only people who can afford to move in here are the well-off who want to get out of London. So Pierce and his mates build hundreds of executive homes and an army of the retired rich move in, and the local kids have to move out to the cities, and Ledwardine starts to lose its identity ... doesn't even look like a village any more, just a chunk of suburbia with an open-air museum in the centre. I ... Sorry.' She fanned the air with her gloves. 'Don't usually go off like that.'

'Look.' James smiled thinly. 'Let's see how things progress. If English Heritage finds some value in the archaeology, then it's all academic. If you have something to say, save it for the sermon. Or, on second thoughts, don't. Night, vicar, Robinson. Ah—' He looked at Lol. 'Believe you've been asked to give us a bit of a concert?'

Lol didn't say anything.

'At the Swan?' James said. 'Christmas Eve?'

'Not sure about it yet,' Lol said.

Over a year after beating his fear of audiences, he still hadn't played Ledwardine. No big deal … and yet it was.

'Shame if you couldn't,' James said.

They watched him leave, plucking his umbrella from the rack. The chances of James ever having heard one of Lol's songs were slight.

'That mean he's on our side?' Lol said.

'Best not to rely on it.' Merrily struggled with the zip of her coat, then let it go. 'Lol, I don't look ill or anything, do I? I mean, the way you …'

'No.' Lol smiled at her. 'In fact, much as I hate to paraphrase Clapton, you look—'

'Oh, *please*. Come on, let's go and put the kettle on.'

'Would that be a euphemism?'

'No! I actually need a cup of *tea*. And an earlyish night – Tom Parson's funeral tomorrow at Hereford Crem.'

Lol nodded.

'I was thinking,' he said, 'if it wasn't time for us to …'

She looked up from the bottom of the zip.

'To what?'

He didn't reply and Merrily saw, for a moment, the former Lol – detached, uncertain, wearing his past like a stained old overcoat. She thought of the way he'd faced up to the man responsible for smashing his beloved Boswell guitar. Making him pay for it in full but then, instead of replacing the Boswell, giving the money away, splitting it anonymously between three local charities. Tainted, Lol had said.

Last week he'd been to London to record his first-ever TV appearance, but he was still scared to play Ledwardine. Scared of what it might be telling him if he bombed.

They were almost alone now, under the cold strip lights. She worried about him. And worried about him worrying about her. *God.*

'Time for us to what?' Merrily said.

Rain blasted into one of the windows and the glass rattled in its metal frame. Lol drew Merrily towards him and did up the zip for her.

'Doesn't matter.'

7

Thing with the Eyes

A BIG KILLING carried its own light. The wild electricity of it had brought the place alive, and Bliss could almost see it connecting across the shining rooftops of this low-slung brick and timbered city, magnesium-white sparks hissing in the brimming gutters.

And there was nobody in the Job in Hereford tonight who wouldn't get a charge out of it.

No detective, anyway. Never let them tell you any different: this was why you were here, why you hacked through all the paperwork, wiped off the abuse like spittle, merely rolled your eyes at the latest edict from a Home Secretary who looked like she might be good at running playgroups. Young cops liked mixing it on the street, tossing yobs into the back of a van, traffic cops liked burning rubber and screaming through red lights. And detectives – no getting round it – liked murder. A headline-grabbing, incident-room, unlimited-overtime murder.

The thing was, *Acting* Superintendent Annie Howe, fast-tracking at Headquarters, already had one. On her own doorstep, in Worcester, a witness in a high-profile paedophile case found dead in his garage.

Was that not enough for *anybody*?

Why did the bitch have to nick his?

Bliss put down the phone. Gerry Rowbotham, the greybeard duty sergeant at Gaol Street, looking up and sniffing theatrically.

'I smell Worcester on the wind?'

'Well, it wasn't me, Gerry.'

She'd given him an earful for not alerting her sooner. Calling from HQ, where she'd just dropped in to *pick up some people* before coming over.

Coming over.

Shit.

Pick up some people .

Fuck.

'She's only appointed herself SIO,' Bliss said. 'She's only bringing her own bastard crew.'

'Well, you know why,' Gerry said.

'No, we *don't* know why. We're not *sure* yet.'

Gerry nodded at Bliss's laptop.

'Would it help if I had a glance?'

'That's the idea, Gerry,' Bliss said. 'If you don't mind.'

Slim Fiddler, the senior techie, had been the first to venture an ID. He'd done a few courtesy pictures once during an official visit to Gaol Street by the police authority. Pretty sure he'd had this head in his lens when it was still turning on a neck. The pathologist, Billy Grace, also thought he knew the face, but he'd shaken off civic functions years ago so couldn't be sure. Only one thing Billy had been fairly sure about.

'Power saw, Francis. So I'd say wherever it was done …'

'Looks like a spam factory?'

'Definitely take a while to hoover up all the bits. I'd say chainsaw.'

'McCullough or Stihl?'

'Ha.'

Back at Gaol Street, Karen Dowell, divisional computer whizz, had fed some piccies into Bliss's laptop and Bliss had spent some of his precious time hawking them around. But with what had been done to the face nobody could be quite sure. Bliss had Karen ring the wife, ask for the guy. The wife said he was out. Didn't know when he'd be back.

'All right, then.'

Bliss planted the lappie in front of Gerry Rowbotham, who'd been in Hereford since coppers were allowed to slap kids round the ear for pinching apples off the backs of carts in High Town. Through the glass, he saw Karen Dowell coming in through the main door, taking off her baseball cap, shaking a cupful of rain off it.

Gerry put on his reading specs as Bliss opened the laptop's lid and clicked on the photo icon.

'There you go.'

The head trembling into focus, coming up sharper and brighter than it had looked in the flesh. And yet artificial, somehow, like it had been sent over from props. Bliss zoomed it up to full screen, looked at Gerry.

Gerry winced.

Bliss said, 'This *is* Ayling. You're sure?'

'He bought me two pints once. You don't forget that level of generosity.'

The old feller quite pale in the bilious light. Stepping back, taking a couple of breaths and risking his ticker with another good long look. 'This was summer, Francis, we'd be turning off all the fans. Gonner throw up more shit than my brother's muck-spreader.'

A light cough. Bliss waved Karen in.

'Anything?'

'Nothing dramatic so far, boss. Problem is, most of the neighbours are elderly people. Almshouses, you know? Doors locked, curtains drawn, tellies on, mugs of Horlicks.'

'CCTV?'

'Couple of possibles. One or two iffy hoodies. Trouble is, in this weather everybody's a hoodie. A live witness would be nice.'

'Keep at it. Somewhere there's an old dear who sees all. I want her.'

Preferably before Howe arrived with the entourage.

'Er ...' Karen trying not show excitement. 'Actually right, is it, what they're saying?'

'Well, yeh.' Bliss accepted a Polo mint from Gerry Rowbotham. 'Does indeed begin to look like it. So much for gangland, eh?'

'God,' Karen said. 'What happens now?'

'It gets corporate. Doesn't it, Gerry?'

'Francis,' Gerry Rowbotham said, 'You haven't actually *said* ...'

'What?'

'What's happened to ... you know, what they've done to his eyes?'

'Ah, yeh,' Bliss said. 'The eyes.'

You didn't need to be much of a detective to know that the thing with the eyes was going to be central.

THURSDAY

But we should not criticise councillors because of their ineptitude. We wouldn't berate an idiot for not comprehending quantum theory.

Reader's letter to the *Hereford Times*,
February 2008

8

Viler Shades

THE HEATING, SUCH as it was, was due to kick in at seven, for a strict one and a half hours. A cost-of-oil thing. You could get twenty-five per cent of your fuel costs from the parish, for business use of the vicarage, but Merrily had never bothered. Stupid, probably, but too late to start now, at these prices. So she and Jane had cut back. Lost the old Aga, for a start.

Merrily moved rapidly around the kitchen, putting the kettle on, activating the toaster, feeding Ethel, and then running back into the hall, calling up from the bottom of the stairs.

'Flower?'

Her lips could hardly frame the word, all the nerves in her face deadened by the cold. On the wall by the door, Jesus Christ looked down from Holman-Hunt's *Light of the World* with a certain empathy, obviously not drawing much heat from his lantern.

'Jane!'

The kid was definitely up. She'd been wandering around at least half an hour ago. Probably trying for stealth, but when there were only the two of you in a big old vicarage you developed an ear for creaks.

No reply from up there, no sound of radio or running water. Merrily went back to the kitchen and cracked three eggs into a bowl. Tom Parson's funeral was at eleven at Hereford Crem. Old Tom, local historian, one-time editor of the parish magazine, now the third village death in a fortnight. Another funeral, another empty cottage up for grabs at a crazy price, removal vans more common in this village now than buses.

The cold came for her again, and she went scurrying back into the hall.

'Jane!'

Nothing. Merrily pulled her robe together and ran upstairs, two flights, to what Jane liked to call her apartment, in the attic. A big bedsit, essentially, with all the kid's spooky books, her desk, her stereo, her CDs. The door was hanging open. Merrily snapped on the light and saw the duvet in a heap, one pillow on the floor.

What was *this* about? Jane waking up aggrieved because her craven parent hadn't stood up at last night's meeting and fought for Coleman's Meadow? She hadn't *seemed* annoyed last night, but Jane ... one day she might become vaguely predictable, no signs of that yet.

Merrily sat on an edge of the bed, wondering what it would be like this time next year when Jane was gone. Was she really going to carry on here on her own? With Lol on *his* own in Lucy's old house? If they put this place on the market, the Church could clean up. *The Old Vicarage, Ledwardine, 17th century, seven bedrooms, guest-house potential.* One day they'd do it, transfer the vicar to one of the estate houses, and on mornings like this it didn't seem such a bad idea.

A videotape was projecting from the vintage VCR under Jane's analogue TV. Give the kid her due, she'd never pined for home cinema – on a vicar's stipend, still many years away.

The tape was labelled *T-1 Feb.* Recorded last winter, long before Jane had been drawn towards a career in archaeology. *Trench One* was never less than watchable but not exactly crucial viewing. Why this one now?

Oh, and you'll never guess – the kid calling back casually over her shoulder as she went upstairs to bed last night – *who's going to be in charge of the dig.* Merrily waiting in vain for a name, but Jane always liked suspense.

Activating the VCR and the TV, Merrily shoved in the tape and watched pre-credit shots of a sinister grey landcape under a sky tiered with clouds like stacked shelves.

A man appeared, solid, bulky, shot from below the tump he was standing on. *Trench One* had three regular presenters who took turns to direct an excavation, present a different viewpoint, argue over the results. It was about conflict and competition.

'So we've studied the reports of the original 1963 dig ...'

He was wearing some kind of bush shirt, with badges sewn on, an

Army beret and jeans with ragged holes in the knees. In case anyone had any doubts, the caption spelled out:

Prof. William Blore.

'… been over the geophysics, taken a stack of aerial pictures, and it now seems pretty clear to me that this is where we need to sink …' Lavish grin splashing through smoky stubble. '*Trench One!*'

Blore jumping down from the tump and standing for a moment rubbing his hands like he couldn't wait to get into the soil, and then the sig tune coming up in a storm of thrash-metal as he slid on his dark glasses and people began to gather around him.

Young people, his students. *Trench One* had begun as an Open University programme on BBC 2. Very rapidly acquiring a cult following, which built and built until they gave it peak screening. The format had altered slightly: Blore as guru, channelling youthful vigour. Merrily recalled a profile in one of the Sunday magazines describing him as *genial, profane and disarmingly intolerant.*

She stopped the tape. Red herring, surely. No way would Coleman's Meadow be put into the hands of the man who'd told *BBC Midlands Today* that anyone who thought the Bronze Age builders of the Dinedor Serpent were primitive obviously hadn't met the philistines running Herefordshire Council.

Wondering how *genial, profane and disarmingly intolerant* might translate.

'What do *you* think, Lucy?'

She looked up at the framed photo over a stack of Jane's esoteric books. An elderly woman in her winter poncho. The wide-brimmed hat throwing a tilted shadow across bird-of-prey features blurred by the process of turning away. Jane had found the picture in the vestry files and cleaned it up, had copies made and framed the original.

The only known portrait of Lucy Devenish who, like the old Indian warriors she'd so resembled, had probably thought cameras could steal your soul.

Merrily thought the picture looked unusually grey and flat this morning, lifeless.

*

The river was still frothing like cappuccino in the lamplight, but at least he wasn't going anywhere new.

And the rain had eased. There was some ground mist, but the sky was clearing. Looking up, Jane saw the morning star pulsing like a distant lamp.

A breathing space. She walked slowly back up Church Street towards the square. Most of the guys at school hated getting up in the morning, but she'd never found it a problem. Around dawn you were more receptive to … impressions.

Was that weird? Was *she* weird? Over the last couple of years, she'd done all the usual stuff – been totally hammered on cider, got laid – but somehow it wasn't enough. Was she alone at Moorfield High in thinking it wasn't enough?

Probably.

There were very few lights in Church Street, none in Lucy's old house where Lol lived now. Sometimes, pre-dawn, you'd see him by lamplight, working on a song for his second solo album, at his desk under the window. But Lol had been at the meeting with Mum, listening to Pierce's New Ledwardine bullshit, which was enough to sap anybody's creativity.

A breeze blundered into the square, ripping away the mist like a lace-curtain and rattling the stacks of morning papers barricading the doorway of the Eight Till Late. The only sign of life. Not long ago, even in the bleak midwinter, you'd have had clinking milk bottles and the warm aroma of baking bread. Preparations for a day. Now even the morning post wouldn't be here for hours, and the milk came in plastic bottles in the supermarkets, and soon nobody would be seen on the streets of Ledwardine until about ten when the dinky delicatessen opened for croissants.

Jane stopped on the edge of the square and looked out, over the crooked, 16th-century black and white houses and shuttered shops, towards Cole Hill, the first point of contact with each new day. Hearing Mum again, from last night.

I won't dress this up, flower. When the stones are exposed and studied or measured or whatever happens, they want them taken away. Possibly erected somewhere else. Or … not erected.

This was Lyndon Pierce plus transient scum like Ward Savitch, of pheasant-holocaust fame. Mum had admitted she'd managed to say nothing; as the meeting was supposed to be for public information only, the words *powder* and *dry* had seemed appropriate. Jane was aware of trembling.

The church clock said 6.30, just gone. Still a while off daylight, and Mum wouldn't be up for another half-hour. Jane walked under the lych-gate and into the churchyard, switching on her lamp, cutting an ochre channel through the mist which put ghostly wreaths around the graves.

The beam seemed to find its own way to the only stone with a quotation from Thomas Traherne:

> *No more shall clouds eclipse my treasures*
> *Nor viler shades obscure my highest pleasures ...*

Jane knelt. If she was late for breakfast, late for school, it didn't matter. This was important. This was the person to whom she'd have to answer if the village lost its ancient heart.

'Lucy,' she whispered to the headstone, 'the bastards want to have them ripped out. Put on a flatbed truck and taken away.'

Sometimes, when she was on her own in the early morning or at twilight, calm and focused, she'd almost see Lucy Devenish, eagle-faced and huddled in her poncho on the edge of some folkloric otherworld.

'So, like, if there's anything you can do?'

She'd been coming here every day for weeks now, far longer than she'd been going to the river. Talking to Lucy, keeping her up to date. It was important.

Jane looked up to see only steeple, mist and morning star, felt damp seeping through the knees of her jeans. She stood up, on the edge of the old coffin path along which the dead of Ledwardine had once been carried.

As she walked away, there was a tiny sound like a snapping twig on the path to her left, as if someone was walking beside her. Only some small mammal, but it made her smile as she set off along the ancient trackway which would later proceed, in perfect alignment with the gateways at each end of Coleman's Meadow, to the Iron Age camp on Cole Hill.

It was like you were walking the border between worlds. Walking with ghosts. Could be down to Bill Blore, now, to stop the sacrilege, let Lucy walk in peace.

A voice came bubbling in the soggy air.

It said, 'Who's Lucy?'

Lol lay listening to the gunslinger wind prowling Church Street. Scared now. For a couple of days after London, it had been simple bewilderment and gratitude to whatever had got him through it. But this morning he'd awoken into darkness, the swaggering wind, anxiety.

Five days ago now, London, and reduced to a dream-sequence. Last night, to put it in its place, he'd been set on doing something real. Like maybe standing up and laying into Lyndon Pierce, this bastard who last summer had said to him, *If certain people who en't local don't like the way we do things round yere, seems to me they might think about moving on.*

Moving on? In London for just two days, Lol had been semi-paralysed by a fear of *not getting back.*

He looked up at the oak beam over the bed, thinking about its permanence, how it had become stronger with age. How, if you tried to bang a nail into it now, the nail would snap off.

A lot like the woman who used to live here.

But how unlike either the woman or the beam *he* was.

Remembering the routine cowardice assailing him as he'd climbed on the stool with his guitar to do 'Baker's' in the big BBC studio, surrounded by an audience top-heavy with *real* musicians. Superstitiously sure he was going to fail because he was playing the Takamine rather than the ill-fated Boswell.

I want to know about everything, Jane had demanded when he finally did get home. *Everything and everybody.*

Lol had said they'd probably view the performance and then decide to lose him from the final edit. Jane had looked sinister. 'Only if Holland and his producer want to be stalked for the rest of their lives by a vicar's psychotic daughter with a machete.'

He'd smiled and told her everything. Everything he could remember about his big day out in the big city, recording 'The Baker's Lament' for BBC 2's flagship music programme, *Later With Jools Holland*. The New Year's Eve programme. Hadn't realised until he was in the studio that this was the one where they all had to feign excitement as the hands of the big clock closed in on midnight and the pipers waded in. A producer had said they'd have to do it live next year, in line with the BBC's new drive towards truth and honesty.

Lol had been the cameo act, of course, the one-song guy – the big stars did three numbers – but it had been preceded, unexpectedly, by an interview with Jools. The great man decently glossing over Lol's weird years, before screening a 30-second clip from the award-winning independent film about the death of village life, for which Lol's music was the soundtrack. The micro-budget movie that was turning 'The Baker's Lament' into a fluke Christmas minor hit, turning Lol's long-dormant career around.

What he remembered most about the actual recording was not the cameras, or the one chord-change his fingers fluffed, but a bunch of people in the studio audience, swaying and mouthing the words of the chorus:

> *… we paid for all that we used*
> *Now the money's all spent*
> *That's the Baker's Lament*

One of the mouthers, unless he'd imagined all this, had been Michael Stipe of REM, benignly smiling and inclining his long bony head. Jane had been wildly impressed. Lol, too, at the time, obviously. Before it was all put into a hard perspective by his next clear memory, of a guy approaching him afterwards, explaining that he was putting together an American tour for Original Sin and how would Lol feel about being considered for the support?

Five weeks, in the spring, the guy said. Someone else, who he'd declined to name, had pulled out, so they'd need to know fairly soon if Lol was up for it.

Five weeks.

All Lol remembered about his own response was,

'*I'm thirty-nine.*'

The guy laughing and slapping him on the shoulder, telling him that America didn't have an ageism problem on anywhere near the scale of Britain's and, anyway, Lol looked younger, and the Sin guys loved his music. Adding, with unmoving eyes, '*You may never get a time like this again. You know what I mean by a time? When the right people know your songs?*'

Lol hadn't told Merrily. Whatever she really felt, she'd be twisting his arm to go for it. Fifteen years ago, if he hadn't, at the time, been a guest of the psychiatric health system, he'd have signed the contract before he left the capital.

Now he thought only about the wearying cycle of soundchecks and encores curtailed because the audience had paid to see the act that came next. Bars and towns, towns and bars that all looked the same, clapboard motels with sunken beds and rusty showers.

Plus, there was a message on his answering machine from Barry at the Black Swan. *Need an answer today, Lol. Before lunchtime, preferably. I can get posters done in a couple of hours, but I need to know.*

Unnerved, Lol rolled out of bed, went to the window.

He was panting.

He looked across the narrowing street to the matching black and white timber-framed 17th-century terrace with its winter-empty window boxes and the holly wreaths on its front doors and a few lights still on, more than usual because half of the houses were holiday homes now, coming alive for Christmas.

Lol turned, his face against the wet glass, to see the front garden of the vicarage and …

… Merrily, in jeans and a big sweater, looking up and down the dripping street in the half-light, as if she'd lost something. Her face soft and pale, hair over her eyes.

Lol just wanted to run down and hold her.

The condensation was cold on his cheek.

Merrily. Merrily and the songs. Nothing else. OK, maybe occasional gigs to keep your hand in and your mortgage payments met, your professional confidence afloat.

You only had one life and his was half gone and if he couldn't spend all of the rest of it with the woman who'd *really* turned him around, what was the point?

You know what I mean by a time? When the right people know your songs?

Lol looked up at the oak beam. How old? Four hundred years? Longer, maybe twice as long, because it had been a tree, born into red Welsh Border soil.

The guy had been wrong.

The right people *didn't* know his songs.

He'd toured a wide area of western Britain, but not within ten miles of this village. All the times Barry at the Black Swan had invited him to do a gig, and Lol had backed off.

Because, apart from Barry, nobody who lived here had ever acknowledged what he did. None of the locals, none of the incomers. He doubted anyone in Ledwardine had ever bought his solo album and certainly not anything he'd done years ago with Hazey Jane.

A cold audience. He'd played twice, in the past year, to cold audiences. He'd played in bars where they carried on drinking and chatting amongst themselves. He'd played one pub where a dozen people had carried their drinks outside because they couldn't hear themselves laugh. It hadn't mattered that much; he just wouldn't go back there again.

But this ... was where he lived. In Lucy's old house – there should be a blue plaque outside. This was where he wrote the songs that were so much a part of who he was. That, in some ways, were *all* that he was. If he said no to Barry, it was cowardice. Ledwardine would have good reason to despise him.

But if he said *yes*, and Ledwardine despised him ...

Lol saw Merrily looking down the street directly towards this window, and pulled his face away, stood clutching the wooden sill with both hands while the west wind rattled the panes as if it was trying to shake some sense into him.

The whining of the wind seeming to echo Councillor Pierce.

Grow or die.

9

Where the Dead Walk

TWO WOMEN IN a graveyard before dawn … this was not the kind of encounter you could easily walk away from. A sense of déjà vu had thrown Jane off balance, but she kept on walking along the side of the church, the woman and the wind keeping pace with her.

'Been out every morning for about a *week* or something,' the woman said, 'and there hasn't been anything much in the way of decent light *at all*. Rather hoping today was going to be the breakthrough. *No* chance.'

Jane's lamplight had found the costly lustre of a big camera with a fat lens, the kind of kit that made Eirion's prized SLR look like a budget disposable from Tesco.

'Yeah.' She looked up; the sky was paler, but there were none of the pastel streaks that preceded an actual sunrise. 'We get a clear night, and then it all closes in again.'

'What are you, a poacher?'

'Do I look like a poacher?'

'Dunno. Too dark to see. I was thinking, the lamp? Don't poachers lamp things?'

'So I believe,' Jane said. 'But, like, not often at a quarter to seven in the morning.'

Incomers: what could you say?

Be a bit rude to lamp her directly, but the haze on the edge of the beam had revealed bushy red-gold hair, and the posh, musky voice suggested fairly young – probably a bit younger than Mum, maybe early thirties? Still sexy, anyway, and aware of it.

The déjà vu had explained itself – Jane recalling meeting another photographer, from the *Guardian*, one afternoon last summer when they'd been trying to get publicity for the campaign. This had also followed a visit to Lucy's grave. It was like Lucy was the catalyst, her grave a *live* place. The idea made Jane feel happier. She asked the woman where she was from and got a vague arm-wave towards the orchard.

'Oh ... down there.'

'No, I mean who are you with? Which paper?'

'Oh, I see. Freelance. *Observer, Independent on Sunday* ... magazines. I write the words, too, sometimes.'

Jane nodded. Wasn't as if hacks and snappers were scarce in Ledwardine, not since the village had been identified as the principal centre of the – *retch* – New Cotswolds.

'Lensi.'

'Sorry?'

'People call me Lensi. Used to be Lenni, but now it's Lensi – L-E-N-S-I. For obvious reasons.'

She had what Jane was starting to think of as a New Cotswold accent. Posh, but a trace of London. And ... jolly. The only word for it. Super-confident, no sense of intruding.

'Right,' Jane said. 'Cool.'

'And you are?'

'Jane.'

They'd come through the small gate at the top of the churchyard and out onto the still-deserted square, where the fake gaslamps exposed a biggish woman in light-blue Gore-Tex, gleamingly new. Wide face, wide mouth, lovely even, white teeth. Also sapphire earrings and Ugg boots – Chelsea wellies.

'Well,' Jane said. 'I'd better be—'

'So who *is* Lucy? I mean, you haven't got a dog or anything with you?'

God.

'She was a friend.'

'Was?'

'The graveyard? Flat stones with, like, names carved into them?'

Jane stopped by the unlit Christmas tree, over twice her height and swaying in the wind. She could see lights in the vicarage. Should be getting back. Mum had a funeral; she wouldn't be in the best of moods by now.

'Her name was Lucy Devenish. Used to have a shop just over there, called Ledwardine Lore. Got knocked off her moped. Killed. On the bypass.'

'And you ... still like to chat with her, do you?'

'Look,' Jane said, 'if you want to catch the best of the early light, you could go down that alley, and you'll come to a stile which takes you into the remains of an old orchard, with a gateway into—'

'Coleman's Meadow. I know. It's the way I came.'

Jane stared at her, silent.

'I live near there,' Lensi said. 'For nearly seven weeks now, on and off. We're in a barn conversion.'

'Cole Barn?' Jane backed up into one of the oak pillars of the market hall. 'You've bought Cole Barn? But it's—'

Blighted was Gomer's word. Been on the market for a while, very desirable property and everything, but who wanted to lay down big money and maybe wind up living next to an estate of luxury executive homes?

'Just renting it, actually,' the woman said. 'We're checking out the area generally, to see if we like it, before deciding whether we should buy ourselves in.'

Buy ourselves in?

'And I was reading about all this kerfuffle over prehistoric remains, so now I'm sort of keeping an eye on it for the *Indy*, in case it blows up into something ...' Lensi stood back and stared openly at Jane. 'You're not Jane Watkins, by any chance?'

Damn.

'They sent me some cuttings, including a picture of the girl who started all the fuss. Objecting to the housing, if I've got this right, because it was on a ley line or something? That was before they found the stones.'

Jane said nothing. Lensi peered at her, the camera swinging free, dense coppery hair falling over one eye.

'You *are*!' She began flapping her jacket. 'Jane, what fun!'

'*Fun?*'

'Sorry!' Lensi backing off, palms raised. 'I know – serious matter. I realise that. Is it true you didn't know *anything* about the buried stones when you started your campaign?'

'Nobody did. And if you were at the meeting last night then you already know all this.'

'Oh ... none of *that* came out. It was quite disappointing. Jane, look, I'm sorry if I offended you. I just want to get this right. How you found out about the stones – just for information, I'm not writing it down or anything.'

Jane sighed. Eirion, who was planning a career in journalism, was always saying that pissing off the media was counter-productive. How could you expect them to publish the truth if you didn't tell them the truth?

'Please?'

'OK ... I'm like standing on Cole Hill.'

'That's the—'

'It's the only hill around here worth calling a hill. It was one evening last summer, and I had this ... I'm not calling it a vision or anything, it was just some things coming together.'

How could you explain it to a stranger? How could you convey the sudden awareness, at sunset, of this dead straight ancient track, passing like quicksilver through the field gates at either end of the meadow in direct alignment with the church steeple?

Perfect example of a *ley*, as first discovered by Alfred Watkins, of Hereford, nearly a century ago, in this same countryside. Alfred Watkins wasn't *known* to be an actual ancestor of Merrily and Jane Watkins, but who could say? She'd certainly felt he was there with her, like Lucy. Well, maybe not *quite* like Lucy.

'Leys are ... nobody knows for certain what they are. Just straight tracks from one ancient site to another, or maybe lines following arteries of earth energy. Or spirit paths. Where the dead walk?'

Lensi said nothing. The sky was shining dully, like a well-beaten drumskin.

'The dead are very important,' Jane said. 'To a community. You need continuity.'

'Really.'

'Ancient people knew that, in a way we don't today. It's important, for stability, for the spirit of the place, to have the ancestors around, keep them on your side. Which is why we need to keep this ancient path open … passing through the church, through the graveyard and the medieval orchard … then through the standing stones, to the top of Cole Hill, the holy hill.'

'Why is it holy?'

'It's like the guardian hill for the village. *Cole* is actually an old word for juggler or wizard. And Coleman's Meadow, at its foot … The Coleman … the shaman? So, like, if you uncover the old stones after centuries and then take them away and build an estate of crappy exec-utive homes for wealthy—'

The sapphire earrings twinkled.

'If you build houses we don't even need,' Jane said, 'then you're breaking the only link we have with the earliest origins of the village for purely commercial reasons. So we set up the Coleman's Meadow Preservation Society—'

'*We?*'

'Me and my … ex-boyfriend.'

'This was a pagan sort of thing, was it?'

'Kind of.'

'As in worshipping old gods?'

'The sun. The moon. Yeah, I suppose old gods. But obviously it's not *only* pagans, it's everybody who's concerned about preserving what's important. We've had a lot of support from all kinds of people, all over the country … abroad, even.'

'Old gods.' Lensi smiled in her patronising way, like all this was so incredibly quaint. 'It was a stone circle?'

'Just a stone row, they think.'

'And that's where the dead walk, is it?'

'It's a big subject.' Jane looked up as a few isolated raindrops fell. 'Look, I'm sorry … if I don't get back I'm going to miss the school bus. I need to change.'

'Of course. Jane,' Lensi looked down at her camera, 'I'd like to take a few pictures of you, if I may. I don't mean now, obviously …'

'Some people reckon we'll have floods in the village,' Jane said. 'Could be some pictures for you there.'

'Ordinary local news … that's not really my thing.'

'It's just I got a lot of stick over it last time.'

'Because of your mother's job? What kind of pagan *are* you, exactly, Jane?'

'I'm sorry – why are you interested?'

Lensi shrugged. Maybe she was just looking for a coven or something to join. It happened. Happened a lot these days, apparently. Like in the old days incomers would want to know about the tennis club or the bridge circle.

And this was a set-up, wasn't it? This woman had recognised her and followed her into the churchyard. Didn't really give a toss about the sunrise.

'Look, I've go to— Going to be late for school, OK?'

The rain came on suddenly, like all the taps in heaven had been turned on. Lensi was shielding her camera, Jane backing off towards the vicarage, dragging up the hood of her parka, then turning to run, hard against the downpour.

Hearing Lensi calling after her, but she didn't stop.

10

Peace on Earth

THERE WAS A sourness to it, this weather. The rain was rolling down from the Black Mountains like bales of barbed wire. It was relentless, and it sapped you.

Merrily slowed the Volvo behind a tractor and trailer. About five roads were closed, diversions in place. The route to Hereford took you through hamlets you'd forgotten existed, past flooded fields with surfaces like stretched cellophane. Was there such a condition as rain-sickness?

'*Why do they never dredge the rivers? That's my point.*' Phone-in voice on Radio Hereford and Worcester. '*How do they expect us not to get flooded if they don't dredge the flamin' rivers? Can you tell me why, Colin?*'

Studio voice: '*I'm afraid I can't, Robert, but it's a good point and one we'll be putting to our expert from the Environment Agency who, of course, should've arrived by now but he's – yes, you've guessed it – been held up by the floods.*'

On days like this, virtually every programme on Hereford and Worcester turned into a flood programme. Which was useful but not the main reason Merrily was listening.

Finally showing up, with about ten minutes to spare, Jane had claimed she'd only been checking on the river.

Been away too long just for that, of course, but there was no time to go into it before the kid was off to catch the school bus, carrying a slice of yolky toast across the square. Merrily guessing she'd been over to Coleman's Meadow to make sure nobody had come in the night and dug up the stones.

As if, having been the first in the new millennium to identify something odd about Coleman's Meadow, she was now feeling personally responsible for it.

Was *obsession* too strong a word for this? Lucy Devenish, Thomas Traherne, Alfred Watkins, Nick Drake ... a pale company of dead people with whom Jane felt—

'*Christ!*'

The old Volvo was suddenly bucking against a wall of water, as the tractor and trailer up ahead plunged into a flooded dip in the lane where the ditch had overflowed. Merrily frantically wrestling for control as the black tide rose around the car, and the force of it, the *weight* of it, was unexpectedly frightening.

Then she was through.

But, hell, you could see how easy it would be to get trapped – tonight's TV news screening a video clip, shot on somebody's mobile phone, of a woman in a cassock being pulled by firefighters out of a side window of her drowning car.

She was testing her brakes, letting out her breath, as Colin on the radio suggested that, with Bishop's Meadow already annexed by the swollen Wye, Hereford's crucial Belmont roundabout would be closed before the evening rush hour. Colin sounding quite excited. However, as flood-relief seldom involved detectives, it seemed unlikely this was what Frannie Bliss had meant when he'd suggested that Merrily kept the radio on.

She'd called him on his mobile after Jane had caught the bus.

'Norra good time, madam,' Bliss said.

Not referring to her by name a signal that he was in the CID room. Understandably, Bliss had never liked to advertise a working relationship with the diocesan exorcist.

'Any chance you could call me back, Frannie? Only wanted to ask one question.'

'Yeh, I've heard that before.'

'What would your Special Branch colleague be doing in Ledwardine?'

'When?'

'Last night.' No use pretending she might've been mistaken; it *was* him. 'At a parish meeting about the Coleman's Meadow stones. He'd obviously come in after everybody else, sitting near the door, first one out.'

'No idea, Merrily, I'm not one of his confidants. Maybe he's bought himself a holiday cottage in Ledwardine. They're on good money, the funny boys. Fringe benefits.'

'I didn't even know he was still around. Thought he'd gone back to the Met or wherever they hang out.'

'Look,' Bliss said, 'I've gorra go. I'll get back to you when I can, all right?'

'Has something happened?'

'Put your radio on,' Bliss had said. 'And keep it on.'

The travel update warned of serious flooding around Bromyard in the east, which could be a problem; she'd need to get over there within the next few days to pick up Lol's Christmas present. Couldn't leave it much longer – too much to do around the big day, and there was the delicate issue of introducing the midnight meditation on Christmas Eve.

Always a problem to alter anything in a village.

'*And if you're having problems in your particular part of the two counties,*' Colin said, '*ring in and tell us … our lines are open all day, every day right through Christmas.*'

Christmas. Why did the glow always seem to fade, the closer you came to it? Why was there always some damn crisis? Peace on earth, goodwill to all—

'*—However, as you may have heard on the news, the floods aren't the only problem in Hereford. Police have sealed off part of the city centre in the wake of last night's—*'

Ah …

'*—shocking discovery of a human head in the ruined Blackfriars Monastery in the Widemarsh Street area. Our reporter Arabella Finch is at the scene. Bella, what's happening now?*'

Merrily slowed, crawling into tree-fringed King's Acre in the city's western suburbs. The female voice came back in low quality, probably from a radio car.

'Colin, I'm talking to you from one of the back streets between Widemarsh Street and Commercial Road from where it's usually possible to see the ruins of the medieval Blackfriars Monastery. But not this morning. The whole area's been completely screened off by the police who've set up an incident room at the Cantilupe School next door to the monastery. I've been told a press conference has been scheduled for twelve noon, when obviously we hope to learn more. But I can tell you that the head was found last night by a member of the public on or near the medieval preaching cross in the rose garden at the front of the monastery ruins.'

'Bit of a shock for someone, Bella. And of course, this all happened when the city was absolutely packed with Christmas shoppers, in town for the traditional Wednesday evening late opening.'

'There probably weren't as many shoppers as usual, Colin, because of the floods, but obviously it's made the police investigation a lot more diffi-cult. With so many extra people about, it would be far easier for whoever left the head to come and go unnoticed.'

'Now it's a … it's the head of a man, is that correct?'

'That's what we understand, Colin.'

'And is this someone who was actually, you know, beheaded?'

'My information is that it was done after death.'

'Do they know who it is yet?'

'Well, personally, I think they do, and there's quite a buzz about it. I can't see that they won't be revealing a name in the course of the day, but relatives will have to be told first, of course. There has, obviously, been an extensive search for the rest of the body, but no suggestion that anything's been found yet.'

'And what about local people, Bella? The people living and working in a very built-up part of the city. How are they reacting?'

'Well, as you can imagine nobody here can quite believe that something so, you know, horrific and barbaric should have come to Hereford. Earlier this morning, I talked to people living in the streets behind Blackfriars Monastery, as well as some coming to work in shops and offices around lower Widemarsh Street—'

Merrily switched off the litany of shock and disbelief and what's the world coming to?

A black Christmas for somebody. No surprise that Bliss didn't have time to speculate about what Jonathan Long might have been doing in Ledwardine.

Peace on earth, goodwill to all men.

Yeah, right.

Under a sky the colour of wet mortar, she came off the White Cross roundabout at the fourth exit, for the crematorium.

11

A Sense of Eternity

Quite a turnout for Tom Parson, and Merrily had known him well enough to make it meaningful – as much as you ever could with another funeral party waiting outside, stamping its feet and rubbing its hands.

Tom had been Old Ledwardine – at least, that was what she'd thought until she'd talked to the family.

'Tom was … a *character*,' she said in the chapel at the crem. 'Someone of whom, now he's gone, we say, *We won't see his kind again.* Someone who was part of the fabric of the village. Old Ledwardine. I'm … not exactly Old Ledwardine, and I just assumed Tom's family had been around the village for generations.'

In fact, she'd discovered, Tom Parson had been an incomer, a retiree. OK, thirty years ago and only from Shropshire. But there was surely a message here about how a community – even a landscape, or, as Jane would insist, the spiritual essence of a place – would absorb and condition people.

If it happened slowly. If it happened naturally. And if you kept open a few pathways to the past. If you had that *grounding*.

She didn't say any of that. There wouldn't be time – that was her excuse. Anyway, there'd be a memorial service for Tom back in the village after Christmas, followed by interment of the ashes in the churchyard; she'd be able to do a better job then. Tom's niece had sent her away with a pile of his historical notes which she thought the parish ought to have. Maybe Jane could go through them.

But that was it for today. Merrily drove into the city centre and found a parking space on the corner of Broad Street and King Street, just across from the Cathedral, its sandstone tower wadded in charcoal cloud.

There was a light on, up in the Deliverance office in the gatehouse, and she could see Sophie Hill standing at the window, quite still, poised like a mannequin in some discreet dress shop for elegant women of a certain age.

But the composure was illusory. By the time she was halfway up the stone steps, Sophie was looking down at her, rigid now, in the office doorway.

'Merrily—'

'Just dropped in to see if you fancied a bit of lunch?'

'Can't. I'm sorry.'

'Soph?' Following her into the office, Merrily noticed that the white hair was coming adrift and a silver-blue silk scarf lay discarded in the correspondence tray. 'Is there something …?

Looking into Sophie's eyes. On any other woman's face, the expression would convey maybe mildly disturbed. On Sophie it suggested horribly distraught.

'Merrily, you're not in a hurry, are you?'

'Well, no, I—'

'Could I ask you to mind the office for an hour? I wouldn't ask if it wasn't important. You're not in a hurry, are you?'

'You just asked me … No.'

'Good. Thank you.'

Sophie pulled her coat from the peg. Merrily took off her black woollen funeral coat and went and sat down behind the desk. In the centre of it was the leather-bound pad Sophie used to take down the Bishop's dictation. Nothing else.

'There's nothing I can …?'

'If you could just look after the office for an hour. If the Bishop of Bath and Wells rings, tell him Bernard will get back to him tonight. If I'm going to be longer than an hour, I'll call. If you have to leave, lock up, would you? You know where the keys are …?'

'Of course I know where … *You're* OK, aren't you? I mean—'

'Yes,' Sophie said. 'I'm fine.'

Had the Bishop's secretary ever looked this pale?

Jane said, 'You ever heard of a photographer known as Lensi?'

'What?'

'L-E-N-S-I.'

She was in a cubicle in the girls' toilets, with the mobile. Keeping her voice down.

'This a joke?' Eirion said.

'Irene, would I really be ringing you this time in the morning to tell you a joke?'

Was he *glad* she'd rung? Had his fancy phone ID'd her, with LED red stars glittering around her name? Was he excited to hear her voice, the way, if you twisted her arm, she'd have to admit it was really good to hear him, even to hear herself calling him *Irene*?

A few months ago, they'd been in one another's phones all the time, like this was for eternity. But situations changed.

'What's she do?' Eirion said.

'She takes pictures. Photojournalist.'

Had to admit this was an excuse to call him. Yeah, yeah, she accepted she'd been looking for one and this would probably be the best reason she'd get this side of Christmas.

'I don't really know many photographers, except for a few TV cameramen,' Eirion said. 'I'm … as you know, I'm just another student.'

'*You* don't think you're just another student, Irene.'

He read all the papers, in a professional kind of way. He remembered the bylines, who was a good writer, who got the biggest stories.

'What's her full name, Jane?'

'I've told you, I don't know her real name. She does pictures for the *Independent*.'

'That's a start. What's she look like?'

'Like … early thirties? Red-haired. Not small. Not exactly plump but certainly, you know, voluptuous.'

'And you want to know about her *because* …?'

'Because she's just moved into the village and maybe has an interest in witchcraft or something. Not that she seems to know much about it. She's probably just attracted to the nudity and fertility rites. And she wants to take my picture.'

'Without your clothes?'

'I can see I'm wasting my—'

'*If*, however, you were just looking for a reason to call me, I'm flattered,' Eirion said.

'I was *not*—'

'Jane, you're doing your smoky voice.'

'I'm trying to be *discreet*, you smug Welsh git! I'm at school, in the bog.'

A silence. Eirion drew breath.

'A proper name would help. Jane, look … seriously, we haven't really seen much of each other since the summer, have we?'

'If you remember, you went off to university.'

'It's *Cardiff*. It's less than a two-hour drive away, and I'm home at weekends. As you know.'

'A lot can happen at university. You're young – young*ish* – and unattached. Universities are full of loose women.'

'Let's not go into all that again,' Eirion said. 'I can assure you there hasn't been anybody for—'

'Longer than one night?'

'For just over four months, I was going to say. Which, in case you've forgotten …'

'No, I—' Jane's voice died on her. But could she believe this? 'I haven't forgotten.'

'So I was thinking … Well, my dad and Gwennan were supposed to be going to France for Christmas, with the girls and I was thinking you could maybe've come over here.'

'Where we'd have the house to ourselves. Kind of thing.'

'Only that's not going to happen now. Sioned sprained an ankle skating and they're putting it off until the New Year, when you'll probably be back at school. So I was wondering about maybe coming over there. Like for a few days?'

'And stay where – the Black Swan?'

'Yeah, on my massive student grant. I was actually thinking … the vicarage? You've got a lot of spare bedrooms. I'd pay, you know, reasonably normal rates. B-and-B?'

'That's—'

'What do you think? Just to see if there's … you know … anything left? You know what I'm saying.'

'Irene, we were childhood sweethearts. It's a phase.'

'A phase.'

'And like, if you really don't know if there's anything *left*—'

'On *your* side. I meant *your* side. My side I know about.'

'Oh.'

'Jane, would I really be sitting here getting all sweaty and embarrassed and stuff, if I wasn't still …?'

She didn't say anything. She realised she was smiling.

Realising he'd never really gone away. That her life was full of Eirion cross-references. Although that wasn't necessarily a good thing, was it? They were young, they were supposed to be putting themselves about. *Why* was she smiling?

'It was just a thought, all right?' Eirion said.

'Of course, if the dig's on in Coleman's Meadow,' Jane said, 'I was supposed to be, you know, helping?'

'And that's limited, is it, to people who've belatedly applied for archaeology courses on account of they've been watching *Time Team* and *Trench One* and can't think of any quicker way to get on TV?'

'*Au contraire*, Welshman, I believe I can bring to the study of antiquities something new and meaningful.'

'As distinct from your usual pseudo-pagan New Age bullshit.'

'And I'm thinking, could I stand this for a whole week?'

'Jane, you'd love it.'

'I'll talk to Mum,' Jane said.

Somehow excited. Despicable, really.

Sophie, nun-like in her long charcoal-grey coat and her silk scarf, was walking rapidly across the Cathedral Green towards the Castle Street entrance, furled umbrella under her arm.

She lived back there, in one of the posh terraces behind the clois-ters and the Cathedral School. Her husband was an architect, semi-retired now, the golf club a second home. An adopted son lived in Canada.

Merrily watched her from the office window. Some domestic crisis? Domestic, for Sophie, usually meant the Cathedral. Which she *served*. Living within its ambience, more a part of it than any of the bishops she'd worked for. Whatever had happened, it had to be serious for Sophie to be walking *away* from the Cathedral at not yet one p.m. on a working day.

When she passed out of sight, between the bare trees, Merrily switched on the computer, opened the Deliverance file.

Still just one entry for this month: a vague report of what Huw Owen would call a *volatile* – poltergeist activity, alleged, at a small warehouse on the Holmer trading estate. Request for assistance withdrawn before it could be checked out. Pity, really. There was always a reason for reported phenomena, always something interesting. But the Deliverance Ministry wasn't the police; you went where you were invited.

The report, however, would stay on file in perpetuity, in case some future Deliverance adviser should be approached by some future tenant of the premises.

If nothing else, this job gave you a sense of eternity.

If *nothing else* …? In many ways, Deliverance gave you too much – too much to question, too much strangeness. Too much that seemed to have very little to do with faith and the yearning for transcendence, more with a basic, primeval fear of the unknowable. Sometimes the roles of priest and exorcist didn't seem wholly compatible.

Time on her hands now, Merrily put the computer to sleep and tapped Al and Sally Boswell's number in Knight's Frome into her mobile, to check on the progress of Lol's Christmas present.

'Well, I *think* it's nearly ready,' Sally said. 'Probably tomorrow, all being well.'

'And I do want to pay the proper price.'

'Al says you'll pay what he asks. He's quite annoyed with Laurence for not telling him sooner about what happened to the other one.'

'Lol blames himself. Whereas I blame *my*self because it was smashed on the instructions of a man he was approaching on my behalf.'

'It was a *guitar*, Merrily, not some holy relic.'

'Sally, to Lol, a Boswell guitar is as close to a holy relic as you can get with steel strings.'

Sally laughed and said Al would understand. Al was of Romani descent. The lute-shaped bodies of his guitars contained many different kinds of wood, most of them pulled from the hedgerows and the copses and dingles of the Frome Valley where the Romani used to come annually to pick hops.

Sally, very *olde English gentry*, said, 'I probably forgot to mention, he's finally taken on an apprentice. Becoming more aware of his mortality, perhaps, and the need to pass on his skills. But that does mean he needs to turn out more instruments per annum, if only to pay the boy a reasonable wage. So, you see, they aren't *quite* so rare and precious any more.'

'How about I come over at the weekend? Is a cheque OK?'

'Do watch out for the floods, though, won't you, Merrily?'

'The Frome's out?'

'Not yet,' Sally said, as the office phone began ringing. 'Well, not here, anyway, but Al tells me he's seen the snails moving uphill.'

'What?'

'Hundreds of them, Al says. It's an old sign. Slugs, too, apparently. A scramble for higher ground.'

'Blimey. Look, Sally, I'll have to go, I'm on my own in the office and the phone's ringing.'

The Bishop of Baths and Wells? God, who *was* the Bishop of Bath and Wells now? As Merrily clicked off the mobile, a gust of new rain skated over the window behind her, like brushes on a snare drum, and she glanced over her shoulder. The way you did, now that something as drably prosaic as rain had turned sinister. She picked up the phone.

'Merrily.'

'Sophie?'

'I wonder if you might join me.'

'Now? Me? Where?'

'I can meet you on the corner of Castle Street and Quay Street – do you know where I mean? It will take you no more than about three minutes on foot.'

'Probably need to bring the car, Sophie, I think I'm about to get nicked for outstaying my welcome in King Street. What's happened?'

'I'll meet you in *ten* minutes, then.'

'Has something happened?'

A clock ticking at Sophie's end. A big, old clock.

'Sophie?'

'You may not have heard, but there's been a particularly horrific murder in the city. Or at least—'

'I heard on the radio, yeah. You mean where the victim was ... beheaded?'

Merrily stood up. Down below, Broad Street was like a sepia print, all its colours draining away in the downpour, and the Cathedral Green was deserted.

'I'm with his widow,' Sophie said.

12

Throwback

SOPHIE WAS WAITING in Castle Street under her pink and yellow golf umbrella. Surreal, like a bad dream in which you somehow understood that pink and yellow were the colours of foreboding and death.

'Nobody here knows yet,' Sophie said. 'When it comes out, all hell—'

Her face looked thinner, with hollows. They were alone in what had been the medieval heart of Hereford. No shops here, no obvious public buildings, only timber-gabled cottages and three-storey Georgian town houses. Quiet, except for the beating rain and the murmur of old money, what was left of it.

Never mind Baghdad, think how many heads must've rolled routinely down here, below the walls of Hereford Castle.

Merrily had found a parking space near the footpath to the Castle Green. Not a stone left of the castle now, unless some remained in the foundations of these steep, solid, private dwellings, one owned by Sophie and her husband, another by ...

'What's her name?'

'Helen,' Sophie said. 'Ayling. We've ... known one another for some years.'

'I've heard that name ... Ayling ... have I?'

'Well, of course you have.'

But the connection wouldn't come. Merrily felt damp and uncomfortable in her funeral clothes.

'She hadn't reported him missing,' Sophie said. 'Hadn't seen him for more than twenty-four hours, but it wasn't the first time.'

'Oh my God, she had to identify ...?'

'No, they spared her that.' Sophie nodded down the street towards a three-storey terrace of old red brick. 'It's the middle one, with the cream door.'

She pointed the umbrella, began to follow it into the road. Merrily stayed at the kerb, getting very wet very quickly.

'Sophie ... why me?'

'Because you're ...' Sophie came back, held the umbrella over them both '... because you're a widow and ... and a priest. And you mix with these people.'

'People? You mean the police?'

'And because you're here. Helen doesn't have any relatives.'

Didn't sound right. A touch nervous now, Merrily let herself be steered into a narrow alley at the end of the terrace, Sophie deciding they wouldn't use the front door.

'They'll see us.'

'Who?'

'You didn't notice the car parked on a double yellow line?'

'The police?'

'Watching the house. They wanted a woman to come in and stay with her, a ... what do you call them?'

'Family liaison officer?'

'Well, even *I* know what that's really for. Someone following her around, being solicitous, making tea, hoping she'll let something slip.'

'What?'

'Here.'

Sophie pushed at a mossy, Gothic-pointed door in a high brick wall.

They were in a substantial walled garden. A dead fountain in an overflowing stone pool, rain bouncing angrily from a small conservatory backing on to the house.

'We were in the Cathedral choir together,' Sophie said.

As if this explained something.

'How come no relatives?'

'Well, not in Hereford, anyway. She met Clement in London when she was a secretary with the Association of County Councils, and he—'

'Clement?'

'Clement Ayling.'

'Christ,' Merrily said.

A high-ceilinged drawing room. The grandfather clock doing its hollow *thock thock* in the shadows. Tall windows silvered by the rain, a pastel green glow from a small reading lamp on a coffee table and a crimson glimmer from the fireplace. Pictures on the walls of the same man shaking hands with various notables: Princess Anne, Margaret Thatcher.

'Merrily lost—' Sophie coughed. 'Lost her husband some years ago. In a car crash.'

Helen Ayling looked up, confused, from a brown leather wing chair. 'And had *he* stormed out after a row?' She steadied the white china cup and saucer on her knees. 'I'm sorry, I—'

'After several rows, actually,' Merrily said. 'Sometimes he walked out, sometimes I walked out. But it's ... hardly the same.'

The atmosphere was different from the dimmed death houses she often had to visit. Unstable here, still slippery with congealing shock. She and Sophie were sharing a creaky leather chesterfield. On the wall behind his widow's head, Councillor Clem Ayling stood shoulder to shoulder with Bill Clinton – but only, Merrily guessed, for the photo.

'It was rather stupid of me,' Helen Ayling said, 'even to mention the row. But you don't think, do you? You *can't* think. It's as though everything around you is collapsing.'

No make-up, and her eyes were dry. She was slim and tidy and her short brown hair, though tangled, looked freshly washed. Merrily had imagined she'd be around the same age – who knew? – as Sophie, but she was younger, maybe late forties. So about twenty years younger than Clem Ayling.

'They said to me, what was it about? What were you arguing about? I said, it's none of your business, it's a private matter – we had a row, like couples do, he walked out and he didn't …' her voice gave out and she swallowed '… come back.'

Merrily looked up at Clement Ayling in the Thatcher photo. A bulky, beaming man with grey hair, crisp and wavy, and an almost-Edwardian moustache. She'd never met him, knew him only by reputation: an old-school Tory, a dinosaur, a throwback.

Merrily's mouth was dry. Someone had killed a former leader of the city council and cut off his head. All hell *would* break loose.

'He'd done it before,' Helen Ayling said. 'Last time he booked into the Castle House, just up the street. He has an office, with a change of clothes, and he'd go directly there the following day. After he retired, the council became … most of who he was.'

Merrily nodded.

'The police said, why didn't you report him missing? I tried to explain , but they didn't seem convinced.' Both hands gripping the cup. '*Oh, dear God.*'

'When you say the police …?'

'Man with some sort of Northern accent.'

'Liverpool?'

'Perhaps.'

The strategic hypocrisy of the cops. As if they'd have reacted at all, the same night, to a report of a man walking out on his wife. Even if it *was* a face from the *Hereford Times*.

Helen Ayling sat up, placing the cup and saucer on the table, shaking her head.

'I still can't take it in. The sheer horror of it. When did they do it? He was on foot. Were they waiting somewhere *here*? Did they take him somewhere to—?'

'*Don't.*'

Sophie reaching over, taking Helen's hands. Sophie's eyes suddenly blazing with outrage. That it could happen *here*. In this most protected, select part of town. This conservation area. Under the Cathedral that Sophie served.

'The police were all over the house,' Helen said. 'And the garden. Putting all the lights on. The *tool-shed* ...'

Yes, they would have to look in the tool shed.

'You'll stay with us tonight, Helen?'

'Sophie, thank you, but ... I have to stay here, don't I? For as long as ... Have to get used to it.'

'I'm not sure that's a good idea, Mrs Ayling,' Merrily said. 'I'm afraid you're going to get them all hanging around outside – national press, TV. That's one reason the police suggest a family liaison officer stays here with you. Protect your privacy when your ... when they release your husband's name.'

'They can't protect you from your thoughts, though, can they?'

'With regard to that,' Sophie said, 'I thought Merrily could perhaps do something ... pray with you?'

'Sophie ...' Helen Ayling, perhaps understandably, looking less than eager. 'I rather think ...'

'I understand that at times like this,' Merrily said, 'prayer can be difficult, so ...'

Helen Ayling nodded, her eyes falling shut like an old-fashioned doll's. 'It's not real to me yet. They can't even—' Her eyes flicked open, looking into Merrily's. 'Your husband ... was *he* ... his body ... able to be identified ... by you?'

'No. His car went into a motorway bridge. At speed.'

Sean's body pulped and shredded and mingled with the remains of his mistress.

The front-door knocker crashed twice; Helen Ayling and Merrily both flinched.

'Stay there.' Sophie came to her feet, moved to the door to the hall. 'I'll see who it is.'

Helen nodded wearily, pulling a dark green cardigan around her shoulders. Merrily sat there feeling all wrong in her cassock, like some kind of attendant angel of death. Noting that Helen Ayling's eyes remained dry, without the hollow shining light that came with real grief. Pain was there and revulsion, but if this had been a marriage made in heaven something in heaven was malfunctioning.

'The Blackfriars priory,' Helen said. 'Monastery. I've never even been there. I'm sure my husband never mentioned it. And the ... the Preaching Cross. *Why ...?*'

And then Sophie was back, carrying her grey coat and Merrily's coat and the wet umbrella.

'It's the police again. Not Bliss this time, Merrily. It looks as if he's been relieved by his superior officer.'

'Howe?'

Sophie nodded. Merrily stood up at once. If it was Howe, better she wasn't here.

'Helen, we can probably both wait in the kitchen,' Sophie said, 'if we're quiet.'

'Please make yourselves some tea. Anything you want.' Helen crossing the room, head bowed. 'I'll let them in.'

At the door, she turned. She looked small and devastated, like a lost child in a department store.

'Why do they keep coming here? I'm not *part* of this. He was a *public* man. Even in ... death.'

She went out quickly, almost running, and Merrily followed Sophie into the inner hall leading to the kitchen, the way they'd come in, Merrily looking back once, thinking, yes, in many ways this *was* the same as her and Sean.

When a man you were supposed to love and didn't any more came to a sudden and savage end, it messed you up in all kinds of unforeseeable ways.

13

All of Him

OBVIOUSLY ANNIE HOWE *would* come in for this one. This was high-profile in every respect. This would be national news. And besides ...

'My father knew your husband for many years,' Annie Howe was saying. 'He's asked me to express to you his—'

'I'm sorry?'

'County Councillor Howe? Charles Howe?'

'Charlie,' Helen Ayling said. 'Yes, of course.'

Yes, there was *that* very useful connection.

Merrily stood listening in the inner hall, with its stained panels and yellowing mouldings. The door to the drawing room wasn't quite closed. She'd put on her coat and her gloves, and it was still cold, *looked* cold in the blue-grey light from a single frosted window at the far end.

There was a radiator, but it was off. Evidently not a man to waste money, Clem Ayling. At least, not his own.

Annie Howe said, 'I spoke to my father this morning. In confidence – he's an ex-police officer. He asked me to convey to you his regret at what's happened to your husband.'

His *regret* that someone killed your husband and cut off his head? The Charlie that Merrily knew would have said far more but, like New York cops on TV who tossed out a cursory '*Sorry for your loss*' before cutting to the chase, Annie Howe didn't do warmth. Or even, come to think of it, fury.

Helen said, 'Charlie was here ... I don't know, some weeks ago.'

'Mrs Ayling, I'd like to ask you a few more questions relating to your husband's council work.'

'I'm afraid he didn't—'

'If you could bear with me … the last day you were together, that's the day before yesterday, you told my colleague your husband was out all day, at meetings. Do you remember precisely *which* meetings?'

'The morning, I'm not sure, but in the afternoon I know he had a meeting of Hereforward.'

'Hereforward – could you remind me …?'

'It's where they discuss radical, long-term ideas for the future of the county, with various appointed consultants. Clem always hated going, but he didn't like the idea of anything like that even existing, unless he was there to monitor it. Bunch of outsiders, he used to say, who couldn't care less about Hereford. But then he also used to say that about most of the council officials.'

'He didn't get on with certain officials? Can you think of anyone in particular?'

'Not really, Superintendent. He used to say most of them simply saw Herefordshire as a stepping stone to somewhere more important.'

'But nobody in particular.'

'I don't think he singled out … He also thought some of them were giving jobs to their friends who weren't up to it. As well as having too many parties and drinking sessions. I'm sure Charlie's told you—'

'Yes,' Howe said, 'but I'd like to hear about it from your husband's perspective.'

Sophie had appeared in the doorway with a white china cup and saucer, the cup's contents steaming. Merrily followed her across the passage to the kitchen. All this was no business of hers, but sometimes – and she wasn't proud of this – it helped to have inside information to trade with Frannie Bliss.

'God knows, Sophie, I've tried to like that woman. Cold, no people skills and she'll be chief constable before she's forty – that's what Bliss says.' Softly shutting the kitchen door behind her, she unbuttoned her coat, pulled off her gloves. 'How am I doing for Christian charity so far?'

'You look starved.'

'That's because I haven't eaten.'

Aching for a cigarette, Merrily sat down at the round central table. The kitchen was lofty and oppressive, all dark wood and high cupboards. She drank some tea and looked at Sophie, who was standing with her back to the stove – a Rayburn, not an Aga.

'How long have they lived here?'

'*He* lived here for over thirty years,' Sophie said. 'They were married … ten, twelve years ago?'

'Not a first marriage, then.'

'His first wife died. Two grown-up children, both … away.'

'So how much will Helen …?'

'Inherit? I don't know. If she gets the house, she'll sell it. It's entirely impractical, just a symbol of Clement's status. Bought it when his business was flourishing, in the 1970s.'

'What *was* his business?'

'Electrical goods, small chain of discount shops. Lucrative in their time. Gone before you arrived here, I think. His daughters weren't interested in taking it on.'

'You don't think Helen will stay?'

'I think she'll be off as soon as he's buried.' Sophie came to sit down. 'It was a dream gone sour. A rather naive dream. I don't know what he promised her, but she had this vision of an elegant, graceful life in the Cathedral Close. Civilised dinner parties, receptions, nights at the theatre. This is just … just a market town with a cathedral.'

Sophie looked up at the soiled ceiling, wrinkled her nose. 'All the changes she was going to make to the house and wasn't allowed to. *What's wrong with it?* he used to say, and I think he really didn't know. Self-made man, you see, his father was a manual worker. Mrs Thatcher – you saw the photo?'

'Mmm.'

'His idol. The small-businessman's daughter. Waste not, want not. He loved it when she was advising us to stock up on tinned food. He'd go to Tesco and come back with nine tins of stewed steak. Also thought – like Mrs T – that the worst thing to happen to the twentieth century was the 1960s.'

Merrily said nothing. If there was a margin between this and Sophie's own philosophy, it was slender.

'And she actually didn't realise any of this before she married him?'

'He was – I've heard this from quite a few people – a very different man when he was away from home. He was always dynamic, in a heavy sort of way, full of a sometimes alarming energy. And away from Hereford he became … expansive. Generous, charming. As if he saw himself as an ambassador. Helen was exposed to the full force of it, at a particularly vulnerable time in her life.'

Sophie got up and went to the door to check if the police were still in the house.

'Familiar story. Still living at home, caring for her disabled father. And then he died, leaving a void she had no idea how to fill. Clement Ayling was rather good at filling voids.' She came back and sat down. 'I'd guess it barely survived the wedding. Within two years she was almost suicidal. But wouldn't leave, you see – couldn't. She'd made her bed.'

'So this row they had – what do you think that was about?'

'She's not going to tell anyone *now*, Merrily. To be quite honest, I'd've thought a row would have been almost a positive step. Most of the time they hardly communicated any more. Helen said the council was most of what he'd become … I'd go further. Since he sold the business, the council was all of him.'

'So …' No way of edging around this. 'Frannie Bliss suspects that Helen might have had something to do with Ayling's death? Is that what you're thinking?'

Sophie stared at the closed door, her hands around the small brown teapot. A tea-for-two, waste-not-want-not kind of teapot.

Merrily said, 'That why I'm here, Sophie? Second opinion?'

'Given—' Anxiety bloomed in Sophie's eyes. 'Given the nature of his death, that seems … barely conceivable.'

'We don't *know* the nature of his death. Only what was done to him, presumably afterwards. His whole body could be in … portable fragments.'

Sophie was rigid now, palms flat on the table.

'Oh, look,' Merrily said, 'Bliss would just be going through the motions. When there's a murder, the first person who needs to be eliminated is the partner. Because … in most cases, the partner did it. And you just said yourself that she was desperate. Suicidal.'

'I said *almost* suicidal. She got used to it, Merrily, as people usually do. As women of my generation almost *always* did.'

'No, you're right,' Merrily said. 'It's ridiculous.'

Dismissing the image of a wretched, half-demented Helen Ayling carrying her husband's head through the Christmas crowds in a shopping bag. But it was no surprise that they'd checked out the tool shed.

Merrily sat back. Her stomach felt like an empty fridge. She wanted to pray, preferably over a cigarette.

Sophie said, 'If Inspector Bliss thinks—'

'Sophie … whatever Bliss thinks doesn't matter any more. It's what …' Merrily nodded at the door. 'It's what *she* thinks.'

'We should go.'

Sophie was on her feet, carrying the crockery to the sink, numbly turning on taps. Merrily found a tea towel, and they performed, in silence, a domestic ritual which might never seem as comfortingly familiar again.

They left by the back door, not speaking until they were in the alley. The rain had thinned; the sun was a voyeur behind dirty curtains of cloud.

Merrily was thinking that Howe and whoever was carrying her bag might be closeted with Helen until dark.

'I'll come back later,' Sophie said. 'When they've gone.'

'Be slightly careful, Sophie.'

'I shall sit and listen. Without questioning.' Sophie had put up the golf umbrella, a garish blossom in the drizzle on Castle Street. 'Do you want to come back for something to eat, Merrily? It really won't take me—'

'No … thank you. Really, I need to get back. Get out of these clothes.'

Merrily saw that there was still a car across the street, parked on the double yellow lines. Sophie turned to walk home, looking back over her shoulder.

'I'll call you tonight. After I've talked to Helen.'

'I'd be glad if you would.'

Walking back to the Volvo, Merrily felt choked up with doubt and uncertainty about something that was not her business. And apprehension about Sophie, about whom she harboured no doubts, no uncertainties.

As she reached the unmarked police car, another car pulled in behind it, a window gliding down.

'You got time for a coffee, Reverend?' Frannie Bliss said.

14

Joy to the World

IN A CHROMIUM cafe on Broad Street, Bliss was taking his filter coffee black, to match his mood. His face was sallow with freckles, his hair had been eroded beyond comb-over to the shaven stage, never totally convincing in December.

Not yet forty, looked older.

'She wants me out,' he said.

At barely four p.m., the day was signing off. The winter-holiday lights over the street were ice blue and sea green. No angels, no Santas, no reindeer.

'Hang on in there, Frannie,' Merrily said. 'She might be up for a transfer to the Met or something.'

Bliss looked up over his bitter coffee with a bitter little smile. 'Merrily, I meant Kirsty.'

'Oh God.' Merrily lowering her mug. 'I thought you'd managed to … deal with things.'

'You can only paper over the cracks so many times before the paste stops sticking and the frigging paper falls off.'

'What about the kids? It's … Christmas.'

'Oh, Christmas *helps*. We always went to the in-laws' farm for Christmas. Gorra lot more going for it, for kids, than a semi in Marden.'

'That's where they've gone?'

'The farm, yeh. Only this time they won't be coming back on Boxing Day. The house … the house we can flog, for less than we paid last year, or I can buy Kirsty's half – the options were efficiently outlined for me in an email waiting on me lappie. By *wanting me out*, I meant out of her life, not necessarily off the premises, if I can buy her out. Lucky me.'

'God, I'm so sorry, Frannie. Look, if there's any—'

'Got in, in good time for breakfast, she's already buggered off. Even turned the heating off. Shut the frigging heating down! Must've stayed up half the night working out the details in this state of cold rage she can keep up for hours. So …' Bliss leaned back on his stainless steel stool '… there goes another happy family Christmas exchanging presents round the tree, watching *Harry Potter* with the kids …'

Merrily said nothing. Never met Kirsty, but she could only ever imagine Bliss *half*-watching *Harry Potter* with his kids and hoping the phone would ring before the Quidditch game was into injury time.

'I mean, you *were* right,' he said. 'Howe – goes without saying – would also love to be attending me farewell piss-up. Not happy that she wasn't informed as soon as it was found.'

'So why wasn't she informed?'

'Because somebody said, you know, let's not bother her, it's Christmas …'

'*Frannie.*'

Nobody could say Bliss allowed other people to dig his grave. 'Under normal circs, I'd be number two on this, but she's brought her own feller over from Worcester. DI Brent, PhD. A Ph frigging *D*! What's happening, Merrily? All these higher-educated, fast-track police persons together … in a school.'

'The incident room?'

'Taken over the school next door. Packed the kids off home. So we've got Howe as headmistress, Brent as deputy. Kevin Snape as school secretary, fortunately.'

'What *are* you on about?'

'Office manager – that's the bloke responsible for organising the show. Kevin's a mate, so I get to keep tabs.' Bliss poured himself more coffee. 'Quite like to have seen Annie's face when she found you and Sophie in Ayling's back parlour.'

'She didn't. Annie Howe doesn't know I've been anywhere near Ayling's parlour.'

Merrily explained. Giving him the edited version, Sophie's role minimised. Telling him what little she'd heard from behind the drawing-room door.

'Played the dad card, Frannie.'

'Charlie?'

'Mmm.'

'Bloody Charlie Howe. West Mercia's finest, as was. Still walks around Gaol Street in his capacity as a member of the Police Authority. Always your mate. *Leave it with me, brother, I'm on your side.* Tapping his nose. Bent old twat.'

Merrily said nothing. Ex-Chief Superintendent Charlie Howe. Had he helped cover up a murder many, many years ago? Never proven, never would be, and now Charlie was this ever-popular senior councillor with a daughter doing awfully well in the police service, and not a mark on her.

'Does it still count for much round here, do you think?' Bliss said. 'Ancestry? Roots? I'm standing in the middle of town last night with Kirsty and the progeny, and I'm looking round and I'm thinking, what the *fuck* am *I* doing here? *I* don't fit in. But, then ... I might still feel like that if I *had* roots and saw what was happening to Hereford under Charlie and his mates. I remember what happened to Liverpool.'

'It's still not a bad place, Frannie. And you've had your moments. More than Annie Howe.'

'Yeh, and which of us is the frigging acting superintendent? Look, you wanna bun or something? Jammy doughnut?'

'Yes.' Merrily slid down from her stool. 'I'll get them.'

Waiting at the counter, she exhaled, closing her eyes. *Christmas.* The wonderful, life-affirming festive season. Joy to the world.

The doughnut energising him, Bliss said that if Howe hadn't taken over he might well have had Helen Ayling brought in this morning for some serious Q and A.

'A bit too quiet, that woman. Not many tears.'

'She was a secretary. Discreet. And maybe it wasn't exactly a love match.'

'That was your impression, was it?'

'Frannie, I'm just a priest.'

Bliss wrinkled his nose. Like much of Merseyside, he'd been raised a

Roman Catholic. His idea of a priest didn't include Anglicans, never mind women.

'*An old-fashioned man*, Merrily. That was what she said about him. Well, we knew that – old-fashioned in the sense of insular, pig-headed, bigoted ... And the wife would be property, like a car, best kind being cheap to run and not too much engine noise.'

'Maybe.'

'So Helen ... Think about it. She's been brought into a strange city. She's isolated, unhappy, and it gets no better. Trapped with Mr Hereford in a five-bedroom mausoleum, last decorated in 1973. And then old Clem does or says something that finally flips her big red switch, she pulls a kitchen knife off the rack and ... sometimes it's quite easily done, Merrily. You'd be surprised.'

'And then?' She looked around; a few other people in the cafe, none of them close enough to hear. 'And then this quiet, discreet, middle-aged secretary gets a hacksaw from the tool shed and saws him up? You really think that?'

'Actually, we borrowed the hacksaw, and it's clean. They're almost 100 per cent on a chainie now, which would mean lots of blood spatter and there were no immediate signs of that. But some ladies are a whizz with a mop and a bucket of Flash.'

'Frannie—'

'Merrily, it *happens*. Most killers never meant to be killers, and they panic. And then they either become very calm and sensible and give themselves up or they get increasingly wild and irrational.'

'All right – what about the rest of him?'

'Yeh, he was a big man. To move him far she might need help, I'd concede that, unless—'

'Maybe a bunch of burly Liberal Democrats?'

'—Unless he was reduced to manageable pieces. But chop-up jobs, butchery, it's usually men. Takes a strong stomach and a fair bit of strength unless you've a lorra time to play with.' Bliss looked down at his second doughnut for a few seconds, then back at Merrily. 'No, all right, for what it's worth, *I* don't think it's her.'

'Then why the hell have we spent the last ten minutes—?'

'Because I think that's what Howe was hoping. That she could hang it on Mrs A. Because … what's the alternative?'

'Ayling's council work?'

'Which is sensitive. Which is why Annie's here.'

'Because of Charlie?'

'Now wouldn't it be lovely …' Bliss beamed '… if Clement Ayling was killed by Charlie Howe?'

'You jest, right?'

'Regrettably, I probably do, but Charlie's always gorra lot to hide, and Annie knows that. And if we start poking into council business, who knows what might else be uncovered? If Charlie goes down for *any* small indiscretion, where does that leave Annie's glittering career?'

'And, as Annie probably knows, that wouldn't totally break your heart, would it, Frannie?'

'I'm saying nothing until my lawyer gets here,' Bliss said.

'So you think Annie Howe's stepped in – taken over – to steer the investigation away from anything close to Charlie? I mean … how close *is* it to Charlie?'

'All right, here's the scenario,' Bliss said. 'Ayling leaves a meeting of this think-tank committee, Hereforward, held at the Green Dragon at around three-thirty p.m., just before it starts to go dark. Home is a five-minute walk across the Cathedral Green. He never makes it.'

'So he was killed soon after leaving the meeting?'

'Or taken, anyway. Somebody – perhaps, considering the size of him, more than one person – got to him between the Green Dragon and Castle Street. Maybe he got into a car. Maybe he had something to follow up from the meeting, went off with somebody.'

'Is Charlie Howe—?'

'Yeh, Charlie's on that committee. In fact, I've just fixed up to meet one of the Hereforward officials tomorrow, find out what they were discussing. Ayling might've made himself unpopular over some issue – you never know, do you?'

'So Ayling could've actually been attacked on the Cathedral Green itself?'

'Possible,' Bliss said. 'But unlikely. Too many people about. But he must've been *taken* somewhere, that's the point. Somewhere ... his head is removed, the body disposed of.'

'But why was the head then taken to Blackfriars?'

'You tell me. I gather you know a bit about religion.'

'Bit before my time, pre-Reformation monasteries.'

'It's a public place,' Bliss said. 'But not so public that installing a favourite councillor's head would attract a cheering crowd. Even in the daytime, people don't go in that garden. It doesn't lead anywhere – there's a great tall fence round it. It's not like the Cathedral Green, a short cut to all kinds of places. Blackfriars, after dark, you could position your trophy without being disturbed.'

'Trophy?'

'I think so.'

'The way medieval heads were displayed? Traitors and turncoats?'

'Making a point,' Bliss said.

'And that point *is* ...?'

Bliss shrugged.

'It's an age of extremes. Lorra anger in this county at the moment, Merrily. Anger at a government that doesn't give a shit for rural areas. Anger at the council because it gets squeezed by the Government and pushes council tax through the roof, goes for easy cash cuts.'

'Wholesale school closures?'

'All carried out, of course, on the advice of senior officials. Career rats, with no attachment to the area, and most councillors don't have the brains to argue. But they're the ones who take the shite. Frustration boiling over into rage across the city and the fields and orchards of this once-glorious county. Or hasn't it penetrated to leafy Ledwardine?'

'Are you kidding?'

Bliss was right. If rage was smoke, this inherently laid-back county would have suffocated. But it was a big step from cursing the local authority in the pub to hunting down and killing a senior member, decapitating him, putting his head up like a trophy.

'Or maybe some individual has had a particularly bad time because of some aspect of council policy. Social-services issue, maybe. A feller can go crazy if his family's lost their home or they've had a kiddie taken away by social workers.'

'Ayling was on the social-services committee?'

'At one time or another, Ayling was on *everything*, Merrily. He had more fingers than they had pies. And he was vocal. Big noisy feller. Never kept his opinions to himself. Not the way it's done these days. You filter it through the Press Office first.' Bliss ripped off a corner of his doughnut. 'I actually came up with something fairly interesting by the simple expedient of Googling Clement Ayling.'

'*Not* relating to his council work?'

'Well, yeh, but not in quite the same way.' Bliss looked at the segment of doughnut, then put it back on his plate as dark jam seeped down his fingers. 'In my desperation to remain at the forefront of the investigation, I've floated it to Howe. We're waiting for a forensic report that might confirm it. In fact I may get back to you, Merrily, if it comes up positive.'

'Me? Why?'

'Talk about it then, if we need to. Don't want to complicate your life unnecessarily. You're not going away anywhere for the festive season, I take it?'

'I *work*, Frannie. Night shift on Christmas Eve. We're having a meditation into Christmas morning.'

'What happened to Midnight Mass?'

'That will follow. Quietly. But maybe no raucous carols until the morning.'

'You little radical, Merrily. That's not gonna please the drunks. Part of Christmas, staggering into church at five to twelve, belting out, "Oh Come All Ye Faithful" to the tune of "Silent Night".'

'Before throwing up their curry and chips over somebody's headstone. We don't have that kind of person in the New Cotswolds, Francis.'

'Oh, yeh ...' Bliss fingered up some jam '... I was gonna tell you ... Our friend Mr Jonathan Long of the Overpaid Public School Twats Division. Why he might've been in Ledwardine?'

'Blimey, I'd almost forgotten. What a difference a day makes.'

'Yeh, well, forget about it again. I *was* gonna tell you, but now I can't.

I'd suggested it might help if you were aware of a particular situation, but … apparently it wouldn't. So that's that.'

'You've brought me here to tell me you can't tell me?'

'All I can say is, it's a temporary thing and it's something you'll probably be glad you didn't know about at the time.'

'Thanks.'

'Odd, though.' Bliss licked raspberry jam from his fingers. 'All the picturesque backwaters in all the world … and they have to pick on yours.'

He laughed.

When Merrily got in, there was a heap of Christmas cards on the mat, the post getting later and later and bigger and bigger. She sorted out the brown envelopes from the white. Only two, thank God, but one looked like the big one, the one you opened now with trembling fingers. The heating-oil bill. Couldn't face it tonight; she put it on the hall table.

The other brown envelope, local postmark, contained a white card on which two severe-looking angels formed an archway to a tunnel. At the end of it was a glowing circle, in mauve.

THE CHURCH OF THE LORD OF THE LIGHT

We are praying that at this holy time you will
turn away from the **old darkness** and open
your heart to the **TRUE LIGHT**.

The underlining of TRUE LIGHT had been done in ink. Underneath, someone had scrawled:

> Before it is too
> late for you

A poison-pen Christmas card. Unsigned, but the name of the church was familiar.

Merrily put the card back in the envelope and the envelope on the table, underneath the oil bill.

'Thank you, Shirley.'

15

The Badge

'JANE ...' MERRILY HESITATED '... don't think I'm being old-fashioned, prudish, illiberal and all that stuff, but—'

'Yeah, I do know what you're going to say.'

Jane finished wiping down the refectory table, tossing the cloth from hand to hand. This kid who was a kid no longer. Who was, in fact, less than two years from the age Merrily had been when the pregnancy test came up positive. How terrifying was *that*?

'Separate rooms,' Jane said. 'That would be part of the deal.'

'It would?'

The issue had been raised after they'd eaten, washed the dishes and made some tea.

'OK, let me be totally frank and upfront.' Jane pulled out a chair at the kitchen table and sat down, arms folded. 'Adult to adult.'

'I hate it when you say that. Can't help feeling you've not been one long enough to qualify for the badge.'

'The point about Eirion,' Jane said, 'is I do need to know where we stand. I've hardly seen him since he went to university. I mean, people change, don't they?'

'Sometimes.'

'When they're mixing in like a different *milieu*.'

'Erm ... good word.'

'What I'm trying to say, is that if he thinks he's coming here to start where we left off.'

'Left off,' Merrily said. 'Mmm.'

This was adult to adult, was it? She knew, of course, that Jane and Eirion's relationship had long been consummated. In fact she knew precisely when – Eirion, in an honest, innocent and rather touching moment, having told her himself, the morning after. A summer morning, here in the vicarage kitchen, sitting at this same refectory table. Seemed a lifetime ago. It was, what – eighteen months?

Hell of a long time for teenagers, though.

'So I said I'd ask you,' Jane said. 'And I have. And it's your decision, Mum, and if it's inconvenient or you say no for any other reason, I'm not going to take it any further. I am not going to argue.'

'In other words, you're saying you want me to make the decision for you.'

''Course n— Well, I mean your advice would obviously—'

'Do you *want* to see him?'

'Probably.'

'Probably?'

'Well … yeah, I do. But I just … I just feel it may not be right. That I might be looking back on it in years to come and thinking, *that* was when it all went wrong, that Christmas. Because Christmas is an intense kind of time, isn't it?'

'It can bring things to a head.'

'Like in Hereford last night.' Jane raised an eyebrow. '*Head?* Never mind.' She twitched her nose. 'Bad taste.'

'You heard about that, then.'

'All over the school by lunchtime. Lots of sick jokes. You know what kids are like.'

'Erm … yeah.'

'So what I'm really thinking is, like, are we *too young* to have been together for *so long*? That's it, really.'

'Sorry?'

'That's the dilemma.' Jane's mind was like a pinball machine. 'Also, I'm thinking … you and Dad?'

'That was *entirely* different.'

'How was it different?'

'Because we … because we'd known each other for a lot shorter time than you and Eirion and there were a lot of things about him I didn't know, and … are you *trying* to embarrass me?'

Jane grinned.

'And because you and Eirion will not, unless you're incredibly stupid or incredibly drunk, *have* to get married. So unless, at some stage, you …' Merrily slumped at the table. 'Sorry, flower, been a difficult day. Has there been anyone else in the interim I don't know about?'

'He says not.'

'No … I meant you.'

'Me?' Jane's eyes widened. 'Listen, I don't do *that* any more – I mean go behind your back. And if you were thinking Neil Cooper, I *quite* fancied Coops. Especially when I— All right, maybe we shouldn't be talking like this.'

'Especially when you what?'

'When I … found out he was married, I had a weird little fantasy about being the Other Woman. But I didn't *do* anything, Mum, I didn't make any approach and neither did he, and I've got past it now.'

'Erm … good.'

'Have I shocked you? Anyway …' Jane sprang to her feet. 'Let's bring it in, shall we?'

Meaning the too-big Christmas tree that Merrily had called for at a farm shop outside the village. She'd forgotten. She prised herself to her feet as Jane went out to untie the tree from the roof-rack of the car.

'Jane …?' Merrily thought for a moment and then called after her. 'OK, tell Eirion I'd be happy for him to come.'

It was a time for commitment.

She watched Jane turn and bow – '*Thank you*, single parent' – as the phone starting ringing in the scullery.

'*Always* liked Eirion. Just didn't like to say it too often.' Going back into the house, alone, murmuring, 'In case it put you off him.'

'*Four* television crews!' Sophie said with distaste. 'Marching up and down, filming the house from various angles. Reporters knocking on doors, reporters under lights, talking to the cameras. Satellite dishes! It's quite unbearable.'

The rain chattered inanely on the window pane. Merrily shifted the

Bakelite phone from one ear to the other, switching on the Anglepoise at the same time.

'So when did they reveal his name?'

'I don't know. Early this evening, I think. How long will this go on, Merrily?'

'It'll seem like for ever, I'm afraid. But I suppose tomorrow will be the worst day. Surely they have police with Helen Ayling now?'

'No, Merrily, she's here.'

'Where?'

'Helen's staying with us. It was, in the end, the obvious solution. The press have been encouraged to think she's left the area, with unnamed relatives.'

'God, Sophie, is this a good idea?'

'It was either that or some family liaison officer in the house. Besides, I've discovered I'm fairly competent at driving the media from my doorstep. Wanted *us* – neighbours – to talk about Clement. On television.'

You could feel the shudder in the phone.

'I noticed *you* went off with the police,' Sophie said.

'Bliss.'

'And what did you learn?'

'He seems to be looking for a connection with Clement Ayling's council work. Fairly obvious, I suppose. Councillors make enemies.'

'Yes.' Sophie sounded calmer. 'You were right. They begin by eliminating the spouse. And then they get to the heart of it.'

'Which is … what?'

'It seems that Clement had been receiving abusive letters and phone calls. In relation, as you say, to his council work. Or a particular aspect of it.'

'What – rage against school closures? That kind of thing?'

'Road rage, actually,' Sophie said.

Jane insisted that a Christmas tree should only be borrowed from the earth. By the time Merrily finished on the phone, she had the tree up in the hall, surprisingly perpendicular, in one of the stone tubs from the garden. Damp soil and stones around the roots – cold enough in here to ensure survival well beyond Twelfth Night.

'Sunday, then?' Jane was sitting on the stairs with her mobile. 'No, that's fine … Yeah, it will be.'

Eirion, evidently. Merrily sensed Jane trying not to sound too affectionate. She waited in the kitchen doorway.

'Sure. I'll certainly tell her. No, couldn't make it up, could you? Bloody hell. Yeah, right. Bye.' Jane looked up. 'He says it's really good of you. He wanted to thank you himself, but I said you were working. Mum, look, there's something else you—'

'Spare me a few minutes, flower?'

'Sure.' Jane sprang to her feet. 'What's the problem?'

Jane was happy, hadn't even objected to being addressed as 'flower'. She stood up. Open boxes of tinsel and tree-lights sat at the foot of the tree, Ethel checking them out, pawing delicately at a coloured ball, then dancing away.

No point at all in keeping quiet about this, now Clement Ayling's name had been released. Of course, it was nothing to do with her really, but with Sophie involved …

'Could I consult you about something?' Merrily said. 'Something you know much more about than I do.'

'Fine wines? Jane Austen? *Vampire Weekend*?'

'The Rotherwas Ribbon.'

'Oh.'

'Or as you probably know it, the Dinedor Serpent.'

'Say no more.' Jane came downstairs, shedding her smile. 'What can I tell you about those bastards?'

16

Patio Gravel

A FUZZ OF viridian forestry, a band of lime-green field and, in the fore-
ground, a vast open spread of red clay where the surface had been
peeled away by the road contractors.

Sitting at the scullery desk, Jane had opened up the picture to full-
screen. You couldn't see the top of Dinedor Hill, where tall trees
enclosed the Iron Age camp, but you *could* see the Dinedor Serpent. For
what it was worth.

'This is what it was like before they covered it up again,' Jane said.

In the middle of the exposed clay, a greyish trickle of small pebbles.

Merrily said, 'That's *it?*'

You might not agree with him, but you could see where Ayling had
been coming from. *Clement went with a delegation to view the site,*
Sophie had said. *Afterwards, he was quoted in the* Hereford Times *as
saying it just looked like, ah … patio gravel.*

Succinct. And probably forgivable, if you weren't an archaeologist. *His
opinion was that anyone who thought a vital relief road should be abandoned
or even diverted to preserve* that *must be quite insane. He said that, even if it
was* preserved, *it was hardly going to be a tourist attraction. Adding that
Herefordshire Council couldn't let itself be dictated to by hippies and outsiders.*

An old-style local politician. Like Bliss said, Clem Ayling's younger
colleagues would have been crouching behind some trite press statement.
Ayling would hold forth … railing against the idiots and the cranks.

Jane, of course, had been following the story from the other side, with
frequent explosions of Jane-rage: another example of the jackbooted
bastards at County Hall sacrificing Herefordshire's sacred past in the
cause of dubious progress. A crime against history and the environment.

But it still looked like patio gravel.

'You're not getting the full picture here,' Jane said. 'That's not possible with hardly any of it uncovered. Take it from me – if it was fully exposed, this could be the most amazing archaeological discovery of the last century. Anywhere in the country. And far, far, *far* more important than another stretch of crap tarmac.'

She'd found the images on the website built by the protesters: SAVE THE SERPENT. On its homepage was a picture of what was said to be one of the only comparable monuments in the world – a hillside seen from above, with sculpted mounds on it protected by new walls. Above the picture, it said:

This is the imaginatively preserved and presented Ohio Serpent.

And below:

Imagine what would happen to it if Herefordshire Council were in charge.

'The Ohio Serpent mound is probably the only comparable monument anywhere in the world,' Jane said. 'That tells you how significant this is.'

'The Dinedor Serpent's not actual mounds like this, though, is it?' Merrily leaned over the back of Jane's chair. 'It just looks like ... chippings.'

'Yeah, well, that's what they thought at first – that it was a road, a prehistoric pathway, maybe going all the way to the top of Dinedor Hill. A *ritual* pathway, for ceremonial processions.'

'Like your pathway to Cole Hill.'

'Except Cole Hill's only an alignment, with no actual visible path, other than the one across the meadow. And that's a straight line, whereas the Serpent is ... serpentine. But the archaeologists decided it couldn't've been an actual pathway, because it has nothing under it – no base, no support. If people had walked on it, the stones would just've been trodden in. Wouldn't've lasted a year, never mind a few thousand.'

'So if it's not the remains of a road or a track ...? I'm sorry, I should know this, shouldn't I?'

Ought to have paid more attention to the Serpent dispute, but other things had been happening at the time. Also, access to the site had been restricted because of the work on the new road, so few people had actually seen it. Not even Jane, apparently.

'Everybody *should* know about this, but most people don't,' Jane said. 'The truth is totally magical. Archaeology to die for.' She looked up. 'You OK, Mum?'

Sophie had said Helen Ayling remembered her husband receiving at least half a dozen angry phone calls and several abusive letters, half of them unsigned. How many had been actual threats she didn't know. If Clement took the call, he simply hung up and wouldn't talk about it afterwards. The letters he burned. Nothing to worry about. Part and parcel of local government service.

Bloody cranks, he'd say. *As if we'd block the city's economic development for their juvenile fairy stories.*

Actually sparing the time, for once, to explain to Helen why the Rotherwas relief road was of such strategic importance, issuing as it did from Hereford's primary industrial sector and perhaps eventually forming part of the city's long-needed bypass.

Opening up this side of Hereford, the commercial possibilities were enormous, Clem said. Only cranks and drug-addled hippies would even want to get in its way, and at least they were relatively harmless. Sophie said Helen had been less convinced of this – recalling coming home one evening, about four months ago, and finding a message on the answering machine warning Clem to stay away from Dinedor Hill if he didn't want to be buried there.

Dinedor Hill: implications here. The city's mother hill, the site of its Iron Age origins. Aligned with the Cathedral in the same way that Cole Hill was aligned with Ledwardine church, but on an altogether more impressive scale. Some people in Hereford felt an almost obsessive attachment to Dinedor. Running a new road too close, cutting off the city from the mother hill, was always going to cause unrest. And if the roadwork itself had exposed even more evidence of Dinedor's sanctity ...

Sophie said Helen had been concerned enough by the tone of the message on the answering machine to hang on to the tape. Had thus been able to present the evidence to Howe when Howe brought up the issue.

'I'm sorry,' Merrily had said. 'I don't understand. *Howe* brought this up?'

'Well, yes, I think so. She seems to have specifically asked Helen if Clement's attitude to the Dinedor Serpent had led to threats.'

'As if she already had reason to suspect the murder was Serpent-related?'

'I thought I'd made that clear,' Sophie said.

Merrily looked down at the seated Jane from behind, really not liking where things were going.

'So when the Council decided to go ahead with the road … people were very angry?'

'You think they didn't have good reason to be?' Jane turned her chair round. 'Soon as the council learned about the Serpent, they hushed it up. They didn't want it to come out until they knew they could bulldoze the road through regardless. One guy chained himself to a machine.'

'You sure about that – that they were hushing it up?'

'It's obvious. They didn't even want to hear any arguments. Wouldn't allow any public debate. It was discussed by the so-called *Cabinet* behind closed doors. All *we* heard was this reactionary old bastard Clement Ayling going on to *Midlands Today* and the *Hereford Times* about how crap the Serpent was anyway and how it wasn't even worth preserving.'

'Mmm.'

'They didn't even take any steps to protect bits of the Serpent they'd uncovered – like against the elements? So it was all filling up with water during heavy rain, causing untold damage.'

'But as I understand it, that's why it *needed* to be covered up again, even if it was by a road – to protect it against bad weather.'

'And people nicking stones as souvenirs, sure. But you could cover it up and still make a feature out of it. Look at Ohio. No, it was the way this was done – hushed up. And like when a few civilised protesters turned up at the council offices and refused to leave they were actually arrested? By the cops? You must remember that.'

'Well, I do, but it came to nothing, surely? Nobody was charged.'

'*Mum* ... they were thrown into police cells! These were just ordinary people disgusted at the way the council was behaving. And two of the ones arrested, they were, like, over eighty?' Jane's eyes wide now, with outrage. 'And some of them got taken all the way to Worcester because like there weren't enough spare cells at Hereford? OK, the charges *were* withdrawn, but banging elderly people up in cells just for standing up for some kind of democracy ... Like they were terrorists or something?'

'You're sure about this?'

'Why do you keep saying that? Of course I'm sure. And the *reason* I'm sure is because some of the protesters are also members of the Coleman's Meadow Preservation Society. Same problem, same council. I'd've been with them myself if it hadn't been a school day – wow, does that sound pathetic or what?'

'Actually, it sounds sensible. If you can cope with sensible.'

'I should've been there. Wimped out.'

Jane turned back to the computer and brought up another SAVE THE SERPENT page, which said:

Please support by adding comments and taking online actions including a petition to the Prime Minister.

Merrily stood looking at it, but not seeing it. Seeing the greater pattern. Dinedor Serpent/Coleman's Meadow. The trouble with this county, it was just too damn small. Everything interconnected. Everything eventually trickling down into your own community, your own home, your—

'Mum! You're digging your fingers into my shoulders!'

'I ... sorry.'

'OK.' Jane stood up. 'What's wrong?'

'You mentioned Clement Ayling.'

'Fascist of the first order. We truly live in a police state, you know? Nobody's allowed to object to anything any more. I mean, you only have to look at pictures of Ayling with his phoney smile, the smug, fat, arrogant—'

'Jane.'

'What?'

'Sit down, huh?'

17

River of Light

THEY DRESSED THE tree. A pagan ceremony, Jane always used to say, and she was probably right.

Merrily climbed on a chair to attach their slightly frayed Christmas fairy, or maybe angel, to the topmost branch. She thought of the offerings at Whiteleafed Oak in the Malverns. She thought of the little lights that were supposed to be visible in the orchard here in Ledwardine, where cider apples known as the Pharisees Red had been grown. Pharisees from *farises* – local slang for fairies.

As if we'd block the city's economic development for their juvenile fairy stories.

Jane was applying herself, with serious, numbed concentration, to the decoration of the tree. When she'd spoken it was only to point out that they needed more glass balls or strands of tinsel.

You could almost hear her mind turning over and over like an engine trying to start. And then she said, as if the words had just drifted out, '*Do what thou wilt, though it harm none.*'

She had the Christmas tree lights stretching up the stairs to untangle the wire.

'That would be the motto of the Pagan Federation?' Merrily said.

'Actually, it's a Wiccan saying. But, yeah, if they had a motto it would be something like that.'

'Right.'

If you were a vicar, a parish priest in the Christian faith, and you were fully aware that your daughter was wearing, next to her skin, a fine silver necklace with a pentacle hanging from it, what were you supposed to do about that? Come over all Shirley West? Ban her from keeping pagan books in your vicarage? Watch her every move, find out who she was meeting, phoning, keep a check on her emails and pray for her deliverance from the arms of Satan?

Or did you, seeing through to the person underneath, remember when you were a teenage Siouxie and the Banshees fan in black lipstick and let it, for God's sake, lie?

'Mum, these lights are just not coming on.'

'They never come on first time. You have to go round screwing every one in tight, and then … pray.' Merrily came down from the chair. 'So what you're trying to say is … no supporter of the Dinedor Serpent or the Coleman's Meadow stones – and certainly no modern British pagan – would even contemplate something so brutal and barbaric.'

'*You* think they would?'

'I wouldn't know, Jane. Some of the modern pagans I've encountered, it would be difficult to imagine them sacrificing lunch. But if you look at their forebears in the Dark Ages …'

'Which weren't dark, but go on.'

'If you look at ancient Celtic paganism, as practised, presumably, by the Iron Age people who lived in their round huts on the top of Dinedor Hill … and Cole Hill, come to that—'

'So that would be like two thousand years ago? Three thousand?'

'Whatever, they were very into removing heads, the old pagans, weren't they?'

'*No!*'

'All I'm—'

'That's disgusting!' Jane glared down from the stairs, holding the dead lights. 'I don't know anyone who could do that.'

'Well, I don't either, so let's not worry too much about it. It's all circumstantial, anyway.'

'These are gentle people. Well-meaning.' Jane looked down at the limp necklace of bulbs. 'They're just people who think we should be aware of our origins.'

'Well, me too, but—'

'And like just pushing out cities and towns and villages in all directions, ruining the countryside for more and more houses and factories that close down after a couple of years ... that's just mindless. Building that road is ... thrusting a spear into the countryside.'

Merrily sighed.

'It's like nobody ever really thinks any more,' Jane said. 'Like the way they just went into Iraq and nobody considered the consequences. Nobody *thought*.'

Tears in Jane's eyes.

The fairy lights blinked once and then came on, like jewels on her fingers. She looked down at them.

'God, it's just like the Serpent.'

'Sorry?'

'It's like ... I never told you, did I? Let me show you, OK?'

Jane picked up the end of the wire and dragged the lights up the stairs to the first landing, where she took off one of her trainers. She wrapped the end of the wire around it to hold it firm on the landing, and then came downstairs backwards, arranging the lights.

Somehow, they all stayed on.

'This is how it worked, right? The theory is that the Serpent may run all the way from the top of Dinedor Hill down to the River Wye.'

'How far's that?'

'Not as far as you'd think. So it's connecting what, in ancient times, would have been the two main features in the landscape, pre-Hereford – the biggest hill and the river. The most important river in the west of England and Wales, so very sacred. And the wavy pattern of the Serpent is actually simulating the meandering of the river.'

'Who's saying that?'

'That's come from the archaeologists themselves – the guys in charge of the rescue excavation. I got it from Coops. Obviously, they've only uncovered a small section of the Serpent, but that's what they reckon. These guys don't say anything until it's looking pretty solid.'

'I see ...'

'I don't think you do. Not yet. Listen ... this is the cool part – the little stones include fragments of quartz, which was probably quarried in the area. So if you imagine this river of stones – with a high quartz content – rising from the Wye, across Rotherwas. Imagine Rotherwas when there were no factories there, no warehouses, only open countryside. So imagine the river rising up the side of Dinedor Hill. Now …'

Jane went across the landing and snapped off the lamp over the stairwell.

'… Imagine a full moon …'

Before her eyes adjusted, Merrily saw this shining chain against smoky blackness. Ascending lights.

'On the night of a full moon,' Jane said, 'all the fragments of quartz would've been reflecting the light. So you'd be seeing like tens of thousands of little lights. An incandescent stream down the sacred hill to the banks of the Wye. You see?'

'The whole Serpent lights up? That's what it was for?'

'Awesome, isn't it?'

'Yes,' Merrily said. 'It must have been.'

Light against darkness. My God.

Realising that Jane had said something about this before but it hadn't really registered. There really wasn't anything like this, was there, possibly anywhere in the world?

'Jane, why was this not talked about?'

'Because the council kept it quiet. You think *they* wanted everybody to know how exciting it was? Mum, it's like Bill Blore said, these people are not fit to make decisions on anything important. Anything you can't take to the bank they don't even understand.'

That night, as the squally rain spat at the bedroom window, Merrily lay awake, thinking about the Serpent, the stones of Coleman's Meadow and several other recent finds suggesting a rich, unsuspected, ancient heritage along the Welsh border. When you considered the emotive and mystical power of this illuminated umbilical cord and the impact of its severance by a road carrying heavy commercial traffic …

Who cared?

Not the council, evidently. Most of them probably hoping the serpent would be washed away by the rain.

'It's clear what's happening, isn't it?' Jane had said, when they'd put the lights back on the tree. 'Hereford's pagan past is rising again, all around us – and it's more beautiful and spectacular than anyone ever dreamed. And they hate that.'

'The Council?'

'The Council, the secular state. And the Church, what's left of it.'

Ah, yes, the Church. All this was pre-Christian, not the Church's problem – official.

And whatever was in Coleman's Meadow wasn't a problem for the Vicar of Ledwardine. Yet the beauty and – yes – the *sanctity* of it all … Jane was right, nothing of spiritual value should be discarded. Whether or not you could understand it, there was something you could *feel*. Something to seize and lift the spirit.

Archaeology to die for.

But archaeology to *kill* for?

Merrily rolled over. She'd forgotten her hot-water bottle, was feeling chilled, like the vicarage would always be, and she was resisting the warm fantasy of being across the road in Lol's little terraced house, in the little cosy bedroom with Lol's warm—

'Mum?'

The landing light had come on, and Jane stood in the bedroom doorway, bare-legged, a fleece around her shoulders. Flashback to the days after Sean's death, when she'd stand, bemused, in another bedroom doorway, hugging her oldest teddy.

'Mum, I forgot – sorry.'

'What time is it?'

'Only about half-twelve.'

'Oh, only half-twelve and you having to go to school in the morning, even if it *is* the last day of term—'

'Mum, I forgot, OK? I was going to tell you about it before you asked me about the Serpent and all this Clem Ayling stuff came up, and it got … pushed out.'

'Couldn't it have waited till morning?'

'We never seem to have time in the morning, and I want to check the river, and—'

'OK.' Merrily reached over to the bedside chair for her bathrobe. 'Tell me. Quickly.'

'It was this woman I met yesterday morning. In the churchyard?'

'You've never mentioned a woman.'

'No, it didn't seem important, and I was late and ... Anyway, she called herself Lensi, and she had this posh camera. Said she was a press photographer, freelance, working for ... I think it was the *Independent*? She knew about the stones, and she, like, she wants to take some pictures of me?'

'Not another one.'

'Yeah, well, I didn't encourage her, I'm a low-profile person now.'

'Can't actually say I've noticed.'

'Anyway, I asked Eirion if he could check her out with his media friends? And, good as gold, he did, and when I rang to tell him it was OK to come at the weekend he told me who he thought she was.'

'Madonna?'

Merrily dragged the robe around her shoulders as Jane came into the bedroom, pushed the door to behind her and sat down at the bottom of the bed.

'*She* says people call her Lensi, right?'

'You said that. And why am I interested?'

'That's what I said to her.'

'What?'

'I'm like, why are you interested? This was when she started asking questions like, what sort of pagan are you, Jane?'

'Oh God.'

'I didn't *tell* her. Not that I'm any *kind* of pagan, anyway. It's just like an ethos, isn't it? But it came up, because she'd been asking about the stones and Lucy Devenish. And then you, a bit.'

'Me?'

'She obviously knew who you were. And, like, Eirion always says if you avoid answering journalists' questions it'll only make them think you're covering something up and they won't let it go.'

'Jane—'

'Anyway, Eirion knows this guy who's like Wales correspondent for the Indy? And *he* knows this woman photographer who calls herself Lensi. Like, nobody *else* calls her that ... it's about giving herself this kind of professional-photographer image? They used to laugh at her, didn't take her seriously because she was posh. Rich family in the country. Finishing school, that kind of thing.'

'And what exactly was the posh photographer doing poking around the churchyard?'

'She lives here. This is the point. She's renting Cole Barn. With her husband.'

'Well, yeah, I heard that had been let, but—'

'They've been here several weeks. Eirion says her real name's Leonora Phelan. But it's her husband you're more likely to have heard of. Mathew Stooke?'

Merrily sat up. The strip of yellow light from the landing was like a knife blade.

'Yes, *that* Mathew Stooke,' Jane said. 'We're pretty sure.'

FRIDAY

'This is an exciting find, not just for Herefordshire and the UK, but apparently, so far, it is unique in Europe. It has international significance.'

Dr Keith Ray,
Herefordshire County Archaeologist
Today, BBC Radio 4

There has been some misapprehension that the whole monument is affected by the road scheme course, and that the intention is to destroy the monument. Neither of these is true.

Herefordshire Council website

Working Relationship

THROUGH HIS MUCKY windscreen, Bliss watched Annie Howe powering out of her car in the schoolyard, aiming an unfolding umbrella like a harpoon gun into the rain. Stepping between police vehicles, in her white trench coat – well, not exactly a trench coat and not exactly white, but you got the idea.

Kevin Snape, the office manager, had served the summons last night, leaving the message on Bliss's mobile: *'Ma'am wants to see you first thing, Francis. Eight a.m. sharp. At the school.'*

That would be before morning assembly. Before the main team got in. Suggesting Annie wanted to tap him on some background angle, something she didn't want to share with the whole class. Probably just with DI Iain Twatface Brent, PhD, after Bliss had gone.

He waited until she was in the building, then got out of his car, got wet – never been an umbrella kind of person. Inside the school-hall-turned-incident-room he shook himself, looked around. Kevin Snape at a computer, Terry Stagg on the phone.

Seeing all the kiddie things pushed into corners reminded him that sometime over the weekend he was going to have to tell his folks up in Knowsley that Kirsty had left him and taken the beloved grandchildren.

This jagged tear in life's fabric. Hadn't been able to face going home last night. Cod and chips in the car at ten p.m., not getting back to the house until he was too knackered to do anything but crunch through the Christmas cards on the doormat and crawl upstairs. What he needed was for the Ayling case to roll on through Christmas, turning all the festive shite into a merciful blur.

'Francis – in here, please.'

The SIO had bagged a classroom for her office. Bliss went meekly in. How come, when Annie Howe was younger than him, she still made him feel like a spotty kid?

'Sit down, Francis.'

Ma'am at the teacher's desk, kiddie chairs stacked against the walls. Bliss thought of detaching one and squatting in it, looking up respect-fully at the Head, but there was already a teacher-sized chair waiting.

He sat down. Ice-blonde Annie was dressed for the day's press conferences in a dark green suit with deep lapels, dazzling white shirt, no jewellery. Morning papers in front of her, the *Western Daily Press* on top.

BEHEADED:
Massive hunt for
city chief's killer

'So what's the state of play with your Worcester witness murder, ma'am?' Bliss said. 'Still thinking contract killing, are we? Knowing who ordered it but not who actually did the deed.'

Howe looked up slowly. Clearly aware that what he was really asking her was what the hell she was doing over here, with the Lasky case still live.

'Actually, it's the other way round: we're fairly sure we know who did it, but we *don't* know who ordered it. We're looking at a ring. Two more in Droitwich, another in Evesham. Plus Lasky in Worcester. And the father.'

'Scumbag.'

The father was the worst of them, in Bliss's view. Selling sex with his kids? If it hadn't been for his brother-in-law going to the cops, it might've gone on for years.

Now the brother-in-law was dead. They'd found the poor sod knifed in his own garage, two weeks before he was due to testify against the father and the family's paedophile solicitor, Adrian Lasky. Annie Howe never thinking the man might need protection – all paedophiles being cowering wimps who couldn't deal with adults.

'Under the circumstances, however, it seems unlikely that Lasky directly commissioned it,' Howe said. 'However … my boss is handling it and, as I take it *you*'re not in a position to assist us, let's move on.'

'Contract boys.' Bliss shook his head. 'Even ten years ago, a rarity. Now you've got kids who'll do it for a few hundred, knowing the worst that can happen is six years and they come out with a degree in sociology, courtesy of the prison—'

He stopped, Annie giving him the cold stare.

'Kids,' she said. 'We'll need to return to the subject of *kids*. Remind me.'

'I'm sorry?'

'Meanwhile …' adjusting her cuffs now '… you'll be interested to know that we were right about the connection with the archaeology at Rotherwas and Dinedor. Proven.'

'*Wooh!*' This was too good. 'Samples matched up?'

Unbelievable, though, this woman. *We* were right. Not *you* were right. No *Well done, Francis, nicely put together.*

'So we now have confirmatory reports from forensics and from the archaeologist in charge of the project.'

'Good,' Bliss said. 'Excellent.'

'On which basis, you'll need to follow it through. I'm having copies of both reports run off for you now, and Iain Brent's arranged for the archaeologist to be on site at eleven-thirty. Iain will give you the details when he comes in.'

'You want *me* to talk to this boffin?'

'What we need from the guy is a list of people who'd be au fait with the latest findings at Dinedor. We also need to know who's had permission to visit the site and who's expressed a more than superficial interest. We need— Is this a problem?'

'It's just …' That it was a job for a frigging DC. 'If you remember, I'd arranged to see the feller from this Hereforward committee – Ayling's last meeting?'

'You can leave that for now.'

'Leave it?'

Leave the meeting relating to the quango of which Clement Ayling had been a member and Charlie Howe still was.

'It's not of immediate importance, is it?' Howe said. 'I want this thing wrapped, Francis. Obviously, I'm refocusing. I'm looking, as you yourself suggested, for environmental extremists. I'm looking for pagan-oriented fanatics—'

'What, like the residents who were banged up for aggravated trespass for refusing to leave council premises?'

'We ...' Howe shrugged. 'We *may* talk to them, but mostly they're a little too old for the profile, wouldn't you say?'

Bliss eyed her.

'You've got something else, haven't you?'

Howe's expression, if you could call it that, didn't change. She'd finally lost the Gestapo-issue rimless glasses – contact lenses now – but she still hadn't learned how to smile without using her fingers to prise up the corners of her mouth.

'Ayling ... had received a number of threatening phone calls. In relation to his support for the relief road and his derisive remarks about the Serpent.'

'*How* threatening?'

'Sufficiently. We have a tape, from his answering machine, so that gives us a voice. Male.'

'You got this from Helen Ayling?'

'Something jogged her memory.'

Bliss struggled for control. So this had turned up last night? And Howe hadn't even told him. Seeing Dinedor had been his idea, any other SIO he'd worked with on a case this big would have called personally to fill him in, no matter how late. When your wild card came up, it was acknowledged.

It was called a *working relationship*.

A knock on the door and Howe said, 'Come.'

Come. She probably said that, in the same detached tone, in bed, if you could imagine that. Word was that one of the desk boys in Worcester had run a book on which team Annie played for and had to give back all the money because nobody had ever managed to find out. Figured. Even Bliss wasn't sure, but he was horribly afraid she might actually, in theory, be straight.

Kevin Snape came in with some papers. Howe nodded towards Bliss, and Kevin put them down in front of him, winked and buggered off. Copies of the forensic and archaeological reports. Bliss didn't touch them.

'And of course you might like to consider,' Howe said, 'if you know anyone else with a knowledge of religious fanatics in this area and the borderline insane.'

Uh oh.

'Yeh, I'll have a think,' Bliss said, cautious.

'I'd make an approach myself but the person I'm thinking of is clearly not comfortable with educated women.'

Bliss didn't laugh.

'There's also the daughter. The daughter, as you know, is … maladjusted and seems to have contact with many of the crank elements in this area. I'm interested in who she might know.'

'You want *me* to—'

'Get what you can, but be careful how much you disclose. Nothing, obviously, from those particular reports. Not that I need to—'

'No, you don't.'

Bliss stood up, needing to get out before he said anything he'd regret.

'Sit down, Francis,' Howe said. 'I haven't finished with you.'

Haven't finished with you?

Mother of God, you could only take so much of this shite. Bliss put his hands on Howe's desk, took a breath.

'Look …' close enough now to notice she wasn't wearing perfume '… whatever's on your mind, why don't you just frigging come out with it, Annie? Because I'm getting a bit pissed off with—'

'Sit *down*, Bliss.'

Howe hadn't moved. Bliss sat down. The next ten minutes brought him closer to throwing in his warrant card than at any other time in his nineteen years as a cop.

19

Hole

PICKING UP SOME cigs in Big Jim Prosser's Eight Till Late, Merrily saw that Hereford had exploded, debris all over the morning papers.

The *Birmingham Post* had Clem Ayling pictured last summer at the opening of a new woodland craft centre. Wearing a yellow hard hat, symbolically holding an axe, lavishly smiling. A grinning death mask now, glaringly surreal.

'I met him just the once.' Jim stacked up more papers near his checkout, stooping over them. Last of the old-fashioned shopkeepers, four pens in his top pocket. 'Odd, really. You couldn't dislike the feller, whatever you think of his council. An ole rogue, but you expect that.'

'Don't expect this, though, Jim. Not here.'

'Aye. Lyndon Pierce was in earlier. Never seen him look as shattered. Like it might be him next. No such bloody luck.' Jim smiled. 'Sorry, Merrily.'

'You can't be *totally* against the village doubling in size.'

'Can't I?'

'They'd all want papers.'

'Aye ...' Jim dropped the papers; a nerve had been exposed. 'From some bloody supermarket where the village hall is, when Pierce swings his lottery grant for a new leisure centre. It stinks, Merrily. It's not the place we moved to.'

'It hasn't happened yet, Jim, we can still ob—'

'I meant the whole *county*. Nobody's ever gonner forget it was Ayling who stuck to it as half the secondary schools would be gone within five years because of the council getting squeezed. But that en't how I see it. If they can afford new shopping centres, they can afford to keep the schools open. We got more bloody supermarkets in Hereford than any city of its size in the country – did you know that? All the time, they're expanding on what we *don't* need and cutting back on what we do, and it … it's bloody wrong.'

Merrily nodded. What could you say?

'No,' Jim said, 'I never thought anything like this would ever happen yere, but then I never thought to see so many strangers in the city – criminals, a lot of 'em – only gotter read the court cases in the *Hereford Times*. It's out of control, it is. We're all rushing to the edge of the bloody cliff. I dunno how you do your job – trying to find the good in people.'

'Jim, if we—'

'Brenda wants to sell up,' Jim said.

'The shop?' Merrily looked up at him, one hand in her wallet. 'Leave the shop?'

'Gonner be sixty-six next time. Old enough to remember how, when you caught a youngster nicking sweets, you clipped him round the yearole and told his dad, and his dad'd give him a good hiding on top. Nowadays you just gotter raise your voice, bloody dad's in threatening to take you apart.'

Merrily sighed.

'You know what done it for Brenda? That armed robbery up in Shropshire – you see that on the local news? Country village, shop *just* like this, with a post office at the back. Brenda says, that's it, time to get rid.'

Merrily glanced up to the top of the store, where Shirley West hunched behind reinforced glass. It was widely known that Brenda Prosser had never wanted to take on the post office, for this very reason: all that money on the premises. But with the Post Office flogging off most of its premises, it was the back of the Eight Till Late or nothing.

Neither Jim nor Brenda was qualified to run a post office, but if they'd refused it wouldn't have gone down at all well in Ledwardine. Fortunately, Shirley West, having left the bank in Leominster for reasons undisclosed, had been looking for a job. And Shirley had once worked in a post office.

'I don't know what to say, Jim. It just wouldn't be the same.'

'It already isn't the same,' Jim said. 'Anything else I can get you?'

'No, I don't— Yes. Well, just information. The people at Cole Barn ...?'

'The Wintersons? If you're thinking of trying to get them into church I wouldn't bother, they're only renting. Nobody was gonner buy at the kind of price that French outfit were asking. Not now.'

'No.'

Cole Barn had been acquired, derelict, for conversion by a subsidiary of the company which now owned the Black Swan. Speculators, in other words, and nobody was too upset when it backfired. Executive homes or standing stones, neither would be good news for the privacy of Cole Barn, still on the market after over a year.

'Yere today, gone tomorrow, these folks,' Jim said. 'Not worth the bother.'

'I'm not allowed to say that. What are they like?'

'They're ... from the Home Counties somewhere. Woman's friendly enough in an eyes-everywhere kind of way – I'll have one of these, some of that ... Bit hyper. The husband I've never seen. Something you've heard, Merrily?'

'Me? When do I ever hear anything?' Merrily picked up her cigarettes. 'You're not *really* thinking of going, are you?'

'Likely next spring. Look at it this way ... what's this shop gonner be worth with a Tesco or a Co-op down the bottom of Church Street? Bugger-all.'

'I don't know what to say.'

'Say nothing yet, eh?' Jim said. 'We don't want talk.'

Merrily nodded, zipping up her coat. It had held off raining for all of half an hour but as she left the Eight Till Late it was starting again, like some automated cyclical sprinkler. She moved along the side of the square and under the market hall, walking to the end where, between the oak pillars, you could see into the window of the new bijou book-shop called – God forbid – Ledwardine Livres. Nine-thirty, and it was opening a good hour earlier than usual – Christmas market. The blind went up to reveal a narrow window with a display including, she noticed, Richard Dawkins, Ian McEwan and Philip Pullman. Healthy balance towards atheism, then. Or was this paranoia? Maybe not. Above Dawkins's *The God Delusion* was a book with a silver-blue cover. *The Hole in the Sky.*

The O in *Hole* actually had a hole in it. Merrily went in, collecting a wry smile from the proprietor, Amanda Rubens, late of Stoke Newington, when she laid a copy on the counter.

'Know thine enemy, vicar?'

'Something like that,' Merrily said.

She hadn't noticed any books in here about local folklore, mysticism, earth mysteries. How things had changed since the shop had been Ledwardine Lore, run by the late Lucy Devenish.

The car was still stinking of last night's chips. Bliss sat in the parking lot, behind Gaol Street, the session with Annie Howe replaying itself in his head like one of those sick-making seasonal supermarket tape loops of Slade and Roy Wood wishing it could be frigging Christmas every frigging day. Bliss wanting to beat his head on the dash to dislodge Howe's final ringing dismissal.

'*Go!*'

Turning away, like she couldn't bear to look at him. Like he was some kind of old shit the police service needed to scrape off its new boots. Unbelievable. The Senior Investigating Officer in the crucial early stages of the biggest murder case in Hereford since Roddy Lodge, making time in her schedule to tell him—

Bliss let the window down.

—about one of the consultant orthopaedic surgeons at the County Hospital preparing to file a complaint regarding the treatment of his son by a plain-clothes officer of this division in an incident which had occurred—

Bliss turned his face into the rain.

—two nights ago, during the extended opening period for Christmas shopping in High Town.

'Mr Shah …' Howe fingering a report on her desk '… alleges that the boy and two friends were being harassed by an over-zealous community support officer who had wrongly accused them of dropping litter.'

'*Wrongly* accused them?'

'When they began to protest their innocence, a man identifying himself as a police officer intervened, threatening to throw Mr Shah's child into a cell and, I quote, *beat the shit out of him.*'

Bliss sitting there, staring at Howe. The other side of the glass door, the hall was filling up with cops.

'The officer did not give his name but, when he began to scream obscenities at the boys—'

'*Scream ob*—?'

'—They noticed he had what was described as a distinctive northern accent. Similar, according to one of the boys, to the comedian Paul O'Grady.'

'How much flattery can a man take?'

'You're not denying you were the officer concerned.'

'Annie, what I *am* denying—'

'Even though, for some reason, *DI Bliss*, we can't seem to put our hands on your report of the incident.'

'That is ridiculous. It wasn't an *incident*, by any stretch of the— *How* old d'you say the kid was?'

'Thirteen. And why do we *have* incident reports? Remind me?'

'This thirteen-year-old was drinking Stella. Not exactly the weakest of lagers.'

'Orange squash—'

'Balls.'

'—According to Mr Shah.'

'Mr Shah. Right. OK. Let's deal with that aspect first, in case you're about to— It was night and half the shops were shut. I did not even *notice* what colour the kid was. I assure you – and community support will corroborate it – that this kid was chugging full-strength lager and appeared intoxicated. And he *did* throw it down in the street, after spraying lager at this long-suffering anti-drink campaigner in a monkey suit. As for the *obscene language* … I told them to piss off. That was it.'

'You told a thirteen-year-old boy to piss off.'

'You should've heard *him*!'

'And did you also call him a *twat*?'

'Aw, Jesus, I call everybody a twat! It's hardly ...' Bliss shut his eyes. After all his efforts to tone down his language, successfully reducing *fucking* to *frigging*, for the sake of his kids, he just wasn't having this. '*And* – you can confirm *this* with the plastic plods – I never laid a hand on any of those kids, nor did I threaten to. I most certainly did *not* threaten to beat the shit out of him. Come *on* ... in the centre of town? In public?'

'It seems you expressed a preference for somewhere *less* public. Like a cell stinking of vomit?'

'Jesus, it's what you *do*, isn't it? You give the little— You give them a bit of a scare and send them on their way. It saves a lorra ...' Paperwork. Bliss shut up. Howe's entire career had been fabricated out of paper.

Silence. Even the frigging rain holding off.

'No.' Annie Howe's voice like ice splitting on a January pond. 'It *isn't* what you do. It's what some stupid, crass policemen *used* to do. In the bad old days.'

And then she'd filled in the background for him – why this was not something he could just walk away from, with two fingers in the air. Seemed that most of what happened had been witnessed by a neighbour of Shah's from Lyde, north of the city. Thought next day that he ought to tell Shah that his son had been involved in what appeared to be a binge-drinking incident in the centre of Hereford. The little twat had obviously lied through his teeth about what had happened to avoid a backlash at home.

A public incident; now this Mr Shah wanted a public apology.

'In that case,' Bliss had told Howe, 'I will personally pay a visit to Mr Shah and put him fully in the pic—'

'You will not go *near* Mr Shah.'

'*Jes*—' Bliss gripping his knees. 'All right, what about the plastic plods? You've presumably got *their* statements?'

'We have.'

'And?'

'The community support officers say that while the accusation of littering *was* legitimate—'

'Exactly.'

'—Both agree that what happened was an entirely manageable situation and they had not – nor would have – requested any assistance.'

'Aw, come on, there was no way—'

'They say, in fact, that the situation was undoubtedly *inflamed* by your uncalled for and unnecessary—'

'*The lying shites!*'

'Bliss …' Howe finally rising up. 'I don't *care* which of you is lying. What I *do* care about is having a senior officer implicated in a trivial but potentially damaging and highly public incident while the rest of us are working flat-out on what's turning out to be the most—' Howe waving the *Daily Press* in Bliss's face '—high-profile homicide investigation in the history of this city. Now, I don't know what your problem is … my information is that it's personal and domestic. But you'd better either keep it under control or seek counselling … and meanwhile give some serious thought to drafting a suitably arse-licking apology to this bloody man before he takes it any further.'

'Ma'am, I think you ought to—'

'Don't say *anything else*. Get out of here. Talk to the people we discussed and give me a report. You know what I'm looking for.' And, as he was leaving, she'd told him explicitly where he stood, looking down at the papers on her desk, making the odd note, delivering the message as a partly absent afterthought.

'If anybody can get you out of this,' Annie Howe had said, 'it will probably have to be me.'

She hadn't looked up. No need to.

Bliss laid his head on the steering wheel, forehead against the fuzzy tiger-striped cover the kids had bought him last Father's Day. Remembering the hollow quiet in the incident room, half-full by then, when he went back that way, looking for Karen Dowell.

Aware also that, having been briefed by Howe and sent out on his own by nine a.m., he'd effectively been excluded from Morning Assembly and was in no position to complain.

Lol ran downstairs and flung open the front door. The rain washed Merrily inside. Lol was exasperated.

'You've got a *key* ...'

Why did she never seem to use her key, like she might be some kind of intrusion into his space?

'Yeah, I know.' Slipping out of her coat, hanging it over the newel post at the bottom of the stairs, where Lucy Devenish used to hang her poncho. 'I forgot it. I just ... walked out. Needed to talk to somebody.'

'Somebody?'

'Sorry.' She put her arms around him. 'This is ridiculous.'

'What is?'

'This.'

Merrily went back to her coat, pulled a brown paper bag from a pocket, handed it to him. Lol shook out the paperback book, recognised it at once, from hoardings in London and the sides of bus shelters.

It was the hole that did it. It wasn't a black hole, just grey. A grey hole in a shiny, silver-blue sky, and when you opened the cover it exposed not a title page but a blank page, all grey, at the bottom of which it said:

nothing ... what did you expect?

'I don't get it,' Lol said. 'You *bought* this?'

'Just now.'

'You bought Mathew Stooke's best-selling guide to living—' he read from the back cover '—*a balanced, guiltless life without the pointless tedium of God* ...?'

'Begrudging every penny,' Merrily said. 'But I suppose we ought to support our neighbours.'

20

Government Health Warning

THE WOOD-BURNING stove wasn't very big, but was more than enough for this room. One of the newer ones with glass that didn't fog, two reddening logs melting into one another, the whole chamber flushed pink and orange, a beacon in the greyness of the day.

Sinking into the sofa under the giant Mars Bar beam, legs extended into the heat, Merrily almost fell asleep. Damn it, *so* much cosier here than the big, draughty vicarage.

Marry me, Lol. Take me away.

She blinked, shocked at herself, sat up. Lol was coming in from the kitchen with mugs of tea. She put out a hand, looked up into the eyes behind his round brass-rimmed glasses.

'Where am I? How did I get here?'

'I don't know.' He bent, kissed her hand before placing a mug in it. 'But you're rather attractive, so hang around if you want.'

'Yeah, OK.'

She sipped her tea. Lol had been working. Scrawled lyrics on paper upon paper on the desk under the window, his acoustic guitar leaning next to it. This was the Takamine, plugged into the old wooden-cased Guild amplifier that looked like a big valve radio set from the 1950s or something, its red power light aglow.

This was where the Boswell used to sit. Lol never mentioned the Boswell. She hoped she was doing the right thing; it was going to be an awful lot of money, more than she'd ever spent on anything – even a car, come to think of it.

'Does anybody else know this Stooke's living here?'

Lol was leaning over the back of the sofa, arms either side of her, his mug of tea in one hand. Merrily shook her head.

'I'm guessing not. He's here under a false name, anyway.'

'He's not exactly inconspicuous, is he?'

Lol opened *The Hole in the Sky* to the inside back cover: full-page photo of a man with shoulder-hugging black, curly hair, a full dark beard.

'And I believe he weighs in at about eighteen stone,' Merrily said.

'Who told you that?'

'Got it off the Internet. I couldn't actually get back to sleep after Jane broke the news. Sitting in front of the computer at half past two, frantically Googling Mathew Stooke.'

'Of course that might not even be him,' Lol said. 'Maybe they borrowed the reserve bass-player from Iron Maiden.'

'To disguise his identity in the wake of all the threats to his life?' Merrily shut the book. One of the reviews on the back said, *In the current climate, Stooke must be seen as almost insanely brave.* 'You see, that's completely wrong for a start,' Merrily said. 'In the current climate, Stooke's right in the vanguard. The current climate is aggressively secular.'

'It means Islam, doesn't it? The fact that Christians hate him ... with all respect, no big problem. Not in this country, anyway. But when you offend the Muslims ...'

'To my knowledge, they haven't stuck a fatwa on a writer since Rushdie. And fundamentalist Islam ... terrorism – that's the main *reason* for the growth of the secular state. Secularism's become a kind of refuge. A political safe haven.' Merrily put the book on an arm of the sofa. 'That's what's so depressing about it. Nobody'll admit it, but it's all about fear.'

'God gets a government health warning?'

'That's next.' Merrily sank back wearily into the sofa. 'Still, at least this resolves one issue.'

Reminding Lol about the guy in the three-piece suit she'd spotted after the parish meeting. Jonathan Long. Special Branch. Telling him what she'd learned – or hadn't learned – from Bliss.

'So it *is* political,' Lol said. 'Or it'd be the ordinary cops. It's national security.'

'All these guys get death-threats. The publishers are probably disappointed if they *don't* get death threats.'

'So this Long would've been organising some protection for him?'

'Possibly. I don't know. It doesn't entirely make sense. I mean, he's not exactly in deep cover if Jane's rumbled him inside a day. And why here, Lol? What's he doing *here*? And why – this is the real issue – why's his wife cosying up to my daughter?'

'Well, if she's a journalist ...' Lol finished his tea, put the mug on the floor. 'They're living on the edge of Coleman's Meadow. Coleman's Meadow's a story. Or it will be.'

'What do you think I should do about it?'

Lol lay back, stretching his legs towards the stove.

'Out him, maybe?'

'Does that really sound like the kind of thing I'd do?'

'Or you could go round, see if he's interested in attending church.'

'I did think of that, yes.'

'Merrily ...' Lol turned to her. 'Have you *read* what he thinks about the clergy?'

'It was a joke. But no, I haven't read anything he's written. But I will have by tonight.'

She stared into the stove, where two logs were making a molten Gothic arch, like the gateway to hell.

All the picturesque backwaters in all the world ...

In the silence, Lol said, 'Did I tell you they want me to tour America?'

Merrily sat up, hard.

Of course he hadn't told her. He knew he hadn't told her.

'Who?'

'Guy called Jeff Caldwell. A promoter I met at the BBC. Prof Levin knows him.'

'And?'

'Prof says he's on the level.'

'Well ...' Ice sliding into Merrily's stomach. 'That's fantastic, Lol. That's ... you know ... Erm, when?'

'I don't know. Early next year. Someone backed out. It's colleges, mainly, but ...'

'Well ... congratulations. You ... you've made it.'

'You think?' Lol sat down next to her. 'People who've done it say it's all motel rooms and ... other motel rooms.'

'Exciting. Wish I was coming.'

The rain was heavier now, the slow, sinister beat of individual drops on the glass giving way to a gusting, shuffling rhythm like a whole drum kit out there.

'Well ...' Lol said. 'I *had* wondered about that. If there'd be any possibility?'

'Of what?'

'Going to America. I mean you.'

'Me? Who'd pay?'

'Me.'

'No, that's not— How long for?'

'Five weeks, apparently.'

Merrily said nothing. They both knew how impossible that would be for her, for too many reasons to list. Inside the stove the gates of hell had collapsed in an orange starburst.

'OK, I'll ring the guy this afternoon,' Lol said. 'I mean, it's not really what I—'

'Lol.'

'What?'

'You have to do it.'

'I like it here too much,' Lol said. 'And it's too late.'

'No! *Listen*. It was like when you didn't want to play in front of an audience. When you thought you were incapable of doing it. And then you were forced to. And you didn't look back, and now you're so much more comfortable with yourself. You ... function better.'

'Um, thanks. But I don't think it *is* that important. What's more important ... is what happens on Christmas Eve. At the Swan.'

She sat looking at him, saying nothing.

Christmas Eve ... she'd made a point of not trying to influence him one way or another. He had a few friends – good friends – in

Ledwardine, but she wasn't sure if he had fans. A gig at the Black Swan could be a triumph; it could also be a disaster, especially on Christmas Eve. And he didn't need it. He'd done Jools Holland, he'd been asked to do America. He'd seen Michael Stipe singing along with 'The Baker's Lament'. If he passed on the Swan, what was lost?

'I've … said OK.'

'Oh.'

'Pushed it to the wire and then rang Barry and … he's having posters done.'

'What, erm … what decided it?'

'Well, it …' Lol looked uncomfortable. 'I suppose it was Lucy.'

'Oh God. Not you as well.'

'Sorry?'

'Talking to Lucy. Like Jane?'

'Not quite,' Lol said. 'It was strange.'

Merrily said nothing; anything to do with Lucy Devenish usually was. Lol managing to acquire Lucy's house – this house, *his* house now, for God's sake – had meant, for him, a responsibility. The need to keep Lucy's spirit sweet.

'The lines of a song came to me. I've got a bunch of songs now – I've been putting them together for the second album.'

'The risky second album.'

He rarely played his songs to her – and never, she suspected, to anyone else – until he thought they were as good as he could make them, and even then they were usually on tape.

'Same theme as "Baker's",' Lol said. 'Rural change, rural decay. And other stuff with relevance to what's happening here. I've also adapted three of Traherne's poems.'

'That's a brilliant idea. Was it hard?'

'Not as hard as I thought it would be. And then I was just sitting around, playing with ideas when these lines kind of came out of nowhere.'

He didn't sing them, only spoke them in a whisper.

'*Miss Devenish … Would ever wish it so …*'

There was silence. Almost immediately, Merrily heard the words again, in her head.

'God, Lol. Lucy in a song? You're actually writing a song about Lucy Devenish?'

The only song he'd ever written, specifically naming a real person, was 'Heavy Medication Day', the one about Dr Gascoigne, the psychiatrist big on sedation, who'd caused him problems in the psychiatric hospital. And look at the trouble *that* had caused.

'It's halfway there,' Lol said.

'You've got a song about Lucy Devenish, and you're planning to play it for the first time at the Black Swan, in front of people who knew her?'

'No, the first time, I'm going to play it here, in her house. And if I feel she doesn't like it …'

'You know she'll like it,' Merrily sighed. 'Because, however it turns out, you'll think she gave it to you.'

A chiming, tiny but strident, came out of the hall. Merrily jumped. It was her mobile, in a pocket of the waxed coat hanging where Lucy used to drape her poncho.

'Won't you?' she said.

'You'd better get that.'

She stood up and went out into the tiny hall. The rain was a muffled roar, like a big audience, as she fumbled out the phone.

'Reverend.'

'Oh.'

'Where are you?' Bliss said.

'Does it matter? Where are *you*?'

'I'm in the car. Outside your vicarage.'

'Ah.'

'I need to talk to you.'

Merrily went back into the living room, where Lol sat, looking down at his hands clasped together below his knees.

He looked up and smiled, but she sensed a thick wedge of anxiety behind it.

She bent and hugged him, the phone still at her ear.

'I'll come over,' she said to Bliss.

21

Pebbles

THERE WAS A crack in the cast-iron guttering over Lol's front door, and a cold stream of water sluiced into Merrily's hair as she stumbled into the street, pulling on her coat. All down Church Street she saw gutters spouting and drains gulping vainly at the muscular coils of water pumping between the cobbles.

Bliss had seen her, his Honda pulling into the kerb, headlights on, the passenger door already swinging open. She grabbed it, slotting herself in, and he was off like a getaway driver.

'God's sake—'

'Remarkable,' Bliss said. 'Don't think I've ever known a woman get dressed that quick. I do hope Robinson appreciates what he's got.'

'What do you want, Frannie?'

'Long term, a whole new life would be nice.' He drove down Church Street towards the river bridge, waited there for a van to come across. 'Meanwhile, have a listen to this.'

An MP3 player was wedged behind the gear lever and plugged into the sound system. They were halfway across the bridge, Merrily connecting her seat belt, when the man's voice came through the speakers. A phone voice, close-up, muffled but precise.

'*You are a disgrace, Ayling. Like the rest of your stinking council, you are a disgrace to Hereford.*'

'Oh.' She let the seat belt come apart. 'This is Ayling's answering machine?'

'*You have betrayed your heritage. You have tried to smother the Serpent, in the cause of naked, corporate greed ...*'

Bliss reached out a hand, put the player on pause.

'You recognise the voice, Merrily?'

'It's local.'

'Local varies.'

'Hereford, rather than real border.'

'That's what I thought.'

'Sounds like he's reading it. Like an agreed statement.'

'Through a handful of Kleenex.'

Bliss drove slowly past the village hall, where the puddles on the car park were starting to join together, forming a moat which continued, deepening, when Church Street became a country lane.

'I'd turn round when you can, Frannie. Only the four-by-fours are risking it down here.'

'Always defer to local knowledge.' Bliss pulled into a passing place, began a three-point turn, the wipers on high speed. 'And you've not answered me question yet.'

'If it wasn't for the bypass we'd be almost an island by now. Why are you asking *me*?'

'I'll give you the honest answer, Merrily. Your name was mentioned as someone whose work sometimes brings her into contact with religious eccentrics.'

'Mentioned by ...?'

'The headmistress.'

'Just that religious *eccentrics* didn't sound like her kind of term.'

'It wasn't, I just didn't want to offend you. In truth, her experience of you – can't for the life of me think why – seems to be as someone who is generally hostile and unhelpful.'

'That is so hurtful.'

'Yet seems to have the impression that you and I have a certain rapport. Me being raised a lapsed papist and all.'

'She instructed you to sound me out?'

'In her way.' Bliss put out a hand to the player. 'Let me give you the rest.'

'*... But the Serpent is not dead. Your storm troopers cannot trample the Serpent underfoot. Under tarmac. The Serpent will not sleep, but will writhe in anger under the hill and grow a new skin. Do not imagine it's*

*over, Ayling. When your road is open and strewn with wreckage and blood
… you will remember the Serpent. You will remember what you did.'*

Pause.

'We are the Children of the Serpent.'

Click.

'That's it?'

'That's it.' Bliss switched off the player. 'You heard of them?'

'The Children of the Serpent? Can't say I have.'

'You quite sure?'

'Frannie, what *is* this?'

'Do you recognise the voice?'

'No.'

'That was a frigging long time coming.' Bliss leaned back, his hands
slackening on the wheel. 'You know it's important we eliminate people.
You do realise why? Otherwise a lot of innocent loonies are gonna get
harassed.'

They were back in Church Street. Before the square, Bliss turned left
into Old Barn Lane, accelerated towards the bypass. Evidently determined not to take her home. Wanting her in *his* car, next best thing to
an interview room. She'd never known him like this.

'Are you OK, Frannie?'

'This tape, by the way – you haven't heard it. I'm not supposed to take
it out. Got it from Karen, who gets trusted with copying stuff onto hard
disk and MP3.' Bliss slowed. 'And you're not surprised, are you? You knew
about it. What happened – Helen Ayling told Sophie and Sophie …?'

'Something like that.'

'I don't know why I bother. You wanna hear it again?'

'Frannie, I really *don't* know the voice.'

'Maybe Jane?'

'Can we leave Jane out of it? She's—'

'An adult – correct? I'm gonna leave you the player. Let her hear it.
You'll know if she recognises the voice, won't you?'

'What, so you and Annie Howe can bring her in and shine a bright
light in her face until she fingers somebody?'

'Now let's be sensible.'

'All right then, let's talk about Mathew Stooke.'

Bliss braked, his hands squeezing the wheel.

'You little sod, Merrily.'

'Calm down, I didn't make any inquiries. It just … reached me. From another source.'

'What … God?'

'And nobody knows, as far as I'm aware, outside my … immediate family.'

'You've *seen* Stooke?'

'No, I … If Long's involved, does that mean Cole Barn is some kind of safe house? I mean, there've been threats, right?'

'My, we are au fait with the spook terminology. *Safe house.* I ask you. Nothing so melodramatic, Merrily. Yeh, there've been threats, but it's considered low-risk.'

'Islamic, though?'

'Just threats. It's even been in the papers. He made a statement through his publishers. Said, if you remember, that he stood by every-thing he'd written and he wasn't gonna hide from religious maniacs.'

'When was this?'

'When the book came out in paperback. Two months ago? Bit of a coincidence, some people thought.'

'What are you saying? He was claiming he'd had death threats to get publicity for the paperback?'

'Always a first thought. Especially as publicity, in this case, had been subcontracted by the publisher to an outside PR company. Naturally, they denied it.'

'How were the threats made?'

'Anonymous letters. I think there were three or four of them within about a fortnight.'

'Long told you this?'

'Merrily, it was in the frigging papers. Don't you *read* the papers?'

'Well, it's been a bit … So what's he doing here?'

'Keeping a low profile. He wants a bit of privacy to finish his next … whatever shite he's working on now. And his wife wanted to live in the country. She likes to walk. Apparently.'

'Actually,' Merrily said, 'a village is not a bad solution. You get gossip *within* a village, but it very rarely transfers to the outside world. So Jonathan Long …'

'A formality. I gather Mr Winterson, as I believe he's known, has been left with a phone number, for if he spots anything suspicious.'

'Like a woman in a dog collar?'

'Merrily, he eats vicars for breakfast. He'd destroy you with his withering logic.'

'Thanks.'

'You just want to see if he's got little horns, don't you?'

'Well, that too.'

'I gather you wouldn't recognise him. He's lost a lot of weight. Anyway, avoid. Don't betray my trust.'

'It didn't come from you. No trust involved. Where are we going?'

'God knows,' Bliss said. 'It's been a crap day.'

'You want to talk about it?'

'Not really. Howe's under pressure to wrap this up quickly. Probably political, and naturally we're all getting the heat.'

'*Political* pressure?'

'Killing a senior councillor is tantamount to sedition.'

'Only if it was done for political *reasons*. You surely can't be letting your whole inquiry be dominated by one message on an answering machine. Does nobody remember the Yorkshire Ripper hoax tape? *I'm Jack*? Put the whole investigation back months, and he was still … ripping. And all the cops charging down the wrong alley.'

'This is different.'

'Really?'

They were on the bypass now. Not the costliest of bypasses, less than a mile of it before it joined the original Leominster road near a nineteenth-century bridge across the river at a spot known as Caple End. But maybe this was the best kind: not really a bypass at all, when you thought about it, just a more direct way in and out of Ledwardine. Bliss pulled into a long lay-by the other side of Caple End bridge. It was wider than the village bridge, a place where summer tourists would stop to picnic by the river.

'Gorra feller coming over from Worcester in about an hour. Archaeologist in charge of the excavation of the Dinedor Serpent. I've been directed by the headmistress to meet him on the site.'

'You going to play *him* the message?'

'Word is some of the archaeologists aren't too pleased at being told to wrap up their dig and bugger off so the new road can go in. So ... no.'

'You think the Children of the Serpent could be disgruntled archaeologists?'

Bliss wrinkled his nose.

Merrily said, wanting to help him, '*Wreckage and blood*? You know what that might be implying, do you?'

'Remind me.'

'Can I have a cigarette?'

'It's a *police* vehicle.' Bliss let go the wheel, sagged in his seat. 'Yeh, go on. But open your window a bit.'

Pulling out the Silk Cut and the Zippo, Merrily wondered how Jane would explain this. Think it out.

'OK, sometimes ... when there's an accident black spot – the kind where there's no obvious cause, no blind bends, whatever – some people may suggest drivers' concentration could be impaired, or their perceptions altered, because the road is aligned with – or crosses—'

'A ley line?'

'Let's call it a line of energy. Which our remote ancestors apparently knew about but we, with our dulled senses, can no longer perceive.'

'Yeh, I know all that. But – pardon me if I'm stating the obvious here – the so-called serpent is not a line, is it? It's a ...' Bliss did the gestures '... wavy thing.'

'Still some kind of energy path. According to Jane, it's possibly connecting the River Wye with the earthworks on Dinedor Hill and reflecting the curves of the river. I'm just trying to give you an idea of how *they* might see it.'

'*Reflecting* the curves?'

'Literally, perhaps, because of the pieces of quartz which would reflect moonlight.'

'So the new road cutting through all this ...'

'Would be seen as breaking an ancient spiritual link. The secular world, with its noise and its exhaust fumes bursting through the coils of the serpent.'

'Which our friend insists is writhing under the hill.' Bliss sighed. 'I can't believe we're discussing this.'

'Isn't this what you wanted? How whoever made that call might be thinking? But the person who made the call ... how likely is that, really, to be Ayling's killer? As Jane's always saying, these are people who abhor violence.'

'Go on, all the same. Finish it.'

'Well ... the theory might be that you've got all this rogue energy misdirected now, affecting the attention of drivers, if only for a second. So whenever there's an accident on that road ...'

'Certain people will be nodding their little heads knowingly. Which people?'

'Frannie—'

'Members of the Coleman's Meadow Preservation Society, for instance?'

'Look ... I just can't. I can't give you a list, OK?'

'It might ...' Bliss looked at her steadily, finger-drumming the vinyl in the centre of the wheel. 'It might be the soft-option, that's all I'm saying.'

'It's ridiculous. These people—'

'Merrily, eight of them were arrested for refusing to leave the council offices when the cabinet was meeting to discuss the new road. That shows a certain ... determination.'

'Frannie ...' Merrily heard the echo of Jane: *We live in a police state! Nobody's allowed to object any more* 'It's bollocks. I doubt any of the eight people arrested were even pagans, practising or otherwise. Just ordinary people with an interest in their heritage who didn't think the democratic process was being followed. You really have no *solid* connection between the Dinedor Serpent and the murder of Clement Ayling.'

'Wanna bet?'

She turned to face him, her back against the door, smoke from the cigarette wisping out of the open window, stray raindrops spraying in. She said nothing.

'What I'm about to tell you, Merrily ... there's always something we like to keep in our back pocket, right? Something known only to the investigating team and the killer?'

She kind of nodded, not entirely sure she wanted to become the third party.

'So you know what that means,' Bliss said. 'It means not a word, Reverend. Not to Lol, not to Jane ... *especially* not to Jane.'

Merrily saw the water whirlpooling around the arch of the bridge. One of those moments where you backed away from the edge or you got pulled in.

'Look, whatever it is, you really don't have to tell me. You know how I hate to feel compromised.'

'Yeh, well, on past experience,' Bliss said, 'I prefer to have you compromised.'

'Thanks.'

'And it's been a crap day.'

'So you want to ruin someone else's?'

'His eyes were gone,' Bliss said.

Merrily swallowed some smoke, coughed. An empty stock lorry came rattling over the bridge, headlights full on, yellow smears on Bliss's blotched windscreen.

'Ayling's eyes had been gouged out and pebbles placed in the sockets. Bits of gravel, it looked like.'

'Gravel?'

No ...

'Which turned out, on examination last night, to include fragments of quartz.'

'Oh God.'

'Almost certainly originating in the so-called Dinedor Serpent. Somebody'd carefully jammed bits of the serpent into Clem Ayling's eye sockets.'

Merrily squeezed out the cigarette, burned her thumb.

'Being a cynical, case-hardened detective, I never let on, but I'll admit it spooked even me at first.'

'As it was ... meant to?'

'Yeh. Me or somebody. Torchlight, see. Councillor Ayling's severed head, with the eyes lit up like little bulbs on a Christmas tree. Not something you easily forget, Merrily, to be honest.'

22

Watery Lane

It SHOULDN'T BOTHER her, of course. With less than ten per cent of the population of Ledwardine ever showing up at a service, there had to be scores of atheists in this village.

On the other hand, the others simply *didn't show up*. Said the occasional good morning to the vicar, ignored the church. Entirely inoffensive, your atheists, as a rule. Didn't make a thing out of it. Except for fundamentalists like the celebrated geneticist Richard Dawkins, who had opened his book *The God Delusion* by hailing the *bravery* and the *splendour* of atheism. And Mathew Stooke, who'd taken it a little further. Who, according to his website, was demanding – how seriously wasn't made clear – an official bank holiday, some of kind of Atheism Pride Day. People parading with blank banners, singing 'Glad to be Godless'?

Merrily lit a cigarette, studying Stooke's face on his website, like there was the smallest chance of him being the first to blink.

Not an edifying image. Black hair, black beard – touch of the Charles Manson, even – but better than imagining the heavy head of big, smiley Clem Ayling with eyes of shining quartz.

No matter how much he'd changed, she thought she'd recognise Stooke's eyes. Quiet eyes that were looking past you towards a finite horizon. No *visible* rage.

For ten years, Mathew Elliot Stooke was a Religious Affairs correspondent for the *Guardian* and then the *Independent* newspapers. He travelled all over the world, meeting and interviewing religious leaders – archbishops, cardinals, ayatollahs, the Dalai Lama, and various powerful evangelists in the US.

And then, one day, I had what the religious would call a religious experience.

Most people lose their faith as a result of personal tragedy – for example, the failure of prayer to alleviate the suffering of a loved one. In my case, I simply awoke, as if from a ridiculous dream and realised in a single moment of revelation – a word much inflated by the Christian church – that it was all a despicable fabrication.

Immediately, a great weight dropped away from me and for a few moments I had never felt as free or as happy in my life.

This, of course, was before the anger set in.

Not even a physicist or a geneticist. Just a journalist.

The *Independent* had kept him on as Religious Affairs correspondent after he'd come out as an atheist. Well, they would, wouldn't they? Merrily sat in the computer-lit scullery, remembering, from her childhood, the Troubles in Northern Ireland. Catholic against Protestant, religion synonymous with hatred and violent death.

Around the same time, John Lennon had been imagining wistfully that there was no heaven. Easy if you tried, and she *had* tried but never found it that easy. Nothing colder than an empty sky: clean, pure, bleak, pointless.

Like the scores of Islamic suicide bombers who'd given their lives to promote the cause of secularism in the West. Blow yourself up with a few dozen innocent infidels and there's a queue of virgins waiting for you in paradise.

World Cup tickets for all martyrs.

Insane.

All religion, therefore, was insane.

Mathew Stooke continued in his job with the *Independent* for another year. During this time, viewing the world of religion through new and penetrating eyes, he wrote the remarkable series of articles which would become the basis of the international bestseller *The Hole in the Sky*.

Merrily cross-reffed to Stooke's Amazon listing, found *The Hole in the Sky* ranking number 34 in the Hot One Hundred. Which, since it had been around for more than a year, was disturbingly impressive. Whatever it was costing to rent Cole Barn would be small change, these days, for Mr Winterson.

'A man who embraces glorious, guiltless blasphemy like an expensive whore.'

New York Times.

Yeah, right. She scrolled into the Amazon reader reviews.

This book came out of rage and it made me angry too. Stooke is a diamond. I salute him.

... The guy beats Dawkins hollow because he seems to have started out as a believer and he knows what that's like. The sense of betrayal comes across so much more powerfully than the smart-arsed science-boy stuff you get from Dawkins. It's time for the pope and the archbishop of Canterbury and a few imams to get scared. Stooke is the goods.

I got this book for Christmas, which I thought at first was a bad joke. By the time I was halfway through the book I realised it was Christmas that was the joke.

Merrily watched the cigarette browning in the ashtray. So what did *you* get for Christmas, Merrily? *Apart* from Britain's premier evangelical atheist as a parishioner.

She picked up the cigarette and tamped it out in the ashtray. She had a parish to work, the open desk diary reminding her to drop in this afternoon on Sarah Clee, who provided summer flowers for the church from her garden in Blackberry Lane, and should be back home after a hip replacement.

Real life. She spooned out some lunch for Ethel, scrambled herself an egg and carried it, with a slice of toast, back to the computer. On the desktop was an icon marked *Sacred*.

Cole Hill Preservation Society. The membership database. Jane had all the names on her laptop but, for safety's sake, she'd copied the file onto the scullery computer.

All the names of all the decent citizens concerned about their heritage. All the gentle pacifist pagans. And maybe one or two loonies. No worries about her mum prying, because of the new trust between them now.

Merrily's hand hovered over the mouse. The paperback copy of *The Hole in the Sky* lay at the edge of the desk like a time bomb.

Bliss stopped the car on a forecourt in front of some shops on the edge of the Rotherwas Industrial Estate, got out his mobile and checked in with the incident room.

'Hold on a moment, Francis.' And then – a knowing, calculated insult – Iain Brent, *PhD*, didn't even bother to cover the phone. 'Don't need Bliss for anything, do you, ma'am?'

Bliss didn't hear a reply.

'No, Francis,' Brent said. 'Unless you have anything for *us*?'

Twat.

Bliss spent a couple of minutes staring through the dirty windscreen at the dirty sky, trying to lose the tightness in his chest.

On the way out, after his dismissal by Howe, Kevin Snape had called him back.

'Nice one, Francis. The Dinedor connection – staring us all in the face, but nobody else spotted it.'

'Deductive flair, Kev. Sadly out of fashion nowadays.'

'No, come on, what put you on to it?'

Just a hunch, Bliss had said. And contacts. Like he was going to tell them the truth – that all he'd done, because he knew bugger-all about local councillors, was Google *Clement Ayling, Hereford* and then watch two full pages of links to the Dinedor Serpent come bouncing up at him. And then Google the Serpent.

Bliss started the car, looking for Watery Lane which apparently gave access to the new road site. His mobile went off. He pulled in again. 'Yeh.'

'Inspector Bliss? It's Steve Furneaux, Planning Department, Herefordshire Council. You wanted to talk to me, I think, about Hereforward. And then my secretary said you'd rung an hour or so ago – she wasn't sure whether it was to cancel or postpone.'

Bliss thought about it quickly. Yeh, he'd done that. He'd called to cancel. Just like he'd been ordered to by his superior officer – daughter of the ex-copper, bent, who was also a member of Hereforward. *Not of immediate importance, is it?* Annie had said.

Right, then.

'No worries, Steve,' Bliss said. 'All it was … small problem about me getting to your office before lunchtime. Where is it you actually *go* for lunch?'

'Oh, various pubs. And Gilbies bar.'

'Gilbies would be fine,' Bliss said. 'Shall we say half-one?'

When he turned along Watery Lane it was rising to its name, the ditch on the left overflowing, half the road swamped.

Bliss drove through regardless.

Over seven thousand people worldwide had signed Jane's online petition, calling for the preservation of Coleman's Meadow as sacred space. Merrily hadn't realised there were so many. Easy to underestimate the Web's ability to draw together threads of dissent.

> from Dr Padraig Neal, Co. Wexford.
>
> The warmest of greetings, Jane, from Ireland.
>
> I most fervently applaud your courageous stand against the barbarian bureaucrats and would respectfully draw your attention to our own battle royal. As you may have read elsewhere, Ireland's most venerated ancient site, Tara, seat of the pagan High Kings, is threatened by the construction of the M3 motorway, powered by Euro-grant millions.
>
> Tara represents, in the words of the poet Seamus Heaney, 'an ideal of the spirit'. But the secular state is without ideals. Heedless of tradition, it will thrust a spear into our spiritual heart and fill the hole with money.

Several like this. She kept on scrolling down, looking for a specific reference to the Dinedor Serpent. Although there seemed to be a direct parallel here, if on a far smaller scale, to what was happening at the hill of Tara, the various Irish protesters didn't seem to have been aware of the Serpent.

A hard copy of Jane's petition had already gone to Herefordshire Council, although Merrily guessed that some of the messages accompanying the names and addresses of supporters had been edited out first.

These are gentle people. Well-meaning, Jane had said.

From Helios, Chichester:

This is to confirm that my Order has now placed a suspended curse upon The Herefordshire Council. If a single modern brick should ever be laid upon Coleman's Meadow, it will come into effect and you will – be assured – have local by-elections within the year.

Bright blessings to you, Jane!

Merrily found several like this, also, some of them far more local and even more weird.

One, from a man in Malvern, said:

Dear Jane Watkins,

I thought I should write to you as I have visited Coleman's Meadow on a number of occasions in the past few months and wondered if anyone else had had similar experiences to me.

I should point out that I am an experienced pendulum dowser and also, I suppose, a sensitive, in that when I visit neolithic sites I can usually sense something of their origins and the purposes for which they were created.

The essence of it is, at Coleman's Meadow I believe you have a very active site-guardian.

(I presume you know what I mean by this term. In the unlikely eventuality that you do not, I append a list of relevant websites – I trust, Miss Watkins, that I do not insult you.)

Most site guardians are, as Shakespeare has it, 'all sound and fury signifying nothing'.

Not so at Coleman's Meadow. I rather think that anyone working on or near this site who is not well-intentioned will have cause to regret it.

Please post this message on your website so that this information is available to anyone who may wish to comment or even to use it, in the defence of this site against negative intentions.

Yours sincerely.
Charles Miller
Inst. of Chartered Surveyors
Member, British Society of Dowsers.

Merrily closed the database, switched off the computer. Sometimes logging on to the Net was like turning over an old log in the woods, a whole unexpected ecosystem under there.

Gentle people. Well-meaning.

Yes. Most of them.

23

The Hill, the River and the Moon

'IT'S NOT GONE,' the archaeologist said. 'Just gone back underground, it has. Like a big earthworm.'

His name was Harri Tomlin, from the South Wales Valleys, now based in Worcester with the team in charge of the Dinedor/Rotherwas excavation. Young guy. Blond curls fringing his orange hard hat. Bliss had been given one too, before he'd been allowed on the site. Health and Safety. At least it kept the rain out.

'When I say *worm*,' Harri said, 'that's not much more than conjecture at this stage. Worm, dragon, serpent ... we have nothing to measure it against, see, that's the problem. There's nothing quite like it anywhere.'

They were standing on a bulldozed mound of clay. Caterpillar tracks below it had filled up with cloudy water. A bunch of trees had been sawn down, their trunks lying around like dead soldiers on a battlefield. Behind the site was the sprawl of the Rotherwas Industrial Estate and the civic waste tip – on the edge of that, unexpectedly, the Rotherwas Chapel, medieval and Tudor, an historical gem.

Mass of contradictions, this part of town. Directly ahead was Dinedor Hill, wooded and misted, towards which the Serpent apparently coiled.

'So let me get this right,' Bliss said wearily to Harri Tomlin. 'You're saying it definitely wasn't an ancient road.'

'We very quickly ruled out an actual road, Mr Bliss, because it doesn't have any substructure, see. It's also built on undulating ground, rather than having the ground flattened as you'd do for a road. So it has this kind of *flow.*'

He'd talked about fire-cracked stones, sourced nearby. The Bronze

Age guys would heat up big stones, then drop them into cold water which would break them up into the kind of small pieces they could use.

'And it contains a lot of quartz?' Bliss said.

'Fair amount.'

'And it was exposed for a while after you found it.'

'For too long. Even after a few weeks, there was some erosion. We were actually glad to get it covered over again.'

'Weeks,' Bliss said. 'So in that time anybody could've nipped up here, under the fence, and pinched a handful.'

'Or a bucketful. That's what worried us. Sightseers often like to go home with a souvenir.'

'So people *were* actually nicking stones?'

'It's ten metres wide. How could we tell? Why do you want to know if some were missing, Mr Bliss? If you don't mind me asking.'

'How long is it?' Bliss said.

'How long's a piece of string? We cleared sixty metres, but that might be just a small segment. May go all the way up the hill, to the Iron Age camp on the top, behind those trees. The Serpent is *pre*-Iron Age, obviously, but then there could've been something interesting up there before the camp.'

'I'm not really getting an image, Harri.'

Bliss was cold and his hands were going numb and whatever the Serpent had been they'd reburied it, so the council could put their road across it. Just another construction site now.

'Ever seen the Uffington White Horse in Berkshire, Mr Bliss?'

Bliss shook his head. Didn't recall ever being in Berkshire. He did remember a white horse in Wiltshire, in the context of a miserable camping holiday with Kirsty before they were married. Kirsty whingeing the whole week.

'May have seen one on the Wiltshire Downs. Chalk?'

'That'll do. Now, forget the chalk and instead of a horse think of a snake. Or, if you like, think of a river. Think of the Wye. Could our structure have been designed to replicate the actual course of the Wye, winding from the top of the hill to the banks of the river itself?'

'That far?'

'It's not very far. The river's down there, behind those industrial buildings. This is about the hill, the river and the moon.'

Harri told him the theory about this sinuous spectral form winding its moonlit way to the top of the hill.

'Prehistoric *son et lumière*?' Bliss said.

'The sound would be chanting. A sacred hill, see. A lot of hills were sacred. And the river. Water was always very significant, and the Wye's a magnificent river so it would be venerated above all others in the west. Therefore, if we imagine ...'

Harri walked to the top of the mound and started weaving his arms about, the way blokes used to air-sketch a voluptuous woman.

'... If we imagine something mystically – and very visibly – connecting the hugely powerful River Wye with the highest hill in these parts. Something suggestive of a coming-together, a confluence, of these great power symbols, the hill, the river and the moon.'

'Now about to be trashed by a new road slicing through the middle, courtesy of the Hereford Council,' Bliss said. 'Would that be a fair assessment?'

'Hey ...' Harri Tomlin put up his hands. 'Wasn't me done him, guv.'

'So much for a quick result. Where do you lads go from here, Harri?'

'Probably try to extend the excavation in the direction of the river, see how far the Serpent goes. Which means digging on private land, so may take a while to organise.'

'And when you say these places are sacred, what's the significance of that, in terms of what they were doing here back then?'

'Ritual.'

'Meaning?'

'Search me. That word covers up a lot of ignorance. We don't know what rituals were involved, of course we don't.'

'Human sacrifice, maybe?'

'Ah, see, people *like* to think there was human sacrifice all over the place, but it probably wasn't all that widespread. It's common to think of Bronze Age people as primitive savages, but they must've been quite sophisticated.'

'Savagery itself, Harri,' Bliss said quietly, 'can sometimes be quite sophisticated.'

Harri Tomlin looked across at the stripped ground and the slaughtered trees, his legs apart, his fluorescent yellow jacket gleaming with rain. Then he looked at Bliss.

'What are you after? You really think somebody killed Ayling because he was being so negative about this discovery? I mean, you actually think that's a possibility?'

'It's a possibility, Harri.'

'Can you tell me *why* you've made this connection, because from my point of view—'

'Nothing personal, Harri, but it's not my decision how much we reveal and when. I *can* tell you there was a ritualistic element. And the connection with this site … that's beyond argument.'

'Which is why you borrowed some quartz chippings from us yesterday?'

'And if you can think of anything else that might help us, I hope you won't hold back.'

Bliss let the silence dangle, looking at Harri Tomlin through half-closed eyes.

'Look,' Harri said. 'You want me to get fanciful here, is it? I mean, I'm not going to have to repeat all this in court at some stage?'

'I'm not writing it down, Harri, and I'm not wired. Be as fanciful as you like.'

'All right, then,' Harri said. 'Heads.'

'Heads, plural?'

'I'm not so much thinking of the guys who laid out the Serpent, I'm thinking the people who built the camp or fort on Dinedor Hill. The Iron Age Celts, who came over here from Europe, two or three thousand years ago. They were very into heads. They believed that the seat of consciousness – the soul, if you like – was located in the head. So the Celts tended to take off the heads of their enemies.'

'That a fact.'

'After death, this is. And, from your point of view, it possibly gets better. A contemporary Roman account tells how they'd preserve the head of a distinguished enemy in cedar oil and keep it in a chest for display. Or they might offer it up to the gods. Skulls have also been found, in quite large numbers, at shrines and other sacred places.'

'Like the old Blackfriars Monastery?'

'No, no, Mr Bliss – medieval, that is.'

'Couldn't be a Celtic site or something underneath?'

'If there is, we haven't found it yet. Sorry.'

'So, let's look at this a minute, Harri. We've gorra mixture of historical periods. But wouldn't this serpent ... wouldn't that still have been around in Celtic times?'

'We think not. A Roman ditch cuts across it, so it was certainly silted over by then. However, the hill itself would still have been venerated and perhaps a memory of the Serpent remained. Perhaps it still ... For instance, while I've been working here, people have told me how families used to follow a path to the top of Dinedor on special days, like a pilgrimage?'

'To this day?'

'Near enough,' Harri Tomlin said. 'That's a ritual, too, in its way, isn't it? Beliefs and customs often last longer than physical remains. There's also – I don't suppose this helps you, particularly, but there's a link between heads and water – specifically wells and rivers. Skulls have been found in rivers.'

Bliss was gazing up at Dinedor Hill, trying to stitch all this together. The important thing was that Harri Tomlin was strongly supporting the ritual element in the killing.

'You get many ... I dunno, *modern* pagan-types coming to see the site, Harri?'

'Oh, some days ...' Harri was smiling '... you'd look up from your trench and they'd be coming out of the woods like the Celts of old. Home-made, multicoloured sweaters and dowsing rods. Harmless enough. Quite respectful, in general. You tell them not to walk across the site, they won't. Very respectful. Give me pagans any day, rather than bored kids.'

'You get to know any of them?'

'Not by name. One weird beardie is much like another, I find. We don't get them now, mind – had to be a lot more strict about sightseers since the accident.'

Bliss blinked at him.

'Two of the boys cutting down trees. If it's a big one, one of them goes some distance away to get the wider view and then gives a whistle when he can see it's clear. Boy with the chainsaw, he swore he'd heard the whistle, see ...'

Harri put a hand behind an ear by way of illustration. Bliss waited.

'Well, the other fellow never whistled because he wasn't out of the way himself. Tree comes down, *wheeeeeee*.' Harri lowered his arm, slowly. 'Fractured skull, smashed shoulder. Two operations on that shoulder.'

'You were here at the time?'

'Worn my hard hat religiously ever since, Mr Bliss.'

Bliss handed his back. Five past one. Time to leave, if he was going to make Gilbies by half past.

'All the way to the ambulance, he was swearing he hadn't whistled,' Harri said, like Bliss might want to make something of it. 'Funny how your senses can play tricks in a big open space like this.'

24

Poisoning the Apple

MERRILY WENT INTO the church, up into the chancel, to meditate ... pray.

Taking off Jane's red wellies and sitting, thick-socked, in the old choir-master's chair. Hands palms-down on her knees, eyes almost closed, breathing regulated. This was how she went about it now, when she was on her own. Less liturgical, more meditative. Feeling for answers ... truth.

Feeling for anything, actually, today, as the rain tumbled on the roof, rushed into the guttering, roared inside her head – a punishing noise. Her reward, probably, for opening *The Hole in the Sky* at random.

> ... understand this: Christianity has already entered its final phase. By the end of this century, 'Jesus Christ' will be nothing more than a mild oath, the origins of which will be a mystery to most people under the age of seventy.

She'd put the book down. Not thrown it down, just laid it next to the sermon pad.

It was not the issue. It was meaningless, like the arrival in Ledwardine of Mathew Stooke. No significant coincidence here – *all the picturesque backwaters*, forget it, the guy had to live somewhere.

This was *not* the reason she needed to go into the church.

Merrily had spent about twenty minutes mentally laying out the real issue, walking all around the house and ending up in Jane's attic apartment where there were stacks of old magazines: back copies of *Pagan Dawn*, *Pentacle*, *White Dragon*, other homespun journals representing Wicca, Druidry and all pagan points in between. Bought and absorbed by thousands of people far too shy to dance naked around a woodland fire.

And people who weren't. And people who did.

A long-established subculture was renewing itself, Jane would insist, while Christianity withered, in these days of industrial abuse, greed, neglect and consequent climate change. As the Earth bled, paganism was the only *practical* belief system and if the Church wanted to survive it needed to alter its remit accordingly.

Jane's view of it was rose-tinted, of course – paganism just this all-embracing term for Earth-related green spirituality, a striving for oneness with the elements, sometimes personified as gods and goddesses, the male and female energies in nature. Pagans were more aware of their immediate environment, more connected to the land – *this* land, *these* hills, *these* fields. And when the land was raped and its ancient shrines desecrated by secular governments, pagans felt the pain, almost physically. Felt the violence. *A spear into our spiritual heart,* as the Irishman, Padraig Neal, had put it.

But this wasn't some enlightened, half-faerie super-race. Pagans and green activists were just more flawed human beings, prone to anger, frustration, irrational hatreds, mental imbalance ... and firing off inflammatory emails.

Emails were not like letters. Emails were shot from the hip and, by the time you'd realised you'd gone too far, it was too late, you'd sent it. Sure, there was a lot of anger about, but there was a big difference between sending a knee-jerk email and going out there with a knife or a machete.

And yet ...

you will – be assured – have local by-elections within the year.

What was she supposed to do about this?

Perhaps sit down tonight with Jane and have a long discussion in the hope of convincing her that they should go through the entire correspondence of the Coleman's Meadow Preservation Society, compiling a list of possibly dangerous extremists. Which would take most of the night.

And then what?

What?

What if there was another killing?

*

At lunchtime, when she got the call on her mobile, Jane was still smouldering.

Last day of term, and in morning assembly they'd all had to stand up and do a minute's silence for Councillor Clement Ayling, who had apparently been Chairman of Education. Morrell paying a sincere tribute to Ayling's vision and all that crap. Meaningless to the little kids at the front of the hall. Jane, at the back, glowering down at her shoes, thinking, *What a total hypocritical scumball.*

Another *Catcher in the Rye* moment. Been getting them a lot lately. This was the situation: Morrell – who insisted his job title was *School Director* – was the worst kind of New Labour, and Ayling had been this lifelong worst kind of Old Tory. Not only that but he was one of the guys behind the plan to close down a whole bunch of Herefordshire schools, primary and secondary.

Well, not close them down, *merge* them – that was the get-out term. What you did was to put two fairly successful small secondary schools under one big roof.

Thus creating a massive new sink school where nobody learned anything except where to get good crack, and they had to lower the academic goalposts and fiddle the results and the cops spent so much time on the premises you might as well set up a permanent incident room on the playing field.

And *why* was Morrell quietly supporting this? *Why* had Morrell – whose party claimed to stand for *education, education, education* – been up Ayling's bum? Simple. *This* school had a lot of land, and fields all around, perfect for expansion. So, if Ayling's scheme went through, while some other bastard might be out of a job, Morrell could find himself *director* of an *operation* twice the size, with a *much bigger salary.*

That was how much of a socialist Morrell was. Right now, curled up on the rescued sofa in a corner of the sixth-form leisure suite, Jane just couldn't wait to leave this lousy place for good.

'You thinking about sex again, Jane?'

Sweaty Rees Crawford chalking his snooker cue, getting in some final practice for this afternoon's Big Match, the final of the Sixth Form Championship in which he was playing Jordan Hare – Ethan Williams taking bets on the outcome. Jane couldn't decide.

'Look,' she snarled, as her mobile went off inside her airline bag. 'Don't you go projecting your sad fantasies on me, Crawford. You screw that thing around much faster, there won't be any chalk left. Who's this?' Snapping into the phone.

'You don't sound too happy, Jane.'

'Coops?'

'Oh, *Coops*,' Rees Crawford said, leering at her, and Jane gave him the finger.

'It *is* OK to call you now, is it?' Neil Cooper said. 'Your lunch break, right?'

'Sure.' Not like it would matter anyway, the way she was feeling. 'It's fine.'

'Only I said I'd keep you up to speed. It's starting tomorrow.'

'The dig?' Jane gripping the phone tight. 'The dig's *happening*?'

'Officially starting tomorrow.'

'So Bill Blore …'

'He's here. Don't say wow. *Please* do not say wow.'

'He's in the village?'

'He's actually been over a few times, doing geophysics, making sure we haven't got it all wrong and what's under there are concrete lamp-posts or something. You, er … want to meet him?'

'Me?' Jane lowered her feet to the floor. 'You're kidding, right?'

'Actually,' Coops said, 'he wants to meet you.'

'Stop taking the piss. I'm not in the mood.'

'No, really. He's meeting all the people involved with Coleman's Meadow from the outset. You *were* the outset. What time's your school bus get in – half-four? Should still be *some* light. So if you want to come over to the site when you get home?'

'Wow, you *are* serious.'

'All I'd say, Jane,' Coops said, 'is, don't get carried away. Whatever he tells you, *don't* get carried away.'

'You know me, Coops,' Jane said, tingling. 'Ms Cool.'

*

On a good day, Merrily would have been leaving the church nursing some new and unforeseen possibility, the softly gleaming ingot of an idea. Saved again.

Or at least not feeling sick with dread.

When she walked out, in Jane's red wellies, under the dripping lych-gate, it was like Ledwardine was drifting away from her. All its colours washing out, daytime lights in the shops burning wanly behind the sepia screen of slanting rain. Gutted by the feeling that the village was getting bigger and, at the same time, more amorphous, more remote.

Like God?

All she'd seen, in meditation, were the small crises she'd failed to react to, the issues she'd back-burnered. All coming together like coalescing clouds, making darkness.

Crossing to the Eight Till Late, she saw a pale orange poster in one of the mullioned windows of the pub on the edge of the square.

Christmas Eve at The Black Swan Inn.

Ledwardine's own

LOL ROBINSON

('The Baker's Lament')

in concert.

9 p.m.

All welcome.

God, Barry hadn't wasted any time, had he? *All welcome.* Would that work? Already she could hear the background noise from the bars, people talking and laughing while Lol, bent over his guitar, murmured his tribute to Lucy Devenish whom most of the Swan's clientele had either never known or considered mad.

From Brenda Prosser at the shop, she bought a box of All Gold for Sarah Clee.

'They must be mad.' Brenda apparently continuing a conversation she'd been having with the previous customer who'd already left the store. 'Merrily – pardon me for being nosy, but do you get properly recompensed? I mean for all these flowers and fruit and chocolates you keep buying for sick parishioners?'

'Erm ... no. *Who* must be mad?'

'Those archaeologists. All turning up this morning in their Land Rovers. And a TV camera team, too – what's that programme ...?

'*Trench One*? They've arrived? I didn't know that.'

'And a big tall crane. We didn't know there was going to be TV. What can they hope to do in this weather?'

'I actually think they like it, in a way,' Merrily said. 'Makes it look more dramatic on TV if they're fighting the elements and they're all covered in mud. Makes archaeology look like ... trench warfare?'

'Rather them than me.' Brenda shivered. 'All the farmers have moved their sheep from within about half a mile of the river, did you know?'

'Doesn't surprise me.'

'Give Sarah my love, will you?' Brenda said.

Not possible, as it turned out. The rain had slowed, but there was no promise of brightness in the swollen sky when Merrily reached the age-warped cottage in Blackberry Lane, with its window boxes of yellow and purple winter pansies. Brian Clee, retired postman, had the front door open before she was through the garden gate.

'*I'm* sorry, Merrily, should've rung you.' He looked worn out, frazzled 'She was only took in this morning, see. Another ward closure – some infection. Half the hip ops postponed.'

'That means she'll be in over Christmas?'

Merrily followed Brian Clee into the house, his white head bent under the bowed beams in the hall. She left Jane's red wellies on the doormat, took off her coat and stayed for a cup of tea, listening to Brian's opinion of the county hospital, its unfriendly, automated rip-off, too-small car park, its smoking ban in the grounds so you couldn't even have a fag to calm your nerves.

'She'll be fine, Brian. We prayed for her last weekend, and we'll do it again on Sunday.'

'Thank you, Merrily.'

Brian nodding as she left him with the chocolates. Not displaying much conviction, though, that virulent hospital infections could be neutralised by prayer.

The word 'prayer' will, in turn, reflect memories of something quaint and rather childish. The nightlight on the bedside table. Something grown out of.

'*Sod off, Stooke!*'

Merrily stopped in the lane. Had she actually said that out loud? She was furious at herself for letting this get to her. There was no earthly reason …

And yet there was. She kept forgetting this – Stooke's wife coming on to Jane like that, asking too many questions. *That* was a reason. She'd even Googled Leonora Winterson, finding next to nothing. No picture, anyway; Lensi took pictures rather than appeared in them – and certainly not with her husband. In fact, Google Images had only one shot of him – the ubiquitous Charles Manson pose. His website said he didn't do TV, and cameras were banned from his bookshop signings.

I'm not a personality, just an investigative journalist who investigated a god and found two thousand years of lies, fabrication, abuse, corruption, hypocrisy …

Couldn't get rid of him. Like he was her nemesis or something. Merrily splashed angrily through a chain of puddles into the church-yard, arriving at the modest grave of Lucy Devenish.

It had come to this.

'I don't know what the hell *I'm* doing here, Lucy. I'm supposed to minister to the living.'

Standing in the grey-brown rain with her bare hands on the rounded stone, remembering the first time she'd encountered the indomitable Miss Devenish, on an ill-fated night of wassailing in the orchard. Lucy with her hooked Red Indian's nose, wearing her trademark poncho and a sense of unease.

Amply justified that night. During the traditional loosing of shot-guns through the branches, to promote a good year of apples, old Edgar Powell had blown his own head off. They used to say – kids, mainly –

that Edgar haunted the orchard, and if you looked up into the branches of the Apple Tree Man, the oldest tree, you might see him. The tree had been chopped down. A mistake, Jane had said; old Edgar could appear anywhere in the orchard now, smiling through the branches and the blood. It didn't scare pagan Jane.

You know what, Lucy? Merrily's grip tightening on the headstone. *I think I'm losing it. Thought it was going all right. The regular congregations weren't exactly huge, but the Sunday-evening meditation ... word was spreading and we were getting people actually interested in searching for something inside themselves. I was finally beginning to see what you meant by the orb.*

Orb was a word Lucy had borrowed from Traherne, the 17th-century poet, drunk on Herefordshire. Lucy using it to describe the ambience of Ledwardine, the confluence of tradition, custom, history and spirit. The orb was an apple, shiny and wholesome.

Who's poisoning the apple, Lucy?

Blinking back tears, she turned away. This was Jane's place. Jane did the dead. Jane, who felt herself so far from death as to be able to deal with it almost lovingly. Merrily walked away, following the route Jane had identified as a coffin path, a spirit road, into the lower orchard where Edgar Powell had died.

Haunted or not, the orchard in winter was a reminder of loss. The village had once been encircled by a density of cider-apple trees, nurtured, it was said, by the fairies whose lights could be seen glimmering at twilight among the branches.

If there were lights now, they were corpse candles. The trees were slowly dying off, gradually getting cremated on cosmetic open fires in the Black Swan.

A village of smoke and ghosts. The recently dead and the long, long dead.

Curiously, she was feeling calmer now. Standing on the path inside a rough circle of spidery, winter-bare apple trees, thinking about Lol who would sometimes play Nick Drake's tragically-prescient song 'Fruit Tree' which suggested that, for some people – for Nick, certainly – nothing would flourish before death.

Merrily looked up. With the trees gradually getting turned into scented ashes, the only active life forms here were the unearthly balls of mistletoe, suspended like alien craft high among the scabbed and blackened branches, always just out of reach.

Kisses for Christmas, out of reach. She walked on, knowing exactly what she was doing now, where she was going.

When you left behind what remained of the orchard, the fields opened up below you. One was Coleman's Meadow with a temporary barbed-wire fence around it, a parking area marked out with orange tape, and something like a fairground on it now: a dark green tent, like an army canteen, two caravans, two Land Rovers and one of those cranes that they used for a cherry-picker TV camera. About a dozen people in waterproofs around a mini-JCB, laughter rising frailly through the rain. Cole Farm itself, served by a narrow lane, was wedged into a clearing in the trees ascending Cole Hill. But Cole Barn was exposed on the edge of a small field adjoining the meadow, with a pool of flood water in front, beginning to encroach on a tarmac parking area.

Well, it was *called* Cole Barn, but it had never been an actual barn, according to Gomer Parry, just an old tractor shed. So there was no glazed-over bay, like you usually found with barn conversions, just an ordinary front door, probably not very old.

From which a woman emerged. Turquoise waterproof, coppery hair. She came out quickly and ran through the squally rain to a new-looking black Mercedes 4x4 parked in a turning circle. Merrily stood on the edge of the dripping orchard, as the engine growled and the 4x4 spun, skidding and squirting gravel, into a dirt track full of puddles that led into the lane.

It was, she guessed, quite an angry exit. She herself could now make a discreet one, turning away and melting back among the geriatric apple trees.

Or she could go down, knock on the door and, if anyone was in, do the bumbling-vicar bit. Welcome to the parish, Mr Winterson.

You just wanner ...

Before she could reconsider, she'd scrambled down to open up the field gate, and then she was crossing the strip of rough grass spiked with the skeletons of last year's docks, to the front door of Cole Barn.

... See if he's got little horns.

25

Outside the Box

'BASICALLY,' STEVE FURNEAUX said, 'I liked Clem. He was like an old bulldog. Barked at you from a distance and then he'd gradually come sniffing around, always suspicious, until you threw him a biscuit or two.'

Gilbies was in an alley behind High Town, the tower and spire of St Peter's church pushing up suddenly behind it like a rocket on a pad. A bar, for the upwardly-mobile. By the time Bliss had got there Steve had eaten; Bliss had bought coffees.

'We coped with him,' Steve said. 'You couldn't actually heave him out of the way, but, like I say, you found ways of getting round him.'

Bliss figured Steve Furneaux was about his own age, but with better hair. A middle-ranking official in the planning department at Herefordshire Council. Londoner. Crisp, dapper, sandy-looking feller. No shit on *his* shoes.

'Because we're all quite excited about Hereforward, Francis. It's a new concept, experimental, and we don't want it to crash.'

'Well, I'm just a thick copper. Perhaps you could you explain it to me very simply. As to a child with learning difficulties?'

'I'll explain it as I would to a new councillor,' Steve said. 'Which is pretty much the same thing.'

He paused to check out Bliss's reaction. Bliss put on a smile. Harmless Terry Stagg had already talked to the chairman of Hereforward, assembling the nuts and bolt of Ayling's last meeting. When Bliss had suggested it might be worth looking at some of the issues Hereforward was involved in, Howe could hardly say no at a briefing. Only privately pulling the rug when she had Bliss over a barrel.

Bliss had picked out Steve, looking for an official, an employee, rather than a slippery councillor. It was proving a good choice. Steve was slippery, too, but in a different way, and he oozed personal ambition. Therefore no loyalty to Hereford or its councillors.

'This is how it came about,' Steve said. 'There was some new funding available for a number of local joint committees to be set up to consider the long-term economic prospects and cultural directioning of particular areas of the West Midlands.'

'Cultural conditioning,' Bliss said. 'Right.'

So this would be a clutch of councillors, council officials, sharks, leeches, token ethnics and tame gays tolerating each other over a free lunch. Not a new concept at all, then.

'Hereford was encouraged to go for it, as we're out on a limb,' Steve said. 'Geographically more Wales than West Midlands – but of course Wales is a different country now with its own government.'

'And this would be another way for us to get quietly reined into the Midlands, would it?'

Steve laughed, glancing across at the bar-huggers. Wiped his nose with a red-spotted handkerchief and lowered his voice.

'Think of it as a much-needed shot of adrenalin. We get to think outside the box. We were almost certainly the first to float the idea of a University of Hereford, which is now on the wider agenda.'

'Blue-sky think-tank, in other words.'

'Exactly. Look, Francis … sorry, is it Frank?'

'It's not Frank,' Bliss said.

Through his teeth.

'I mean, you're obviously an outsider, too,' Steve said.

'I just talk like this to sound cool. Go on. You want to educate the hicks.'

'The point is, there hasn't been enough *overview*. Local government gets lost in details and, inevitably, parochialism – individual councillors nursing their pet projects and nothing getting done. Our brief is to come up with radical, global ideas which we feed directly to the cabinet, so that they've been fully shaped *before* they're put before the authority en masse.'

'I see.' A fait-accompli machine, in other words. 'And Clement Ayling ...'

'... was initially suspicious of us, as he always was of anything new. But he had a lot of influence and got himself co-opted onto Hereforward. More to keep an eye on us than anything. I think he saw us as some sort of central-government infiltration.'

'Perish the thought,' Bliss said. 'So ... what global concepts were you discussing at the meeting on Wednesday, Steve?'

Steve looked doubtful about being able to answer this one, maybe on the grounds that a report had not yet gone to the cabinet, or some bull-shit.

'All right,' Bliss said, 'answer me this. Was Councillor Ayling in any kind of, shall we say *heated discussion* during the meeting?'

'Not that I recall, Francis, no. He seemed to spend most of it sitting there with his chin sunk into his chest, conveying a certain boredom with the proceedings'

'He leave with anybody?'

Terry Stagg had spoken to the Hereforward committee secretary, confirming times and stuff, but going over the same ground would often throw up an anomaly.

'He left with me, actually,' Steve said. 'As I told your colleague.'

'And what did you talk about?'

'Oh ... trivia. Date of the next planning meeting, that sort of—'

'Did Hereforward have a view on the Dinedor Serpent?'

'Ah,' Steve said.

'Because Clem Ayling had very definite views, didn't he?'

'Ah, well, you see, Clem ...' Steve leaned back on his stool. 'I'm afraid poor old Clem couldn't see the romance in it. Old-fashioned Herefordian, wanted the city to expand and prosper, offer more jobs and, yes, have its own university, he was with us on that ...'

'But couldn't get excited about a trickle of gravel.'

'No, I— Francis, where's this going?'

'You tell me, Steve.'

'Well, we ...' Steve picking up his coffee for support. 'We had quite a debate about the Serpent some months ago. Yes, the tourist potential of a world-famous prehistoric monument … if that's what it is, we can't easily ignore it.'

'So, in saying it was worthless, Ayling was at odds with the rest of the committee?'

'Ahm …' Steve putting down his coffee. 'Essentially, no. This was one of the few issues where Clem and the rest of us were broadly in agreement, although most of us were more tactful about how we phrased it.'

'I see,' Bliss said.

'Obviously, if we'd been talking about something on the scale of Stonehenge … but, as you said yourself, this is a trickle of gravel. The tourism potential is always going to be minimal. That was how we saw it. And we certainly need that relief road – Hereford being the only substantial centre in the country without a bypass. This is a move in the right direction. Vital, really.'

'Had to go through …'

'*Had* to go through.'

'So Hereforward didn't manage to come up with a brilliant compromise solution.'

'We're working on it. We've asked to be kept informed of developments. If the Serpent does turn out to be something unique, then it's our job to capitalise on it. But the council would need some convincing, and the more they get slagged off from outside the more they'll resist.'

'Who's been slagging them off? In particular.'

'The archaeologist, Blore, didn't help an awful lot did he? Considering we were paying him …'

'Who were?'

'Hereforward used him as a consultant on the Serpent.'

'Must've been costly.'

'Not particularly, and we wanted an educated viewpoint.'

Big name, more like, Bliss thought.

'And then he shoots his mouth off to the media. My colleagues weren't pleased.'

'Why? Blore's a notorious loose cannon. They'd been thinking they could buy his opinion?'

Steve shrugged, wiping his nose.

'I hear he's in charge of this other local dig now,' Bliss said. 'Ledwardine?'

'Got in by the back door. Not our problem, that, thank God – strictly a local issue. Local councillor wanted us to intervene, but a bunch of upmarket houses is not the same as a road and I suppose big stones would have more tourist appeal than pebbles.' Steve looked at his watch – wafer-thin, and an extra dial, probably for New York time. 'I'm afraid I've a meeting at three at Ross and Belmont's close to impassable, so if you have any *major* questions ...'

'Would hate to hold you up, Steve. You look like a man in a hurry.'

'Always,' Steve said. 'Surprised I haven't seen you around, Francis. Which gym do you use?'

Bliss stared at him. This was a man who would get on well with Annie Howe. Christ, this man might even be able to *seduce* Annie Howe. Bliss kept on staring, but Steve Furneaux seemed quite relaxed in the company of a fellow incomer, an ally against the hicks and the rednecks.

'Out of interest,' Bliss said. 'You being a blue-sky thinker, Steve ... a *radical* thinker—'

'I'm a planning officer. But, you're right, Hereforward lets us off the mental leash.'

'So who did it, Steve? Who killed Clement Ayling?'

'You're asking *me*?'

He looked thrown for a moment. Kind of feller who'd hate ever to be caught without an informed opinion.

'I was thinking you could give me a blue-sky idea,' Bliss said. 'An independent assessment.'

Steve Furneaux actually looked, for a moment, like he was drawing up a shortlist. Or maybe – call this blue-sky thinking – wondering how best he could convince Bliss that Hereforward was a blind alley.

But he never found out who'd be in Steve's frame; his mobile went off. 'Excuse me a moment. *Yeh.*'

'Boss?'

'Hello, Sergeant.'

'Oh.' Karen Dowell picking up his signal. 'Right. I'd better keep this short, then.'

Bliss fiddled with his sugar spoon while Karen told him that Howe was calling the class together for 2.30 p.m. On account of they'd found the rest of Ayling.

'Well ... more or less,' Karen said.

Bliss put the spoon down gently.

'Where?'

'In the river. Half in, half out, kind of thing. Up against Bredwardine Bridge. You know where I mean?'

'So that would be ... the big river.'

A magnificent river, Harri Tomlin breathed in Bliss's head. *Venerated above all others.*

'Even bigger at present, as you can imagine,' Karen Dowell said. 'Well high, and a lot of debris, fallen trees and stuff washed up against the bridge. The body was apparently somewhere in the middle of all that.'

'Intact?'

'Still in the suit.'

Bliss had tuned out the background chat, and his mind was back in the mist with Harri Tomlin.

'This is getting a bit spooky, Sergeant.'

'Best if you tell me later, is it, boss?'

'Karen, when you said *more or less* ...?'

'In relation to the body? Well, it just leaves the eyes, doesn't it? The eyes are still missing.'

'Ah.'

'Got to go, boss. Sorry.'

'OK. Thanks, Sergeant.'

'Developments?' Steve Furneaux said.

Was that a flicker of relief in Steve's eyes?

Maybe, maybe not.

'It's the old story, Steve. No lunch, as they say, for the wicked.' Bliss slid down from his stool. 'Oh ... before I go ... was Charlie Howe at the meeting?'

'Yes, I believe ... Yes he was. We were surprised to see him because he was only just out of hospital. *Ah ...*' Steve raised a forefinger. 'Of course ... ex-policeman. Old colleague of yours?'

'Bit before my time,' Bliss said. 'But a mate, you know. A good mate.'

Bliss had left his car at the back of the Gaol Street pay-and-display, away from prying police eyes. He sat in it for a while. One hand was trembling. Maybe the caffeine and no lunch.

Bitch had excluded him again, frozen him out. It had taken Karen to call and tell him that they'd found Ayling's body. Nothing from Howe, not even via Brent.

This was about more than just the Shah kid. More than just him trying to keep her out of the Ayling case from the start. This was about Charlie, for definite.

Well, sod her, he'd make sure he was there at 2.30. Drop into the school at the last minute, so neither Howe nor Brent could head him off at the pass. Maybe he'd walk there a bit late. Bide his time and then casually explain the possible significance of the bulk of Ayling turning up in the Wye.

Why the body, not the head? Didn't know, but it didn't matter, there was *something*.

As he took his key out of the ignition he saw something sticking out from under the passenger seat. A small, scuffed book.

He bent and retrieved it.

My Little Pony. Naomi's. For a moment, he couldn't breathe.

What had he done?

Naomi. Seven and a half years old. All her mother's best qualities, without the difficult bits. Bliss leaned back, holding the book on his knee, eyes squeezed shut. Even trying to focus on Kirsty's difficult bits, he was reminded of one tender moment somewhere under that white horse in Wiltshire. A feeling of yes, this was right, this was the right thing.

What happened? Where did that go?

He sat up and put the book in the glove box, got out of the car and locked it and walked away, feeling closer to breaking down than at any time since his solo breakfast of burnt toast and brown sauce.

26

Dated Masquerade

As soon as Merrily had rung the bell she pulled back, appalled.

The front door was new. Polished hardwood, expensive. 'Cole Barn' carved tastefully into an oak plaque.

She backed away from it, disorientated. Looking around and not recognising anything. As if she'd come here without thinking, taken the wrong turning, walked into the wrong room.

Looking back towards the orchard, you almost could believe there *was* some primeval energy around that path. Not so much a healing, life-affirming force as something that amplified your anxieties into obsession.

If you were vulnerable. If you'd prayed for advice and received nothing. If you were afraid your daughter was unwittingly linked with someone who had killed and butchered a man. If, wherever you looked, you saw people losing control of their lives and threatening shadows cloaking the same implacable figure: the enemy of faith, the spirit of the secular state. The worm in the apple.

Nobody answered the door.

She breathed out hard, finally turning away. Anticlimax or relief?

Whatever, just get out of here. Walk away. Go home. Consider your-self saved.

All the same, Merrily was reluctant to go back on that same path. Just didn't want to.

On a ridge at the top of the hedged paddock there was a wooden stile, giving access to Coleman's Meadow, the platform crane arching over it as if it was offering lifts into the meadow. If she went back that way, at least she'd have something to tell Jane tonight.

The rain was in remission again, the air felt a little fresher. Walking up the sodden field, she became aware of the bell-shaped Cole Hill rising on the other side of the meadow.

So perfect from this angle. Robed in cloud, somehow lighter than the sky. She was aware, for the first time, just how breathtaking it would be, viewed between standing stones.

And stopped, strangely moved, touched by a *connection*. Was this how Jane felt all the time? Was this what Jane would interpret as pagan consciousness? It didn't matter. All she knew was that the destruction of this view by Lyndon Pierce's upmarket estate of fake Tudor executive homes with double and triple garages would be the worst kind of insult both to the living and the long, long dead.

This wasn't myth. It was the only certainty she'd felt all day.

She felt lighter stepping down from the stile alongside the platform crane, its great arm half raised from the back of a black and yellow truck marked *access hire*.

Behind it, two men were arguing, blocking the path, one scowling from under a green waterproof hat, the other wearing a red hiking jacket and an expression somewhere between pained and placating.

'True,' the hat guy was saying. 'We did know about it, we knew it was happening, but we were definitely *not* told it was going to be televised, with all the crap that involves. And I'm not trying to be awkward, but I came here for a bit of peace. To work, you know?'

'Which I fully— I do understand your situation, and I'm sorry. But with this weather we've got way, way, *way* behind schedule, and we just can't afford to delay it any longer. I mean, have you any idea—' the man in the red jacket indicated the crane '—what that costs to rent?'

'With respect, mate, that's really not my—'

'All I'm saying is we absolutely *need* to get a couple of days in before Christmas. And *then* – I promise you – most of us will clear off for a week or so and leave you in peace. OK?'

'Where are you getting your power?' the man in the hat said. 'Electricity – for lights and things.'

'Generators.'

'All of it?'

'Of course all of it.'

'No cables leading out? You've got any uncovered cables?'

'Is there a problem?'

'Doesn't matter.' The man in the hat abruptly turning away. '*Oh*—' Nearly walked into Merrily. 'I'm *so* sorry ...'

'My fault, I think I crept up on you.'

'No, no, it was my— Look, I'm sorry, are you local? Can I ask you – do you mind? – did *you* know about this?'

'Well, I did *know* about it,' Merrily said, 'but I've not heard of an official announcement, and I don't think there's been anything in the papers.'

'We *never* put anything out to the papers in advance,' the red-jacket guy said. 'Simply because we don't want a huge crowd of spectators. Which I'm sure wouldn't be in your best interests, either, Mr—'

'Winterson.'

Merrily took a step back, the red-jacket guy saying, 'Yes, of course. I was going to come round to see if we could talk to you.'

'You *are* talking to me.'

'I meant on camera. I'm sorry, my name's Mike Brodrick. I'm not an archaeologist, I'm a director with *Trench One*. What happens, we usually interview either the owner of the site or the person living closest, to learn something about its recent history. I now realise that, in your case, that—'

'Look, Mike, just ...' Mr Winterson shaking his open hands, irritated '... carry on, yeah? Do what you have to do.'

'Well ... thank you. It won't be anywhere near as disruptive as you think, I promise.' Mike Brodrick gratefully walking off, calling back over a shoulder. 'And we'll have a security man on duty throughout. Day and night. Meanwhile, you know, stroll around if you'd like to. Check us out.'

'I'll do that.' Mr Winterson moved away from the path, turning to Merrily. 'Sorry about that. Must've sounded like one of these awful city types who move in and then start complaining about the cock crowing and the church bells.'

He took off his hat. He didn't have a beard and his greying hair was short. He was nowhere near eighteen stone. His smile was rueful. 'Elliot Winterson.' He put out his hand. 'You look absolutely soaked.'

'I'm getting used to it. Merrily Watkins.' She shook his hand; it wasn't limp and it wasn't cold. 'TV guys, huh?'

'Think they walk on water. I was a journalist for years – print jour-nalist, scum of the earth, you know? While the TV boys are *personalities*. And don't they know it. I mean, did you hear that? Offer the neighbours a chance to be on the box and watch all their complaints melt away. I'm sure it never bloody fails.'

He looked at her. She found she'd opened her coat, exposing the dog collar, like you brought out the big cross and the sprig of garlic.

'Ah.' He didn't look fazed. 'Yeah, I thought I'd heard the name. Did I see you at the meeting the other night?'

'But not in uniform.'

Merrily was trying not to stare at him. Black fleece and grey trousers. His hair looked as if it was growing back after being shaved tight to the skull. The beard stubble was younger, maybe two days' worth, making a mauvish circle around his entirely friendly white smile.

'Quite interesting,' he said, 'the way people were divided over this dig.'

'Not so much the dig as what happens afterwards,' Merrily said. 'Whether the stones get re-erected in situ.'

'We certainly felt as if we were intruding on a family dispute.'

'Pretty dysfunctional family.'

'All communities are. Who was that woman who thought they repre-sented satanic evil?'

'Our postmistress.'

'Member of your church?'

'She comes to services, but I think she finds me a bit disappointing.'

He laughed. He looked relaxed now – more relaxed than Merrily felt. So much for the reprieve. A van drew into the field from the lane. A white van with a grey cromlech symbol on the side, the word *Capstone* across its lintel.

'So you, erm, don't really like it here, Mr Winterson?'

'Elliot. No, look, it— the village itself is perfectly pleasant and unex-pectedly civilised – nice pub and that bistro place. It's just— you don't think they'll have great big floodlights at night, do you?'

'Hard to say. I don't know much about archaeology.'

'Me neither. *Shall* we have a walk around? You can spare ten minutes, surely. I feel safer with the vicar.'

Huh? Another line from *The Hole in the Sky* came back at her, the kind that lingered, smarting, like your arm after an inoculation.

> ... the pathos of the modern-day clergy. These sad, vacant players in a dated masquerade.

'Someone local, anyway,' he said. 'My wife— have you met my wife?'

'I think my daughter did.'

'Ah yeah. Jane? Jane who started all this. Jane who we have to blame.'

Two men were taking something that looked like a complicated Zimmer frame from the back of the van.

'She's eighteen,' Merrily said. 'She's hoping to become an archaeologist.'

'Seems to have made an impressive start. She told my wife about her ... visionary experience.'

'You don't sound convinced.'

'She's ...' he shrugged, the rueful smile again '... young.'

'It did lead, eventually, to the discovery of the buried stones.'

'Yes.' His eyes didn't flicker. 'My wife's hoping to shoot a photo-sequence for the *Independent* when they get going.' He smiled. 'I suppose, now I've made myself into a possible thorn in their side – a potentially *difficult* person – these chaps'll be more inclined to give Lenni access, to keep me happy. Not that that was any kind of strategy, you understand. Can we *see* any of these famous stones yet?'

'They had at least one virtually exposed,' Merrily said. 'I'm not sure how big it was, but it looks like they've covered it over again. Probably because of the weather. There are at least another two, apparently, but I'm not sure where exactly.'

They walked down from the ridge towards the unturfed area, where a young woman was pacing something out between two khaki-coloured tents. You could see where the turf had already been removed in stripes, two orange-coloured mini-JCBs facing one another like adolescent dinosaurs squaring up for a fight.

'So what do *you* do, Elliot?'

'Me?'

'You told the TV guy you were here to work.'

'Ah.' He grinned. 'Bit of an exaggeration, I'm afraid. I'm on a sort of self-imposed sabbatical. I was working in America when my father died suddenly, leaving—'

'Oh, I'm—'

'Leaving me with a lot to sort out.' Waving away the sympathy. 'And enough money to buy time to consider exactly where we wanted to be.' He grimaced. 'Back in London, frankly, might've been quieter, but my wife ... perhaps she'll get the country out of her system. Or perhaps I'll get used to it. I'm ... looking at a few ideas for books. Nothing I feel confident enough to talk about yet. I'm sorry, that sounds a bit ...'

'I wasn't prying.'

'No, really, you have every right to pry. It's not fair arriving some-where being mysterious. People want to know. People need to know. Mystery wastes everyone's time.' He glanced at her, little smile. 'And, er ... I gather from my wife that you're not *just* a vicar.'

'Nobody's *just* anything, Mr Winterson.'

'Suppose you don't like talking about it. Understandable.'

'No,' Merrily said. 'Not at all. It's usually more a case of people who don't like asking me about it. Think I must be a bit weird.'

'Surely not,' Mathew Stooke said.

She could almost see the hot coals being laid out for her to walk along. There were, of course, ways of explaining Deliverance that even an atheist would buy ... almost.

She was thinking about Nigel Saltash, the consultant psychiatrist introduced by Canon Siân Callaghan-Clarke to help modernise Hereford's *deliverance module*. Saltash with his trim beard, his sports car and his undisguised disdain for the paranormal, which you could very plausibly translate into terms like *mental imbalance* and *psychological projection* and then go on to discuss the many forms of schizophrenia. On the other hand, that was the coward's way out, and Nigel Saltash hadn't lasted the course.

'Well, somebody has to do it,' Merrily said.

'Really.'

'At least one person in every diocese, sometimes a group or a panel.

We're very aware of the need to avoid sensationalism, which is one reason it isn't talked about much.'

'People gossip, though. I mean locally.'

'Sometimes.'

'Perhaps because you're not exactly the *archetypal* exorcist, are you?'

'Big hat and a black bag? That would be the Jesuits. In the movies.'

'Untypical?'

'If you start seeing the demonic everywhere, you can very soon lose your balance. Mostly it's about helping people who feel … threatened by conditions they're living in.'

'You make it sound like rising damp.'

Merrily shrugged. Talked about hauntings and perceived hauntings.

'Meaning it all has a rational explanation?'

'Sometimes it does. You need to be aware of that. But, to paraphrase Sherlock Holmes, once you've eliminated the rational …'

'You enjoy it?'

They'd stopped by the galvanised gate, blocking the path which led up Cole Hill. Nobody had ever asked that before.

'I think it's worthwhile,' she said.

'And when you're confronted by someone who believes that he or she is afflicted by some … paranormal presence, what exactly do you *do*? How do you establish if they're telling the truth? Or at least what they perceive to be the truth.'

'Depends on the circumstances. I might begin by just praying with them. Which often proves effective without recourse to … further measures. And sometimes indicates to me whether what I've been told is the truth.'

And didn't it sound feeble?

'Ah,' he said, 'the power of prayer.'

'Don't worry, I'm not going to ask if you'll be coming to church.' Merrily checked herself. Would at least agnosticism be a safe assumption, based on his attitude so far? She could hear the sluggish rumble of a generator, overlaid by laughter from inside one of the tents, squeals, a cry of mock protest. Quite young, some of these archaeologists. Maybe students.

'You get good congregations, Merrily? Despite church attendance being generally in decline?'

'Less so in rural areas. Rural people are always closer to … Anyway, I try not to count heads. And just because traditional services are in decline—'

She broke off again, frowning, her memory for some of Stooke's more cutting put-downs becoming almost photographic.

Christianity only hangs on because of the general mental laziness of congregations and its continuing mix 'n' match reinvention by the Church of England.

'And anyway,' she said, 'it isn't just there for services. Or just for Sunday. Some people prefer to come in on their own, sit and think, walk around. We'll always need places where people can do that.'

He didn't reply. She looked up into the spongy sky as plump new rain-drops landed on her cheeks.

'I think I need to get back. It's starting to …'

Fastening her coat over the dog collar, realising what was happening. Drawing up her hood and pulling it across her face, as if it could conceal her thoughts.

'Sorry if I've delayed you, Merrily.'

'No, you—'

'I've enjoyed talking to you,' Mathew Stooke said as the heavens opened. 'Very much.'

Once Merrily was out of sight of Coleman's Meadow, she headed directly for the main track and the orthodox route to the village centre, walking faster and then almost running through the sheeting rain, getting rapidly out of breath until, halfway up Old Barn Lane, she had to slow down because the water, in places, was flowing around her in a brown tide, almost ankle deep.

She stood panting on the edge of the pavement. Her hood had been blown back, her hair was soaked and water was dripping into her eyes as she walked miserably into Church Street.

Dawkins, you watched him on TV, you sensed the sneer. *Come on,* you felt him saying, with a certain embittered weariness, *hate me. Hate me because you know I'm right.*

But Stooke … Stooke was nothing like his book. Polite, deferential, self-deprecating. God, she'd almost liked him. Maybe *had* liked him.

She walked into the square, by the side of the Christmas tree, not yet lit, although shop lights blazed defiantly. No human life on the cobbles. It was one of those days when you wouldn't even notice the onset of darkness.

And somehow she'd allowed Mathew Stooke to interview her. Done a few interviews with journalists in the past; there was always curiosity about deliverance. What they'd later written was sometimes cynical but usually fair.

But Stooke didn't do articles, he did books, and he didn't do *fair*. Bliss had said, *He wants a bit of privacy to finish his next … whatever shite he's working on now.* Even Lol had warned her to leave him alone. But she couldn't, could she? She'd taken his presence personally. *All the picturesque backwaters.* Just had to go and find him, put herself through the test.

And now he'd contrived to interview her. Just like his wife had interviewed Jane.

Merrily hurried into the drive, past a parked car, both its doors opening. When she reached the front door, she half-turned to find her key and found two people behind her in the wet and muddied half-light.

A woman in a bulky blue fleece and a woollen hat. A blond-haired man in his twenties, ready with his ID.

'Mrs Watkins?'

'Yes?'

'DI Brent, West Mercia CID. This is DS Dowell. May we come in?'

Dowell? *Karen* Dowell? Pushing wet hair out of her eyes, Merrily peered at the woman: stocky, pink-cheeked, thirtyish. Bliss's bagman, right? Bliss always spoke well of Karen. And yet …

She wasn't smiling; she looked tense, her face overlaid in Merrily's thoughts with stark and grainy images from dark dramas and fly-on-the-wall police documentaries.

And one recalled instant of frozen reality. *May we come in?*

When they said that it was never good news.

27

Epiphany

WHEN JANE GOT off the bus, the rain was lighter, and she didn't mess around: throwing her airline bag over her shoulder and hurrying across the square, under the lych-gate and into the churchyard, where she stood for a moment with her hands either side of the curve of Lucy's gravestone, feeling the energy coursing up both arms.

All things in their proper place, the verse concluded, *My soul doth best embrace.*

A place of energy, not death. She had a picture of Lucy's grave up on the Coleman's Meadow website now, alongside the only picture of Lucy because, whatever was being achieved here, this woman deserved the credit.

'We're in this together, right?'

Jane gave the headstone a final squeeze, for luck, and ran off through the churchyard and the wicket gate into the orchard. Leys should be travelled. Every time she came this way, *with a purpose*, she was reinforcing her links with the ancestors and the life-force of the village. The orchard had been the life-force and the church had been at the centre of the orchard, Lucy telling Jane, *Which came first, I wouldn't like to say, though I suspect the orchard.* She'd said that perhaps there'd been a pre-Christian shrine where the church now stood. As if she'd felt it, or perhaps the presence of the buried stones, not so far away in Coleman's Meadow. The way Jane had surely felt it on a summer night on Cole Hill.

Hurrying now along the slippery path through the ruins of the orchard, the light almost gone, the path obliterated by sodden dead leaves, but her feet knew the way. Her heart, too. When she'd got drunk, one long-ago night, on cider, Lucy had said, *The cider's the blood of the orchard. It's in your blood now.*

And although the orchard was looking derelict and moribund, the blood was pounding by the time Jane reached the edge of Coleman's Meadow. Well out of breath, but the excitement fizzing up as soon as she saw all the vehicles.

Mainly 4×4s and a van with *Capstone* on its flank. All parked on the edge of the meadow in an area cordoned off with orange tape. They'd taken away the old stile and ripped down the brutal strands of barbed wire that Pierce had had put up to protect the proposed building site. There was now a less hostile green wire fence with rustic posts and a galvanised farm-gate, and it was open.

Walking through the new entrance, Jane saw that khaki-coloured tents had gone up and two portable lavatories between the two caravans, which had been there for a few days now. About a dozen people were wandering around and looking up at the charcoal sky.

And Jane ... standing on the edge of the meadow her gaze inevitably drawn towards Cole Hill's dark Iron Age ramparts behind naked trees, Jane was bathed in a moment of what James Joyce and those guys had called *epiphany*.

Like the long, heavy velvet curtains were going back to reveal the next, crucial stage of her life. This sense of pure joy. And she was fully aware of it. How often did that happen?

'Got a pass, have we, my darling?'

The guy who'd come out of the smaller caravan wasn't much older than Jane. He was wiry, had gelled hair and wore leather jeans and a security armband. Wandering over, kind of springy and officious, but Jane was too high to be brought down by some jobsworth.

'Pass? Listen, I *live* here. What sort of—?'

'Hey! Whoa! I dunno! They just told me to be sure and keep the riff-raff out.'

'I look like riff-raff?'

'I'm not sure. Don't move.' He came up close, smelling of something pungent in the way of aftershave. 'Hmm.' Putting on a thoughtful look and then breaking out a black-stubbled smile. 'You could always bribe me. What you got on tonight?'

'She's feeding her bloody kids, what do you think?' a guy in a suit said. 'Probably doing her homework, Gregory. Back *off*, you randy oik.'

The security guy stepped back, put on this stiff, solemn face and saluted. 'Whatever you say, Mr Blore, sir.'

'*Professor* Blore, you little fuck!'

The security guy grinned, and Jane jumped back as the man in the suit turned and examined her, and – wow – it *was*. Hadn't recognised him, not in the suit and tie, and with his hair brushed. His accent was posher, too, encased in a bigger and deeper voice. Resonant, Jane thought. Out of the earth.

She saw that Coops was with him, looking young, wispy and spare, because Bill Blore really *was* a big guy. Bigger than on TV. Well, certainly wider, built like Hadrian's Wall or something. He'd grown his hair – like for the winter? – and it was swept back and tied in a ponytail, and you didn't see many of those any more.

Coops said, 'Bill, this is Jane Watkins.'

Maybe she blushed. She certainly felt like blushing. In fact, oh God, she felt like running away.

She didn't move.

'Jane.'

His face was just like on the box, good-looking in this kind of swarthy way, his eyes maybe just a bit more bulgy, his smile … fun. She'd seen that smile so many times, usually when he'd proved the geophysics guys wrong, taken a gamble and they'd found some Roman's thigh bone in *Trench One*.

'Hi,' Jane said.

It came out like the smallest mouse-squeak.

'Uh, it was Jane who …' Coops giving Bill Blore an unsure kind of glance '… first got the idea there might be something here?'

'Cooper, I *know*.' Bill Blore bent, this big, callused hand coming out. 'Jane, it's a privilege to meet you.' The hand closing around Jane's like the bucket of a JCB as he turned to Coops. 'Where's Declan?'

'I think he's putting his gear away.'

'Why does that bastard always go to earth when it goes dark? I *like* dark. We do have *lights*, don't we?'

'I think he's put those away, too.'

'Arse,' Bill Blore said. 'I was rather thinking we might shoot Jane.'

'I think quite a lot of people would go along with that,' Coops said.

Jane frowned, but Bill Blore didn't get it. He looked up the sky, then back at Jane.

'All right. Tomorrow, then. What are you doing tomorrow, Jane?'

'Erm, nothing. That is, like … whatever you want?'

'What *I* want is to keep it in sequence.' Bill Blore turned back to Coops. 'If it starts with Jane, then that's where *we* should start, before the site gets too mucked up.'

'Right,' Coops said.

'How about ten o'clock? Ten a.m., Jane, that OK for you? We'll shoot you at the top of the hill or something.'

'You mean …' The sodden ground below Jane's muddied school shoes had become suddenly unsteady. 'For, like … TV? For your programme?'

'Well, it's certainly not going to be for young Gregory's private DVD collection.'

'Wow,' Jane said. 'I mean … sure. I'll be here. I mean, I didn't really think you'd want to …'

'We'll get you on the hill, and you can take us through the story of how you found the stones, yah?'

'Well, it wasn't *just* me.'

'Sweetheart …' Bill Blore put his big hands on her shoulders, looked into her eyes, his own eyes brown as lubricating oil. 'For the purposes of my film, it *was* just you.' He looked up. 'Look, excuse me, there's a guy I need to grab …'

Spinning away, raising a hand to somebody, and Jane thought of something important.

'But I can still help … can't I?'

'Hmm?'

'Neil said I could probably help? With the dig? Like I don't expect to be allowed a trowel or anything, but I could … you know, carry stuff around, take messages.'

'Oh … absolutely,' Bill Blore said. 'We're fighting the weather on this dig, so we'll need all the help we can get. Excuse me, OK?'

As he tramped off, his suit trousers tucked into tan leather boots, Coops came and stood next to Jane.

'Yeah, yeah,' Jane said. 'I know, don't get carried away. He's a bit of a presence, though, isn't he?'

Watching Bill Blore striding across the dark meadow, planting a hand on some guy's shoulder, giving him instructions on something.

'Yeah,' Coops said. 'A presence.'

Jane felt a bit sorry for him, remembering the afternoon last summer when she'd followed him here. When the grass had been all churned up after Lyndon's Pierce's bid to destroy the straight track, making the meadow – Pierce thought – unsuitable for anything but building on. Remembering Coops's excitement as he'd shown her those first partly exposed stones.

Jane had been like, *These are real, actual prehistoric standing stones?* And Coops – she was always going to remember this – had said, *I'd stake my future career on it.*

And Jane, beyond euphoric, had, in that moment, fallen just slightly in love with him. Seemed a long time ago now.

'He's really ready to go tomorrow?'

'So he insists, Jane. He seems to've got it scheduled for early in the next series of *Trench One* – and that starts in the New Year.'

'Wow, that's tight.'

'I don't think the ratings were fantastic for the last series. Too many big digs that yielded a couple of pottery shards and not a lot else. He needs something spectacular, and he's not going to let the weather or Christmas stop him getting it.'

They watched an orange-coloured digger manoeuvring through the entrance. Shame they couldn't've employed Gomer, but Jane supposed they needed somebody used to archaeological procedure.

'Tell you one thing, Coops – *he*'s not going to let Pierce get away with moving the stones, is he? They've lost the Serpent, he's not going to let us lose this.'

'I never count on anything,' Coops said.

It started to rain, but not too heavily. Nothing was too heavy tonight.

'Hey … I'm going to be on *Trench One*, Coops. He did *say* that, didn't he? I mean, I didn't just dream it?'

'No.' Coops let a smile fade through. 'No, you didn't dream it. And by early spring I'd guess you'll be having your picture taken next to the raised stones.'

'Makes you kind of shiver to think about it,' Jane said.

Jane walked back on to the square to find it aglow. The fake gaslamps reflected in the swimming cobbles, warm amber light in the mullioned windows of the Black Swan. Plus the Christmas tree's lights, just white ones this year – more sophisticated, apparently, which was incomer bollocks, but Jane couldn't be annoyed about anything tonight.

Mum's car was in the vicarage drive, and there was another one outside. Jane let herself in through the side door, near the back stairs, and slipped into the kitchen just as a man and a woman were going out the other way, through to the hall, watched by Mum, still in her wet coat.

The woman was carrying a computer, its wire wound around an arm. She smiled kind of stiffly.

'You'll have it back very soon, I promise. Maybe tomorrow.'

'I hope so,' Mum said in this dull, flat voice. 'Because—'

The man said, 'Is this your daughter?'

'Because all the parish stuff is on there as well,' Mum said.

The woman nodded. The air between Mum and these people was like cling film stretched tight.

28

Shaking the Cage

FOR CONFIRMATION, MERRILY had the radio tuned to Hereford and Worcester, the floodline programme with news inserts. The teatime studio presenter was talking to a reporter out on location; you could hear the rain splattering a car roof.

'... one of those places everyone knows. Almost like a seaside resort in the summer because there's a kind of pebbly beach, and people go bathing in the river.'

The reporter was on the phone. Bella Finch again, out on location, talking about something they'd found in the Wye.

'... level's extremely high, and a lot of debris has been washed downstream, up against the bridge. What looks like a whole tree and lots of branches, and apparently that was where the body was found, entangled in debris. Must have been a terrible shock for somebody.'

'Do we know who found it?'

'No, we don't, and the police have been quite sparing with information. It was only, as you know, after we received a call to the floodline from one of our listeners about police activity around the bridge that we learned about this.'

'Yes, and please keep those calls coming in, because we're all aware that the flood situation isn't getting any better in the two counties. But what are the police saying, Bella?'

'Very little, I'm afraid, Kate. They won't even confirm at this stage whether—'

Merrily switched off, watching Jane shrug.

'They found the rest of him, then. Had to turn up somewhere, sooner or later.'

Jane was sitting at the table, a mug of tea going cold in front of her. Her face smoky and mutinous in the kitchen's amber lamplight. It was progress. A year ago she'd have been screaming and storming out.

'Bodies and rivers,' Merrily said. 'You know the Celtic stuff.'

'*Heads* and rivers,' Jane snapped. 'Because the head was the home of the soul and water was the entrance to— Anyway, what would *they* know about any of it?'

'They *do* know about it. They know about the theory that the Serpent connected Dinedor Hill with the Wye. They also have very strong forensic evidence linking Clem Ayling's murder with the Serpent.' Merrily sat down. 'Jane, they're in a hurry.'

'So?'

'It means all I could do was delay them. No way I'd be able to stop them. And any attempts to delay them would just make them more suspicious and more determined.'

'Who cares? If I'd been here—'

'If you'd been here and refused to give them your laptop and gone on about living in a police state, that guy Brent might well have formed the wrong opinion. He doesn't know you, he doesn't know me—'

'Where's bloody Bliss, then?'

'I don't know. The woman, Karen, I thought she was Bliss's regular assistant, Andy Mumford's replacement. But not today, apparently.'

'You're saying they might've *nicked me*?'

'They'd have made life very difficult. Brent wanted those names and he wanted them tonight. He actually said, for heaven's sake, he said, *Mrs Watkins, there's an easy way and a hard way ...*'

'How did they even *know* we had the names?'

'Jane, you were in the *papers*.'

And Frannie Bliss knew. He'd even laid out a broad hint this morning in the car, suggesting that giving him a list of Coleman's Meadow activists *might be the soft-option*. Where was he now? Once or twice, she'd caught Karen Dowell's eye, and Karen had given her a harassed look that said *this is not my fault*.

'I've betrayed them,' Jane said.

'No,' Merrily said. '*I*'ve betrayed *you*. But it seemed like the best solution.'

Jane looked at her, still some anger in her eyes but mainly confusion, bewilderment.

'You're eighteen,' Merrily said. 'I wasn't in a position to give them your laptop, nor would I have.'

'So you handed over *your* computer, with the database on it. Hoping to get it out of the house before I came back.'

'Basically, yes.'

'Do not *dare* say you did that to protect me.'

'No.' Merrily ached for a cigarette but didn't get up. 'I just didn't have time to think. You don't. It's how they do it. Doorstep you.'

The last time it had happened – serious-faced police at the door, *May we come in?* – had been when they'd arrived to tell her about Sean.

'I was tired and wet, and I couldn't see a way out and I ... still can't. If they'd had to come back with the paperwork ...'

She'd looked at DI Brent's bland, detached, civil-servant face and seen School of Annie Howe. Remembered how Bliss always said that, where the police were concerned, a refusal often offended and offence usually led to a blind determination to nail you to the wall.

'So what will they do with it?' Jane said.

'Copy everything. Then go through the names. They'll start straight away, probably with the local ones. The local ones who seem most ... extreme. Jane, have you ... ever heard of a group calling itself the Children of the Serpent?'

'Who are they?'

'They haven't been in contact with you?'

'No. I've never heard of them. You think I wouldn't remember something like that? Who are they?'

'There was a threatening message on Clem Ayling's answering machine from someone claiming to represent the Children of the Serpent.'

Jane looked genuinely blank.

'Good,' Merrily said.

'OK,' Jane said. 'What's to stop me sending out a round-robin email to everybody on the Coleman's Meadow database saying we've been raided by the police and had our computer seized and warning them there's going to be a witch-hunt.'

'Nothing.'

'And what's to stop me ringing Eirion and getting him to tell his media friends? Getting it out in the papers?'

'Nothing,' Merrily said again.

'But?'

'But ... I suppose, in most other situations it would look like some kind of breach of civil liberties. But this is a high-profile, decidedly horrific murder. It's on the cards that somebody on that database, if they didn't do it, at least has links to whoever did. So it's one thing protecting somebody over a cause you believe in ... shielding a murderer is something else. And what if ... Let me get you a fresh cup of tea.'

'What if he does it again, right?'

'Mmm.'

'This is a totally, *totally* shit situation.' Jane lowered her head into her hands. 'And things were going so well. I just ...' she looked up '... just met Bill Blore.'

'*You* did?'

'At the Meadow. They're all set up.'

'Yes, I was going to tell you about that.'

'I had a call from Coops at school. He said Bill Blore wanted to meet me. And, like ... he did. He's going to interview me tomorrow. On camera.'

'That's fantastic.'

'So I get interviewed for *Trench One* at the same time as friends of Coleman's Meadow, people who I got to sign my petition, people who rallied round to help me are—'

'Jane ...'

'Getting pulled in by the—' Jane gripped the edge of the table. 'By the cops. Maybe old people again, taken down the cells and ... I dunno ... beaten up ...'

'All right.' Merrily stood up. 'I'm going to ring Bliss.'

*

At just after seven, its cobbles glazed with rain and milky light from the Christmas tree, the square looked like an ice tableau. Certainly felt cold enough, and looking at Bliss made Merrily feel colder. Off duty now, he wore jeans and an old Stone Roses T-shirt under a thin jacket. She guessed he didn't want to go home to an empty house, but he wouldn't come into hers either. Probably didn't want to face Jane. Even case-hardened cops had a cut-off point.

'I didn't know about it,' he said. 'I'd've told you. Maybe Karen didn't get a chance to call me.'

He'd parked next to the market hall, and they were standing under it, alone on the square. It wasn't raining; an intermission, that was all. But it was coming back; it always came back.

'Actually, I thought if they ever went that far they'd send me,' he said. 'I was prepared for that. I'm sorry. I really am sorry, but ...'

'I suppose it was finding Ayling's body in the river.'

'They told you about that?'

'Karen Dowell told me when we were alone in the scullery for about thirty seconds, while Brent had a snoop. And it's since been on the radio.'

'I met this archaeologist at Rotherwas. He made the connection with the river, I put in a report. And *that* ...' Bliss leaned into the car, hands on the edge of the roof like he was about to start a sequence of push-ups '... that was the grand finale of my contribution to the Ayling inquiry.'

'Frannie?'

'I've been returned to what are laughingly described as "normal duties".' He straightened up. 'More specifically, this petty suburban coke dealership we've been eyeing up for a few weeks. Chickenshit, basically. Nobody who's running away.'

'So why—?'

'Why now, you ask, three days before Christmas when we're already stretched to buggery?'

'You're still thinking Charlie Howe?'

'I went too near him once before. He doesn't forget. Charlie spots large dollops of the brown stuff floating inexorably towards the Xpelair, he calls his only daughter.'

Bliss leaned back against the wet car and told Merrily about getting carpeted by Howe this morning for failing to report a face-off with three drunken teenagers, one of them a hospital consultant's son now claiming he'd been threatened with violence by a foul-mouthed cop. He didn't need to explain how the Ice Maiden was manipulating the situation.

Merrily dug her hands down into her coat pocket, recalling how Bliss had once helped Lol put the screws on Charlie, to get Annie Howe off *her* back. Maybe that was when his name had been added to Charlie's blacklist.

'You think she really knows what Charlie got up to in his police days? Because whatever else you think about Annie Howe ...'

'He's her *dad*, Merrily. Any shit coming off Charlie makes the greasy pole Annie's squirming up even greasier. Whether she's bent or straight doesn't come into it.'

A white car pulled into the square, an elderly couple getting out, along with handbag, gloves. Dinner at the Swan.

'Come over to the vic, Frannie. Have something to eat. Jane's not going to scream at you.'

He shook his head.

'I'm not that crap a cook, am I?'

'You're *fairly* crap,' Bliss said.

'You look tired.'

'I've always looked tired, Merrily. Me ma used to say I looked like a little old man at three.'

'No word from Kirsty?'

'I'm guessing I'll be hearing from her solicitor first.'

'And is that what you want?'

'Is that what *I* want?'

'Sorry,' Merrily said. 'I just had a feeling you—'

'We never should've patched it up. Maybe I realised that, some part of me. The part that kept shaking the cage.'

'You were deliberately shaking the cage?'

'Possibly.' He started pushing at the car again. 'Thing is, you can keep walking the tightrope, carrying this fragile thing in both hands, keeping it dead steady, one foot in front of the other, not daring to blink ... and then one day you think, Shit, is this a *life*?'

'It is for some couples. I suppose.'

'Sad cases, Merrily.'

He talked about coppers who started out all bright-eyed and *let's nail the bad guys*. All the boyish enthusiasm getting rapidly suffocated by paperwork, regulations, baseless complaints, time wasted enforcing crap new laws.

'And when it's going right, when you've had a result and you come home full of it, and you wanna talk about it to somebody ...' He shook his head. 'She just didn't get it, Merrily.'

'Kirsty?'

'Never got it.'

'And ... I mean ... were you getting what *she* wanted from life? Sorry, Frannie, I don't mean to ...'

'Doesn't know what she wants. Only what she *doesn't* want.'

'You still love her?'

'I need an early night.' Bliss beeped open the car door. 'I have to orchestrate a *dawn raid*. How'm I gonna cope with the excitement?'

'Frannie ...'

'What?'

'I don't want Jane's name ...'

'I've tried to explain, Merrily, I've no influence any more. All I can do is ask Karen to keep me in the loop.'

'Then you keep me in the loop?'

He nodded.

'Just so you know,' Merrily said, 'I went through some of the Coleman's Meadow petition emails. Not thoroughly, but I didn't see any mention of the Children of the Serpent. And Jane says she hasn't heard of them, and I believe her.'

'Good.'

'Although there *was* somebody in Chichester claiming to have cursed Hereford Council.'

'Yeh, well, we've all been down that road.' Bliss slid into the car, started the engine, ran the window down and leaned out. 'Maybe I'll jack it in. Join Andy Mumford, go and work as a private eye for Jumbo Humphries, videoing straying husbands. What do you reckon?'

'I reckon you're overtired.'

Merrily walked into the Eight Till Late for cigarettes. Now Jim Prosser had told her they were planning to leave next year, the atmosphere in here, the whole feel of the place, seemed dimmer and more melancholy, like low-energy bulbs when you first switched them on. Or perhaps it had been gradually changing since the coming of Shirley West, caged at the bottom of the store.

Jim was on his own at the top till.

'Hell, Merrily, you're looking ...'

'Knackered?'

'Let's say careworn,' Jim said.

'Been a wearing sort of day.'

'You too? Brenda's been in bed all afternoon, she has. Touch of migraine.'

'Oh, I'm sorry.'

Jim sighed, rueful smile.

'Kind of migraine brought on by proximity to certain folks.'

'Oh.'

Jim looked from side to side, as if someone might be hovering, and then along the single aisle towards the post office, with its blind down, its big CLOSED sign, its ... was that a metal cross on the wall?

'Truth of it is,' Jim said, 'that's another reason Brenda reckons she can't stick it n' more. One hand, it's a good thing having the post office here. Good for business, passing trade. Other hand ...'

'Shirley.'

'When that office shuts, it's like a bloody weight's been lifted. I got nothing against religion, as you know, but nine hours a day?' Jim looked uncertainly at Merrily. She put down a ten-pound note, pointed at the cigarette shelves.

'This church she goes to, in Leominster ... she mention that much?'

'She do, but I don't listen.' He picked up the tenner. 'Wanted me to put a poster up for it. I said, no, we got a good church yere, and a good vicar.'

'Thank you. How did she react?'

'Scowled. I said, why'd you wanner go to two churches?'

'She explain? Sorry, Jim, it's just I had a strange kind of card from this church. Maybe I should ask her. Try and have a talk.'

Jim laid a packet of Silk Cut on the counter, with Merrily's change. 'I wouldn't do that.'

'Sorry?'

'Let her be for a while, I would.'

'You have a particular reason for saying that?'

'Well, it ...' Jim started fiddling with the biros in his top pocket. 'It's clear she's keepin' an eye on you. I don't suppose I'm saying anything you don't ...'

'Priests shouldn't smoke or have boyfriends? Or enter church when not suitably attired?'

'Or spurn the meat the Lord has provided,' Jim said.

'What?'

'She was asking me why you never bought meat from us – I don't know what that's about. She watches, see. All the time she bloody *watches*. Main thing now is the, er.... the blasphemous book.'

'Oh, for God's *sake* ... how does she even *know* about that?'

'Running a post office, you learns everything sooner or later, I reckon. Like a confessional, it is, behind that bulletproof screen. Learns more than's good for her.'

Well, thank you Amanda, of Ledwardine Livres.

'That book,' Jim said. 'Hole in the front of it?'

'There is, yes.'

'All the way down to hell,' Jim said. 'Apparently.'

'And that's where I'm going, is it?'

'I'd been thinking I'd be broken up to leave this place,' Jim said. 'But mabbe not.'

SATURDAY

... a Bible which is presented
to be without error or contradiction
is a dangerous and possibly
harmful weapon in the hands of
fallible and corruptible human beings.

Stephen Parsons
Ungodly Fear

29

Nutters

DIRTY PINK LIGHT had fallen on Jane's face in the bathroom mirror. A drawn and worried face. A face reflecting the awareness that today could actually be more life-and-death crucial than she'd figured.

She'd awoken long before daylight, heartsick about selling out the Coleman's Meadow Preservation Society – turned against her own people by the disgusting police state. Yet there was a painful logic in Mum's argument about possibly sheltering someone who thought barbaric violence could further the cause. In the pre-dawn sludge, the slaughter of an old man and the taking of his head was real and frightening, and when she tried to summon the startling excitement of yesterday – the *epiphany* – something else came bobbing up like a cork in a toilet. Something Coops had said, in Coleman's Meadow last night, about Bill Blore and *Trench One*.

… got it scheduled for early in the next series – and that starts in the New Year.

As she rolled out of bed, the implications came crunching into place. She had two university interviews set up for late January. If Bill Blore's programme on Ledwardine was near the start of the new *Trench One* series, then the university guys doing the interviews would almost certainly have seen it.

Seen and heard Jane Watkins talking about Coleman's Meadow. And they'd remember. As soon as they met her they'd remember. So this just had to be good. Didn't it? However bad everything else was, she had to make this interview work for her.

By six-thirty, she was dressed and out there. When the dawn came, the signs were not too scary: a salmony sheen on the horizon, no menacing cloudplay. Certainly better than last night's TV forecast had implied. Jane went to see the river and found him still dangerously high, brown and racing, clearly recalling what it was like to be young and hungry, and she reminded him that he was part of this, that he'd been around in the Bronze Age when the stones had been erected and Ledwardine had come into being.

She stood on the bridge ... could lean over the wall and almost touch the rushing water. She needed some of that – his energy. Needed to sound enthusiastic and driven. But in an authoritative way. Not just some kid who'd accidentally stumbled on something of major importance that she didn't really understand. Because she *did* understand, that was the whole point. She understood what the stones had *meant.* And what they meant now.

'You OK?' Mum said over breakfast.

'Yeah. Fine.'

'Hmm.'

Mum was in Saturday civvies, jeans with a hole in one knee and an old Gomer Parry Plant Hire sweatshirt.

'No, really,' Jane said. 'I have to go for this, don't I? The words *bastards* and *don't let them grind you down* occur.'

'Erm ... my advice – not that I've ever exactly distinguished myself on TV, as you know, so maybe you can learn from my mistakes – is not to actually think about it too much beforehand. Know more or less what you want to say but don't rehearse how you're going to say it.'

'No, I wouldn't do that,' Jane said.

Having just spent twenty minutes mouthing at herself in the mirror. *Bill, I have to say I couldn't believe it at first. It seemed just too perfect. But over the next couple of days I checked out all the points on the line, and it became clear to me that Coleman's Meadow must've been a very significant location. So when the stones were actually found ... no, I wasn't too surprised, actually.*

Wondering what the chances were of getting in a mention of Lucy Devenish, as the person who'd awakened in her this heightened awareness of the underlying landscape. Maybe Bill Blore's crew could get a shot of Lucy's grave.

'And don't arrive too early,' Mum said, 'or you'll just be hanging about in the cold, getting more and more on edge.'

'It'll be fine,' Jane said. 'Look, I never got around to asking, with one thing and another, but were you able to check out Mathew Stooke? Like, apart from buying his book?'

'Who told you about that?'

'Mum, it's on the desk. He's a tosser, isn't he? Next time I see that bloody Lensi—'

'No! Don't mention it. Don't indicate you know who they are. It's better if we don't at this stage.'

'Why?'

'Because … I don't know, really, something's not right. Call it a feeling.' Mum was admitting to *feelings* now? Be the full Traherne in no time at all. For some reason, Jane felt a little lighter.

'We seem to be talking all round something here, don't we?' And Jane would have pushed harder, but time was short, and she needed to go up to the apartment and figure out what to wear that was casual but authoritative.

'Go on,' Mum said. 'Make yourself look wonderful for the telly.'

In the end, Jane dressed down. Jeans and a big dark sweater. A smudge of make-up. Too glam, too sexy would give the wrong impression. Well, *sexy* was all right, in a *cerebral* way; when Bill Blore interviewed her, there should be a little chemistry. Bill liked women, was renowned for it.

Jane was cool with that.

She drank a mug of tea with extra sugar and Mum told her to break a leg. As she walked across the square, she felt destiny nudging her, the sensation of standing on the cusp of something. The red earth giving up its long-buried secrets, the Dinedor Serpent and the Old Stones of Ledwardine linked by ancient electricity and connecting with Jane's own nervous system.

In the churchyard, she didn't spend too long with Lucy, who would surely understand. Pausing only to give the shoulders of the gravestone one squeeze, for luck, before proceeding directly into the dank and dripping orchard.

She imagined a short, lyrical video-sequence of her and Bill following the ley, with music playing underneath – maybe Nick Drake's 'Hazey Jane 2'.

The oldest part of the orchard, gnarled and primeval-looking, was loaded with big balls of white-berried mistletoe. Perhaps she'd come back here before nightfall, with secateurs, and try to reach some. After all, Eirion would be here on Sunday. Feeling kind of turned on now, Jane spun towards the pale light at the end of the orchard, and ...

Wow. If she'd thought it was crowded last night ...

Standing under the exposed waxy sky, she was looking down at something like a reduced rock festival. More tents, an extra caravan, a camper van, the big crane ... cars parked at all angles, including a police car. Big clusters of people turning Coleman's Meadow into another village. A separate community had mushroomed overnight.

Jane counted three separate TV units, guys shouldering cameras, and a bunch of other men and women were hanging around the new galvanised gate by a smaller green caravan.

Adrenalin spurting, she ran down to where Neil Cooper was standing, on his own. Fair-haired, wafery Coops, jeans and a canvas shoulder bag – his day off, too, but who'd miss this?

'Bloody *hell*, Coops, I had no idea there'd be all this ...'

'Jane.' Coops taking Jane's arm, drawing her away and saying nothing until they were behind the bloated bole of an old oak tree. 'It's not quite what you think.'

'What isn't?'

'The media circus. Nothing to do with the excavation.' Coops shedding his shoulder bag and undoing it. 'It's about this.'

Handing her a folded paper.

Jane opened it up. The *Daily Star* was unlikely to be Coops's usual choice.

But then, it wouldn't usually carry a picture on its front page of someone as old and boring as the late Clement Ayling under ...

HEADHUNTERS!

Town hall boss
topped by
pagan nutters

It was as though a fist had come through the paper, smacked her full in the face. Jane stepped back into a puddle.

'It was the only one left on the rack at your local shop,' Coops said. 'But I gather the others are similar.'

She read the whole story, which wasn't long. The police were quoted as saying that fragments of stone found 'with the head' had been confirmed as coming from the Dinedor Serpent, 'an ancient path which local pagans say is sacred'. But which Clem Ayling, whose body had now been found in the River Wye, had dismissed as 'patio gravel'. As a result of which, he and his council had been attacked by 'pagan groups' and 'top TV archaeologist Bill Blore'.

'Oh.' Jane stepped out of the puddle and handed the paper back to Coops. 'So now they all want him.'

For one agonising moment she'd thought the headline meant the cops had been acting on stuff from the Coleman's Meadow database. But, of course, it would've been impossible for any of that to make this morning's papers.

'Fame rules,' Coops said.

'Did you know about these fragments of stone, Coops?'

'Not a thing. If the police consulted my boss, he hasn't told me about it.'

'But like, even if it's true, how can the cops just say it's down to pagans? I mean, how *dare* they—?'

'They probably didn't. They just let the press run with it. Most of the others seem to have been a bit more restrained than the *Star*.'

'Where's Bill Blore now?'

'Somewhere wishing he'd kept his famous gob shut.' Coops didn't look entirely displeased about Blore being caught on the back foot. 'Shut himself in the site caravan to phone a friend. Always assuming he has one left.'

Jane pondered the implications, looking at her watch. Six minutes to ten.

'Coops, is this going to affect my interview?'

'He's pretty pissed off, Jane. Been here since before eight. Wanted to make a good start while the rain was holding off, and now he can't. He's actually—'

Jane heard a few ragged cheers. Coops moved around the oak tree, went to peer over what was left of Lyndon Pierce's barbed-wire fence. Came back yawning.

'Looks like he's coming out. Like some bloody racing driver with his support crew.'

'Can we watch?'

'If we must. But look, Jane, when he gets rid of this lot I'd keep away from him for a while if I were you. Don't push. Let him decide when to remember you.'

'By which time it'll be raining again.'

'Yeah, probably.'

'And I'll look like shit.'

Jane looked around for something to kick.

Bill Blore didn't actually come off the site, went no further than the gate. Leaning over its top rail, wide shoulders hunched under a scratched leather bomber jacket. His thick hair was bound back by some kind of bandanna, his eyes still and steely like ball-bearings, his voice ... big.

'All right, you bastards.'

When he raised a hand it was clenched around a flat-bladed trowel, edged with red mud, like he'd been interrupted in the middle of his work.

Laughter from the hacks, and the stills photographers began taking pictures. The security guy, Gregory, and an older guy with the same armband were standing at either end of the metal gate. Jane was with Coops, hanging back, well out of shot as a rising wind rattled the gate and Bill Blore tapped the top rail with the handle of the trowel.

'OK, hacks, here's the situation. I'm happy to talk to you, but I really *don't* have time for individual interviews, or we'll be here all fucking day. So you're just going to have to ... you know ... gather round, throw the shit at me and I'll bat it back. Five minutes max, OK?'

'Some of us've come a long way, Bill,' someone moaned, but Bill Blore wiped it away with both hands and his big voice.

'Not trying to be difficult, whoever you are, but I've got a job to do and it's rather more important to me than whichever fucking lunatics took an axe to some poor old bugger from the local authority.' Pointing with the trowel at a raised hand. 'OK, go ...'

'Susannah Gilmore, Sky News. Presumably you've seen today's papers, Bill?'

'Gave up reading comics when I turned ten, Susannah, but I've been given a digest, yeah, so I can just about put together a reason for you vultures swooping.'

'Can we get directly to the point, then?' one of the other TV guys said, and Blore bowed and spread his hands. 'Professor Blore, first of all, if you can give us your reaction to the suggestion that County Councillor Ayling was actually murdered because of his negative attitude towards the so-called Dinedor Serpent.'

'Well, that's not my ...' Bill Blore looked down at the trowel, puffed out his lips, looked up again. 'All right. Here we go.'

A few seconds of silence. All you could hear was the slap of one of the nylon tent flaps and some cameras going off. Two uniformed cops looked at people's faces.

Bill Blore took a breath.

'Archaeology's my life. But I couldn't say it's worth the loss of someone else's.' He paused. 'So if you're saying did *I* do it ...?' Bill Blore looked down at the media, the wind lifting his hair. Photographers were snapping him from below and Jane saw that one of them was Lensi, her red hair glowing against the grey sky.

The TV guy said, 'So who *would* you—?'

'Oh, come on, what am I supposed to say to that? Kind of people who'd do this? Not the foggiest. If you're asking me about pagans, yeah, I've met plenty of *them*. Always find them hanging around prehistoric sites. Ask me a couple of days ago, I'd've said they were just bloody comics. Harmless. Didn't think they also included total bloody maniacs. Shows how wrong you can be. *Next.*'

Two questions collided.

'When you say you've met plenty—'

'—Yourself had some pretty hard things to say about the Herefordshire Council—'

'True. And I don't take any of it back. I *do* think local authorities should be better informed about the dangers of destroying our heritage with hastily planned developments. I do indeed wish that bloody road was going somewhere else. And if the late Councillor Ayling had kept quiet about the Dinedor Serpent then so would I. But ... we all have a right to free speech. Without, I might add, facing summary execution.'

The Sky News woman said, 'Bill, you said a moment ago that you'd met plenty of the sort of people who you think might be responsible for the murder of Councillor Ayling. Would you care to—?'

'I did *not* say that, you ... I *said* that I'd encountered some people I thought were comics ... rather than *killers*. But this – as all of you guys should know – is a rapidly changing world. World that's daily becoming more brutalised. Suicide bombers, children shooting other children on the streets, torturing old ladies ... Is it any *great* surprise to me when some second-generation neo-hippies out of their heads on methamphetamine start chopping people's heads off because they think their noble Neolithic ancestors have been *disrespected*? I mean, do I really have to *answer* that?'

'Professor Blore, to what extent do you think that inflammatory statements made by ... iconic figures like yourself can inspire extreme behaviour in ... shall we say people who might already be a bit unstable?'

'*Oh, for ...*'

For a moment, Bill Blore seemed to bulge through the gate, and you thought its bars might actually bend, like in an animation movie, as his patience snapped.

'Look,' he said. 'I think I've said all I want to say about this issue, so why don't you all just piss off now, eh?'

Then he turned and strode back through the cold red mud towards the tents, leaving the security guy, Gregory, to mind the gate, and Jane going, like, *Wow.*

Impressed as hell, but maybe just a little bit scared of him now.

30

A Cold Heart

Sitting on a corner of his desk, Bliss jabbed a copy of *The Times*.

'What is this? I mean *why*? What's she hoping to achieve, letting this stuff out, a frigging witch-hunt?'

It wasn't the lead story, like in the redtops, but prominent enough down the side of the front page and in more detail.

'I think it's already started.' Karen Dowell quietly shut Bliss's office door, came and sat down. After a long night on computer duty, Karen had the rest of the day off. 'Tried to get you last night, boss. Two things. A – Ayling's body had stab wounds, B – they were bringing someone in.'

'When was this?'

'Half-eleven?'

Bliss came off the desk. Nobody had told him. Nobody downstairs had even hinted. But perhaps *they* didn't know either, the way Howe had walled herself up in the Blackfriars school with this little coterie of cronies, safe from prying eyes and the Gaol Street telegraph.

'Your phone was switched off.'

Yeh, it had been. He'd gone to bed, slept like the dead. If anybody called him, well, tough; DI Bliss was in recovery.

'We were systematically working through the names on the Watkins computer,' Karen said, 'and we found a handful they thought were worth looking at who were, you know, within easy pulling distance. This particular guy – *great* excitement. Terry Stagg phoned him. Bingo.'

'Same voice?'

'He's even admitted it.'

'Who is he?'

'Wilford Hawkes,' Karen said. 'Real old hippie. Has a smallholding with his wife and two other women – gay partners, looks like – up beyond Dinedor village. They plant stuff in accordance with the phases of the moon.'

'That makes them Serpent-worshippers?'

'Well … pentagram weather vane on the roof, that kind of thing. But I reckon the real issue is that when the road's built, they'll have heavy-goods traffic about twenty metres from their hedge.'

'And he's put his hand up?'

'To the *call*. Nothing else so far.'

'No charge?'

Hoping there wasn't. Wanting these twats to struggle all the way – at least, all the time he wasn't part of it.

'Not when I left,' Karen said. 'But who knows?'

Bliss pictured Howe and Brent patting themselves on the back, toasting each other in decaff.

'Why did they put this out about the quartz?'

'They didn't mention quartz, boss. Just stones. Didn't mention the eyes, either. Just said "stones found with the head". It went out late afternoon – press statement issued before the body was found in the river. And then we brought the computer in and it all took off,' Karen said.

'What about the wife and the other women?'

'Interviewed but not brought in. Ma'am's still keen on Wilford.'

'You seen him?'

'I've seen the first interview.'

'And?'

'Hard to say. You're better at this than me, boss. Look, I'd better be off, it's my boyfriend's birthday.'

'Yeh. OK. Have a good one,' Bliss said. 'Thanks, Karen.'

She was a good girl. When she'd gone Bliss pressed the heels of his hands into his eyes, sat down. On his desk, an early Christmas present from Howe, was the thin file containing copies of computer-printed letters purporting to come from anonymous residents of the same Hereford suburb and identifying a cocaine dealer in their midst. Normally, given the location, it would have been quite interesting.

With the Ayling case on it was a job for a DS, at most. At the top of the first letter, Howe had written, *Francis – we should go for this one ASAP.*

Bitch.

Bliss picked up the top letter.

We have decided that we can no longer put up with this filthy trade in a decent area. Some of us have teenage children or younger and we do not want them to grow up thinking this is how all adults behave.

Two anonymous letters saying much the same, arriving at Gaol Street in the same post, naming the same man, Gyles Banks-Jones. Gyles ran a jewellery business, sometimes marketing his designer products at home gatherings, like the old Tupperware parties Bliss's mum used to host. Other products as well, allegedly.

We understand he keeps the drugs at his home and can be expected to have plentiful supplies for Christmas. We urge you to take action.

Some quite detailed information about specific parties held in this particular area of the city where Banks-Jones lived. So many that the residents must be dripping with designer bling. The letters, Bliss decided, were a committee job. Sounded like residents must be seriously split on the question of whether Mr Banks-Jones was a good or a bad thing.

Wearily, Bliss unwrapped a packet of chewing gum. This complaint had probably been lying around for weeks. Recreational drugs ... it was going on everywhere, and you could waste manpower for months watching a guy like this: no form, a cleanskin, cleaner than clean. And anonymous letters were bugger-all use; you needed names, serviceable witnesses. Punters never seemed to be aware of the requirements of the CPS.

Then, a couple of days ago, the third letter had arrived.

It had gone directly to Headquarters.

And it was signed. It came from Alan Sandison, a recent arrival in the area, who had attended a party with his wife at which Mr Banks-Jones had brought out his glittering wares along with a number of small packages which had been eagerly opened in the kitchen and widely snorted.

The neighbours who had invited the Sandisons to their party had failed to realise – probably too stoned to work out why he wasn't down the pub on a Sunday lunchtime – that Alan Sandison was a Baptist minister.

Sometimes you had to laugh.

Mr Sandison stated that he was prepared to give evidence in court against Gyles Banks-Jones but not against his immediate neighbours who, he believed, had been led astray, poor lambs.

Well. Bliss mouthed a shaft of chewie. Not a brilliant time of year for a dawn raid. Would cost a fair bit in overtime. But when the Ice Maiden requested action, whatever her private reasons might be for diverting your attention, you acted.

Tomorrow morning, Sunday? Have to be, wouldn't it? Monday was Christmas Eve. Besides … get the frigging thing out the way. Gathering the papers together and picking up the phone to call Mr Sandison, Bliss noticed a cardboard carton containing an unlabelled DVD.

Karen must've slipped it under the file. Karen, the computer whizz. Bliss put down the phone, scraped together a smile and slid the DVD down his inside pocket.

She *was* a good girl.

Like Sophie, Amanda Rubens wore her glasses on a chain. Unlike Sophie she had a lot of other chains and long beads, like some 1920s flapper, over her black polo-neck woollen frock.

'Yes, all right, I'm sorry, it was out before I realised what I was saying. Could've bitten my tongue off, but that bloody woman … "*You besmirch our village with this vileness?*" Can you believe someone would say that … *in a bookshop?*'

The interior of Ledwardine Livres was full of Christmas lights, twinkling between displays of mainly children's books. No bookshop in Hereford or Leominster would rely on atmosphere lighting; either Amanda Rubens was seriously naive or shoplifting in Ledwardine was still confined to the Eight Till Late.

'It was my last copy. Seemed to be going rather well, so I immediately ordered another half-dozen and they were here in the afternoon. Put three at the front of the window, which I suppose was what caught the attention of the postmistress. I suppose it hadn't occurred to me that some people might find it tasteless at Christmas. And that was why I said what I said when she came in and began to remonstrate with me. It ... it simply came out. I simply ... I said, *For heaven's sake, the* vicar's *just bought a copy!*'

Merrily sighed. Amanda played anxiously with one of her chains. 'Anyway, surely nobody in this day and age expects the clergy to limit their reading to the New Testament. Look, I'm sorry. I'm not a gossip. I *never*, as a rule, broadcast what my customers buy for themselves. I suppose this was ... self-defence, as much as anything. She'd never been in here before, and she was quite ... quite fierce. She rather ... filled the shop. I was intimidated.'

Possibly understandable. Amanda was built like a cocktail stick; Shirley could have snapped her.

'I can only say, Mrs Watkins, that if you can bear to shop with us again, I will *never*—'

'What else did she say, Mrs Rubens? You said something about vileness?'

'*You besmirch our village with this vileness.* That one's rather stuck.'

'Did she go further? It's just ... there are things I need to be aware of.'

'Oh, well, I suppose this is right up *your* street ... She said the book was part of the Devil's attempt to take control. In the Final Days. She went on about the Final Days.'

'Something of a buzz phrase,' Merrily said, 'in born-again circles.'

'A dark doorway to eternal damnation – that's what she called the book.'

'Did she say anything about the author?'

'Spin doctor.'

'Sorry?'

'She called him the spin doctor to the Antichrist. She said if I wanted to know the truth about this man I had only to look on the Internet.'

'And did you?'

'I've been rather busy.'

'Thank you,' Merrily said. 'I suppose I'd better check it out. See if I can save my immortal soul before it's too late.'

Amanda Rubens smiled nervously, her veneers gleaming evenly in the soft Christmas light.

'Whole world's gone mad, Mrs Watkins. You think you can opt out of it, don't you, by moving to a place like this?'

'A common misconception, Mrs Rubens.'

'I never encountered a woman quite like Mrs West in London.'

You found this. For city people, used to mixing in confined circles, the country was often a shock to the system.

'And now, when they're saying that Hereford councillor was murdered by some *sect* ...'

'Sect?'

'You haven't seen the papers?'

Amanda opened out the *Guardian*, under the coloured lights, pointing to a story in the middle of the front page.

Usual picture of Clem Ayling. Pastoral colour picture of Dinedor Hill.

Oh God.

Wilford Hawkes was completely bald, white beard down to his chest, an earring with a red stone in it. Bit of a cliché, really.

'You don't understand, do you, my love?' Off the phone, his accent was more distinct. 'We don't need to *kill* people. We don't need to do nothing. They're doing it theirselves. All those JCBs, they're digging theirselves a great big grave.'

'Mr Hawkes.' Annie Howe's voice. 'I am *not* your *love*.'

Bliss smiled. He had his car shoved under dripping trees in this secluded little car park across the main road from Gaol Street. Karen's interview-room DVD in the laptop on the passenger seat.

'All I'm saying,' Hawkes said, 'is when you knowingly damage a sacred site, you expect repercussions. I can give you stories of farmers digging up old stones, ploughing burial mounds. Next thing, sudden electric storms, directly overhead, and then their crops fail and their stock die.'

'Mr Hawkes—'

'All I was doing was giving him a friendly warning.'

'That's your idea of friendly, is it?'

'All right, it was a bit beyond, out of order. I wasn't thinking straight.'

'You were drunk?'

'I don't drink alcohol, my dear. I was, shall we say, in a state of herbally heightened relaxation.'

Mr Hawkes settled back with his hands behind his head, eyes half closed, a faint smile on his lips. The cockiness of a killer? More likely the daft old twat was actually enjoying it. Memories of his lost youth, getting busted by the pigs.

'*Wreckage and blood*, Mr Hawkes,' Howe said. 'You warned him of wreckage and blood.'

'I never mentioned his *personal* blood, did I? We knew we had to lay this on the line, look, in a way the bastards would understand how strongly we feel. They're pushing the ole city out in all the directions it don't wanner go, and they're cutting it off from Dinedor Hill. And then, right on cue, the Serpent shows up after thousands of years just in time to warn us all, and what do they do? They smother it. What they gonner do next, build a supermarket on top? After all, we only got seven already!'

'Are you *sure* you wouldn't like a solicitor, Mr Hawkes?'

'Oh, you'd like that, wouldn't you?' Mr Hawkes sitting up. 'They talk your language, those predators. Always been my policy to have nothing to do with the blood-sucking bastards. Possible to go through your whole life without ever meeting a lawyer.'

'But probably not *your* life, Mr Hawkes, the way it's shaping up. The Children of the Serpent – how many of you are there?'

'How many?'

'How many children,' Howe said icily, 'does the Serpent possess?'

'None. I made it up.'

'You made *what* up, exactly?'

'The whole thing. Children of the Serpent. I thought it sounded good. You think about it: I ring Ayling up, say this is Willy Hawkes, I'm just calling to give you a gentle warning, what's that gonner do? He's gonner laugh down my earole. *Children of the Serpent*, that's got a bit of menace. That works.'

'Mr Hawkes, I shall ask you again, did you kill Clement Ayling?'

'I can*not* believe ...'

'Please answer the question.'

'No! Did I bloody hell kill Clement Ayling! I wouldn't've gone anywhere near him or any of the shabby bastards on that council.'

'Do you *know* who killed Clement Ayling?'

'I been trying to tell you, I don't mix with them sort of people.'

A silence. Willy Hawkes's mouth tight shut behind his beard.

'You're a pagan, Mr Hawkes.'

'I'm British. It's our own faith. Christianity, Islam ... all that was imported for political reasons. Paganism's from the earth. Roots religion.'

'The so-called Serpent. That was supposed to connect Dinedor Hill with the River Wye – is that right?'

Bliss sniffed. She knew it was right, she'd got it from his report.

'I know where you're going,' Willy Hawkes said. 'You found Ayling's body in the river.'

'And what does that tell you, Mr Hawkes?'

'Would've made more sense if you'd found the head in the— Aw, I've had enough of this, lady! You don't know nothing about pagans, do you? Throughout the past two millennia we've not been killers, we've been the *victims*. Witches hanged and burned for curing sick people, saving the lives of the poor. Hanged and burned, by the likes of you! You got the face of a witch-burner, you have.'

Bliss thumped the steering wheel. He loved this feller.

Hawkes leaned over the table.

'Do I *look* like the kind of man who'd behead somebody? Me and my lady and my spiritual sisters, we're peaceful, pastoral folk. What happened to Ayling ... whatever kind of man he was, what you're looking at there is just plain evil. You're looking for somebody devoid of all spiritual feeling. You're looking at a cold heart.'

'There's a pagan network in this area, isn't there?'

'Nothing so formal. Folks knows each other, but we're all different – Wiccans, Druids, what-have-you – we all got our own ways. How long you gonna keep this up before I can go home?'

'Mr Hawkes, you've admitted threatening behaviour. You've admitted threatening a man who was later murdered. Don't think you'll be going home tonight.'

'That's outrag—' Willy Hawkes coming out of his seat, uniformed arms putting him back. He sat there shaking. 'It's the Winter Solstice. Do you know how important that is? I need to be on Dinedor Hill! It's an important time. You can't keep me yere for the Solstice. God damn you!'

Howe didn't react. Hawkes sat twisting his head. He straightened his shoulders, looked down into his lap for a few moments. Then he looked up, smoothed out his beard with both hands.

'I'll tell you as far as it went. If I tell you as far as it went, will you let me go home?'

'I don't make deals,' Howe said. 'However, if you're seen to be cooperating …'

'There's a Wiccan group …'

'A witches' coven.'

'If you like. They gathered for a ritual of restraint to bind the Council, tie their hands. They also put a protective spell on the fields below Dinedor Hill. And they done a ritual of invocation.'

'What does that mean?'

'To awaken the guardians.'

'Mr Hawkes—'

'Every ancient site – well, not *every* ancient site, but a fair few – they got a guardian, see. A spirit or an elemental force to repel invasive influences. What causes the thunderstorms and what-have-you.'

'Doesn't seem to have worked, does it?'

'They lifted it,' Hawkes said. 'Things don't always work the way you think they're going to. We're dealing with forces beyond our comprehension and out of our control, which is why I won't personally work with spells.'

'What are you saying?'

'There was an accident, wasn't there? During the tree-felling. Bloke was hurt. Well, it wasn't his fault, was it? He didn't make the decision, he was just a humble tree-feller. Quite a few people said, no, take it back, get it lifted, bad karma. We can't play their game, we gotter be above all that.'

'And that was when they lifted their ... spell?'

'And then Ayling died. *Everybody* got cold feet then. Me in particular. I'd phoned him. I'd left a bad message on his machine. I'd *made the connection.*'

'Who are these witches?'

'I won't tell you that. They've lifted the spell, that's all you need to know. They got nothing to do with it now.'

'I need their names.'

'Well, you won't get them from me. Not if you keep me yere all week. I'll tell you another thing. We met – a bunch of us – for a meditation.'

'When was this?'

'After Ayling's death. 'Cos we never wanted that.'

'Really.'

'We *didn't.*'

'Where was this meeting?'

'Our barn. We had some very psychic people, and they all came up with the same thing ... a big darkness, an unquenchable evil.'

'And were they given a name, Mr Hawkes?'

'It don't work that way.'

'How unfortunate.'

'But they got a feeling of it. People've forgotten how to listen to their feelings. One of the ladies was quite ill afterwards.'

'I can imagine,' Annie Howe said.

31

Neither Horns Nor Tail

ON JANE'S LAPTOP ... a screenful of apocalypse, grey angels straddling an arid land.

'I'm not sure I can face this,' Merrily said.

A false light gleamed in the kitchen's highest window. On the lunchtime radio news, a big voice was battling the wind.

'—*chaeology's my life, OK? But I couldn't say ... worth the loss of someone else's.*'

'Classic soundbite,' Lol said. 'Do you think he's done this before?'

'*The archaeologist, Professor William Blore, talking this morning in Herefordshire,*' the newsreader said. '*In Zimbabwe—*'

Merrily switched off, frowning.

'The archaeologist, Professor William Blore, was supposed to be interviewing Jane on the top of Cole Hill.'

'Which probably explains why she isn't back.'

'She was very excited. Almost took the heat out of having the computer impounded.' Merrily held the kettle under the cold tap. 'I shouldn't imagine they invited Professor Blore to hand over *his* computer.'

'You had no choice,' Lol said. 'If they'd been forced to come back with a warrant they'd've turned the whole place over. Jane's apartment, anyway. And Jane would've gone wild.'

'Well, that's what I thought, but ...' Merrily plugged in the kettle. 'They said I might get it back today. As if.'

Lol had turned the laptop towards him on the kitchen table. He would often come over on Saturday mornings, when Jane was usually out. Quality time. Or something. No time for any something today.

'*Thelordofthelight.com.* You heard of this one?'

'There are scores of them, Lol. Probably hundreds in the US alone. Full of raging paranoia and an unforgiving Christ I have problems with. But have I heard of this one? *Oh yes.*'

Lol had Googled *Mathew Stooke, spin doctor to the Antichrist.*

'It's the name of Shirley's church, in Leominster,' Merrily said. 'They sent me a lovely Christmas card.'

'Looks bigger than that to me. Bigger than Leominster, that is.'

'Maybe the source is in America. Often is. What's the approach?'

'It's an endgame thing,' Lol said. 'Not too many laughs. Unless you can spot the hidden jokes in the Book of Revelation. *Is* this Revelation? *In the last days, difficult times will come ...*'

'Maybe Paul.'

Merrily came to sit next to Lol. The depressing angels had gone; the screen had faded to the colour of dried blood and stark words in white.

> ... for men will be lovers of self, lovers of money,
> boastful, arrogant, disobedient to their parents,
> ungrateful, unholy, unloving, unforgiving, malicious
> gossips, without self-control, brutal, haters of good,
> treacherous, reckless, conceited, lovers of pleasure
> rather than lovers of God ...

'All looks worryingly familiar,' Lol said. 'How long do you reckon we have left – two weeks, three weeks? Or do we, um, need to go upstairs now?'

> In later times some will fall away from the faith,
> paying attention to deceitful spirits and doctrines
> of demons. By means of the hypocrisy of liars
> seared in their own conscience as with a branding
> iron, men who forbid marriage and advocate
> abstaining from foods which God has created to be
> gratefully shared in by those who believe and know
> the truth.

With a white screen and normal print, implications of the prophecy were explained in detail for *LordoftheLight* browsers: veggies were spurning the animals God had given them to tame and slaughter. 'Now that's interesting,' Merrily said. 'I never quite saw it that way myself, but it explains Shirley's interest in how much meat I don't buy.' While the Green movement, with its worship of Mother Earth, was luring people into pagan ways and modern churches were straying from the laws of God by accepting homosexuality and embracing New Age practices.

'Like meditation, do you think?'

The dour doctrine of Shirley West was unscrolling before her eyes.

Then came the red silhouette of a naked man.

> It has been predicted that, close to the Endtime,
> Satan will incarnate. He will have neither
> horns nor tail. His true identity will not, at first,
> be apparent. He himself may not, at first, realise
> who he is. He will believe that his mission is to
> explain. He will show that everything can be
> explained by science. He will be a hero, hailed
> a genius.

'Who do we have here, then?' Lol wondered. 'Hawking?'

'You really see a very seriously disabled man as the Antichrist?'

'I don't. *They* might. Black humour's a key tool of the prince of darkness. Let's give him the benefit of the doubt. What about Dawkins?'

'Doesn't have the charisma.'

> The Antichrist will create marvels, but will insist that
> they are not of supernatural origin.

'Got him,' Lol said. 'It's that Derren Brown.'

'You're bloody well enjoying this, aren't you?'

'It's interesting watching you getting all embarrassed by your own—'

'This is not *my*—' Merrily caught his smile on its way out. 'Sod.' Lowered her head wearily to an arm, looking up at him sideways. 'Lol, what are we doing?'

'We're uncovering the motivational psychology of Shirley West. It's worth knowing. Ah ...'

> The New Labour government, elected in Britain
> in 1997, was largely a product of spin and the
> manipulation of the media. Nobody seemed
> even to be aware of its policies, responding only
> to its apparently clean and youthful image,
> its demolition of the reputation of the existing
> government and its promise that 'things can only
> get better.' In the same way, the Antichrist has his
> own spin doctors, men and women skilled in
> the craft of communication, lending their services
> to Satan in the same way that the journalist
> Campbell made his available to New Labour.
> In line with the Endtime prophesies, these men
> are already amongst us, one of them the author of a
> book which sneers openly at God. Doubters may
> care to count the number of letters in each of his
> names.
> MATHEW ELLIOT STOOKE.

Merrily sat up slowly.

> In this context, it is pertinent to ask why he chose
> to drop the second T from Matthew, if not to embrace
> his destiny.

Lol said, 'It *is* a bit curious, isn't it?'

'It's *crap.*'

Merrily abruptly killed the images on the laptop. Stood up and walked over to the window overlooking the garden and the churchyard wall, the rain slanted by a rising wind. She felt twisted up inside. Behind her, Lol's chair scraped on the flags.

'Merrily, it's only a—'

'I wonder if he knows about this.'

'Of course he knows,' Lol said gently. 'There must be five pages of links to this garbage on Google alone. He's had threats, hasn't he? That's why he's here.'

'And I wonder if *she* knows.'

'Shirley?'

'If she knows he's here. Or at least suspects he might be somewhere in the vicinity.'

'Why would she?' Lol's hands on her shoulders. 'We don't *know* there's a link between the website and Shirley's church. And she'd hardly think that because you bought his book ...'

'If I hadn't bought it, Amanda Rubens wouldn't've reordered so fast. Extra copies? The same day? Which she puts at the front of the window?'

'Maybe she thought you were going to slag off Stooke in a sermon, thus generating a few extra sales.'

'Whatever, I wish I'd left it alone. And I wish I'd ...' Merrily stared out over the wall at the dulled sandstone of the church '... never met him.'

'Oh Christ ...' Lol backed off. 'You *didn't* ...'

'Frannie Bliss said much the same as you. Leave well alone. Stooke eats vicars for breakfast.'

'So naturally you had to rise to the challenge.'

'It wasn't like that.' Or maybe it was. She turned away from the church and the rain. Everything seemed to be out of control. Everything was futile. Stooke was looming larger in the great scheme of things than he ought to have done. And Bliss saying, *All the picturesque villages in all the world and he has to pick yours.*

'No coincidence,' Lol said. 'Wherever he ended up, there was always going to be a vicar.'

'Anyway, we had a talk. Me being careful not to suggest I knew who he was.'

'Wouldn't the very fact of you turning up at his house convey that impression?'

'I didn't. Or rather I did, but he wasn't in, and in the end I ran into him in Coleman's Meadow. Checking out the dig. And got chatting, as you do.'

'Not me.'

'Yeah, well, in my profession, you can't *afford* to be a recluse. And he was curious about what I did. I mean deliverance. Or rather he knew about it and he wanted to know more, and if I'd shown any reluctance, it would've looked ...'

'No, it wouldn't. It's the Bishop's secret service. You keep saying that, and you don't like giving talks to the WI, so why should you feel obliged to talk about it to a guy you just met in a field?'

'It was how I felt at the time, because he wasn't ... what I expected. You read his book, you sense this colossal self-righteous rage. I mean, why, for God's sake? Guy writes an angry book, we think he spends his life smashing things and beating up his wife?'

'Nice person, then,' Lol said.

'Relaxed, balanced ... almost charming. Don't look at me like that, I'm being objective. With hindsight.'

'You liked him.'

'I ... yeah, I probably did. It was an odd situation. I knew who he was, he didn't *know* I knew, but he knew what I did. And then afterwards it's all turned full circle and I'm annoyed with myself, I'm thinking, you idiot, he's probably writing his follow-up to *The Hole in the Sky*. Am I going to be in it now, or what? The loopy exorcist with the pagan daughter?'

'Bit of a comedown from the Dalai Lama.'

'Oh God ...' Merrily started to laugh. 'I *could*, on the other hand, be going just a little crazy, but it ...'

Somewhere beyond the scullery a door banged.

'... It all *fits*, doesn't it? I was expecting anger, I got mildness. I was expecting monstrous ego, I got ... almost self-deprecating. If I was Shirley West ...'

'Don't even imagine what that would be like.'

'No, listen. The atheist is an angry man, but Satan's spin doctor is a charmer, who puts you at your ease, allays your susp— What's the *matter* with that door?'

Banging again in the wind. It sounded like the side door to the yard, by the back stairs. Like something coming in and slamming it behind … Oh God, *never* log on to a born-again Christian website.

'Excuse me a minute.'

Merrily went through into the low passage leading to the back stairs, where she caught the side door about to slam again in the wind. It hadn't been closed properly. But then it shouldn't have been open, rarely was these days since Jane had stopped regarding it as the private entrance to her apartment.

Odd.

She shut it firmly, locked it at the catch and stood there for a moment, listening.

'Jane?'

No reply. Back in the scullery the phone was ringing. She heard Lol going through, picking up.

'No, I'm sorry, she's not here at the moment. Could I —? Oh …'

Merrily went quietly up the narrow back stairs to the main landing. No sound up here but the rain. The glass in the window at the top of the main stairs was in freeflow. She went up the second, narrower, stairs to the attic apartment.

Its door was ajar. She stopped outside, thought she could hear a faint snuffling.

'Jane, is that …?'

Hesitated for just a moment before going in and seeing – heart-lurch – Jane lying face down on the bed. Fully dressed, with a damp pillow bent around her head.

32

In Your Veins

'Lol,' Eirion said. 'Wow. Amazing.'

Standing in the entrance to the vicarage drive, bags either side of him on the wet gravel. His red and white baseball sweater looked too big. He'd lost weight. Less stocky, less archetypal-Welsh.

'Bad down there?' Lol said.

'The Valleys – terrible,' Eirion said. 'It's like somebody's trying to turn them into reservoirs. I was thinking if I didn't come today I might not get here at all. Tried to call Jane about six times. What's the point of having a mobile if you keep it switched off? So I thought I'd better ring Mrs Watkins, make sure it was all right.'

Eirion looked around in the damp air. Lol sensed his nerves about meeting Jane again, more than three months since their lives had divided.

The light was still on in the attic. Not knowing any better, Lol had told Eirion on the phone that Jane was still out at Coleman's Meadow, but they were expecting her back any minute. Putting the phone down just as Merrily had come briefly downstairs. Jane was up there. Jane had been badly upset. They needed some time.

'So,' Eirion said. 'How are you, man? You're looking well. Bit tired, maybe.'

'Late nights.'

'You're working on something?'

'And time's running out.' Lol picked up one of Eirion's bags. Maybe take him in the parlour, get him something to drink. 'Actually—'

'So how did it *go*, Lol? I couldn't believe it when Jane told me. When's it on?'

'When's what—? Oh, yeah, sorry. New Year's Eve.'

'What they need to do is erect a big flat-screen TV ...' Eirion looked back towards the square and all the bulging, crooked black and whites leaning over it. 'Over there. By the Christmas tree.'

'Eirion, it's *one song*. Might even get cut.'

'No way.' Eirion rubbed his hands. 'Strange, it is, coming back here. I've dreamt about it, Lol. Couple of times recently. One of those places that come up in dreams. Perhaps because it never changes.'

'No.'

'Anyway, I'm glad I've seen you first. Got presents in the car. Nothing much, but I was wondering, would it be OK if I left them at your place?'

Lol looked back at the vicarage. The light in the attic had gone out. 'No problem at all,' he said. 'In fact, why don't we do that now?'

In the scullery, the rarely used third bar of the electric fire was glowing neon-red and making these little zinging noises, like open nerves. Merrily lit a cigarette and carried her tea to the window overlooking the dank Decembered garden.

'Have you ever thought of leaving here?' Jane said.

'Not really. Well ... once or twice. Have you?'

Surely not. Surely never in a million years.

Jane, sitting on the old sofa, expressionless, made no reply. Not since Lucy ...

No, that wasn't the same. When Lucy was killed, Jane had lost control, pulling her hair and screaming abuse at God, even Merrily failing to realise at the time how big a death this was. But Jane had been a kid then and Merrily a nervous, novice parish priest, and their relationship was on a permanent cliff-edge.

'I ... heard Bill Blore on the radio at lunchtime,' Merrily said. 'They'd been asking him about Clement Ayling's murder.'

Jane said nothing. She'd insisted on washing her face before she came down. Washing it over and over, with cold water.

'It struck me that he might've had to delay your interview. Or even call it off?'

She'd been thinking that Lol might be the one to reach Jane. Lol with his sixth sense for humiliation and despair. But when she'd slipped downstairs, Lol had whispered that Eirion was on his way, a day early because of the floods. Everything happened at once in this house. She hadn't told Jane who, when the front-door bell rang, had still been on the edge of the bed, body language screaming, Leave me alone, like *for ever.*

'He didn't want to talk about it,' Jane said.

'Sorry?'

'Blore. Wanted to get on with his excavation. Naturally, *they* – the media – didn't want to talk about anything else.'

'And that put him in a bad mood? I was thinking maybe he'd kept putting you off and you were hanging around the site getting cold and wet and nothing happening.'

'If only.'

'Flower ...' Merrily on her knees by the sofa, picking up Jane's left hand. 'Just because Blore didn't want to talk to you today ...' Watching the nails of Jane's right hand sinking into the cushion. 'There'll be another opportunity. He clearly needs you for his programme, if he's going to—'

Merrily held Jane's hand firmly in both of hers. No, of course. It was worse than that, wasn't it?

'You don't understand.' Jane's hand was gripping Merrily's fiercely, tears pooling. 'You weren't listening. I've been stupid. *Unbelievably* stupid.'

Eirion had the Takamine on his knee. He'd worked out some chords to Sufjan Stevens's 'Chicago'. He seemed to have improved a lot. He looked around at the whitewashed walls, the orange paint that Jane had insisted should be applied between the beams in the ceiling.

'You've got this place fantastic, Lol. Is that your mother?' Nodding at the picture over the inglenook.

'It's Lucy Devenish,' Lol said. 'The only known photograph. For which she seems to have been determined not to pose. Hence the blur.'

'Ah. *That's* her, is it? That blur over the face makes her look a bit ... unearthly.'

'Mostly, she was very earthly. I always hear her saying … after Alison had left and before I met Merrily, when I was really low and a bit deranged, she said …' Lol did the voice '"*You really are a sick, twisted little person, aren't you, Laurence?*" Never dressed things up.'

Eirion laughed.

'Then she gave me Thomas Traherne to read to straighten me out. "*Have to learn to open up, Laurence. Go into the village on your own and go in smiling. That's what Traherne did. Discovered felicity.*"'

'Did it work?'

'Eventually.' Lol opened a couple of bottles of Westons cider. 'That and a few other things. Always presuming I *am* straightened out.'

'This was her place, wasn't it?'

'Still is. Lucy's house, my mortgage.'

'Jane talks to her,' Eirion said. 'At her grave. Is that healthy, do you think?'

'I always think graves are for us, not the dead. Lucy's grave … Jane thinks it's on an energy line. A spirit path.'

'Well, that's Jane, isn't it?'

'If it gives her energy …'

'What about this house?'

'Who knows? I only got it because the last people moved out after a short time. Claiming it was haunted.'

'But you …?'

'Nothing.'

'Maybe Miss Devenish is happy you're here.' Eirion drank some cider. 'God, listen to me, I've not been here half an hour and I'm talking like Jane already.'

'But I'm always conscious that if I slip back, she'll bloody well manifest with that hooked nose and the eagle eyes and the poncho flapping …'

'Steady on, Lol.' Eirion shuddered, put the bottle down. 'Slip back how?'

'Or it's like I'm only allowed to stay here for some purpose.' Lol sat down on the hard chair at the desk in the window. 'Anyway … I've been putting these songs together.'

He told Eirion about Christmas Eve at the Black Swan and the suite of songs illustrating elements of what Lucy had called the Ledwardine Orb.

'Traherne ... Wil Williams, the 17th-century vicar here who was accused of witchcraft ... Alfred Watkins, who discovered leys ... his friend Edward Elgar, the composer who turned the landscape into music ... and Lucy, who bound it all together.'

'How many songs?'

'Five so far, three more in the works. And a reworking of Nick Drake's "Fruit Tree", which seemed appropriate. Apple trees ... change and decay. Mortality.'

'Nearly enough for an album. Hey ...' Eirion's eyes lighting up. 'This is actually the second solo album? The sequel to *Alien*?'

'Maybe, if I can pull it off, I won't be an alien any more.'

'Like you'll've landed?'

Lol shrugged, uncertainly.

'Sounds a bit pathetic, doesn't it? As for playing the songs for the first time in public, in the Black Swan on Christmas Eve ...'

'Bollocks!' Eirion played a ringing C7th. 'The heart of the village. Couldn't be better, man. It was meant.'

'You could almost think that,' Lol said. 'I came down this morning and the book of Traherne's selected poems and prose was lying on the desk. The one Lucy gave me. Lying just there. No memory of getting it down from the shelf. Picked it up and it fell open at *You never enjoy the world aright till the sea itself floweth in your veins, till you are clothed with the heavens ...*'

'*... and crowned with the stars.*' Eirion looked momentarily embarrassed. 'Jane used to ...'

Quote it when they were in bed, probably, Lol thought. Very Jane.

'Anyway,' he said, 'if you're just the bloke with a guitar in the corner on Christmas Eve, nobody listens, and I've realised I want them to. Want the incomers to know about this stuff – it's a bit of a white-settlers' pub, the Swan. Even if they say *This is crap*, I want them to listen. So ... I was thinking I could use back-projection? They've got some kit at the Swan, and Jane has this collection of old photos of

Ledwardine – and some new photos of Cole Hill, taken by you, I believe ...'

'I look at them often,' Eirion said. 'Too often, really. Especially the one of Jane with her blouse ... *but*, you don't need to know this.'

'So would you be able to take care of that aspect? Make sure the right pictures come up on the screen behind me at the right time? Also, with one song, I need to use a recording of Elgar's Cello Concerto. I'll need fingers on mixers.'

'Hey ...' Eirion put down the guitar. 'Look no further, Lol. Jane, too? Me and Jane?'

'Well ... hopefully.'

Eirion stiffened. 'Lol, she is OK, isn't she? There's not something about Jane you aren't telling me?'

Lol went to the window. Dusk was forming. There were no lights upstairs in the vicarage.

'Oh my God, there's something wrong, isn't there?' Eirion said. 'I felt it as soon as I walked on to the drive.'

'Eirion ...' Lol turned round; he wasn't good at this. 'To be honest, I'm not sure.'

'Listen, you might as well tell me.' Eirion had gone pale. 'Is it this fucking Neil Cooper?'

An hour or so later, with night wrapping itself around the village like an old grey coat, Jane and Eirion went down to the river with a lamp.

The air seemed to be throbbing with unshed rain. Merrily and Lol went back into the vicarage and sat in the kitchen.

'I hope he gets more sense out of her than I did,' Merrily said.

33

A Corridor

THE RIVER WAS in an angry world of his own, heaving himself up against the arch of the bridge. Jane tried to get into his mindset; sometimes anger was a lifeline.

'You think there's room for someone like me in journalism?'

They were heading for the riverside footpath which did a half circuit of the village before veering off and ending up, like all the Ledwardine paths did, in one of the old orchards. Despite the growing darkness, Jane was walking fast and hard.

'Don't like the sound of that.' Eirion scrabbling after her, not really dressed for this, looking fairly respectable for Mum. 'Why would you suddenly want to get into journalism?'

'Because you get to …' Jane didn't stop, climbing over the stile leading to the riverside footpath '… shaft people?'

She heard Eirion sigh, glanced quickly back at him. She'd always been on at him to lose weight but now he had, it was wrong. His face was leaner, more streetwise, less vulnerable, less … manageable.

Jane held the lamp and watched him climb over the stile without stumbling. In the old days he'd have stumbled. She turned and started walking away, against the flow of the river. The other side of it, the lights had come on, the big red Santa plumping out like some gross cyst from the wall of a new bungalow on what Gomer Parry called *the hestate*.

'See, I used to think that was a pretty shoddy thing to do, but now I realise some people deserve it.'

'Well, yeah, obviously,' Eirion said, 'but—'

'Really arrogant people? Bastards who destroy other people without a thought?'

The rushing river beside her was brown with churned-up silt and gassy like cheap draught bitter. Eirion stopped.

'So we're talking about Professor Blore, are we?'

Jane kept on walking, forcing him to come after her. She wished it would start raining, give her an excuse for looking messed-up. Bloody rain, always there except when you needed some.

'Blore?'

Eirion shouting like maybe she hadn't heard. A bit out of breath now, she noticed. So he wasn't doing gym, just missing meals.

'Why would it be?' Jane said.

'Because when you rang last night to set this up, it was like, Oh *Bill Blore's* going to save the Meadow, Bill Blore and me, Bill *Blore* who's like totally cool and—'

'*Shut up, you*—!'

Jane spun and stumbled, one foot going down the river bank, Eirion trying to grab her but she reeled away, fell on her bum on the soaking grass.

'Oh, Jane ...'

'I need to rethink my future, OK?' Jane refusing his hand, refusing to get up, feeling sick and stupid. 'It's no big deal. There are loads of other careers. No big deal. The world's my ... hairball.'

Blinking back tears like some little kid, an auto-reaction to the unexpected.

'It is, Jane.' Eirion standing with his arms by his sides now, shaking his head. 'It's a bloody great mega-deal. You had it all sorted. You knew totally where you were going. You couldn't understand why you hadn't spotted the obvious.'

'I can make a mistake.'

'Yeah, but you usually can't bring yourself to admit it, which is why this is so totally ... What happened? What did Blore do? Is he still around?'

'Dunno.'

'I mean, I can go and ask *him*. Corner him in the pub. Get him up against a wall, like, what've you done to my ...?'

Behind Jane, the river surged and frothed, pitiless. But Eirion had dried up. God, he didn't know what to call her any more: *My former girl-friend? My ex?*

She was shocked.

Eirion came and sat down next to her on the sodden grass in what was clearly a new jacket – worse, new trousers.

'Start at the beginning,' he said.

The hestate behind them now, they were walking more slowly, hand in hand, like thirteen-year-olds on a first date. Or at least like thirteen-year-olds did when Jane was thirteen. Five years ago ... hell, that was a long time ago. So much pressure to grow up fast, pressure to put your life into a Jiffy bag, tick the boxes, meet the targets. Pressure, pressure, pressure.

'He did exactly what he said he was going to do.' Jane took a steadying breath. 'Shot me.'

Eirion looked at her, up and down, like for exit wounds.

'Can't say I wasn't warned, Irene. Like, Coops had said he was prob-ably going to be in a crap mood. He said it was best not to approach him afterwards.'

'Coops.'

'Neil Cooper. County archaeologist guy?'

'I know who you mean,' Eirion said.

'A friend, Irene. That's all. Married.'

'I'm sorry. Go on.'

'I *didn't* approach Blore, I really didn't. I was just, like, standing around, and I could see him keep looking at me, like he was trying to remember who I was and what I was doing here. So I just kind of smiled and didn't go over. I mean, it wasn't just me, everybody was giving him a wide berth. The students, the camera crew ...'

'He's an archaeologist, Jane, not bloody Brad Pitt.'

'He's a *distinguished* archaeologist. He has an entourage – students and ... what's the word ... like fossils?'

'Acolytes?'

'Yeah. So then this other guy was there who wasn't supposed to be. This dowser, with his divining rods?'

A man Jane remembered from a meeting of the Coleman's Meadow Preservation Society last summer. Schoolteacher-looking guy with grey hair and a white beard. A member of the British Society of Dowsers, who said he'd used his rods and his pendulum to track the ley line – the *energy* line – from Cole Hill to the church. Telling Jane to point out to Mum that the energy passed directly through the pulpit and if she ever felt in need of spiritual fuel for a sermon she need only become aware of the line and energy would flow through her. And then telling Jane – like he'd once put in an email – that Coleman's Meadow had a site-guardian attached to it, some kind of elemental force, and anyone who tried to damage it could expect a hard time.

'I mean, he wasn't doing anything *bad*. Just walking round with these copper dowsing rods. He'd been waiting there since first light, apparently. Told Coops he'd been waiting weeks to get into the site, see if the line corresponded to his calculations or whatever.'

'I had a go at that once,' Eirion said. 'Dowsing. Farmer near us hired this bloke to tell him where to sink a borehole. It works, I think, but that was underground water, not … earth energy.'

'Same thing.' Jane looked at the river. 'That's *serious* energy. Anyway, Coops said this guy could have ten minutes. Just don't get in the way and remember that he couldn't come in after they'd started the dig. He was this really polite, inoffensive guy, you know?'

Eirion nodded.

'So he must've had his ten minutes, and he was just walking back towards the gate, following whatever his rods were picking up, when Bill Blore practically walks into him. He's just like standing in his path, like looming over him? And he's, like, what are you doing on my site? And the guy like smiles and starts explaining about the energy line, and then Bill Blore says has he ever calculated how far a dowsing rod would go up his arse before it—'

Eirion winced.

'And looking like he … like he wanted to actually do it? And then … I was outside the gate with Coops, staying out of the way, so he hadn't seen me, and he goes, Where's that fucking girl? Let's get all the shit out of the way, then we can do some work.'

'So that's when you left, is it?' Eirion said.

'No,' Jane said. 'That's when I *should*'ve left.'

It was that feeling of being locked into destiny. That it was all *meant*. That the secret of Coleman's Meadow would have remained undiscovered, if *she* hadn't come here.

Arrogance. She was just as bad as Bill Blore, who ...

'... said we just hadn't got time to go to the top of Cole Hill with the crew. Well, I should've realised then. How could I explain how I first, like, *perceived* the line, if I couldn't stand up there, in the Iron Age ramparts and point to the steeple and the impression of the path across the meadow. You need to see it.'

'Maybe he was thinking they could get some shots from up there afterwards,' Eirion said. 'Or from a helicopter. So they could overlay your description of it with the pictures.'

'Yeah, that's what he said. Don't worry about it, they could overlay it. Whatever, I went along with it and they decided to record it on the edge of the meadow, by the gate, and he's like, "So tell us how you first became interested in Coleman's Meadow." And I'm trying to explain, the best I could with nothing to point to.'

Telling him about discovering Alfred Watkins's seminal work *The Old Straight Track* and realising how magically this line fitted Watkins's concept of ley lines, which actually made a lot more sense than some people wanted to admit.'

Magically. Bill Blore nodding. *I see.*

Jane telling him that of course she knew how archaeologists had rubbished Watkins and ley lines both, back in the 1920s, and how it was lucky they were so much more open-minded now.

'And Bill Blore's like ... he's just standing there with this kind of sardonic smile on his face?'

Occasionally shaking his head, slowly. There were two cameras, one on Jane, one on him. And this director guy, Mike, who was talking more to the camera guys than to Blore, giving them signals and stuff. And, of course, there were all these students gathered round, about six of them.

'You'll have seen how he works with students.'

'Points out how they've got it all wrong,' Eirion said. 'Throwing away what they thought was rubbish and it's actually a tiny piece of Roman mosaic.'

'Like that, yeah.'

Bill Blore had let her ramble on for several minutes about leys and earth mysteries and the incredible moment of illumination she'd experienced on the top of Cole Hill. And then he'd gone, *Thanks, Jane*, and turned to the students, a camera following him.

Interesting, eh? Blore had said. *This, you see, is how myths are created. A youngster comes to the right conclusions ... for all the wrong reasons. Ley lines. Gawd help us.*

Then turning back to Jane, smiling kindly.

All the same, we're grateful to you. What are you going to do next? University?

And Jane had gone, *Maybe ... hopefully, archaeology.* Probably blushing a bit.

One of the students had smirked.

Bill, is there a degree course in ley lines now? Which university would that be at?

Jane wanting to deck the bastard, who was only about a year older than her, probably Eirion's age, and so grateful when Bill Blore immediately turned on him.

George, you are so fucking ignorant!

Bill said *fuck* a lot on TV, like Gordon Ramsey. Like it was part of his contract to get one in every couple of minutes. But the student still backed off, red-faced, going, *Sorry, Bill.*

And Blore had gone after him.

So you should be, George. And then, with a barely perceptible snigger clotting in his throat, he said, *Have you never* heard *of the University of Middle Earth?*

There was about half a trembling second of hollow silence ... before this explosion of laughter, probably shattering enough to distort the soundtrack.

Everyone, including Bill Blore, stepping away. Jane becoming aware that she was on her own, encircled by it. The laughter. Which had been hissing between her ears like some foul tinnitus ever since.

'The bastard,' Eirion said.

'And you know what was worst of all? Because it was him ... because it was Bill Blore who'd said it ... I was laughing, too.'

Laughing in desperation, through the tears gathering in her eyes, the way they were gathering now.

It hadn't even ended there. Bill Blore, still on camera, had given the students a short lecture about the danger of damaging the credibility of their profession by allowing the core disciplines of archaeology to be undermined by fashionable fads and the drivel spouted by gullible New Age cranks determined to prove spurious links between ancient civilisations and all kinds of *sad psychic shit.*

The last thing archaeology needed, Bill Blore said – glancing with this kind of cold *affection* at Jane – was a following of cranks ... however cute they might appear.

Remember that.

All the time, the other camera focusing implacably on Jane, like some gleaming evil eye, and there was nowhere to hide.

When it was over, and the cameras were switched off, Bill Blore had seemed so much more relaxed. Loosened up, smiling at people. Finally, moseying over to Jane, looking down benignly, squeezing her arm. *Well done, girlie.*

Patting her once on the shoulder before strolling away, followed by his entourage, like some high-powered surgeon in a crap hospital drama who'd just saved somebody's life against impossible odds.

Wicked stuff, Bill, the director guy had murmured, within Jane's hearing. *And all done in one take.*

Jane followed the lamp into the orchard. Still some old frost-rotted apples lying on the ground, winter rations for the blackbirds

'Girlie?' Eirion called after her. 'He called you *girlie?*'

Coops had been sympathetic, of course. He'd said Blore was a shit anyway, everybody knew that, and when you caught a shit on a bad day you just put it down to experience, wiped it out of your head. Coops just hadn't realised, and she hadn't even told him what she was now trying to explain to Eirion.

'This is going on TV, right?'

'Well, it … I mean *Trench One* …' Eirion shuffling about, trying to make it better. 'It hasn't got a really *big* audience.'

Even he hadn't quite put it together.

'But what it *has* got …' Jane's throat was parched '… is an audience of archaeologists? Almost certainly including professors of archaeology at, like, *universities*?'

'Oh,' Eirion said.

'Are they going to forget the gullible, airy-fairy, cranky girl who got lucky against all the rules? Ever?'

'They'll probably just … feel sorry for you,' Eirion said.

'Yeah, right, you put your finger on it there, Irene. They'll feel sorry for me.' Jane rocked back against a rotting stump. 'Are you *kidding*? They'll *despise* me. Totally. Terminally. I'm finished with archaeology before I even started.'

She was feeling physically sick. The humiliation would go on reverberating down a corridor as long as the rest of her life.

SUNDAY

The Atheist is a Prodigious miracle in
this world, a walking carcase in the
Land of the Living ...

Thomas Traherne
The Fourth Century.

34

Recovery Space

LIFE ALWAYS SPEEDED up before Christmas. Not yet dawn, but the top end of the secret bypass was already a red river of tail lights.

Bliss could remember when all this used to be country, but good flat land didn't stay green-belt for long. North-west of the city, a mesh of unexplained roads had appeared. No signposts, but what it amounted to was another unpublicised back way round the city, and housing had sprouted around it like pink fungi.

These were the more expensive properties, detached and set back from the road but still built too close together, with shared driveways. Bliss and the van parked round the corner.

As they walked up the drive, a landing light came on in a central upstairs window. Soft red walls, a glimmering in the bubble glass in the front door, and you knew all the radiators would be coming on, and those reassuring standby lights in the big, tidy kitchen.

Bliss thought of his own cold, messed-up kitchen, the heating clock he'd never had to master before. He wiped his mind, like with a wet cloth, and pulled himself into the situation.

Dawn raid. The *go go go* stuff. Coppers in face-shield headgear like international cricketers. The front door splintering under the enforcer. *Police! Police! Police!* Like the FBI without the weaponry.

Some part of Bliss would have quite liked all that. Meanwhile, in the real world …

Under his porch light, Mr Banks-Jones, up surprisingly early after last night's party over at Tupsley, was struggling with the Sunday papers, a too-thick bundle rammed into a too-thin letter box. Clearly unable to pull them through from the inside, he'd come out.

'Idiots. Nobody takes *any* care at all any more. Look at the way the *Observer*'s torn all the way—' He looked over his shoulder, exasperated, then quickly straightened up. 'Oh. I'm so sorry, I thought you were my neighbour.'

'West Mercia Police, sir,' Bliss said. 'Are you Gyles Banks-Jones?'

One of the uniforms was already round the back, on the off chance that Mrs Banks-Jones was on her way down a drainpipe with a carrier bag full of recreational drugs. Gyles stood there in the rain, in his dressing gown, a thin, studious-looking guy in early middle age.

'Oh, lord. I knew this would happen one day. But ... Christmas?'

'Life is unfair, Mr Jones,' Bliss said. 'All right if we pop inside?'

'Look ... I've got two young children.'

'Snap. DI Francis Bliss, my name, and this is DC Wintle, who attended the same party as you last night. Undercover.'

'How do you do. I, ah ...' Gyles Banks-Jones swallowed, moistened his lips. 'Any chance we can be civilised about this?'

It wasn't a lot, really. Bliss wasn't well-up on current street prices, but he reckoned no more than about six grand. Plastic bags in the velvet linings of jewel boxes stacked in Gyles's workshop extension, back of the house.

He'd showed them where to look, then had sat down next to his wife on the sofa downstairs. His kids had slept through it all.

Now, in the interview room. Gyles, gardening fleece over his denim shirt, was telling Bliss that while it wasn't all for personal use, he would certainly object very strongly to being called *a dealer*.

'If it's just for your friends,' Bliss said, George Wintle silent at his side, 'you seem to have quite a wide social circle.'

'Inspector Bliss,' the solicitor said, 'I believe my client has told you—'

'And I don't believe him, Mr Bilton,' Bliss said.

The solicitor looked about nineteen. Glasses, puppy fat, new briefcase and an earring. He'd materialised unusually rapidly for a Sunday morning; even so, Gyles Banks-Jones was in a fairly frayed state by then. As anyone would be, exposed to the smelly street-scrapings occupying the neighbouring cells two days short of Christmas.

'Mr Bliss,' Gyles said, 'I realise that the law of the land obliges you to regard me as a common criminal, but society—'

'Please do *not* give me *society*, Gyles. You can help me, or you can be difficult … with whatever effect that may have on the length of your sentence.'

'Now that's ridiculous. Do you think I'm naive? I watch the news, I read the papers. Nobody goes to prison these days for a first offence of … of this nature. The prisons are overcrowded. Everybody knows that.'

Gyles flashing an imploring glance at his solicitor, but the solicitor pretended he was searching for something in his case. Bliss – leaning back, hands behind his head – let the silence inflate like a breath-test kit, and then he yawned.

'Gyles. Little toe-rags from one-parent families, with only five convictions for TWOC and crack by the age of seventeen – *they* don't go to prison, on account of the System says we have to give them a chance to turn their little lives around. Respectable, middle-class, liberal-minded gentlemen with good incomes, however, who sadly fall from grace just the once …' Bliss dropped his hands, sat up hard. '*Bang!* That was your cell door, Gyles. I'd say five months.'

Enjoying this now. The day having totally turned around when they were leaving Gyles's place in daylight and he'd looked up at a window of the house across the double drive, and seen a face peering out.

Gyles looked at his solicitor, who clicked his case shut and set it down beside his chair.

'How do you collect the coke?' Bliss said.

'They … bring it to my shop. In cardboard boxes. Cardboard boxes I've given them. As if it's supplies from a wholesaler.'

Banks-Jones's had turned out to be the jewellers – oh, the irony of it – from whom they'd bought Kirsty's engagement ring. Gyles's dad had run the shop, back then.

'And when you say *they* …?'

No answer. For the first time, Bliss smelled fear. There was a particular person here that Gyles really did not want to finger. Someone who very much knew where he lived.

'How was it sourced, Gyles? Take me back. How'd you make the first contact?'

'I … I teach at the art college, one day a week. Jewellery. Someone I met there … I *can't*—' Gyles shook his head as though he'd just woken up. 'I can't do this. I have to *live* in this city. These people are not criminals.'

'Who aren't?'

'Certainly none of the people at last night's party. Or the person who introduced me to … to …'

'… To the real criminals?'

'We keep them at very much arm's length. None of us can be seen to … We're all either self-employed, with all the stress *that* involves these days, or with taxing jobs. We're not … *lowlife*. It's about relaxation, unwinding … *recovery* space.'

Bliss said, 'You're a twat, Gyles. You know that?'

'Do you know what some of these people are *like*?'

'Jes— Of *course* I know what these people are like. On which basis, I'd far rather put them away than you. So let's start again, shall we? Play your cards right, you could be home for Christmas dinner – which I'd guess tastes better from a nice plate rather than one of them tin trays with little compartments. So let's talk about the friends and neighbours whose senses you help to stimulate. Would that include the man next door, by any chance?'

'Why can't you just charge me and—?'

'Let you go round and warn everybody? Please, Gyles, don't insult my intelligence. You know what I'm after.'

'Look … I keep my distance. I don't try to get to know them. And if I'd known what sort of people they were, I would never have—'

'How *do* you know what sort of people they are?'

'I know where they live. Roughly.'

'Let me take a wild guess – the Plascarreg? Don't worry, I gather nobody can get out of there today, with the Belmont roundabout only open for canoes.'

'This is unbearable,' Gyles Banks-Jones said. 'This is an absolute nightmare.'

35

Paganus

Paganism was all over this church: glistening in the holly on the sills, glowing dully in the red apple held by Eve in a window that was more about orchard fertility than original sin.

Merrily paused, looking down into the central aisle, meeting nobody's eyes. She had some lights on, high in the rafters over the nave, and a couple of spots. *Say it.*

'Last week, I was virtually accused of being one.'

A pagan.

Better if there'd been more people to hear it, but the Sunday before Christmas you rarely got many in church. And it would get around – these things always did.

Secretly standing on a hassock, Merrily gripped the sides of a high Gothic pulpit that was too big for her. Never really liked the pulpit. A glorified play-fort.

She'd told them there were things that needed saying about Coleman's Meadow. What it meant for the village.

About thirty-five punters; could be worse with Sunday opening, all those last-minute presents to buy. Which reminded her, with a jolt, that she'd need to get over to Knights Frome to pick up the Boswell guitar. Could she fit that in before tonight's meditation?

No – *phew* – it was *OK*. No Sunday evening meditation this week; it was happening on Christmas Eve instead. Tomorrow. *God.* The medieval sandstone walls seemed to close together under the lights, crushing her like a moth.

She closed her eyes, drew a breath. The noise in the windows was like a battering of arrows. The relentless thuggery of the rain had awoken her well before the sky was diluted into daylight, so vicious you expected to find craters in the road. She raised her voice against it. 'Most of us will be aware of the archaeologists who started work yesterday. They could even be working this morning – I don't *think* I see any of them here.'

Just as well, perhaps.

Last night had been almost unprecedented. Jane looking cowed, hunted. Not even angry, just ... dulled and unreachable. From the moment they'd got back Eirion had kept looking at Merrily, his eyes clouded with worry, wide with mute appeal: *do something.*

In the end, Lol had created an opening, announcing he'd had an unexpected cheque from album sales in Germany. Enough to buy them all dinner at the Black Swan.

Jane had looked immediately panicked, said she was, like, really tired? Merrily, throwing Lol a glance, had said why didn't he and Eirion go to the Swan, talk music and stuff? Eirion having met Lol before he'd even known Jane, back when he was in a schoolboy rock band with the son of Lol's psychotherapist friend Dick Lyden. Merrily thinking that if she didn't get the full facts out of Jane, Lol would at least hear it from Eirion.

When they'd gone she'd built up the fire in the parlour, and they'd sat for two hours going over the implications.

'The bottom line,' Merrily told Lol on the phone, after midnight, 'is that this has virtually destroyed archaeology for her. It's something she's never going to forget – or be allowed to. And if you take away the possibility of some ancient magic in the distant past and all you're left with is ...'

'Bits of pottery and old bones,' Lol said. 'Not enough for Jane.'

'I can't believe he could do that to her.'

She'd been on the mobile in her bedroom, Eirion and Jane in their separate beds a floor apart. Presumably.

'She was in the way,' Lol said. 'He'd had a bad morning, and Jane was in the way.'

'And the dowser he threatened to impale on his own rods?'

'Just warming up. Jane tell you how relaxed he was afterwards, when he'd turned it around?'

'And that tells you what? As a psychotherapist.'

'Failed psychotherapist. It may, of course, be nothing to do with psychology, just cold professionalism. It's the *Trench One* format, isn't it, now? It's had to become one of those programmes founded on friction, confrontation.'

'Cruelty.'

'But the victims have to look like they deserve it. I'm guessing Blore had been encouraging Jane to get carried away with her own discovery, so she'd come over as a bit ... you know, precocious, full of herself. Get the audience on Blore's side before he ...'

'Takes her down?'

'With a beautifully timed joke. At the end of a sequence leaving him looking witty and sharp. Couldn't've been better with a script.'

'You think maybe there *was* a script?'

'Probably nothing that formal, but the way Eirion told it, it just struck me that the student had been set up as a feed. Obviously, you'd never prove that. And if you could ... so what? It's Blore's job.'

'To make an eighteen-year-old girl feel two feet high?'

'I had to stop Eirion going for him in the pub.'

'Blore was there?'

Merrily supposed that was why Jane hadn't wanted to go near the Swan.

'Mr Conviviality,' Lol said. 'Buying nearly as many drinks as he consumed. Eirion wanted to threaten him with bad publicity. It wouldn't've helped. Eirion's not a journalist yet. Blore would've swatted him like a wasp.'

'You think there's *anything* we can do to stop it going out?'

'Probably not by appealing to his sense of moral decency. He's not going to throw away five minutes of great telly.'

'No.'

The worst thing about this was that Jane would feel she couldn't go back to Coleman's Meadow as long as Blore and his crew were there. So she probably wouldn't see the stones raised. *Her* stones.

It had taken Merrily another hour and a half to get to sleep, and then the rain had awoken her twice before she'd given up, struggled into her robe and gone down to make tea before the dawn had arrived like industrial smoke, and the rain had *really* set in.

Enough of the congregation had been at the parish meeting and knew this already, but it bore repeating.

'Coleman's Meadow,' Merrily said, 'was already seen as quite a controversial issue because the archaeology could, if it was significant enough, prevent housing development in the village. But there are other possible housing sites, so that's not so vitally important.'

Except to the people who knew that only full development of Coleman's Meadow could swiftly open the way for the kind of serious, large-scale expansion that would very soon become unstoppable. A *lot* of money at stake here, and she was tempted to talk about that … but, although Lyndon Pierce wasn't here, it would get back to him. And his lawyers.

'The other reason for controversy is that what's being uncovered is a pagan site. Again, not *that* many people would see this as a problem.' Who, in fact, apart from Shirley West? She didn't look at Shirley in the corner of a pew halfway down the nave in her padded raincoat, but she could feel Shirley looking at her. A public figure now, the postmistress, status.

'But, because this is basically a religious issue, I suppose I should be the one to address it.'

Focusing on James Bull-Davies because he *wasn't* looking at her. James was in the old Bull family pew, an elbow on the prayer-book rack, head lowered into forked forefingers, listening. Two rows behind him, Jim and Brenda Prosser glanced at one another.

Merrily had called in at the shop just before eight, on the way to Holy Communion, and Jim had shown her the Sunday paper spreads.

ROAD-RAGE, *PAGAN*-STYLE.

The *Sunday Telegraph* was the only paper to connect the Dinedor Serpent with the Tara Hill row in Ireland, quoting the poet Seamus

Heaney and other luminaries on the way that determinedly secular governments, fuelled by fat bags of Euro-loot, were happy to lay tarmac over sacred ground.

In Hereford, the chairperson of the Save the Serpent group was quoted as saying, *They're cutting the ancient umbilical between Hereford and its mother hill.*

Lower down, a local landowner said, with some bitterness, *If this road was in danger of going through a mosque we'd be diverting it without a second thought.*

But had Clem Ayling actually been killed because of his ridiculing of the Serpent? The *Telegraph* feature writer, maintaining his distance and a healthy irony, had discovered a woman called Sara Starkey, described as a Wiccan High Priestess. Sara, whom Merrily had never encountered, hadn't held back.

The Serpent was sanctified to the Old Ones. I've walked there and, in a psychic state, seen ceremonies of night and fire. I've seen a torchlight procession led by Druid priests, clad all in white, moving slowly down the hill towards the river, where the moon's reflection swims, following the coils of the Serpent. I've felt the anger and the sorrow resounding down the ages, and I'm telling you that this road, if it goes ahead, will be subject to forces which no surveyor can control.

Already, one man has been badly injured felling trees on the site. On any road that goes through there, cars and lorries will go wildly out of control, and there'll be serious accidents. Drivers will be slamming on the brakes for human shapes that do not exist … in their world.

Merrily had smiled. Got that one right, then.

But it was interesting, the way the pagan aspect had been emphasised. You'd think nobody else cared. But even Jane's database suggested that the majority of the Coleman's Meadow protesters were people with no obvious spiritual affiliation, simply an interest in prehistory and heritage, and the Dinedor Serpent campaigners were likely to be even more orthodox. However, somebody – very probably Annie Howe, via the police press office – had inflated the religious angle. Hence yesterday's headlines about pagan nutters.

The *Telegraph* had a picture of Sara, a sharp-faced middle-aged woman with long straight hair standing on the earthen ramparts of Dinedor hill fort.

I'm speaking in sorrow, but from experience. When we ignore the spiritual traditions of the ancestors, in full awareness of what we are doing,
we deserve all we get. However, the idea that a Wiccan or a follower of
any other earth-related spiritual path would commit a murder is proof
only that the accusers know nothing of the pagan way.

Retribution they'd leave to the gods.

Before Lol and Eirion came back from the pub, Merrily had asked Jane about the worst the cops might find on the Coleman's Meadow database.

'Do you want *me* to tell the media that the police took away the computer? I'm prepared to do that. They haven't brought it back, have they?'

'No way,' Jane had said. 'That would just make you look like …' the kid had found the first and last smile of the night '… one of us.'

It wasn't going to be Stonehenge, Merrily said, but even a few modest standing stones re-erected after many centuries – so many centuries that they'd vanished from recorded history – would inevitably be a presence in the village.

'Even if they're not as high as me, we're looking at a significant ancient monument. So was this a *pagan* monument, buried because it had been seen as anti-Christian? Or because this was a nice flat field and the stones were getting in the way of somebody's plough? OK, let's deal with pagan. What do we *mean* by pagan?'

Quick sweep of the congregation. No significant reaction. Shirley West was no longer looking at her. Shirley was hunched, her head bowed, still as an obelisk.

'The dictionary tells us – just to be sure, I looked it up this morning

– that the word comes from the Latin, *paganus*, meaning a rustic or peasant. Meaning *ordinary people*. Like the people who lived here, in this community, before the time of Jesus. Pre-Christian. And what does *that* mean? Means they didn't have the benefit of having known about Jesus Christ, who introduced the human race to a new dimension of love, a new understanding of what love can mean. This was sophisticated stuff, and maybe their society wasn't ready for it.' Merrily stood on tiptoe on the hidden hassock, leaned over the battlements of the play-fort.

'But does that mean they were *bad* people who lived in darkness and sin, with no possibility of eternal life? I don't think so. I look at where these stones were positioned, possibly to catch the first rays of the midsummer sun when it rose over Cole Hill. These were people who had no doctrine to follow, no commandments. Only their feelings. And their feelings told them to reach for the light. And that's good enough for me.'

She looked across at the stained-glass window of Eve with the apple, still, unfortunately, brown and unlustred. Bloody rain.

'I'm not inclined to worry about pagans, past or present. They at least represent some kind of spirituality. The Bronze Age people were aware of higher forces, which they responded to. These were the people who first developed this community, then kept it going, fed it, tended livestock, planted the first orchards ... created what our old friend Lucy Devenish, taking her cue from the poet Thomas Traherne, used to call the Orb.'

She looked up at the apple shapes outlined in the filigree of the rood screen.

'What did Lucy mean by that? I think she was talking about the idea of Ledwardine as a living organism sustained by an energy and an intelligence beyond ours. Don't know about you, but I'd tend to call that *God*.'

Down at the bottom of the nave, the latch went up on the main door, with a clank, and rain swept in, bringing with it Gomer Parry in his old gabardine mac that was soaked through and tied at the waist with baler twine. Gomer shut the door behind him, took off his flat cap, drips falling onto the worn skull indented into the memorial stone of John Jenkyn, d. seventeen hundred and something. Gomer and the stone spotlit from above.

'All I know for certain,' Merrily said, 'is that *this* – this church – became and remains the centre of the Ledwardine orb. So I'd say let's do it. Let's raise the stones, because they're about the dawning of spirituality in Ledwardine – that first reaching for the light. I think they can only strengthen us.'

She looked down at the sermon pad, which she hadn't consulted once. She saw Shirley West stand up, as grey and still as the pillars.

'Can we sing number fourteen in your carol book. "In the Bleak Midwinter". *Softly wind made*—'

'You are *disgusting.*'

Shirley's forefinger quivering, before she turned and went scuttling down the aisle, pushing past Gomer to get to the door, and Edna Huws hit the opening chords.

Gomer shambled up the aisle as Merrily came down from the pulpit. They met at the bottom of the chancel steps.

'Quick word, vicar,' Gomer said under some ragged, nervy singing. 'Only I needs to get back, see.'

In the old days, the bells would have been rung.

Clanging down the valley, peeling through the rain, to be echoed by the bells of Weobley and Dilwyn and Pembridge and Eardisland. A chain of warning, ley lines of alarm spearing across the county.

Merrily went back into the pulpit. Let them finish. Stay calm. James Bull-Davies had seen Gomer. He was looking watchful, not singing. An Army man.

In the old days, the Bulls would have known what to do.

Shirley West's outburst … in a couple of minutes even that would be forgotten.

Merrily let the old carol soak away into the sandstone.

'Erm … something you should all know.'

There needed to be a prayer, but would anyone bother to stay for it?

36

Out

JANE STOOD NEAR the top of Church Street, on the edge of the cobbles, and watched him coming out.

There was this huge, almost peaceful sense of … relief? Beyond the amplified drumming of the rain on the hood of her parka, everything was awesomely silent.

An almost religious hush. A transformation.

It was as if he'd known this had always belonged to him and now, having repossessed it, was turning it into a different place: a drowned dreamscape, an alternative village, Ledwardine-on-Sea.

The village-hall car park was like a harbour, litter bins three-parts submerged like lobster pots. A couple of guys were dumping sandbags around the hall's entrance, Uncle Ted in fisherman's waders quietly directing operations, the swollen scene doused in shades of grey and brown.

Jane, at first, was stunned and then dismayed.

It had all happened within a couple of hours … on the first morning when self-pity had sapped her will to go down at first light and talk to the river.

Even last night with Eirion had just been an excuse to get out of the house; there'd been no contact. Guilt – it was ridiculous but it was there. She'd released something huge, by default. Broken off contact, and now he was out.

Like he'd come looking for her.

She said to Eirion, 'I suppose you've seen all this before?'

'Common enough in the Valleys, Jane.'

'Not here.'

OK, it wasn't exactly a tsunami, and the water hadn't reached any houses yet, and you could still just about see where the river ended and the flooding began. But it was scary. You could smell it, too, she was sure you could smell it. Something dank. The river had always looked clean; this wasn't.

No traffic noise – that explained the hush. No motorists attempting to leave the village, from the south anyway. Well, they couldn't. Across the street Lol had appeared in his doorway, casual, hands in the pockets of his jeans. Raising a hand to Jane and Eirion as an elderly guy Jane didn't recognise started bawling at him through the rain.

'Anybody informed the authorities?'

'Probably, but they could be overstretched,' Lol said. 'If it's happening here, it's happening all over the county.'

'But it's not *supposed* to happen here.' The man was struggling with an umbrella. 'We were formally assured it *never* happened here. We've come down for Christmas, brought everything … wine, turkey …'

One of the second-homers, who'd pushed up house prices. Jane's sympathy dissipating.

'How soon before it goes down again?' the man said, outraged. 'We can't afford to get stranded here.'

'Hard to say,' Lol told him, 'as it's never happened before. But as long as you can get to the bypass, you're—'

The rest of it was mangled under the grinding clatter and rumble of the first vehicle coming through the new Church Street pond, maybe the only one that could.

Jane went cold, thinking about what the man driving it had said the other night when they were on the bridge.

'Oh my God, Irene, I dreamed of the dead!'

'Well, that's you, Jane,' Eirion said. 'I wouldn't expect you to dream of soft green meadows and bunny rabbits.'

'A sign of rain.'

'What?'

'To dream of the dead is a sign of rain.'

'You needed *signs*?'

She'd dreamed of Lucy Devenish. Lucy standing by her own grave, her poncho torn and muddied, and when Jane had tried to talk to her Lucy had just looked right through her, towards the orchard, as if it was Jane who wasn't there. And in that moment of terrifying non-existence she'd awoken, desolate.

'It's like war's been declared.'

Eirion was pointing up towards the square, where people, including Mum in her black cape, were starting to gather near the market hall, a couple of women holding kids back.

'They've come out of church, that's all,' Jane said.

No voices trailed from the assembly. Eirion was right; this was what it must've been like when war was declared. They'd all known in their hearts that it was coming. And now the bell ringers were starting up, all bright and Merry Christmassy. Like the dance band on the *Titanic*. It should be a solemn *dong, dong, dong,* a warning toll wadded in cloud to freeze everybody into stillness and dread. Before they all turned as one, pointing down the street at Jane. *She did this. She let it happen.*

'Well …' Eirion looked up. 'This is going to curtail Blore's dig.'

'He'll probably just erect some huge marquee over the whole site.'

'You want to go and see?'

'*No!*'

'Be a good time,' Eirion said. 'There's nothing we can do here.'

'It's not my place any more. It's his. Blore's.'

'You don't think that. Not in a million years.'

'Doesn't matter what I think. I count for nothing. The sodding cops have got my database, Blore's got my … my future. Squashed in his big hand.'

'Oh, Jane, come on, let's not …'

'Not what?'

Eirion pushed back the hood of his yellow slicker, gripped her arms above the elbows.

'You can't, see. You bloody can't.'

'*What?*'

'Let it go. Abandon it. Even Lol said that. There's too much … emotional investment.'

'Like, wow,' Jane said sourly.

'When we did those pictures in the summer, you were just ... lit up. I was ...' Letting go of Jane's arms. 'I wanted to kick uni into touch, get a job as a gardener or something, just to keep on seeing you.'

He backed away, embarrassed now. She looked into his face, taut with adult anxieties and things he probably wasn't sure he was ready to handle. She didn't know what to say, shaken by his intensity and all churned up like the river man with whom she'd tried to fake a relationship.

Probably fortunate that Gwyneth came rattling alongside, her bucket pulled into her big yellow chest, GOMER PARRY PLANT HIRE in green on her flanks. Gomer leaning over to the open side of the cab, glasses gleaming.

'Takin' her up the square, Janey. Hold the high ground, see.'

'Your bungalow's not—?'

'No, no, but I en't takin' no chances with this ole girl.' Gomer beamed at Eirion. ''Ow're you, boy?'

'I'm OK, thanks, Gomer. And *you're* looking—'

'Good boy!'

Gomer raising a hand, Gwyneth clanking off towards the cobbles.

Eirion shaking his head, bemused.

'He looks kind of ... energised?'

'He is,' Jane said. 'Some people go on about him being too old to be doing what he does, but they won't be saying that now, because a JCB's about the only vehicle that can get through deep flood water. It's got the weight, and its exhaust pipe's really high up.'

And Gomer Parry had the only one in the village. Jane watched the JCB crawling onto the cobbles, Gomer jumping down like somebody thirty years younger.

'Helps to feel needed, doesn't it?'

'You think Coleman's Meadow doesn't need *you*, Jane?'

Jane said nothing.

'Who's it got left?'

'It's a field. That's all it is.'

'Come on. Please.'

'Why? What's the point?'

'It's like a pilot getting back into the cockpit after a crash.'

'I was never *in* the sodding cockpit.'

'You were. You found it. The whole set-up. You were led to it.'

'New Age bullshit, Irene. Pure accident. Even you don't believe it.'

'I'm not clever enough on this issue to know one way or another, but I believe in … well, in you, anyway. The you that gets excited about … Look, if we go halfway, I'll take a look first, OK? If the bastard's there I'll come back and we'll forget it.'

'Irene, I don't …'

'You *do*, Jane.'

Rain on his face making it look like he was in tears. The old Eirion, somehow.

'And Lucy Devenish is dead,' he said.

In a situation like this, Merrily thought, feudalism rose again. James Bull-Davies was too impoverished now to be much of a squire, but it was in his blood, and she was glad to see him taking control.

'Panic's premature – chances are it won't get much higher.'

James, in his holed and etiolated Barbour, talking on the square to a couple of migrant mulled-winos she didn't recognise.

'Only village hall in the firing line so far.' He looked around. 'Where's that bloody Pierce? Suggest he gets off his arse and onto his council. Uses whatever influence he's got to get us some technical assistance.'

'No chance o' that.' Gomer Parry took out his roll-up, cupped in his palm against the rain. 'Pierce don't give a monkey's for the hall getting flooded. He wants a new one, with squashy courts. Part of his master plan. Ole hall sinks, supermarket gets the site, Pierce fills his pockets. *You* know that, boy.'

'You may not be wrong, Gomer, but this is hardly the time for poli-tics.' James nodded at Gwyneth. 'That thing fully functional?'

'Wash your mouth out,' Gomer said.

Merrily smiled, pulled the bottom of her cape out of a puddle and stepped under the market hall.

'What can *I* do, James? How many people do you need at the village hall?'

'Can't do much there apart from sandbags. If they don't work and it floods … well, it floods. Least nobody lives there. Not much you can do for the present, vicar. Couple of us will take a look at the river, work out where we can either build up the bank or create a new barrier … and then rely on the expertise of our good friend Parry.'

'Well, just let me know.'

'Will do.'

She'd need to be prepared. If anyone was made temporarily homeless, there were spare bedrooms at the vicarage, just need to get more beds from somewhere. *And* she'd need to get over to Knights Frome and pick up the Boswell. Get across the county without a boat.

'Mrs Watkins?'

'Oh, I'm sorry …?'

She turned to find a woman standing next to her under the canopy of furrowed oak.

Fulsome red hair against turquoise Gore-Tex and a metal-framed case. *Oh God, not now.*

'My name's Leonora Winterson.'

'Oh … yes.'

'I think you met my husband?'

'Yes, I did.'

'Well.' Mrs Winterson gazed down Church Street. 'This is all looking a bit critical, isn't it?'

'Well, not exactly *critical* yet …'

'Nothing's safe any more, Mrs Watkins. Not even a place like this. All these people moving in looking for Olde England, and Olde England's getting washed away before their eyes. Soon be no more stable than Bangladesh, but I suppose we all have to grab what we can while we can. And I think I …' Stooke's wife pushed her hair back from her pale face '… need to grab *you.*'

'Me?'

Mrs Winterson pushed the strap of her camera bag higher up her shoulder, looking down at the cobbles, like smooth brown stones on the bed of a shallow stream.

'Is there somewhere private we could go?'

'Well, I need to be available, in case …'

'Yes, of course.'

'What about the church?' Merrily said.

Mrs Winterson almost laughed.

'Yes,' she said. 'Why not?'

37

Emperor of Unbelief

THE STONE EFFIGY wore the high-necked jacket of a puritan, had a sword unsheathed by his side. And that feature every tourist seemed to notice.

'Who is he?' Mrs Winterson asked. 'And why do his eyes appear to be open? That's not ... normal. Is it?'

Her own eyes were grey-green and quick with nervous energy. Merrily stepped down into the chapel.

'His name's Thomas Bull. One of the post-feudal lords of the manor who'd have to shell out periodically to stop this church falling down. You probably saw one of his descendants organising things on the square just now.'

'Oh, the ... bossy one. James?'

'A lot less wealthy than his ancestor. But a better man.'

'It's awfully gloomy in here,' Mrs Winterson said.

'But it *is* private.'

The Bull Chapel was one step down from the chancel, behind the organ pipes. It had one leaded window that looked frosty even in summer. 'And all mod cons.'

Merrily pulled two folding wooden chairs from a stack wedged between the tomb and the chapel wall. She opened them out. 'Not long after we moved here, someone told me that, when the tomb was sculpted, the eyes – as with most effigies – were shut. But, because of the iniquities he'd perpetrated in his lifetime, Tom Bull was unable to rest. One day, the vicar's wife walked in, looking for her husband, and the eyes were ... as they are now. It was said that particular vicar's wife never came in here again.'

'And you ... believe that, do you?'

'Well, no, my guess is that Tom Bull left instructions for the eyes to be left open so he could lie here for all eternity ogling visiting women. How can I help you, Mrs Winterson?'

Merrily sat down and gathered her cape across her knees, all prim and priestly. Mrs Winterson didn't join her.

'You're probably thinking I haven't chosen a particularly good time for this.'

'Well, the village is slowly flooding, and I'm sure there must be something I could be doing out there, but ...

'This really is a *horrible* place.'

Merrily nodded. It was, sometimes. Interesting that the atmosphere, which she'd always felt was distinctly unholy, should get to an atheist.

'Well,' she said, 'we *could*'ve gone to the vicarage. Only I didn't want to disturb Jane. She might be in the middle of a ritual to persuade the river god to turn back before the flood water reaches the grave of the high priestess, Lucy Devenish.'

Mrs Winterson stared for a long moment, exhaled a brittle laugh. Then she sat down opposite Merrily, unpopping her jacket.

'All right. Point taken. I listen to gossip. I *like* gossip, I'm a journalist, it's what I do. I'm sorry. I'm guessing you've had bad experiences with the media.'

'Not so far. But then, they usually make a direct approach.'

'I'm sorry. When I met your daughter, I ...' Mrs Winterson hooked an Ugg-booted foot around the strap of the camera bag, dragging it in front of her chair. 'What did my husband have to say?'

'He asked me a lot of questions.'

'It's not something you can easily turn off, professional curiosity. Besides, if you're looking for somewhere to settle, you like to know how the place works. And the people.'

'Yes, he *was* asking how I worked.'

'Look, if we've offended you, I'm sorry. Elliot can be ...'

A bank of rain washed against the leaded window and Merrily sensed the water rising, the sudden urgency of life and what a waste of energy it was, all this tap-dancing around the truth.

'Disingenuous?' she said.

'What are you saying, Mrs Watkins?'

'That's what you call him is it? Elliot?'

'It's what I've always called him.'

'You didn't *like* Mathew?'

Leonora made a small noise in her throat.

'Well,' she said, 'that's saved a bit of time.'

The site was isolated by the rain, Cole Hill mired in cloud. Couple of long tents and the two caravans. Puddles turning into pools, where they'd hit clay. And nobody around, thank God, except Gregory, the security guy, standing in the doorway of his caravan. Jack-the-lad in his bomber jacket, leather trousers, Doc Martens. The caravan behind him a big boom-box vibrating to a hip-hop stammer.

'What a shithole, eh?' Gregory said.

Jane could only agree. It looked no prettier than a building site. If Eirion thought she'd feel better seeing it like this, he was wrong. No connections were made. It wasn't hers, wouldn't be again.

'Last day for me, anyway,' Gregory said. 'I'm out of here tonight.'

'What, there's going to be no security over Christmas?'

'Not me, anyway. I'll be getting pissed with my mates. Will you miss me?'

Jane said nothing.

'He's a bastard, Blore, isn't he?'

'No, really?' Eirion said.

'This your boyfriend?'

'Eirion,' Jane said. 'Gregory.'

'Eirion? Wassat, Welsh?' Gregory stood back, gesturing inside. 'You guys wanna beer? On the house?'

Jane flashed *no* at Eirion.

'Why not?' Eirion didn't look at her. 'Thanks.'

Tight-lipped, Jane followed Gregory. Inside, it was surprisingly respectable, with a bed-settee and a car battery for the yellow and black DeWalt ghetto blaster. Gregory switched off the music, fetched three bottles of Budweiser lager from the kitchen area.

'They're all bastards.' He snapped off the bottle tops, dropped them in a waste bin, handed bottles to Jane and Eirion. 'The students, too. Think they own the place, wherever they are.'

'*All* students?' Eirion said.

'We done a few digs for Blore's outfit. He's a bastard, like I say, but he's straight. He's a straight bastard.' Gregory laughed. 'Look, don't stand around, girl, sit on the bed.'

'It'll get all wet.'

'It'll dry out. Students're a pain in the arse. All wannabe celebs ... like the professor. They come back wetting themselves laughing yesterday, after you and him ...' Gregory pointed his bottle at Jane. 'You were a gift, girl, that's what they were saying. Never do TV with the professor, I coulda told you that.'

Jane took off her parka, sat on the edge of the bed.

'What was *he* saying?'

'Blore? Nothing much, far's I know. TV – he despises it. He come in here, one night – not this job, one we done down the Forest of Dean – and the TV's on, and he just switches it off. Never watch it, he says. And I go, what, not even your own show? And he's like, that's the *last* fucking thing I'm gonna watch. Comes in here quite often, stretches himself out on the bed, where you are, and we have a couple of beers.'

Yeah, Jane thought, he'd do that. Hang out with his security guy to get away from people who wanted to show him their bit of Roman pottery.

'Anybody wants to be on TV, they deserve all they get. Easy meat. We done this one in the Cotswolds last year and Blore's doing a bit of a recce of the site – jeans, jacket covered with badges. Along comes this old colonel type, cravat, bristly moustache, shooting stick, face like a beetroot.' Gregory extended his neck, nose in the air, did the gruff and grumpy. 'Devil's going on here? Don't you know there's going to be an important archaeological dig on this site? You have any idea how much damage is done by you bloody treasure-hunters with your damned metal detectors?'

'I think I saw this one,' Eirion said. 'Blore keeps quiet, playing him along with expressions of dumb insolence. Winding him up, before completely paralysing the poor old boy with a lecture on the history and the potential of the site, with chronological references to every excavation there since about 1936.'

'And then, as the Colonel's walking away, he goes ...'

'*Didn't you used to be in* Dad's *fucking* Army?' Eirion smiled. 'I could never figure how the old boy didn't see the cameraman.'

'Back of the van,' Gregory said. 'Little peephole in the side. They often do it. Then they invite the old guy for a drink, all have a good laugh and he's more than happy for them to use it. Signs the form, no problem. People will take any shit from TV. That's what Blore says.'

'He doesn't *care* what he does to people?' Eirion said.

''Cause it ain't *real*, mate. It's TV. Whoosh, gone. And you pick up the money and on to the next one. It *ain't real.*'

'It is for the viewers.' Jane sat up, both hands around her beer. 'For some people, he's the only thing they know about archaeology.'

'That's their problem.'

'He's right, I suppose.' Eirion said. 'TV's been degraded. Too many channels, it is. Instead of variety, it all goes into a cheap mush. *Trench One* – you used to think quality, but they all go the same way. People interested in archaeology, that's just a minority audience. There's a much bigger one for like ...'

'People getting made to look small,' Jane said.

'*He* don't do it,' Gregory said, 'some other bastard will and he'll be out on his arse. I could show you half a dozen guys here who'd have his job, no messing, if he starts to go soft. Walk over his corpse.'

'That's scary.' Jane drank some lager. She didn't really like lager, but she didn't want to look like a girl. 'I mean, if—'

'It's survival, darlin'.'

'But if the only way you can get on in archaeology is to, like, become a bastard on TV—'

'It's not the *only* way.' Gregory grinned. 'You seen the big caravan over there? Bigger than this, anyway. That's his. Blore's.'

'He sleeps here? I thought he had a room in the Black Swan.'

'It's not for *sleeping* in, my love. King-size folding bed?' Gregory spread his hands. 'I got some spare keys, if you wanna look.'

'Well,' Eirion said, 'that would be—'

'We'd rather *not*,' Jane said firmly.

'Like I say,' Gregory said, 'I've done security on a few of these gigs now. Shagfest, or what?'

'Bill Blore ... and his students?'

'Well, not all of them, obviously,' Gregory said. 'Not the *blokes*.'

Out, then. That wasn't so hard, was it?

Leonora Winterson had relaxed into her seat as if a weight had been lifted from her body. Her turquoise coat was hanging open; underneath she wore a white sweater with a deep neckline, and the tops of her breasts were tanning-salon brown.

'No way he was going to hide,' she said.

'The police actually wanted you to adopt a new identity?'

'For a while. The traditional book-burning by red-neck morons in the US Bible Belt, that's part of the package. Islam, however ...'

'*The religious are as cringe-makingly predictable as the doctrines they follow.*'

'My God, you've read the book?'

'Dipped into it. There was a Muslim threat?'

'Wasn't a *fatwa* or anything, just mutterings by a couple of crazy imams, but the police and the security services have been very nervy since 7/7. But, you see, he's a journalist. We don't *hide*. And if you can't stand up for what you believe in, it makes a mockery of the book.'

'So this is a compromise.'

'Only because we don't want people on our back all the time. He's become a kind of anti-guru, so you get the *disciples*. Almost worse than the religious bigots, for whom just knowing he's around is enough to provoke a need to confront him. As if, by not doing it, they're betraying their faith?'

'Really no accounting for some of these people,' Merrily said.

'Hates being recognised, anyway. Hates the thought of becoming a *personality*. Hid behind that beard for a while and now people have that rather messianic image of him he's got rid of it. The weight – that was an exaggeration anyway. People with big beards always look heavier.'

'So … the Wintersons.'

'His mother's maiden name. Now you know.' Leonora paused. 'Jane, huh?'

'Easy to underestimate Jane.'

'You're not going to out us, are you?'

'That would be unchristian.'

Leonora smiled briefly, stood up and walked over to the tomb, making eye contact with Tom Bull.

'Bizarre. First person in this village I get to talk to without having to watch what I say, and it's the vicar in the bloody church. A vicar and a dead lech.'

'Some irony here that escapes me?'

'I'm from a solid Church family.'

'Ah.'

'Went to Church schools, all the bullshit that goes with that. Why are you nodding?'

'Your reaction to being in here was … somehow, not the reaction of a lifelong atheist.'

'Do *not* …' Lensi levelled a finger '… get too clever.'

Merrily smiled.

'My father worked for the diocese, in an administrative role. My mother was a Sunday School teacher. Not many of those left, even then. Village in Buckinghamshire, not *so* unlike this one. My old man became increasingly, insufferably devout. Anglo-Catholic. Hounding the local vicar into installing a statue of the Virgin. Then finally, in middle age, he was ordained himself, and it all became *seriously* stifling. I used to walk around our church, as an adolescent, muttering obscenities, just for the thrill of the guilt, the almost erotic joy of blasphemy.'

'You're trying to shock me?'

'Hell, no.' In the ice-white light, Leonora's skin looked thin, almost translucent. 'I've met a lot of priests. They don't shock. They simply become lofty and disapproving.'

'But you *were* trying to shock your parents.'

'You wouldn't believe how many honourable God-fearing, High Church public-school boys were around, even fifteen years ago, and I must've been introduced to every one of the genuflecting tossers. Which is why I threw myself at Elliot. Good-looking, ten years older than me. Worldly, married, and a bloody atheist. My *God*.'

'When was this?'

'When I was still at university. London. He was a reporter with the *Guardian* then. I was always attracted to the media, but I didn't particularly want to start off on some provincial rag, so I used to hang around their pubs. He was married but I made myself … you know, hard to resist. Don't ask.'

'You threw yourself at a religious-affairs correspondent?'

'Well, he wasn't, then. Just a general news reporter. That came later, when their religious-affairs guy was off sick and they asked Elliot to stand in. *Guardian* reporters get a fair bit of leeway on how they handle a story, and Elliot … well, you can imagine. Good writer, very funny … and *Guardian* readers are liberal, and liberals tend to be atheist …'

'Not invariably.'

'Well, a higher proportion of them are. You must know that's true. Anyway, shortly after that, he was poached by the *Independent*.'

'And of course the *Independent* doesn't exactly *do* religion, does it? Or at least not from the normal perspective.'

'If the Indy was going to have a religious-affairs correspondent it had to be an atheist, yeah.'

'I can see the logic.'

'Still a while before people started to get the joke. And even then, it's not the biggest-selling paper on the rack. It was quite funny – my parents, when they found out what he did, they actually thought I was coming to my senses at last.'

'When *did* they find out?'

'About the same time as the Archbishop of Canterbury's office, I'd guess. Filtered down, and then the doors started closing. The religious establishments build high walls very quickly. Centuries of practice. By the time it was common knowledge where he was coming from, the damage was done, they'd all been on the end of Elliot's harpoon. Unfortunately, by that time my father was too old for it to be much fun any more. I never actually threw it in their faces – hey, I'm marrying the

Emperor of Unbelief, suck on *that* – but we … haven't spoken for some time. Not since the book appeared, anyway.'

'The book, I suppose, being inevitable.'

'It was – looking back – very much the only way to go. An aggressively atheist religious-affairs correspondent was always going to have a limited lifespan.'

Merrily said nothing for a while, beginning, at last, to see where the Stookes were coming from.

The Emperor of Unbelief. The awful banality of it flagged up against the flaky, fake piety of the Bull Chapel.

38

Wounded Bird

Outside, Eirion, naturally, had to ask.

'So did he …?'

'*No!*'

'No, I wasn't suggesting he actually— I mean, he never even made, like … an overture?'

'He's an archaeologist, not a bloody composer. And two days ago I'd never even met him.'

The rain was mist-thin, clinging to Jane's face like cold sweat as they walked away from Gregory's caravan through coils of chilled mud they couldn't avoid.

'I suppose if he …' Eirion took Jane's cold hand. 'I suppose he'd leave you alone if he had you lined up from the start as a sacrifice to the god of TV ratings. I mean, personally, I cannot imagine anyone who would *not* want to—'

'What *is* this? Let's stop Jane from slashing her wrists before Christmas? Look, it's clear that, if you're a woman, with Blore you're going to get stuffed one way or the other.'

Jane looked back at the excavation. Somewhere a bird was chirping, but Coleman's Meadow was unrecognisable as the place where, on a golden morning in high summer, Eirion had photographed her cupping the sun.

'It's dead, Irene.'

'Just the way it looks now, work in progress.'

'No, something's gone. I don't want to remember it like this.' Jane zipped her parka. 'Let's get out of here.'

'I can't get anything right today, can I?' Eirion said.

'It's not *you*, it—'

Down on the edge of meadow a car door slammed.

Someone called out through the murk.

'*Jane!*'

Neil Cooper was waiting for them down near the wicket gate, where his car and a white van, probably Gregory's, were parked. The ghost of Cole Hill was embossed on the clouds like a pale bell on a minimalist wedding card.

'I'm sorry, Jane – about what happened, I really am. I wasn't able to say much yesterday, and I didn't like to phone you at home.'

He looked older. He hadn't shaved. He wore a patched camouflage jacket and a woolly hat. He was drenched, his jeans dark with damp, like he'd been walking through high undergrowth.

'Not as if you didn't warn me, Coops,' Jane said.

'For what it's worth, if somebody'd warned *me*, I wouldn't've taken any notice either. Is this ...?'

'Eirion Lewis,' Eirion said.

He put out his hand. Coops nodded, shook it limply. Jane thinking the way he was looking today, Eirion would have no reason at all to feel threatened. Pity about that.

'You didn't come here on a wet Sunday to look for *me*,' she said.

'Weather's lousy, half the county's under water, and Blore's in the pub. I just wanted to ...'

He was worried about something. Possibly even upset, and it wasn't about what had happened to *her*. She had a sense of *parting*, the end of something for him, too, and she shivered in the damp, airless drabness of everything.

'Main reason,' Coops said, 'is we've arranged to go away for Christmas, to my wife's parents in Somerset.' He gestured with his head towards the meadow. 'Blore'll be carrying on, with a skeleton crew. He doesn't seem to observe Christmas. This is the last chance I'll get this year to try and see what's going on.'

'But you're in charge, aren't you? You're the county guy ... the employer.'

'That's no longer the way it operates, Jane.'

Coops gave Eirion a sideways look.

'Forget everything you've heard about the Welsh,' Jane said. 'He's absolutely to be relied on.'

'I can die happy now, I can,' Eirion said. 'I am no longer a symbol of the ludicrous English preconceptions about my race.'

Coops smiled faintly, then looked away across the site towards the grey swelling that was all that remained of Cole Hill. He bit his upper lip.

'As the Council – or rather the Council *Cabinet* – are into farming out as much as possible to the private sector, the truth is that half the time we're not quite sure *who* we're supposed to be working for.'

'The council-tax payers? The people?'

'Don't make me laugh. Decisions get made over your head, you don't even know who's made them or why. I ... probably need to get out of this area next year, get a job somewhere else.' He pulled off his hat, wiped his face on the lining. 'You going away for Christmas?'

'Coops, my mother's the vicar. This is the time of year when they do big box-office? So if there's anything you need me to do ...'

He shook his head.

'Hey, it's not as if I've got anything to lose. I'll be looking for a new ... career path or something, in the New Year.'

'No! Jane, listen to me, this is was what I was afraid of. You must *not* let that bastard ruin your life, do you understand? This job needs people like you.'

'Loonies?'

'People who care. People who ... love everything here that's ancient and mysterious, even if it isn't spectacular ... even if it isn't visible. In fact, there's a report coming out from English Heritage next year that will suggest that, the way we're going, less than ten per cent of the ancient monuments we can see *now* will be visible for future genera- tions. No decent money available for conservation, developers ripping up the countryside. We need people who can get angry about that.'

'Blore gets angry.'

'He also gets rich. Easy enough to get angry over lost causes like the

Serpent.' Coops wiped his forehead again with his hat, put it back on. 'I'm probably a bit overwrought, Jane. Couldn't sleep last night, which is not like me.'

'Coops, could you just, like, spit this out?'

'Not that easy. I don't really know what I'm getting at.' He walked away, up the path towards the orchard, as if the site might be bugged. 'OK ... I don't have many friends in the Chief Executive's department. In fact just the one, and no more than a lowly secretary to an assistant, but she ... happened to be in the right place at the right time to notice that someone in that department had received a report. About this dig.'

'From who?' Eirion said.

'Not from us, that's the point.'

'From Blore?'

'It's a report which, in the normal way of things, might have been expected to go to my boss.'

Eirion said, 'Blore is reporting directly to the Chief Executive of the Council? About Coleman's Meadow?'

'Blore was very proprietorial about this excavation from the start. Did all the geophysics personally, with ground radar, and he was working here before any of us even knew he had the contract.'

'And what does that suggest?' Eirion said.

'Well, obviously, it's a prestigious excavation. And it's exciting. We don't often find unknown standing stones, and whatever happens it'll make for some fantastic television. Now, it might *only* be that, or it might be ... he's found something we didn't expect.'

'Like what?' Jane said.

'Well, I don't know, do I? Whatever it is he's— Obvious he'll want to keep it to himself, especially if it could provide an eye-popping climax to his programme. If he *has* got something, he'll let it out no more than a week before the programme goes out, for maximum publicity.'

'Yes.' Eirion nodded. 'That's how it's done.'

'What could it be, Coops?'

'I'm not sure. At the end of the day, he might be a shit but he's a bloody good archaeologist. I've just spent a couple of hours walking round the place, trying to second-guess him, but he covers his tracks.

He had one stone more or less unearthed, the whole thing, but now the soil's gone back, or most of it. As if there's something he doesn't want anyone else to see.'

'Couldn't that just be because of the danger of flood damage?' Eirion said.

'Sure, but …'

'What can we do?' Jane said.

'Nothing.'

'No, I mean, what can *we* do – me and Eirion? We've really got nothing to lose, Coops. We can watch him. We can watch what he does, where he goes.'

'No. I don't want you going *near* him, Jane. I'm serious. He's done enough to you already, but if he really takes offence he can script his programme in a way that will make you look even worse.'

'We don't have to make it obvious. What are we looking for?'

'God … I don't know.' Coops ran a hand over the stubble on his jaw. 'Anything unexpected. Say, for instance, if he suddenly starts to extend the site. In any direction.'

'What would that mean?'

'Well, it … it could mean, obviously, that there's more here than we thought. Originally, as you know, we were thinking in terms of a shortish stone-row, like Harold's Stones at Trelleck. The original geophys suggested three stones, possibly a fourth, fairly randomly arranged, no identifiable pattern and not too far under the surface. But Blore's done his own survey and, although I haven't seen the results, I wouldn't rule out something more extensive.'

'A stone circle?'

'Too early to speculate with any authority.'

'But this excavation,' Jane said. 'You're saying this could be just the beginning of something huge. I mean, like the Serpent? As important as that?'

'Please, Jane …' Coops wiped some dampness from his forehead with his sleeve. 'I wish I'd never …'

'I won't go near him. I'll be very careful.'

Eirion said, 'Jane, I don't think—'

'*We*'ll be very careful. Coops, do you have a number where I can contact you? I know you'll be back after Christmas and everything, and Blore's not going to have *that* much—?'

'No,' Coops said. 'You don't understand, I *won't* be here after Christmas. Not officially, anyway. We've been told to stay out of it. Get on with other things. Leave it to Blore.'

He looked gutted.

'So whatever he finds,' Jane said, 'he gets all the credit?'

'That's ... yes. He gets the credit. And the money. Look ... you've got my mobile number. I'll keep it charged. Just don't get carried away. I could be totally wrong. I don't want to look like a complete idiot. I'm a professional, not a visionary.'

'Yeah, well,' Jane said, 'it looks like I'll never be a professional, but nobody can stop me being the other thing.'

She felt her smile go crooked. She felt a small release, her soul stirring like a wounded bird among the dead leaves.

It had started to rain.

It had probably never stopped.

39

Martyr

'WHAT CAN I say?' Merrily said. 'He seemed a nice man. I confess I didn't expect that.'

The rain fizzed in the chapel window. Leonora Stooke looked amused.

'An atheist can't be a nice man?'

'His book is aggressive, disdainful, derisive ...'

'And funny?'

'Occasionally.'

'He's a good writer,' Leonora said. 'A good writer can write anything. You understand that, don't you?'

'I think the one word we're walking all around here,' Merrily said, 'is *hack*. He did it for the money and the need to cash in on his brief notoriety. Recycle all the dirt he'd gathered, plus a few scurrilous anecdotes he might not have been able to use in the paper. Put it all together, cement with vitriol. Get it out before his star vanished from the ... journalistic firmament.'

The Hole in the Sky.

'You feel better now?' Leonora said.

She was playing absently with Tom Bull's fingers. The poor old sod must be squirming in sexual anguish.

'Yeah. I do, actually.'

Merrily felt angry at Stooke, angry at the Lord of the Light website. Above all, angry at herself, and yet ...

'All books are written for money,' Leonora said. 'Quite an auction for this one. More populist than Dawkins, more outrageous and no screeds of tedious Darwin-idolatry – I'm quoting one of the reviews. It was still a gamble, though. He needed to quit the paper first. Outside of daily journalism, he could drop any pretence of editorial balance.'

'I see.'

'And I have to tell you, Merrily, he is *so* tired of it now. Doesn't want to write another word about religion, one way or the other. Out of his system. Only you don't get away that easily. The publishers want another, and there's a *frightening* pile of money on the table.'

'But the cupboard's bare, right? No more interviews with archbishops and cardinals. No more Dalai Lama.'

'There's the diary of the period post-*Hole*. All the lunacy it spawned.'

'*My life as the Devil's spin doctor?*'

Leonora sighed.

'He even thought of joining one of these fundamentalist sects, dissect it from the inside. Not as if they'd recognise him. But it would just be *too* tedious. And they always turn out to be far less sinister than their websites, don't they? Sad, inadequate little people in search of some kind of imaginary – look, you know the truth about that 666 thing? He didn't *change* the spelling of his first name. His father simply registered his birth in a hurry and didn't realise there were supposed to be two Ts in Matthew. And then they rather liked it. It's that simple.'

'This is the most disappointing day of my life, Leonora. Most people in my profession would give up two years' stipend to come face to face with the man who handles the Antichrist's publicity.'

'I'm very sorry.'

'Still needs new material, though, doesn't he? Might even have to fall back on the story of how he wound up in a crazy village with a priest who doubles as diocesan exorcist while her daughter follows ley lines and worships old gods.'

A silence.

'Don't tell me we weren't earmarked for Chapter 14, Leonora. He was questioning me far too thoroughly.'

'It's the way he is. He collects people. Can't resist it. Professional curiosity.'

'And then there was you and my daughter. At Lucy's grave. *Oh, what sort of pagan are you, Jane?*'

Leonora racked up a smile that was rueful but perhaps not rueful enough.

'You're quite a nice story, you and Jane.'

'It's been done.'

'Only skirted around – I've seen the cuttings. Look, Merrily, you may be right, Elliot will have you in his scrapbook, you and Jane – awfully photogenic, the pair of you. He's an opportunist, seldom wastes anything.'

'Well, thank you for putting my mind at rest.'

'But he isn't going to repay a favour by shafting you.'

Merrily leaned back, listening to the rain hissing and crackling like a fat-frier in a chip shop.

'A favour.'

'Yes.'

'I was beginning to think we'd never get here.'

'We have a problem,' Leonora said. 'Essentially, you're not the only one who knows we're in the village.'

'Oh.'

'It's stupid, but it's causing us a lot of tension. The ravings of anonymous fundamentalist zealots, as I say, part of the package, all grist to the publicity mill, but this is too close.'

'And, erm … why are you telling me?'

'Because it's a member of your church.'

'Am I allowed to ask?'

Leonora leaned back against Tom Bull, so that she was almost sitting on his face. Maybe the significance escaped her, probably it didn't.

'It's the postmistress.'

'Oh.'

'Arguably the worst of all possible scenarios.'

'Mmm. You *have* got a problem, haven't you?'

The day was growing dim. Wrapped in her sodden cape, Merrily stood on the edge of the square and watched reflections of the yellow lights in ancient houses trembling in the flood. No curtains were drawn. If it was coming for them, the residents wanted to know.

And she couldn't lose the feeling, as James Bull-Davies loped through the lashing rain, that the village had changed for ever, lost its nerve, its confident sheen. The old timbered buildings seemed to be leaning closer together, as nightfall turned black and white into grey and white and the dismal rain kept on, and there were no lights in Lucy's old house.

'James, have you seen Lol?'

'Last I saw of him, out working with Parry.' James followed her into the shelter of the market hall. They stood by an oak pillar, looking towards the water. 'Ken Williams, who owns that strip west of the village hall, agreed for Parry to go on his land with the digger, build up the bank. Might save the bottom end of the riverside estate.'

'Save it? You mean—?'

'Well, not yet. Water's a foot deep in some gardens, though. So probably only a matter of time.'

The impact of the continuing rain made the bottom of Church Street look like a choppy sea.

'So if it keeps on raining …?'

James leaned forward, hands linked behind his back, his face long.

'Then we're probably looking at evacuation.'

Merrily looked up in alarm from under the rain-heavy hood of her cape.

'Do people know that?'

'Tentatively suggested to a few families on the estate that they should think about moving valued items of furniture upstairs. Naturally, they're resistant to the idea. As if Christmas confers some sort of immunity, as if nature can't wreak havoc because it's *Christmas*. Gord! Like the blessed river's going to wait till they've finished stuffing their faces.'

'What can *I* do? We have spare bedrooms at the vicarage.'

'Hell, Merrily, don't go broadcasting *that*. We'll be suggesting people find relatives they can stay with, outside the village.'

'Leave the village?'

'Don't like saying it, and some of them don't like hearing it from the likes of me, but what's the alternative? Council's got problems all over the county, some worse than this. Question of priorities. Planning bods're going to get some stick when this is over about allowing new housing on the flood plain, but that's happening everywhere.'

'But what can we do now? What can *I* do?'

'Do? Do nothing. Save your accommodation for emergencies, any people left homeless in the night. Meanwhile, go about life as normal, hope the rain stops, level goes down.'

'And pray.'

'Only try not to do it in the street.' James puffed out his lips. 'Be expedient to lock that bloody woman in a cellar somewhere until all this is over.'

'Shirley West?'

Not a subject she'd raised with anyone before, but it was probably necessary now.

'Much wailing and wringing of hands whenever she can find an audience. Beginning of the end, sort of thing. Great flood come to wash away our sins. Or more specifically, Merrily, *your* sins. Not the best time, I'd have to say, to have unleashed that particular sermon.'

'It needed saying, James.'

'No, it *didn't*.' James shaking his head as if in pain. 'Nobody *cares*, Merrily. Nobody gives a fig about the spirituality or otherwise of whichever bloody savages erected the damn stones in Coleman's Meadow. Nobody apart from you ... and *her*. Truth is, possibly because of your other ... hat, you're dwelling on issues beyond normal people's need-to-know. I'm sorry, but that's how it looked to me.'

'Oh.'

'I'm sorry.'

'No. No, you're right. I overreacted. It's ridiculous. One woman out of a whole village. But she does worry me. Couple of months ago never out of church, full of this slightly suspect humility, but humility none the less, and now ...'

'Hmph.'

'What?'

'Ah.' James shuffled his feet on the cobbles. 'Alison was in Leominster yesterday. Found the place littered with flyers for this Church of the Holy Light?'

'Church of the Lord of the Light. Shirley's other church.'

'That's the crew. Born-again johnnies. Gather in a former warehouse on the industrial estate. Odd set of buggers. Members forbidden to use the health food shop. Beyond me. However, something you should know, if you don't already ... seems to be an offshoot of that revivalist thing that mushroomed in the Radnor Valley, couple of years ago.'

'Ellis?' Merrily spun away from the oak pillar, her hood falling away. 'Nick Ellis is *back*?'

'Gord, no. Calm down. I said an *offshoot*. Can't see that fellow showing his face around here again, ever. Well, actually, you can ... there are pictures of him in his white robes plastered all over the town.'

'I've not been in Leominster for a couple of weeks. God, James ...'

Father Ellis. The hysteria, the speaking-in-tongues, the *internal ministry* for women possessed by the demon of lust. All the charges that ought to have been hung on Ellis, including sexual assault, criminal damage, and he'd got away with it.

'Lord of the Light – he was part of a charismatic Anglican fringe movement called Sea of Light. Became too extreme for them. Last I heard he was in America.'

Merrily felt damp inside, with apprehension. Remembered there'd been a lot of rain when Ellis was dominating his congregation in the hill village of Old Hindwell.

'I was fully prepared to testify, James, but nobody else was willing to, and the Crown Prosecution Service threw it out. As they do.'

'Well ... something of a martyr now, apparently. Hounded out of his own country.'

'A *martyr*? The bastard got off without a ... wasn't even charged. And this is after I actually made a statement saying I'd seen him insert a crucifix into—'

'Yes, quite.' James backed off, palms raised. 'All I'm saying, if there are lunatics going around claiming Ellis was falsely accused, pointing fingers in your direction, might well explain the change in West's attitude towards you.'

'Might, yes. Thank you.'

The last explanation of Shirley West had come from Siân Callaghan-

Clarke, standing in while Merrily was away for a few days. Siân discovering that Shirley had become committed to a rigid form of self-cleansing after learning that her husband – now ex – had been a distant cousin of the Herefordshire-born mass-murderer Fred West. Hanging on to the name, in penance.

'James, if they're in contact with Ellis himself …?'

'Internet.'

'Mmm. Makes it all too easy.'

'Especially if the chap wants to keep the lid on his whereabouts.' James sniffed. 'Never liked fanatics who set up churches in sheds. Seen soldiers turn from perfectly serviceable fighting chaps to Bible-punching lunatics after one week's leave.'

Merrily fell silent, thinking of the website, *Thelordofthelight.com*. How she'd said to Lol, in all innocence, *Maybe coming in from America*.

'Watch your back, vicar, that's all I'm saying. This climate-change business … sometimes think even people's brains are getting over-heated. Avoid her. Anyway, need to be orf. Rain's not going to stop anytime soon.'

'Avoiding her could be … a bit difficult.' Merrily slipped between the oak pillars, pulling her hood back up. 'Better make a run for it.'

40

Moral Void

BACK IN THE vicarage, Merrily went directly through to the scullery, hanging her soaking cape behind the door and sitting down at the desk in front of the black Bakelite phone. She took a breath, let it out slowly, then dialled Huw Owen's number in the Brecon Beacons.

Engaged. She'd wait. This was potentially political. Not a good idea to take it any further without advice from her spiritual director.

She made some tea, picked up *The Hole in the Sky*. Opened the cover, held it up to the window and peered through the hole. All the way to hell?

nothing ... what did you expect?

It made a lot more sense now. Merrily started on page one, twenty minutes of fast-flipping taking her through the entire book.

'God' telling the Yorkshire Ripper to kill fallen women and advising George W. Bush to take Iraq. The Spanish Inquisition, the sectarian horrors in Northern Ireland, all the bloodied roads to 9/11.

Nothing new – how could there be? Not even Stooke's delight in old-fashioned blasphemy. Giving God a good kicking with steel toecaps, trampling on taboos. The Christian God and Jesus Christ, as was the custom in this country, getting a bigger kicking than Allah and *The Prophet Mo*, as Stooke called him with something close to a condescending affection. Apart from the recycled interviews with unsuspecting religious leaders – Rowan Williams was a good one – there was little here not already covered by Dawkins and Christopher Hitchens, a more distinguished hack than Stooke.

The relishing of blasphemy ... when you thought about it, that seemed more characteristic of Leonora than Stooke himself who seemed to have no personal axe to grind against the Church.

She turned to the final chapter.

<u>Predictions? Hardly.</u>

... within fifty years, cathedrals will be art galleries, theatres and concert halls, churches quaint medieval grottoes available for secular weddings and civil partnerships.

The clergy? What remains of it will be unpaid. Little pretence that it's promoting anything more than the first pulp fiction.

The Church of England? Now, what on earth will be remembered of that beyond its origins in the need to legitimise a fat king's leg-over? Future historians will struggle to explain how it managed to go on for so long, flabby with hypocrisy and conceit ...

Merrily dialled Huw's number again. This time it was the machine. Well, it was Sunday and he had a bunch of isolated churches.

'*I'm not in. If it's owt important you'd best leave a message.*'

'Huw, it's me,' Merrily said. 'I have a problem.'

She put the phone down and before she could take her hand away, it rang.

'Gorra favour to ask, Merrily.'

'Frannie. A favour. That's not like you.'

'Ho ho. Listen, that nursing sister at the hospital, your mate, what was her name? Belfast woman, indiscreet.'

'I'd be more inclined to see her as a woman of conscience with a fairly flexible loyalty to the Hereford health authority. Eileen Cullen.'

'Could you get her to find out something for me? Nothing contentious. Just I don't want to be connected with it.'

'But it's OK if I'm connected with it?'

'Nothing *contentious*, Merrily.'

'Your drug thing pan out?'

'Better than expected, as it happens. Yes, indeed. I just need a bit of information that your friend should be able to provide very quickly.'

'You're not going to tell me, are you?'

Silence.

'All right, I'll tell you what I'll do. I'll try and get hold of Eileen Cullen, explain what an essentially decent person you are, underneath, and give her your number. That way you can tell her what you want and she can decide if it agrees with her conscience '

Bliss thought about it. Merrily could hear traffic noise.

'All right,' he said. 'Do that. Give her the mobile. If I don't hear from her in an hour, I'll call you back.'

'It's *that* urgent?'

'My whole life is urgent, Merrily.'

'Where are you?'

'In the car. The car's me office now. A privacy issue.'

'Are you all right?'

'Yeh, I'm rediscovering me faith.'

In the pause, she heard an angry car horn.

'When I was a little lad,' Bliss said, 'I had a hard time separating God from Santa Claus. Our priest, Father Flanagan, used to come round on Friday nights with his bets for me dad to put on for him. And this particular Friday – I was a cocky little twat – I said, Father. I've decided I'll not be coming to church on Sunday, and he goes, Why is that, Francis? And I say, Because I've just turned nine, Father, and I'm too old to believe in God. And Father Flanagan's creased up laughing. One day, Francis, he says, when you least expect it, you'll look up, and there above you you'll see what is unmistakably His face. And when that happens ... *when that happens* ... you'll remember this moment.'

'And you were suitably chastened?'

'No, it was a bit of an anticlimax. I thought he was gonna tell me something interesting.'

'Are you *drunk*?'

'I don't drink.'

'Sorry.'

'Anyway,' Bliss said, 'I looked up, and it wasn't the big feller, it was a face called Steve Furneaux. But I finally saw what Father Flanagan was on about. There *is* a God.'

'And is he on your side?'

'I frigging hope so, Merrily, because no other bastard is.'

A few minutes later Jane and Eirion came back and Merrily cobbled together a seriously late lunch of cheese omelettes and hot mince pies – not good enough, but nobody seemed hungry, the combination of darkness and flood making Ledwardine seem, for the first time, like a perilous place to be. And she kept thinking of Father Ellis and the dark brew of piety and perversity that had poisoned a valley.

Jane was more animated now, but in an agitated way. Her eyes flickering as she ate. There was a thin streak of red mud down her face that looked disturbingly like a knife wound.

They listened to the flood update on Radio H & W. Roads all over the county were being closed, even major roads, east–west routes particularly affected. Merrily had to collect a guitar and was apprehensive. There were few places in the county further east than Knights Frome.

'We'll come,' Jane said. 'Eirion would love to see Al Boswell's workshop, wouldn't you, Irene?'

'I *would*, Jane, but I told Lol we'd go round to his place tonight, see what he wants us to do for this back-projection at his concert. And the recordings?'

'I'd forgotten. Mum, listen, it's not safe out there. Can't you like go tomorrow?'

'Christmas Eve? Not a chance.'

'Or *we*'ll go tomorrow.'

'No, I need to try. If it looks bad I'll turn back.'

'It's just that if I'm going to be an orphan, I'd prefer it didn't happen at Christmas. That would be just *so* Dickens. Do I have time for a quick shower? I feel …' Jane flapped her arms '… yucky.'

'If there's enough hot water.'

When she'd gone up, Merrily drew the curtains, and then – superstitiously – drew them back.

'How is she, Eirion? Really?'

'We, er … we went to Coleman's Meadow. I persuaded her it was the thing to do.'

'Good.'

'Good and ... not so good. We met Neil Cooper – the archaeologist from the council? Not a happy man.'

Eirion didn't look too happy either. Since she'd seen him last, he seemed to have grown up, lost the puppy fat, turned the big corner. She listened to his story about Bill Blore's private memos to the Council – the authority he'd publicly slagged off. It didn't actually strike her as all that curious.

'Maybe it's part of his contract for the excavation. The Council don't trust Blore, and they got into a potentially difficult situation with the Dinedor Serpent, so everything he finds, every step he takes, he has to report back.'

'And he'd've agreed to that?'

'What choice would he have? And anyway, in my experience, the high-profile maverick image is usually a façade. You often find that so-called rebels, when you meet them, tend to be disappointingly orthodox.'

Merrily was thinking of Mathew Stooke. Eirion sighed.

'The older I get, Mrs Watkins, the more disillusioned I become. By the time I'm thirty, the world's going to look like a grey wasteland full of zombies who believe in nothing. In fact, I can see it already. All these teenage suicides, is that any wonder?'

'Hey, come on, Eirion, this is how Jane talks when she's down. I rely on you to lift her out of it.'

'Sorry.'

Eirion pushed back his chair, went over to the window. It was like looking into an aquarium with no lights.

'It doesn't end,' he said. 'She's become obsessed now with finding what-ever Blore's discovered. What it's done to Cooper, that's made her angry, but also ... hopeful, you know? That there's still some mystery to be uncovered there? And she thinks if she can let it out before Blore does it might somehow clear her name, turn it all around. She ... doesn't give up.'

'You noticed.'

'Dragging me all round the boundaries of the site and halfway up Cole Hill, trying to make out the alignment through the rain, trying to see something new. It was ... seemed a bit pointless. Sad.'

'You know what we need to do?' Merrily said, as the phone started ringing in the scullery. 'Somehow we need to persuade Blore either to ditch the interview with Jane or record it again, rather more kindly.'

'How do you propose to do that?'

'Haven't the faintest idea, Eirion.'

Huw's Yorkshire voice, flat and scuffed as an old rag rug, sometimes reassuring, not always.

'Never seemed like much to me, Stooke. Doesn't claim to be a boffin, doesn't refer constantly to Darwinian theory. Doesn't seem to specialise in owt.'

'Except derision,' Merrily said. 'He specialises in scorn.'

'A man of the age,' Huw said.

There was a pause. Merrily thought she could hear the ubiquitous rain bombarding Huw's gaunt rectory in the Brecon Beacons, the crackle of his log fire.

'So Stooke's missus wants you to get this West woman off their backs.'

'Essentially, yes.'

'You told them she's not a member of your church.'

'But she is. She comes every week. But she goes to the other place *twice* a week.'

'A serial worshipper.'

'She's quite clever about it. Never really mentions the Church of the Lord of the Light in Ledwardine. No posters in the post office. A devout Anglican of the old school. My church is her church.'

'But she slags you off. She walked out of your service.'

'She would see that as defending the village's religious tradition against a dangerous subversive influence.'

'Kind of support she got?'

'Not a lot. Some people think she's a joke, some feel sorry for her because she's a lone voice. And, of course, her opposition to the raising of the heathen stones makes her a gift to Lyndon Pierce and the pro-expansion lobby.'

Impregnable, in a way, when you thought about it. Exactly the way she looked behind the big metal cross and the reinforced glass in the post office.

'All right,' Huw said. 'I'm looking at this website, as we speak. *Thelordofthelight.com*. You think this is Ellis again, from the States?'

'I honestly don't know, Huw. It carries his mark. It's not unintelligent, and it's plausible enough. And it would explain Shirley's attitude. Ellis has very good reason to hate me.'

'*It has been predicted that, close to the Endtime, Satan will incarnate*', Huw quoted. '*He will have neither horns nor tail.*'

'That's cows in the clear, then.'

Huw laughed.

'You read the rest, though,' Merrily said, 'what it's almost saying is that Satan is the secular society. The moral void.'

'A persuasive argument in many ways. Where do you stand?'

'Personally, I don't have that much of a problem with unbelievers, unless they try to bully other people into unbelief. But then, I have the same problem with people who try to bully people into *belief*. Like Ellis.'

'Can't bully an atheist into faith any more.'

'But you *can* make their lives unpleasant. The Stookes are getting what I suppose you'd call *ominous* mail and anonymous letters, arguably from the same source, basically reminding them of the various names of their ... satanic master.'

'If Stooke looks different and they're living under a false name,' Huw said, 'how did Shirley find out about them?'

'She's the postmistress. They haven't completely changed their identity – he won't *do* that. So his real name still appears on official documents ... and on cheques. Silly mistake by Leonora. They were late paying an electricity bill because they were contesting it, and in the end she took the final demand to pay it at the post office ... paid with a cheque, with, of course, the name Stooke on it. Not realising at the time what kind of woman was handling the transaction.'

'Shirley must've seen that as a little gift from God.'

'Oh yes. Leonora remembers her looking up with this awful still smile she has – pious going on sinister. *Thank you*, she says, handing over the receipt, *Mrs Stooke.*'

'So how did it go from there?'

'Quite subtly, for Shirley. Or maybe she was being restrained. Say she told someone at the Lord of the Light, and they passed the information up the line to Ellis or whoever – if not Ellis there has to be somebody *like* him – and the word comes back to play it quietly. Not to out him, because then he becomes public property ... a target for fundamentalists everywhere.'

'Aye, and they wouldn't have him to themselves any more. Their private demon for the Endgame. Think they're the chosen ones.'

'Hard to credit the mentality.'

'It's all too bloody easy. These folk are fantasists of the first order. Owt unexpected happens, it's the hand of God. That's all they've done so far, is it, threatening letters?'

'Well ... seems Shirley quite often takes an evening stroll from the orchard to Coleman's Meadow. Taking a good look at Cole Barn from the public footpath. They see her holding out her arms, apparently calling on God to ... who knows? Ties in with what she said at the parish meeting last week – a deep evil in Coleman's Meadow and evil returns to it.'

'Still just one woman, Merrily.'

'Maybe not. They look out of the window around nightfall and quite often there's a man there, at the top of the field, watching the house. And considering how comparatively remote that place is ...'

'Shirley living with anybody?'

'Don't know. But it's only ten minutes to Leominster. Probably some members of the church living even closer than that. When I say watching the house, I don't mean furtively creeping from tree to tree, which *would* be worrying – I mean standing there in the open, not moving.'

'I'm wondering why she came to you if they've got a Special Branch man on the end of a phone.'

'That occurred to me, too. She said – as she'd said earlier – that Stooke refuses to be intimidated by religious cranks. And doesn't trust the security services, which I'd guess is normal enough left-wing journalistic paranoia. And, anyway, what could he do? She's not a terrorist. Basically ... I think Leonora just wants to know if Shirley's mental. I said there was no record of her ever harming anyone. I could've said more but Shirley, strictly speaking, is a member of my, erm, flock and the Stookes, well ...'

'All right,' Huw said. 'I'm going to sit on t'fence here, lass. I'd say talk to them both, but don't get too involved. If Ellis *is* out there in spiritual cyberspace, he won't just have the Stookes in his cross-hairs.'

'Me?'

'Maybe.'

'Sorry ... I was just thinking about something Leonora said. I may have to talk to them again, before I talk to Shirley. Which probably means tonight.'

This could be a *long* night.

'All right,' Huw said. 'You've consulted me. I'm noting this in my diary on the evening of the 23rd of December at 4.44 p.m. precisely. Consider your compact little bum formally covered.'

41

Dark Ones

THE HEAT WAS like urban heat. Penthouse-apartment heat. Or like when you walked into one of those department stores with powerful blow-heaters over the doors, and it made you feel almost faint.

'Coffee?' Stooke said.

'Oh ... please.'

Aware of a small tremor under her voice. Nerves, for heaven's sake. Merrily hadn't expected nerves.

She walked ahead of him towards a stone fireplace, floor to ceiling, with a cast-iron wood-burning stove, logs stacked in stone recesses either side, the room so bright she was blinking.

So what *had* she expected – coldness, absence of light, a sense of *void*?

Certainly not nerves. She hadn't expected nerves. Perhaps she should have prayed for strength before leaving the car.

Perhaps she was pathetic.

'Lenni's washing her hair. Gets rather messed up in this weather. She'll be down in a few minutes.'

'I'm sorry, I tried to phone, but you're—'

'Ex-directory. Of course. She should've given you the number. Probably just slipped her mind. Things do. Not a problem. We weren't going anywhere.'

Stooke took Merrily's dripping Barbour and extended an arm towards a long cream-leather sofa. She sat at the end furthest from the stove, its glass doors shimmering a fierce furnace red, which still wouldn't account for the temperature in a room this size.

All the lights were on. Circular halogen lights, like little bright planets, sunk into the plasterboard between new oak beams. Bracketed spotlights on the walls, all fully lit. No dark corners, no secrets, no mystery. Maybe a message here for the religious. *Mystery wastes everyone's time*, Stooke had said in Coleman's Meadow.

'I'm afraid it's rather *too* damn warm in here at the moment,' he admitted, 'but if one tries to turn something off it can go suddenly quite chilly.'

From where she sat she could count one, two, three … four big radiators.

'Temperature fluctuates hugely,' he said. 'Perhaps the absence of insulation. I'm not used to places like this. The countryside's so demanding of *effort*. Townie to the core, I'm afraid.' His face creased into a lopsided smile. 'Merrily, I'm so sorry about the deception. Winterson … Stooke. It was beyond my—'

'Don't worry about it. Life can be complicated.'

'Yes. Excuse me a moment, I'll fetch some coffee.'

He strolled away through an open doorway, not looking back. Merrily leaned her head back into the sofa. You could see why someone might choose to rent Cole Barn. This room had been converted in broad strokes: the big fireplace, the stone flags, the rough beams of light oak. A room you could move into in about an hour, one size fits all.

The Stookes' additions had been fairly minimal: this sofa and a plush swivel chair, a steel-framed desk, two dense cream rugs and enough utility shelves to hold a few hundred books. She tried to make out titles on spines, but she was too far away.

It was another world. A world of unlimited oil, while she and Jane were shivering over candles, like Scrooge's clerk.

'Merrily!'

Leonora, confident and graceful in a cream towelling robe, towel around her hair. Merrily stood up.

'I'm sorry to just appear like this, but I couldn't—'

'No, I heard. My fault entirely.'

'I won't take up very much of your evening. Just wanted to check out a few things. Something you said in the church about Elliot infiltrating a fundamentalist cult. Something's connected.'

'Sit down … please.' Leonora sank into the swivel chair. Her feet were bare. 'That wasn't really a serious possibility. I doubt he could stand mixing with people like that for more than an hour or two. Especially if they're *all* like our friend in the post office.'

'And was *that* the cult he'd thought about infiltrating? The Lord of the Light?'

'He was angry when they started to target us. He wouldn't have done it, wouldn't have the patience. Merrily, I don't want you to think we're *afraid* of this woman. It's just that if she does expose us, it'll be in a horribly negative way. If we stay, I've no doubt it will all come out eventually, but I wanted us to become known as *people* first. There's more to us than a book, you know?'

Odd, Merrily thought. They'd be disowning it in a minute. A germ of hypocrisy here, somewhere.

'Well,' she said, 'I don't know what your tastes in music are, but if you wanted to meet some people, a friend of mine, Lol Robinson, is doing a little concert in the Black Swan tomorrow night. I could introduce you to a few open-minded people you might not have met, if you ...'

'That would be wonderful.'

'Good. Meanwhile, I'll talk to Shirley. Although this ... may involve more than her. I was wondering if Elliot, in the course of his research into various cults, had encountered a guy called Nicholas Ellis. Fringe Anglican clergyman who ran a fundamentalist ministry just across the border, in Radnorshire.'

'Not sure. There's so many of them.'

'Just I've learned in the past couple of hours that the Lord of the Light church was developed from the remains of Ellis's organisation, and it's possible he may still have some influence. From America. On the Net.'

Leonora called out, 'Darling, have you heard of a man called Ellis?'

'Father Nicholas Ellis,' Merrily said, as Stooke came in with a loaded tray. 'That's not his real name, but it doesn't matter.'

'I've a computer file on him.' Stooke laid the tray on the desk. 'Had some correspondence with a reporter out there. I *think* he was linked to a corrupt itinerant evangelist called ... McAllman?'

'Yes.' Merrily nodding. 'Ellis's was an unpleasant kind of ministry involving sexual exploitation of women. He'll be blaming me, among others, for its demise in this country.'

'This West woman is one of his disciples?'

'It's unlikely she ever encountered him in person. I just wondered if *you*'d had any contact. Couldn't find any mention of him in *The Hole in the Sky*.'

'It would be in the next book.'

'Does he know?'

'Possibly, I don't know.' Stooke looked at his wife. 'Probably does now.'

'Yeah, yeah, very stupid of me,' Leonora said. 'I didn't think. Pretty damned angry that morning. The electricity meter was read after the last of the workmen moved out and before we moved in. Four or five weeks later we had a bill for over £900? Which, even allowing for the way fuel prices are going …'

'Crazy,' Merrily said. 'You do like it warm in here, though, don't you?'

'This is oil. And wood? OK, a lot of lights, but we don't use much electricity otherwise. Eat out most days. It's not that we can't afford to pay the bloody bill, it's just that it's so obviously *wrong*.'

'Thanks.' Merrily accepting a coffee from Stooke. 'And that's why you were asking the guy on the archaeological site where they got their power from?'

'Just a thought that they might in some way be leeching electricity from here.' Stooke brushed a hand through his grey-black spiky hair. 'Bit of a long shot.'

'We had it tested,' Leonora said, 'according to the complaints procedure. They said they could find absolutely nothing wrong. As they usually do. Anyway … that's why I wasn't in the best of moods when I stormed into the post office to pay the final demand instead of just posting it.'

Stooke sat down on the sofa, close to the stove. He didn't seem to be aware of the heat.

'The agents were no help at all. And the firm that owns the place is in France. Places like this, Middle England, they think they can charge what they like for half a job. I'd quite like to move out and try and get some of our money back, but—'

'Darling, I couldn't face it again. Not for a while. The sheer stress of moving, feeling like refugees. We've just ...' Leonora turned to Merrily '... had a run of trivial teething troubles, that's all. It's a barn conversion, nobody's lived here before. Power surges. Bulbs popping. Wake up in the night and one of the smoke alarms is going off, which sets off all the *other* smoke alarms.'

'They saw us coming,' Stooke said.

'So *they* know who you are?' Merrily asked. 'The agents.'

An irrational tension had set in. *Power surges. Bulbs popping. Smoke alarms.* How often had people brought domestic problems like that to her door?

'The security services had a word with the agents,' Stooke said. 'Presumably pointing out that if anything leaked out from *them*, we'd have to move, putting the house back on the market.'

'And they had enough difficulty letting it last time.'

'Did they?' Stooke looking up sharply. 'Why?'

'Because ... the future of Coleman's Meadow is undecided. You either get a whole army of new neighbours or a prehistoric tourist attraction. You were a godsend. As it were. What's the atheist term for a godsend?'

'Are you going to make atheist jokes all night, Merrily?'

'I'm sorry.'

'No, no.' Stooke stood up awkwardly. 'It's me.' He grimaced. 'Fractious. Sorry.'

He folded his arms. Amazingly, in this temperature, he was still wearing the black fleece. Merrily smiled uncertainly. She felt swimmingly disorientated – that uncomfortable sensation of floating one step behind your senses. Too much heat, too much light. She stood up.

'I'm going to have to go.'

'I didn't mean to offend—'

'No, you didn't. I have to drive to the other side of the county and I don't want to be back too late in these conditions. Just one final thing. Shirley's friend ...'

Stooke looked blank. Merrily almost snatched the opportunity to say it was OK, it didn't matter. Get herself out of the heat. She didn't need this kind of complication.

'Oh,' Stooke said. 'You mean the man who was watching the house.'

'Erm … yeah.'

'That made me angry. I don't think Lenni's seen him, but I spotted him a couple of times. He'd just be standing there at the top of the field, on the edge of the wood.'

'The orchard?'

'Yeah, whatever, the trees. I thought he was one of the archaeologists at first, and I shouted to him from the door, but he didn't say anything. He just stood there. Well, it's a public right of way, so you can't actually order people off. I just went back into the house.'

'What time of day was this?'

'Early evening. Just on dusk. Five-ish? Next time I looked he'd gone. Then I saw him again, a couple of days ago.'

'Same time?'

'More or less. It was raining. Lenni'd gone into Leominster, to the shops.'

'Antique shops.' Leonora had pulled off the towels, was shaking out her red tresses. 'So many in Leominster.'

'And there was the guy again, getting soaked?'

Stooke went over to the desk, opened a drawer, took out some papers and extracted one.

Merrily said, 'What was he like? Anybody I might recognise?'

'He wasn't close enough. I thought …' Stooke handed her a folded sheet of A4. 'We'd had that the same morning, and I suppose I saw him in those terms … as, presumably, I was expected to.'

We know why you are here.
We know why you have come NOW.
To call forth the old dark ones from
the woods and reclaim the stones for
your infernal master.
But know that we too are vigilant!

Stooke wrinkled his nose in distaste.

'First time one of these ... missives had mentioned the stones. I should've made the connection after your parish meeting. I suppose when the guy appeared again, I saw him as ... like it says there.'

'One of the dark ones from the woods?'

'Some kind of Stone Age warrior. Short cloak or a skin, and a stick. Couldn't see him clearly, too much mist. I was angry, but I did nothing. Should've gone out, but the field was soaking wet and ... you don't know what drugs these guys are on, do you?'

'Who? The Church of the Lord of the Light? You really think so?'

'Well, maybe not drugs.' Stooke took the paper back, crumpled it angrily. 'But how can they think we're so *stupid*?'

'You're destroying the evidence.'

'It's a copy.'

Stooke looked into Merrily's eyes, and she really didn't know what to make of his expression.

'I'd better be off,' she said.

Merrily stood for a while, leaning against the Volvo, relishing the cold, even the rain, looking back across the hardstanding at what was, essentially, a new house, all its downstairs windows bright.

For a fraction of a second, the lights seemed to flare brighter still, as if there was a flash of lightning inside Cole Barn.

Don't go there.

She got into the car, troubled.

42

Witch-Hunt

WHEN SISTER CULLEN rang from the hospital, Bliss was parked in the entrance of Phase Two of the housing estate where Gyles Banks-Jones lived.

Just after five p.m., and well dark. Phase Two had barely been started and had no street lighting yet. Two hours ago Bliss had slid in next to the site hut, his rear wheels spinning, his lights already switched off. He was sure he could feel the car sinking into the mud, but at least the building site gave him an excellent view of Gyles's house, directly opposite, and the house the other side of Gyles's shared drive.

Steve Furneaux's house. Still no car there, still no lights.

'So would that be all right, Sister?' Bliss said.

'Don't see why I can't find that out, it being Sunday,' Cullen said. 'Although I shall expect some personal intervention from your good self the next time I fall foul of a speed camera.'

'I hate them speed cameras, me.'

Both of them knowing Bliss had nil influence in Traffic.

'Give me twenty minutes, then,' Cullen said.

'This is very decent of you, Sister.'

'Merrily Watkins is a good woman.'

'For a Prod?'

'I don't mess with religion, Mr Bliss.'

'Very wise, Sister.'

Bliss settled back with his Thai Prawn sandwich and a can of shandy. He could afford to give it another couple of hours. Not like his life was going anywhere.

A Christmas tree was lit up in the Banks-Joneses' front window, but no sign of movement behind it. Either Gyles and Mrs Banks-Jones were quietly talking it through, or – easier for Bliss to imagine – they were sunk into the sick, silent aftermath of a blazing row.

However, at some stage over the holiday period, Gyles would be sitting back in his favourite armchair, thinking how pleasant it was here, how warm, how safe. What a nice warm, safe life he'd had. Then getting jerked out of it by the memory of Bliss's rancid Scouser's voice going, *Bang! That was your cell door, Gyles.*

And in case Gyles, full of good whisky and maudlin Yuletide emotion, should then wish to make prison less of a prospect for the New Year, Bliss had given him his mobile number. Pretty sure that Gyles, at some stage, would ring with something he could use. But meanwhile – and more interesting – there was Steve.

Steve Furneaux revisited. Steve Furneaux who kept wiping his nose in Gilbies, but seemed to have no other cold symptoms. Bliss had registered it at the time, but you saw it all over the place these days. Even the red-spotted handkerchief: nosebleeds. If you were constructing the very model of a modern suburban recreational snorter of the white stuff, the computer simulation would be just *so* Steve Furneaux.

Because Gyles was still holding out about his source and refusing to involve his next-door neighbour on any level, Bliss had gone back to Alan Sandison, the Baptist minister.

Making Alan's Christmas by telling him how unlikely it was, now that Gyles had coughed, that he would have to give evidence against any of his new neighbours. Alan had relaxed, much relieved – his conscience clear, all neighbourly relations intact. They'd had a cup of tea, an informal chat ... quality time.

In the course of which it emerged that, yes, Alan did know Bliss's friend Steve, from the council. Indeed, the first neighbourly gathering attended by the Sandisons, before they knew about the cocaine, had been a barbecue in Steve Furneaux's garden.

And surely Alan knew Charlie Howe, didn't he? Everybody knew Charlie ...

Oh, the very friendly white-haired man with the stick, would that be? Nice.

The chances of busting Steve for possession were remote. But Steve wouldn't know that. Very likely that Steve, with his comfy council job and his blue-sky future on the line, was in a state of some anxiety. Which was also nice. No better time for an informal chat about Hereforward, Clement Ayling and – please God – Charlie Howe.

Just don't let Steve have gone away for Christmas.

Bliss ran the engine to demist the windscreen and then, unwilling to push it too far with his old mate God, he rang his old bagman, Andy Mumford.

'Boss,' Mumford said. "Ow're you?'

The sheep-shit accent provoking a surprising tug of emotion, bringing back comfort-memories of the old days – last year, in fact – before Andy's thirty had been up and he'd been shown the door. Poor sod was working with Jumbo Humphries, now – garage owner, feed dealer, private inquiry agent. It was either that or a position as some factory's *Head of Security*, for which read *caretaker, dogsbody, odd-job man*.

'And life's exciting, Andy?' Bliss said. 'Lots of Land Rover chases?'

'What bloody Humphries didn't tell me,' Mumford said, 'was that when there's no case on, I'm expected to work in the bloody warehouse, selling bags of bloody mixed corn to bloody chicken farmers.'

'And how often is there no case?'

'This is the sticks,' Mumford said. 'There's a credit crunch. *You* work it out.'

'I feel for you, Andy. Not as much as I feel for meself, but still ...'

'Made inquiries about getting back – cold-case squad, kind of thing,' Mumford said mournfully.

'And?'

'Seems it would've helped if I'd been a DCI rather than a humble DS.'

'Elitist bastards. Listen, Andy, you still got that little sister on the Plascarreg?'

'Not *my* responsibility.'

'No, don't worry I'm not ... It's just I've had young George Wintle out there, looking for a new coke channel.' Giving Mumford the backstory and the names: Banks-Jones, Furneaux. 'He won't get anywhere, but I was wondering what the buzz was, if any. Who's running the Plascarreg this week?'

'Jason Mebus grows up fast,' Mumford said. 'Real businessman now.'

'I thought he'd been busted up a bit in a car crash.'

'Broke his collarbone rolling a nicked motor, that was all. Young bones heal quick.'

'You don't like Jason, do you?'

'No.'

'Good thought, though, Andy. I'll get George to talk to him.'

'*He* won't talk. Not to the likes of Wintle.'

'Talk to you?'

'Mabbe.'

'Cold-case buggers don't know what they're missing.' Bliss took a breath, went in casual. 'You ever see anything of Charlie Howe these days, Andy?'

Heavy pause.

'No,' Mumford said. 'Nothing.'

This was a little tricky. It was widely rumoured that Mumford had done some cleaning-up after Charlie over the undiscovered murder in the Frome Valley, way back when Charlie had been at Bliss's level and Mumford just a sprog – so that was excusable, just. All the same, a touchy subject. Safer to keep this contemporary.

'You know of any link between Charlie and the late Clem Ayling?'

Mumford found a short laugh.

'Wondered how long it'd be before you got round to Ayling. I did hear your role in that had got a bit shrunk, mind.'

'And you heard that *from* ...?'

'Pint with Terry Stagg. Funny arrangement all round, Terry says. Why would Ma'am set up an incident room within walking distance of Gaol Street?'

'Only if she wanted a soundproof box,' Bliss said.

'Ah.'

'He's never liked me, you know that, Andy.'

'Charlie? No, I don't reckon he has.'

'Not since I got too interested in the Frome Valley.'

No reaction from Mumford.

'Where I won't be going again, you understand. It's history. I accept that.'

Best to underline it: no question of Mumford's youthful indiscretion ever being exhumed.

'All right,' Mumford said.

'But if Charlie's name crops up on the edge of an inquiry I still get interested. And Charlie knows that, and Annie knows it.'

'This connection with Ayling – that *just* the council?'

'Goes a bit further. Charlie and Ayling'd both got themselves co-opted on to this quango think-tank thingy known as Hereforward. Which was Ayling's last meeting. Walks out of it, never seen again attached to his head.'

'Never heard of it.'

'You ever heard of Charlie doing … Charlie?'

'Coke?'

'Or anything.'

'Charlie don't like to lose control.'

'Oh.'

'Women's Charlie's thing. Young women. Always a charmer.'

'Still?'

'Older he gets, younger he likes them. Jumbo was telling me about a divorce case he was working, led to this isolated farmhouse in the Black Mountains where there was what you might call communal activities. Jumbo seen Charlie through his binoculars, once.'

'That's interesting.'

'I will tell you one thing, though, boss,' Mumford said. 'Charlie en't a killer.'

'That's a firm statement, Andy.'

'He's a cover-upper, is what Charlie is.'

Bliss flicked the wipers again. Still no sign of life in Steve's house. He switched off the engine.

'And a bully,' Mumford said. 'Whatever he done, always he done it for the best of reasons and anyone who suggests otherwise he's right in their face and they better watch their step, else they might not have a job for very long. If you see where I'm coming from.'

"I hate that,' Bliss said.

'Power thing, see.'

'Hate it, Andy.'

'What I'm saying, unless you got something real solid, not an easy man to lean on.'

'I realise that.'

'On the other hand,' Mumford said, 'young Mebus, he thinks he's smart but he en't. So if you want somebody to talk to Mebus, on the quiet, like, civilian rules, I'm up for that. Don't take this the wrong way, boss, but you was always good to me. Especially in the last days. And the business over Robbie. I appreciate that.'

'That's very civil of you, Andy.'

'I expect you'd return the favour, any openings come up where you could put in a word.'

'If there's anybody left who listens to me.'

'Bear it in mind, anyway, boss,' Mumford said.

Bliss smiled into the darkness. Mumford's subtext: *anything … just get me away from the mixed corn.*

'I've gorra few problems, Andy.'

'Aye,' Mumford said. 'I know.'

Bliss was finishing off the last Thai Prawn sarnie when his mobile went.

'Not convenient to explain further,' Eileen Cullen said. 'But it's as you said. All right? Have to go now.'

'Thanks, Sister. I owe you one.'

'You certainly do.'

So … the old bastard.

And it would go on, the eternal triangle of Annie Howe, Charlie Howe and Frannie Bliss, until one of the corners dropped off.

He thought about Mumford, a good detective lumbering through most of his career as a DC, kicked out with the digital camera and the inscribed tankard, facing the rest of his mobile years as a part-time PI, part-time corn salesman.

He thought of himself, young Frannie making a fresh start still in his twenties: nice country town, not many streets where you couldn't see a hill. Nice, laid-back country people, not as sharp as Scousers, most of them, but not as bitter either. Thinking he'd have a fair chance of promotion and getting it, too, in the early years.

And then it stopped, and he was looking at a bunch of unexceptional DCIs five years younger than him, then *seven* years younger. Looking particularly at Annie Howe, acting superintendent. A crap detective. A frigging *shite* detective, with a dad who'd been a *bent* detective.

And a bully. All bullies were cowards. His dad was always telling him that when he was kid. You didn't give in to a bully.

The rain was heavier now, and he switched on the engine and the demister. In the old days, someone on the occupied part of the estate would've noticed a car parked without lights and come over to check it out. Not any more. Not with new knife-crime stats on the box every other night. They wouldn't ring the police either, because they knew the police wouldn't come, or maybe they'd drop by next day, if they were passing.

After about two minutes, Karen Dowell called and, for a while, Bliss brightened up.

'It's ridiculous, boss.'

'Where are you, Karen?'

'I'm at home. You see it on the box?'

'I haven't gorra box in the car.'

'Man helping with inquiries?'

Bliss lurched in his seat.

'They've *pulled*?'

'Nah, it's Wilford Hawkes.'

'Karen.' Bliss slumped back. 'You're kidding me.'

'Couldn't believe it either. I actually rang the school to confirm, talked to Terry. What happened, they turned over Hawkes's place and found he'd just put a brand new chain on his twenty-year-old chainsaw. Cleaned it all up himself, like new. So now they've stripped his workshop, sent a vanload to forensic, and they're asking him the same questions, over and over again, in the hope he'll slip up, give some different answers. Which he does, of course, everybody does in the end. Poor little bugger doesn't know what day it is.'

'This is Howe?'

'She's had Brent at him now. Both of them, in fact.'

'Ms Nasty and Dr Nasty. I suppose it's occurred to them that Hawkes is half Ayling's size and nearly as old?'

'It was a single stab wound,' Karen said. 'Not much of a wound, not much blood. In fact, they were still a bit iffy about it till the PM showed what it did to the aorta. Ayling would probably've been dead within minutes.'

'And Willy would've known exactly where to stick it, would he?'

'Could've been luck. On the other hand, he *was* in the Army, way back. Paras. Commando training?'

'But look at him *now*, Karen!'

'Yeah, well, they think he may've had a partner. They're going through Jane Watkins's database, name by name. Paying visits.'

'Witch-hunt?'

'Yeah, funny you should say that. One situation – listen to this – Terry was telling me these witches up towards Ross, friends of Willy's, they thought it was carol singers from the church and wouldn't open the door? And Brent … he had it smashed in? *Smashed in.* All right, maybe there was a bit more to it, and they found some cannabis, but it's still bloody madness, Frannie.'

Bliss thought about his own dawn raid on Gyles.

'Just be glad you're not part of it,' Karen said.

'Yeh.'

Not part of anything. Not even part of a family any more.

'Mind you,' Karen said, 'don't forget it *was* you who first pointed them at Dinedor.'

'Yeh, but that—'

'Goodnight, boss.'

Bliss sat there, shaking his head.

Well, sure, Dinedor needed checking out. But *only* in tandem with the possibility that somebody wanted them to *think* it was all about Dinedor. An investigation this size was more like snooker than frigging rugby – a lot of balls on the table and you didn't just pick one up and run with it.

Unless, of course, you thought your old man might get potted along the way.

Bliss laughed, starting to despise himself. He could stay here all night waiting for Furneaux, and wake up at first light, wheels firmly embedded in the shite, and have to ask Gyles to give him a push, and look like a dick.

When what he was really avoiding …

He leaned back, took a long breath. Well, why not?

Why the fuck not?

He wrenched the car out of the mud at the fourth attempt and put on his lights. He didn't know if this was going to be right, but knew he wouldn't sleep now if he didn't go for it, and the thought of dragging himself back to the empty house at Marden, back to the pile of Chrissie cards on the mat, the spread of white envelopes with a few red ones, like blood in the snow …

On the way to Leominster, he crawled through five pools of flash-flood in the road. He passed twenty-seven houses and bungalows with Christmas lights all over their walls and wrapped around trees and chimneys. Didn't know why he counted them.

Once, disgracefully, he pulled in to the side of road and wept and almost turned back.

In Leominster, there was no flooding, and no lights at all in or outside the Victorian three-storey terraced house where Charlie Howe lived.

43

Lute of the Frome

THERE WAS, INEVITABLY, an element of ceremonial. Merrily had slipped out of her wet shoes in the stone and panelled hall, and that seemed symbolic now, as Al Boswell laid the wooden case on the long oak table below a big copper lantern.

Al must know there was no time to waste. Although the River Frome seemed to be staying within its banks, the duck pond in front of the Hop Museum was brimming, the green and gold gypsy caravan up to its axles in water darker than beer.

'We didn't think you'd come,' Sally Boswell said. 'Nobody should be out on a night like this.'

Sally's long white hair was down. Al was spindly and ageless, like some woodland sprite, Sally the lovely mortal he'd abducted by means of Romani magic.

'The *drukerimaskri*?' Al said. 'Of course we knew she would come.'

He'd had the guitar ready for her. She'd expected him to take her down to his workshop, through the exhibition of hop-growing memorabilia, old pictures of the Romani who had travelled to the Frome Valley for the annual hop harvest. But Al had known there wasn't time.

When he opened the case, the strings of the lute-shaped darkwood guitar shivered in a draught from somewhere.

'God, Al, it's so …'

Merrily leaned over the case but didn't touch. The air felt fresh after the stifling Cole Barn, and the night felt unreal, as if she'd become part of some mythic saga involving the lost lyre of Orpheus or something.

'It's too dim in here,' Al said, 'but if you look into the soundhole when you get it home, you will see, in the wood below it, a quite perfectly proportioned cross.'

'You did that?'

'No, no.' Al laughed lightly. 'The cross was naturally in the grain, and I placed it under the soundhole. In your honour. Would you like to bless the instrument before you take it away? *Drukerimaskri?*'

Romani for a woman priest.

Al bowed and straightened up, spreading his arms, revealing the golden lettering on his black sweatshirt:

Boswell Guitars. The Lute of the Frome.

'I think,' Sally said briskly, 'that we can consider the instrument to be blessed already and not delay Merrily any longer. It's a terribly cruel night. I heard on the radio that all the bed-and-breakfast places in Hereford were full because of people trapped in the city. How will they get home for Christmas? How will *you* get home, Merrily?'

'I don't need to go through Hereford.'

'You should have waited until tomorrow.'

'Couldn't. I've too much on and, besides … he's doing a concert at the Swan in Ledwardine tomorrow night. His first. He's a bit worried about it, playing on his own doorstep and I thought … Well, I was going to give this to him on Christmas Day, but …'

'You've driven across the hell that is Herefordshire on the worst night of the year.' Al's eyes lit up and his face split like a polished wooden puppet's into a crooked but radiant smile. 'This is love, I think.'

'Yes. I—'

'But you're worried.'

'This and that.'

She'd put Cole Barn on hold to concentrate on the road, getting the guitar back home.

Al studied her.

'Tell me … where does Nick Drake come into this?'

'I don't know.' Merrily felt a small seepage of alarm in her stomach.

'I mean, apart from him being Lol's original inspiration. But you knew that, didn't you?'

'Of course he knew that,' Sally said. 'Al's anything but psychic.'

'Alas, she's right. Disregard my whimsy.' Al closed the guitar case, held it out to her like a sheaf of flowers. 'Take her home.'

'Al, you'll have to hold on to her while I get my chequebook out.'

'Pay me after Christmas,' Al said. 'As the sofa retailers say.'

'Absolutely not. Just tell me how much. It's not a problem. I've some money put by—'

'I haven't yet decided on a suitable price,' Al said.

'Please. Let's not quarrel about this. I want to pay the proper price and Lol would want that, too. Especially Lol, because of ... what happened to the other one.'

'Ah, yes. The man who had it smashed, as a warning. Leave a hundred pounds in cash on the table. Do you have a hundred pounds? If not, fifty will do. Don't cross me, *drukerimaskri*, or the curse will come down, and you know how good we are at this.'

'I do have a hundred pounds, but ... it's just a deposit, Al.'

'There we are, then.' Al thrust the guitar case at her and then sprang back, laughing, all limbs, like a grasshopper. 'Tell me ... does Laurence feel guilt, because the young man died unfulfilled, unrecognised, and now Laurence is ... almost halfway famous?'

'Nick Drake?' Merrily said. 'You're talking about Nick Drake again?'

She wasn't about to say that Lol had seen the destruction of the Boswell, the finest handmade acoustic guitar in the country, as a sign of his unworthiness. A confirmation that he'd never be as good as Nick Drake.

'Leave it, Al,' Sally said, and Merrily was grateful.

Before she left the Hop Museum, she put down all the notes in her wallet without counting them.

'A deposit, Al.'

Before she drove away into the cold, liquid night, she sat in the back seat with the guitar case across her knees and, without thinking too hard about whether this was right or reasonable, she asked God to bless the Boswell.

*

In Lol's house, Jane sat with Eirion next to the wood stove in the mouth of the inglenook, sipping hot chocolate, listening to Lol's new music.

> *Can melting sugar sweeten wine?*
> *Can light communicated keep its name?*
> *Can jewels solid be, though they do shine?*
> *From fire rise a flame?*

Her back almost touching the stove, Jane felt this odd, warm shimmer as Lol's voice rose to meet a high guitar note. Lol sat on the edge of the sofa, looking apprehensive, the guitar on its stand under the window.

The room was lit by a fat candle on the low table, the music crisp and real, from the stereo. Lol had made demos on mini-disc of most of the new songs. He could do concerts now, even fairly intimate folk-club-type gigs, but he was still too shy to play live in front of friends. Like he felt that people who knew him would see through the songs to all the flaws in his character, his weaknesses.

Crazy?

Not when you knew the Lol Robinson story. Barely twenty and convicted of sexually assaulting a fourteen-year-old girl while on tour with Hazey Jane. An offence actually committed, while Lol was asleep, by the band's bass-player, who'd walked away, leaving Lol on probation, unjustly disgraced, disowned by his creepy Pentecostalist parents, swallowed by the psychiatric system. His career wrecked, his spirit smashed.

It was Jane's mum who'd finally brought him out of the past. But before he even knew Mum, Lucy Devenish had begun to reassemble him. Lucy and the poems of Thomas Traherne, who'd seen the essence of paradise in this border landscape. Found happiness. *Felicity.*

Before dying at thirty-seven.

Which meant that Lol was older than Traherne now. Oh God, nothing was ever perfect, nothing was easy.

Thus honey flows from rocks of stone
Thus oil from wood, thus cider, milk and wine
From trees and flesh … thus corn from earth …

He'd turned three of Traherne's 17th-century poems into songs, and it couldn't have been easy at all; they all had strange, archaic rhythms.

'We can illustrate this no problem,' Eirion said. 'I've got dozens of pictures from last summer that we shot along the ley. All very lush and pastoral. It's the Elgar stuff I'm not sure about. Maybe I could download some pictures from the Net. Could I hear that again, Lol?'

Lol located it on the disc. The song was just called 'Elgar', dealing with the composer's thoughts as he lay dying, but it wasn't morbid; it was, in the end, uplifting.

When it was over, Lol said, 'People misunderstood Elgar for years, thought he was too grand. Just an ordinary guy, lower middle-class. Insecure …'

'Right.'

Jane was getting a real feel for this now, how it all tied in. Elgar had been a friend of Alfred Watkins and had actually had his picture taken with Watkins in what was almost certainly Coleman's Meadow. Lol had written a new song about Alfred Watkins, using lines from the seminal *Old Straight Track* set to this kind of chugging, pulsing rhythm, like you were following a ley on foot, the music speeding up as you reached what Jane was certain had to be Cole Hill at sunrise, midsummer.

Whether some of the crass bastards who drank and dined at the Black Swan would get any of this was anybody's guess and, for a moment, Jane could hear it all being drowned out by whoops and laughter and inane chat.

And then realised she was actually hearing voices. Raised. Outside the window. Raised voices, excitement. Or panic.

Lol stood up, turned the music down and went over to the window, wiping off condensation with his sleeve.

'Something seems to have happened.'

*

Merrily had taken what seemed to be the safe route, through Bromyard, but who could tell? The entrances to several side roads were blocked by portable signs, some of them semi-submerged.

FLOOD
ROAD CLOSED

She flicked the wipers to double speed, driving like a learner first time out, hands on the wheel at ten to two, unblinking, the radio on low. Halfway to Leominster, the Radio Hereford and Worcester all-night flood special said,

'... *And if you've just tuned in and you're heading into Hereford from the south on the Abergavenny or Ross roads, police advise turning back because the Belmont roundabout has now been closed. Belmont roundabout is closed.*'

Not good. Halfway to becoming the Isle of Hereford.

The wipers strained and the surface water tugged at the wheels, but she made it around Tenbury Wells, its town-centre streets turned into canals, according to the radio.

'*They knew this was coming, look,*' a caller to the station said, '*and they've never spent a penny on flood prevention. When was this river last cleaned out? Tell me that.*'

Merrily switched off the radio. Getting repetitive, the litany of recrimination. She followed a silver container lorry at 25 m.p.h. all the way to Leominster. The town centre was clear, its lights dulled, its swilled streets empty. She drove up the hill towards the roundabout beyond Morrisons supermarket. There was little traffic. She thought she saw Frannie Bliss's yellow Honda Civic, same blue sticker in the rear window, parked at the side of the road, but it couldn't have been.

Back into the countryside. Only ten minutes from home now, in normal conditions. Water was pumping out of the fields into the basin of the road, and the rain ricocheted from the tarmac like a thousand plucked stitches in the headlights.

On the passenger seat the mobile chimed.

Merrily drove up onto the grass verge, kept the engine running, watching the silver container lorry disappearing between dirty curtains of rain.

'Go on then,' Huw Owen said. 'Let's hear it. What happened at Stooke's place?'

All the way to Knights Frome and all the way back she'd been blanking this out. It needed a cool head.

'I was going to call you when I got a bit nearer home. I can't park here, Huw, I'll have to—'

'Christ, you're not bloody well out in this, are you? It's just I rang your landline but t'machine were on.'

'I had to go and see someone. I'll find somewhere and call you back.'

'Just get home.'

'No, we do need to talk about this. Give me two minutes.'

44

Nightwatchman

BLISS WATCHED HIM walking stiffly down the pavement, leaning only slightly on his aluminium crutch. Once, he stopped and lifted it up to point at something. Only Charlie Howe could make a lightweight crutch look like a twelve-bore.

Bliss was relieved to see him. At least somebody was coming home tonight.

Just a chat, Charlie, one to one. Only way to deal with this. Get the elephant out of the toilet cubicle.

Charlie was under a big black umbrella held by a woman with big blonde hair. Not *young* young but had to be a good thirty years younger than Charlie. About Annie's age, in fact. Annie's mother, Bliss had heard, was like Cleopatra – ancient history.

As well as the brolly, the woman was carrying a plastic carrier bag with what looked like bottles in it. Bliss guessed they'd been to Morrisons. Maybe Charlie had even met her there; supermarkets were good for pick-ups.

Whoever she was, she'd need to be persuaded to leave them alone for an hour. Bliss got out of the car as they went in through Charlie's gate, up the short path to the front door, where Charlie started fumbling in his pocket for his keys.

Bliss trotted up behind.

'Hold your crutch, Charlie?'

The woman spun, but Charlie turned slowly, water crashing down on the umbrella, the downpour swollen by overflow from the guttering.

'Least I can do,' Bliss said, 'after all you've done for me.'

Charlie leaned his crutch against the door frame, to show he could manage without it, peered out from under the brolly. He looked like he always had: ski-resort suntan, white hair in a crew-cut out of vintage movies with Elvis in them.

'Brother Bliss, would that be?'

'Just happened to be passing, Charlie. Thought I'd see how you were getting on with the new plazzie hip.'

Charlie said nothing.

'Lucky to get it done before the festive season. I heard they'd been suspended, all the hip ops. Virus? Ward closures?'

'Wasn't affected,' Charlie said. 'Got in just in time. What do you want, Brother Bliss?'

Bliss stood there. He was soaked through already. He could feel the damp on his chest and the weight of dark shoulder pads of saturation. It didn't look as though Charlie was going to introduce his friend.

'We have a chat, Charlie?'

'Certainly. Ring my secretary. Make an appointment.'

'I was thinking now.'

'Not convenient, I'm afraid.'

'Do a good job, then, did he?' Bliss said. 'Bit of a whizz with hips, what I hear, Mr Shah.'

'I'm told it all went very smoothly,' Charlie said. 'You're getting wet.'

'Nice feller, too, everybody says that,' Bliss said.

'A gentleman.'

'Pity about his kid.'

Bliss stared at Charlie, blinking the rain out of his eyes. In truth, he couldn't even see Charlie any more, only a black mist. He just sensed a thin smile.

'What are you doing, Brother Bliss?'

Drowning, Bliss thought.

The Zippo sputtered and sparked before finding a flame. Merrily lit up. She'd pulled into a long lay-by behind a tump of gravel, where the Leominster road let you into the bypass. She was two miles from home and about half a mile from the bridge at Caple End, where she'd sat in

Bliss's car and he'd told her about the pieces of quartz shining in Clem Ayling's eye sockets.

'Now *that*,' Huw Owen said, 'is a bugger.'

Didn't think she'd forgotten anything: fluctuating temperature, bulbs popping, smoke alarms whining in the night, car failing to start, and that staggering electricity bill.

'Something taking the energy,' Huw said. 'There were a fairly well-documented case over at Brecon some years ago, before your time.'

'I've heard about it.'

'Lot of others I've heard about where all that occurs alongside a volatile.'

'If they need the heating on at that level because, if they turn it down, it's suddenly colder than the grave ... OK, you could say that's a case of soft city folk. But *she* isn't from the city.'

'What was the attitude when they were telling you all this?'

'Annoyed. Annoyed at the level of workmanship, annoyed at the electricity company, the owners, the owners' agents ...'

'Nowt more than annoyed?'

'Like it wouldn't even cross their minds, either of them. But, then, they have an image to support. How could they not be in total, one hundred per cent denial?'

'It's a bugger, lass.'

'Don't keep just saying that, Huw. What do I do about it? I get called in all the time on stories far less convincing than this. First rule of deliverance?'

Huw laughed. Both of them remembering their first encounter on Huw's deliverance course in his parish deep in the heart of SAS training country.

First rule of deliverance: always carry plenty of fuse wire.

Second rule: never leave the premises without at least a prayer.

As if ...

'Of course,' Huw said, 'as you say, it might be a scam.'

'Might very well be. She's told me about his need for new material. How book two might have to be just a diary of his adventures since the publication of *Hole*. Thing is, she was very frank about all that, about him being basically a hack with no great evangelical need to convert society to non-belief.'

'Happen lull you into a sense of false security. You wouldn't've gone near that place otherwise, would you?'

'Maybe not. And yet … I'll tell you one thing. There was a look Stooke gave me just before I left – this is Stooke, not Lensi. It was full of almost a kind of pain. Like he's saying, *Denial? Of course I'm in denial. What the hell would you expect?*'

'All right,' Huw said. 'Let's talk about the figure in the field. On the edge of the orchard?'

'It was too dark to get him to show me the exact spot. Apart from it bucketing down.'

'Assuming it's not a scam,' Huw said. '*Nightwatchman*, you reckon?'

Charlie didn't even look at the blonde woman. He didn't stop looking at Bliss. He held the keys out over his shoulder.

'Make us some coffee, Sasha.'

Accepting the umbrella, keeping it well away from Bliss as the blonde went into the house and lights came on.

'You know where my daughter is tonight, brother?'

Still at her desk, popping pills to stay awake? Having Willy Hawkes woken up with a halogen spotlight in the eyes, every hour on the hour till he coughed to Ayling's murder?

'No,' Bliss said.

The water was sluicing over his ears, down the back of his neck until he could feel it cold on his spine.

'Private party in the Home Secretary's constituency,' Charlie said. 'They been good friends for some years.'

'Of course, yeh. Keep forgetting how relatively local the Home Seckie is. Think Annie'll be offered a Home Office consultancy? House of Lords next? Baroness Howe. Has a ring of … I dunno … destiny.'

'In your dreams, boy. Anne's a copper through and through. In the genes, it is. She en't going nowhere she won't be able to pick up the likes of you and drop you where you belong. And neither am I.'

Bliss had started to shiver. You could go through a car-wash on full cycle and not get this wet. And Charlie in the dry, not a droplet on him.

Story of Charlie's life.

'Well, for her sake you can only hope ...' Bliss wiped a hand across his face '... that Annie's DNA managed to bypass the bent gene.'

The rain was suddenly lit up in colours. Bliss turned to see one of those charity Christmas floats rolling past, probably on its way home but the lights still blazing, Bliss thinking, *Jesus, did I really just say that?*

And turning back round to find the rubber foot of Charlie's metal crutch up against his throat.

'Didn't catch that, Francis? Hard to make out what you're saying in this rain.'

Well, he could snatch the crutch away, and then maybe Charlie would lose his footing on the wet, slimy driveway. And the woman would, of course, be watching, from an upstairs window, a witness to this unprovoked assault on an elderly man recovering from hip surgery. Yes, that was one option.

Bliss backed off.

'Why don't we go inside, then? Where it's quiet. Lot to talk about, Councillor. Talk about Hereforward?'

The presence of the woman complicated everything. The woman and the rain. The noise of the rain meant there was no way neighbours or passers-by could overhear anything that might embarrass Councillor Howe and make it sensible to get Bliss inside.

A quiet one-to-one. Even half an hour would do it. Mumford was probably right, Charlie wasn't a killer. Just a cover-upper. Official cover-upper for Hereforward. All quangos had secrets, and this one ...

'Why don't you just go home, Brother Bliss?' Charlie lowering the crutch. 'Modern policing got no use for a one-man band.'

'Yeh, well, that's because no fucker wants to take individual responsibility any more. The new ethos of arse-shielding, Char—'

He was spluttering. The rain was in his mouth. Even the weather was on Charlie's side. This was a waste of time. Nothing for him here. Nothing but more grief, another chance to test his self-destruct button.

'Go home, boy,' Charlie said amiably. 'Go back to Liverpool or wherever it was you crawled from. Long outstayed your welcome down yere, you must see that. You got no friends, you got no—'

'Shah told you the lies his son fed him.' Bliss had started to shout, just needing to get it out. 'You told Shah you'd get it dealt with.'

'—got no wife, now, either. No wife … no kids?'

How the …? Bliss clawed rain out of his eyes.

'You're a sick little man, Brother Bliss. Come down yere thinking you were God's gift to West Mercia. Smart young city copper full of the ole Northern grit, show the country boys how it's done. Make a swift rise to the top.'

'That's bollock—'

'Only it never happened. You weren't good enough. Fooled 'em for a while and then they saw what you were. And now you en't going no higher and you know it and my, that's made you bitter, ennit? Bitter, twisted, sick little man. I know about you, Brother Bliss, known for a long time.'

'You don't know shit!'

'But I do know your father-in-law.' Charlie raising the umbrella so Bliss could see him grinning. 'Didn't know that, did you?'

Shit, shit, shit.

'Same lodge?' Bliss tried.

'Same county, Brother Bliss, that's all it takes. Very small county and you got a big, big mouth. You never deserved Kirsty. Nice girl, good, sensible head on her shoulders. Well rid of you, boy. *Well* rid.'

'You know the truth, Charlie?' Bliss in free fall now. 'I used to love being in this city when I first came. It was small, and it had … this freshness. Wherever you looked you could see a green field or a hill or a wood. You could breathe.'

'Stand there much longer, boy, your breathing days gonner be limited. Get pneumonia and die, and what a mercy that'd be, for all of us.'

'I used to like the way you could breathe. And now …' Bliss took a step forward, soaking socks fused to his frozen feet. 'Now all I can see is frigging greed and opportunism, and I don't enjoy breathing any more because whenever I breathe in I can smell somebody like you. I can fucking *smell* you, Charlie.'

Jesus, how pathetic was this?

Charlie stepped back, and his front door opened behind him. He let down his umbrella, gave it a good shake in Bliss's direction and went into the warm and shut the door very quietly behind him.

Through the windscreen, Merrily saw small smears of light, like glowing tadpoles.

Nightwatchman.

Huw had always preferred his own euphemisms: *visitors, volatiles, insomniacs, hitch-hikers.* Flavouring the unknowable with a measure of comforting familiarity.

'That's your word for a guardian, is it?'

'An entity or thought-form attached to the site to deter intruders who might want to damage or corrupt it,' Huw said. 'We could talk about cases where thunder and lightning resulted from somebody sticking a spade into a burial mound. And horrific phantasms, obviously. But you probably know all them. How close is the barn to the buried stones, lass?'

'Next field. Tell me about nightwatchmen, Huw.'

'Happen less harmful than they look, in most cases.'

'Less harmful? How?'

'Sometimes the images people receive may appear demonic. But that might be more a result of their own conditioning. If we operate on the basis that true demonic is, by definition, satanic and therefore something explicable only in terms of Christian theology, well … Neolithic's a long time pre-Christian. Unless it's been reactivated by more recent activity, you might be looking at no more than an old imprint.'

'By definition, a place memory without soul or consciousness.'

'If you accept, as I would, that ritual sites were usually in places of strong natural energy, that makes sense, aye.'

'What if it's something of human origin?'

'Way back?'

'For the sake of argument.'

'Happen a ritual sacrifice, then. Could even be a willing sacrifice, someone who'd elected or consented to look after the ritual site for all eternity and was then ceremonially slaughtered and buried there, or cremated.'

'But that's all theoretical, isn't it? And can only ever be. Goes too far back.'

'In that case, if there's owt there you've got a few centuries of experience to tap. You could talk to folk. Got to be some memory.'

'But if the people living there have not requested assistance and are never likely to ...'

Merrily paused for a reality check – if the Stookes were lying, all this was academic.

In the windscreen, the tadpoles were still aglow and wriggling. The lights of Ledwardine? Couldn't be. Not from this distance, in conditions of seriously reduced visibility.

'You could still go it alone, if you felt it was necessary. Or you could – as there's already controversy over it – offer to bless the stones. And then make it a bit more than a blessing.'

'That's not a bad idea.'

'You'd have to decide, on the evidence, whether a personality is involved,' Huw said. 'Whether you're asking for the place to be calmed or a spirit to be released. You could argue that if the stones are about to be put back up, with a conservation order, well ... a nightwatchman's entitled to redundancy. Retirement. A nice, long rest.'

'Yeah.'

'Keep us informed, anyroad,' Huw said. 'Now bugger off home.'

He was gone.

Merrily got out a cigarette and smoked half of it before fastening her seat belt and leaning over to make sure that the Boswell guitar case was safely wedged in the gap between the front and rear seats. She switched on the wipers, and pulled into the road. The lights in the windscreen were closer, and they actually *were* moving and some of them were blue. Shadows paddled across the lights. She flipped the headlamps up to full beam.

Two men coming towards her, carrying something between them.

White lettering on blue.

ROAD CLOSED.

Merrily braked.

But hang on, this was the link to the bypass, the great lifeline. It was on fairly high ground, this couldn't be about flooding. *We never looked back*, Lyndon Pierce said. *Benefits of progress, people.*

She lowered her window. Guy coming over – traffic cop, yellow slicker, fluorescent armbands. Merrily leaned out into the rain.

'What's happened?'

'Road's closed.'

'Yes, I can— What is it, a crash? An accident?'

Always seemed to be one, coming up to Christmas. Joy to the world.

'Can I ask you to turn round, please, madam? Just turn round here and get yourself back on the main road.'

'But how long—?'

'And take a different route, if you don't mind.'

'But the other road's going to be flooded, isn't it? How do I get into Ledwardine?'

'You don't,' the traffic cop said. 'Nobody does tonight.' He sighed. 'Or even, I'd say, this side of Christmas ...'

CHRISTMAS EVE

*When powerful interest groups
combine, archaeological guidance
can be subverted or ignored.*

Huw Sherlock, archaeologist,
Third Stone

45

Caple End

GOING TO SEE the Riverman wasn't much of a journey any more. On the edge of the cobbles, Jane lost her footing, swaying like a tightrope walker before going down on one knee into a depth of water that surprised her.

Squatting down to squeeze some out of her jeans before her welly could become flooded, she looked up to see an ovoid moon with a wide halo of dirty yellow, like a tallow candle.

Over a Christmas-card village?

No, not at all. Christmas-card villages were always lit with a warm haze of security. Pre-dawn, in the stillness of no-rain, Ledwardine looked stark and stripped, rigid with shock, its black timbers receded into shadows and its white plaster turned to bone.

Slopping down Church Street under moonlit, mushroom-coloured clouds, Jane was glad Eirion hadn't woken when she'd slid out of his bed to creep back to her apartment to wash and dress.

Last night she'd needed him with her, but afterwards there had been bad dreams. She'd been walking, then running through the churchyard in the blinding rain, trying to find Lucy's grave. Knowing roughly where it was and taking different turnings, the cold mud thickening on her legs, but the graves always had the wrong names on them, and then she'd wind up on the footpath which led into the old orchard, where she didn't dare look up because she knew the remains of old Edgar Powell's blown-off head were up there.

And then she did look up … and awoke.

As one did.

Dreaming of the dead again, but there was no rain this time, only

321

what had already fallen, massively, and now she was alone on the Isle of Ledwardine, under the yellow moon.

She'd thought there might be some people still around. There'd been a few out until well after midnight, bunched together, talking on mobiles, waiting for news. Barry at the Black Swan and his evening staff had kept the long bar open until one, though mainly for coffee. Jane had taken one out to Gomer, waiting on the square with Gwyneth. Who was going to pay Gomer Parry Plant Hire for all this work? Probably nobody. He was doing it for Ledwardine.

Jane stood watching the moon reflected in the deep water at the bottom of Church Street, most of the village bridge invisible now, a few nervous lights on in the hestate, but no more giant Santa's sleigh. No Christmas lights on the square, either: the Christmas tree had been unplugged before midnight, as if someone had felt there was a need to conserve electricity now that the village had become isolated.

Nobody had seen it happen. Everybody had been very confused last night; nobody could quite grasp what it meant. *What are we going to do?* If she'd heard that once, she'd heard it a dozen times, from both men and women.

Possibly her last totally clear memory was of Lol coming back into Lucy's house, where she and Eirion were still sitting by the wood stove, Lol's new music playing low on the stereo.

What? Jane had demanded, suddenly fearful. *What's happened?*

And Lol had said,

It's the bridge.

Jim Prosser had told him. Jim had been standing in his shop doorway telling everybody that the bridge had collapsed.

What? Jane reeling, springing up and rushing past him, out into the rain because she'd thought he'd meant *her* bridge, the bridge at the bottom of Church Street.

But it was worse than that. It was the one at the end of the bypass.

Caple End.

Which wasn't even very old – nineteenth century – and had just given way. Lay in pieces in the river.

Weight of water, Jim Prosser says. Came surging down at about five times the normal— Lol had broken off, then, and stiffened. *Where's Merrily?*

Jane had lied. Well, there was no alternative. Small Deliverance job, she'd said. When she'd tried Mum's mobile it was always engaged. When they'd gone out to join the growing crowd in the street, she'd cornered Jim Prosser. Nobody had been … hurt … had they?

Jim didn't know.

When Mum eventually rang it was from the bastard Ward Savitch's farm. Nearest to Caple End, apparently, and there was a fairly wide footbridge on Savitch's land, originally for getting cattle to and from fields either side of the river. No good for cars, but at least you could get across on foot or a mountain bike or something. The only access now.

Police were sending everybody back, Mum had said, but all the other lanes were flooded. With the bypass cut off, it meant there was no way in and out of Ledwardine for vehicles until the council could get something called a Bailey bridge installed, and that was going to be well after Christmas.

Mum said she'd walk, which might take some time, but at least she had the torch, but Jane had called Gomer, who'd taken his latest old jeep across the fields, all the gates open, now that all the livestock had been taken inside or onto higher ground.

About an hour later, Mum had come stumbling in, hooded and dripping, thrusting the guitar case at Jane: *Hide that somewhere, would you, flower?*

Surreal.

And now it was Christmas Eve and Mum, up till one, was, Jane hoped, still sleeping. One way or another, this was going to be a very different kind of Christmas.

'You've done just about enough now,' Jane told the river. 'You've made your point.'

She noticed how the dark water was creeping like a shadow up the pavement towards the steps of the first of the black and white houses, and heard Nick Drake singing,

'*Betty said she prayed today …*'

Jane spun round.

'... for the sky to blow away.'

'God.'

He was standing in his doorway, in dark clothing and no light behind him. She must've walked right past him.

'You couldn't sleep either, then,' Lol said.

'No.'

She was shaken. It was probably the first time he'd sung to her live, and he'd sounded so much like the dead Nick Drake it was eerie.

'How long've you been there?'

'Couple of minutes, that's all.' Lol pointed down Church Street. 'See how it's actually rising?'

'Even though it's stopped raining?'

'It's coming down from the higher streams now ...'

'That means even if it doesn't rain for a while, it's actually going to get worse?'

'It's got worse in the past few hours. They've put sandbags out at the Ox.'

'God, sandbags for Christmas?'

'And now we won't be able to get the fire brigade in to pump water away. Maybe Pierce is right. If Ledwardine was twice the size it might have its own fire station.'

'Don't talk like that.' Jane had lowered her voice, aware of the echoes they were making in the still, shiny street. 'What's going to happen, Lol? I mean, what are people doing?'

'Bull-Davies and Lyndon Pierce seem to be working together, for once. I think people whose homes are in danger will be encouraged to move out today. Better now than Christmas morning. At least it's still more or less a working day.'

'But how can they *get* out?'

'Special buses. Coaches. They'll set up a pick-up point at Caple End, on the other side of what used to be the bridge. Ward Savitch is making a field available as a parking area – where your mum left the Volvo, I imagine. And then they'll go across his footbridge to the bus.'

'I suppose Savitch is charging an arm and a leg for parking.'

'I don't think he'd dare charge anything,' Lol said. 'Somebody was saying he'd been using bales of straw as some kind of cheap flood barrier, and the whole lot had given way and fallen into the river, blocking up the bridge arches. Which may have been what drastically increased the pressure. Or helped, anyway.'

'*Savitch* might've caused the bridge to collapse?'

Lol shrugged.

'Lol, look … why don't you try and get some sleep while you can? Big night tonight.'

'Won't be that big. Might not be much of an audience left.'

'Well, I put it up on the Coleman's Meadow website. People the world over …'

'That was a kind thought, but they can't get in. Anyway, I might have to go out with Gomer again, if it—'

'Like, no *way*.'

'I might be fairly useless,' Lol said, 'but I think he trusts me to follow orders.'

'What if you damage your hand? What about your shoulder?'

His injury from Garway in October. He never mentioned it but she was sure it must flare up. And anyway, there'd be a lot of blokes available to help Gomer now. It wasn't as if anybody was going to be able to go to work or for last-minute shopping … or anything.

Jane gazed down the skeletal street. It was going to be weird. There'd be no traffic. No one driving in, no one driving out. Nowhere to go.

Almost like a return to medieval times.

46

Pentagram

Around dawn, Bliss's phone was ringing as if from the bottom of a lift shaft. In fact, from the bottom drawer of his bedside cabinet, where Kirsty had made him keep it. He pulled out the whole drawer to get at it and the drawer came apart, like it was reverting to flatpack, whole shoddy sections dropping into the still-sodden pile of Bliss's clothes.

'Boss?'

'Frigging time you call this, Andy?'

Peering towards what light there was. The sky through the bedroom window looked like a badly bandaged wound.

'We got you an early Christmas present,' Mumford said.

Bliss sat up. The bedroom was cold enough to preserve a corpse for a fortnight. Still hadn't worked out the heating cycle; had had to use the immersion heater when he'd squelched in last night to raise enough hot water for a shower – buggered if he was going to make Charlie Howe's Christmas by contracting pneumonia.

'Done a bit of a dawn raid, we have,' Mumford said. 'Just like old times, though not for Jumbo, obviously, as he en't never actually been in the job.'

'Where the hell are you?'

'Think of your favourite housing project.'

'Andy, please tell me you haven't done anything ... stupid.'

'Got a friend with us. I think he'd like a word. Hang on.'

Bliss heard a slurred voice saying something unintelligible but strongly suggestive of split lip. He swung his bare legs out of bed, sat on the side of the mattress in his underpants, shivering. Still aching, but that might be deeply internal.

'Got his own place, now en't you, boy?' Mumford said. 'Girlfriend and a youngster on the way and, like he says, not a good time to go away. Reason he wouldn't mind a word with you, boss, you get my drift.'

'Jesus, Andy, what've you done?'

The phone went dead for a few seconds, then this other voice came on, barking like an old Merthyr mountain ewe in the night.

'Andy've had to walk him round the block, Mr B. Get the circulation back into the boy's cold feet, kind of thing.'

Jumbo Humphries's wheezy laugh.

This was all he needed. Bliss scrabbled in the pile for something that felt halfway dry, his head full of images of ex-Detective Sergeant Andy Mumford beating up some low-life tearaway behind a garage block on the Plascarreg.

'Truth of it is, see, Mr B, he rung me last night, said he couldn't get you out of his head. He haven't heard you talk like that, never. Greatly worried about your state of mind. Figured we oughter do what we could, like.'

'Jumbo … listen to me … who've you got with you?'

'You still there, man? Bloody battery's on the blink, it is.'

'*Who*, Jumbo?'

'You ever see that ole film, early days of special effects, all these skeletons with swords?'

Bliss sighed. *Jason and the Argonauts.*

'We'll be on the spare ground, end of the first row of garages on the left,' Jumbo Humphries said. 'Blue Land Rover, long wheelbase, no side windows. Need to come in from the city. Belmont's still submerged, see. The real thing, this is, Mr B. You won't regret it, man, I'm telling you.'

Bliss threw a stiffened sock at the wall. Somebody save him from middle-aged cowboys looking for kicks.

'Best to come in civvies, mind,' Jumbo said.

Bliss thought about it all the time he was in the bathroom. He went downstairs, stood by the sad unplugged Christmas tree in the hall, picked up the phone, stood with it in his hand until the computer voice reminded him it was off the hook. Then he stabbed the button to get the line back and called in sick.

Jane wore a grey fleece over a pink T-shirt. She looked fresher but pale. They sat on opposite sides of the refectory table with a pot of tea. It was just after eight a.m., Eirion not yet up, a rare chance to talk, just the two of them.

Merrily poured the tea. Apple, mango and cinnamon, Jane's current favourite. They were trying not to talk about the bridge and living on an island.

'Eirion was telling me what Neil Cooper said. About the possibility of more extensive archaeology in Coleman's Meadow.'

'Or beyond,' Jane said.

'Yes.'

'And this is where you say, Don't get carried away about it. Don't get carried away like you did before, and look what happened.' Jane gazed down, addressing the table, speaking very slowly and softly. 'I *know* what happened. I got humiliated. And now half the nation's going to see it happen. And all the kids at school. And Morrell. And the heads of every university department of archaeology in the UK, they will all see me getting humiliated. Maybe it'll even be released on DVD so people who *really* don't like me can watch me getting humiliated over and over again.'

'It's not been televised yet.'

'*Oh* … no.' Jane's head came up. 'You don't go near him. This is not your problem, Mum. And, like, don't give me the old your-problems-are-my-problems line, because that doesn't apply. I'm eighteen, I'm an adult, I need to learn to deal with it. I *will* deal with it.'

'All right,' Merrily said. 'Help me with *my* problem, then.'

She put her cigarettes and the Zippo on the table. Told Jane about the Stookes, the various anomalies, proven and alleged, at Cole Barn.

It was legitimate to share this stuff; Jane had been part of it from the start. She only wished it sounded more convincing in the cold, damp morning. Pre-Blore, Jane would've become excited, full of the implications of this for Coleman's Meadow, the energy line, the spirit path.

She just drank some tea, sighed.

'Well … couldn't make *that* up, could you. Mum?'

Ethel pattered across the stone flags to her dish of dried food, began crunching.

'*I* couldn't,' Merrily said. 'But could they?'

Jane nodded, already resigned.

'Was there anything on your website about, say, site-guardian legends?'

'Mmm. Possibly.'

'And you had an email from a man who said Coleman's Meadow had one.'

'It was the dowser from Malvern who had the argument with Blore in the meadow before he started on me. Lensi was there, doing pictures. She might've talked to him.'

Merrily lit a cigarette, noticed there were only three left in the packet. She missed the rumble of the old Aga, a victim of its oil consumption.

'He seemed a decent bloke,' Jane said. 'I haven't spoken to him about it. If you want, I can email him now.'

'No, it wouldn't prove anything. Let's shelve any discussion about what a guardian is and whether there could be one in the meadow. Let's deal with the prosaic facts. Go back to your meeting with Leonora at Lucy's grave – presumably you'd had the email by then?'

'Weeks before.'

'Did you mention anything to Leonora to suggest there might be any kind of psychic disturbance in Coleman's Meadow?'

'I just told her about the spirit path and the need to maintain a link with the ancestors.'

'You didn't suggest to her that there might be something weird about Cole Farm?'

'I didn't know there *was* anything weird about it. What are you suggesting? They might've put all this together from bits they picked up from people like me?'

'Just eliminating various possibilities. Stooke's looking for material for another book and he's shown a slightly more than cursory interest in me … and you, of course.'

'So the bottom line …?'

'The bottom line might be me telling them their house may have a problem, and they go, well, if you say so, vicar, but what can you do about it? And then I go in and do the business and perhaps they video the whole process from some hidden camera, stupid little priest furthering the spread of primitive superstition … and suppose, instead of being the intelligent, sophisticated types they are, they'd been some poor old couple, et cetera, et cetera. I'm reading it already.'

'That just … stinks.'

'They haven't done anything yet, just told me the kind of stuff that people usually hand me along with a plea for help. But I shall be cool, Jane, I shall make inquiries.'

'What about Mad Shirley?'

'And I'll talk to Mad Shirley. As Huw points out, no need to approach her on behalf of the Stookes. Now she's telling everybody I'm not a fit person to be the vicar, it's … personal.'

'Take her down, Mum.'

'Yeah, and then I'll get on the phone and blast the cops for not returning my computer. God, it doesn't feel like Christmas, does it?' Merrily finished her tea and stood up. 'I'm just going to pop over to the shop before it gets crowded. Nearly out of cigs.'

'What about breakfast?'

'You and Eirion get something decent. I'll just have toast and Marmite or something when I get back.' She grabbed her waxed coat from the peg behind the kitchen door. 'Won't be long.'

Eirion had come down in expectation of central heating, gone back for a fleece, still looked cold. Pampered rich kid. Jane moved away from the sink, picked up a towel to dry her hands.

'She's annoyed with herself for letting things slide. I've seen this before. She needs to walk around the square a couple of times, smoke a cigarette, gear herself up.'

'Something happened I *don't* know about?' Eirion said. 'I mean apart from us being cut off until January?'

'Some people are messing her about, that's all.'

Jane felt suddenly depressed. Everything seemed so … cheesy.

'She's so … not like a vicar, your mother, isn't she?' Eirion poured grapefruit juice into a glass. 'Not like you think of vicars. Especially women. Not what you expect.'

'What – like they don't smoke, don't swear? Don't sleep with the bloke across the street?'

'She doesn't make you go …' Eirion wiggled his fingers like he was getting rid of something cloying. 'In a strange way, she's more human than the rest of us. Forget it, I don't know what I'm talking about.'

'It is odd, actually,' Jane said. 'I think it's something about deliverance people. Something that makes them dispense with the bullshit. I don't quite understand it either.' She looked over to the window. 'I wonder if Blore's going to be back on the site.'

'They'll surely be going home for … See, I was about to say Christmas, but he doesn't do Christmas, does he?'

'The TV crew won't be able to get all *their* stuff out. Unless they moved some of it last night after dark. But then, if the bridge went down around seven …'

'Maybe they'll have vans the other side and carry what they can across the footbridge.'

'We should check it out, all the same. I more or less promised Coops.'

'Your mum might be right, you know,' Eirion said. 'Blore might've found nothing. And Cooper's just embittered because they didn't give him control of— *what?*'

Jane had walked over, put her arms around him. She felt a bit tearful.

'We're destroying your Christmas, aren't we?'

Eirion smiled sadly, running a hand down Jane's hair.

'So far, it's the best Christmas I've ever had.'

'Ah. Right.' Jane looked up at him, solemn. 'Just for a minute, I forgot you were Welsh.'

Dodging neatly away, grinning, clapping her hands and then, as Eirion chased her round the table, snatching an apple from the bowl and throwing it at him. Eirion caught the apple, tossing it from hand to hand, as a vague smear of sun in the high window opened up this white fan of light in the room.

Jane stopped, catching her breath.

'Jane ...?'

'Lucy.'

Jane sat down. Eirion did his wry smile, but his eyes were wary. He put the apple on the table.

'It was just something coming back to me.'

As clear as reality. As clear as if it had been Lucy who'd caught the apple, and Jane was back in the old shop, Ledwardine Lore, the day they cut an apple in half, sideways. Not, as you normally did, through the stalk. She remembered Lucy holding out a half in each hand.

There ... what do you see?

And Jane had seen, for the first time, the slender green lines and dots in the centre of the apple which formed a five-pointed star. The penta-gram that lay at the heart of every apple but which you only discovered if you cut through it sideways, which people seldom did. The hidden magic in the everyday. Lucy saying, *Forget all this black magic nonsense. The pentagram's a very ancient symbol of purification and protection.*

'I think something's staring us in the face,' Jane said.

As if, in that momentary lifting of the spirits, when she'd ducked away from Eirion, picked up the apple, something had opened up for her, like two halves of an idea she couldn't yet put together.

Let no one talk of the humble apple to me, Lucy had said.

Jane sat down. She felt slightly dizzy. Nothing was quite real.

'Irene, could you ...?'

'Anything.'

'If Lol has to go out with Gomer again? Like his hands ...?'

'I'll help,' Eirion said. 'If Gomer will accept me.'

'And tell Lol not to play "Fruit Tree" tonight.'

Most of the village was lying low. Many people had been up late talking in the street, half anxious, half excited, about the implications. Some of them driving out to see the bridge, just to make sure. Lights still burned here and there in the greyness, shimmered in the dark water, but only James Bull-Davies and Gomer Parry were to be seen, at the top of the square, leaning against Gomer's jeep.

'Long ole night, vicar.'

'I don't know how you do it, Gomer.'

He looked scarily happy. Shirley West would be seeing the Devil's light in his bottle glasses.

'Don't need much sleep these days, see. Done all my growin' and never had much in the way of beauty.' He stood looking down the street, rolling a cig. 'Dunno what's left for us to do with the ole river, but I reckon our commander-in-chief yere'll have a few ideas.'

'Well, we can't build a new bloody bridge,' James said. 'Not even you.'

'Erm ...' Merrily sank her hands into her coat pockets. 'Can I ask you guys something? In confidence.'

'Ask away,' Gomer said. 'Like the ole poet said, What is this life if, full of care, we en't got time for the little vicar?'

'Cole Barn. What's the history? It did belong to your family at one time didn't it, James?'

'Gord, vicar, way back everything belonged to my blessed family. Barn itself, no. Ground it's built on, yes – sorry, said I'd check if there was any mention of stones. No there wasn't but the Bulls weren't exactly of an antiquarian bent. If the stones were in the way, they'd've buried them or smashed them up and that would've been that.'

'When did your family last own the land?'

'Cole Farm was ... finally sold, I think, in the 1900s, to Albert Evans, family's estate manager at the time. Inherited by his eldest daughter who'd married into the Pole family, and then finally – as you know – left by Margaret Pole to Gerry Murray, who's now in with Pierce and capitalises on his inheritance by flogging the barn to the Frenchies.'

'Any gossip about it?'

'Sort of gossip?'

'Erm ... my sort of gossip.'

He took it well. Didn't blink. He had, after all, been a soldier.

'Not that I've ever heard. Called Cole Barn on the sales particulars, but Albert Evans built it as a house, for his retirement. Meant his eldest could move into the existing farmhouse with *his* family. Didn't live there very long, though, Albert. Moved down to the village, for convenience. House was eventually gutted, became a cattle shed. That's it, really.'

'First I yeard of it,' Gomer said, 'was when ole Harold Wescott was renting the land from Maggie Pole, and he put his beasts in there, and they made that much noise at night as Maggie, up at Cole Farm, her couldn't get no sleep, so her makes Harold transport the beasts two mile to his *own* barn. That was how it become a tractor shed, see. Tractors don't moan.'

'Never knew about that,' James said. 'Live and learn.'

'I done some drainage work there once, for Harold,' Gomer said. 'Or tried to. Beggar of a job. Nothin' went right. Sometimes you finds ground don't wanner be shifted, see.'

'What made you think that?'

'You just gets a feel that a place is tellin' you summat.'

'Like *bugger off*?'

'Mabbe. Ole digger ... ole digger broke down twice – well, I'm saying *ole* digger, her was new back then, and we never had no real trouble with her since. I goes back to Harold Wescott, I says Harold, en't there nowhere else you can put this drain? Well, I knowed there was, see, but it'd be longer, and Harold, he was always bloody tight like that, so I told him I'd do it for the same price, and that was that. Sorted.'

'This was near Cole Barn?' Merrily said.

'Twenny yards? There was no front on him then, the ole barn, so I'd keep the digger in there while I was on that job.'

'And, erm ... that wouldn't have been when you couldn't get her started, by any chance?'

'You're ahead of me there, vicar.'

'Not been back since?'

'Not likely to, either. Gerry Murray got his own digger, as we all bloody know.'

'Sore point,' James said. 'Murray was hired to do the preliminary ground-stripping for the archaeological dig. Pierce obviously fixed it.'

'Bent bastards,' Gomer said.

The Eight Till Late had only just opened. It was empty.

Apart from Shirley West behind the till.

In the front of the shop, this was. Not in the post office which still had its blind down, concealing the public information posters, the clock and even the iron cross which Shirley had hung very prominently, as if she, definitely not Merrily, was God's representative in Ledwardine. As if the post office was the centre of the real faith.

Merrily looked into the smoky eyes below the coiled hair, summoning a smile.

'Morning, Shirley. Jim not in?'

'Getting his breakfast,' Shirley said. 'He stayed open half the night, the poor man. What do you want?'

Charming as ever.

'What's going to happen with the post office today, Shirley?'

'May not open. No mail going in or out. I'm waiting for instructions from head office.'

'Difficult situation.'

'Yes.'

'I don't suppose they've had this problem before.'

'No.'

'And all my fault, apparently,' Merrily said.

Good a time as any.

47

Beacon

SHIRLEY WORE AN outsize denim shirt with epaulettes, no make-up, no jewellery. Since acquiring the status of village postmistress she'd put on weight, shed femininity. Something ageless about her now, and monolithic.

Merrily stood in front of the counter, small but immovable.

Yes, well …

'A short chat, Shirley?'

Shirley had her fingers entwined below her chest, her eyelids half lowered. Her efforts to avoid scented soap and shampoo had left her smelling like a clinic.

'It's just that people keep saying to me, if Mrs West is a member of this other church in Leominster, why does she keep coming to yours? While making it fairly clear that she doesn't like the way you do things. Never really know what to tell them.'

'You can tell them it's none of their business,' Shirley said.

'And I'd happily do that if you hadn't put on a floor show for them yesterday.'

Shirley said nothing, but the fingers of her right hand, ringless, began flexing on the counter, next to the till.

'Not that I haven't been impressed with what the other place has done for you,' Merrily said. 'The confidence. That sense of certainty.'

Along with a refusal to compromise, a blindness to grey areas and a tendency to regard all other spiritual paths as highways to hell.

Welcome to fundamentalism.

'It's a bigger organisation than I'd thought, too.'

'Worldwide.' Shirley actually smiled. 'And growing day by day. What can I—?'

'But its headquarters are in America?'

'What can I get you, Mrs Watkins?'

'Or in cyberspace. Possible to build a big congregation on the Net.'

'Our congregation is growing day by day,' Shirley said. 'As we approach the Endtime.'

'Ah … right. It all comes back to that, doesn't it?'

'Look around you,' Shirley said.

'The flood?'

'Read the Book of Daniel.'

'I've read it. Not an easy one.'

'And does not Daniel say that the flood will take the Antichrist? Before the Rapture?'

'He does?'

Maybe it wouldn't help to get pedantic over whether Daniel ever had much to say about the Rapture.

'Before we meet the Lord, in our bodies of light,' Shirley said.

American cults had traded heavily on the Rapture. Mass suicide one result.

'Do you … have a particular mission, Shirley?'

'Each of us carries the Light of the Lord, and if we remain steadfast the light will grow within us until we *become* light.'

Shirley West becoming light?

Dear God.

An enigma, though, this woman. Nobody could say she was unintelligent. Former bank branch-manager – good head for figures, presumably, extensive knowledge of business and personal finance, ability to keep customers happy.

What happened?

'We are to keep a vigil at the doorways and raise our lights above them.'

'Which doorways are those?'

And why was this like trying to tease really obvious information out a class of small children?

'*In latter times some will depart from the faith, giving heed to deceiving spirits and doctrines of demons.* Many doorways to hell, look.'

'And there's one here? A doorway here in the village? Is that what you're saying? Are we talking about Coleman's Meadow? Do you have a mission in connection with Coleman's Meadow, Shirley?'

'And the evil in your church.'

'Meaning what?'

'With its pagan carvings and its worship of the orchard.' Shirley's quivering forefinger suddenly extending across the counter. 'Why do you not eat what God has provided for you?'

'Let's not get sidetracked, Shirley, you don't know what I eat. Tell me about the evil.'

'I see what you buy. I know the filth you read. I told that woman, you should *not* allow that filth—'

'Oh, *that* filth.'

'Her shop's cursed. Full of demons. The witch's shop.'

Oh, for—

'You mean Lucy Devenish?'

Not hard to imagine how Lucy would have reacted to a woman able to toss paganism, atheism and vegetarianism together, without any fore-thought, into the drawer marked *hate*.

Shirley drew back her shoulders, bulked herself out.

'And who's lit the beacon for The Baptist to the Antichrist?'

Silence. The strangeness of no traffic.

'That woman was laughing at me,' Shirley said. 'Always so clever, these Londoners. She laughed. She said, *do you know who bought that book?*'

A rare gash of winter sunlight struck white sparks from the chromium rim of a freezer.

'You fooled me at first. Just like you've fooled so many others.' Shirley raised an arm like a club, aiming a forefinger that no longer quivered. 'You are the doorway. *You* lit the beacon!'

Seen soldiers turn from perfectly serviceable fighting chaps to Bible-punching lunatics after one week's leave, James Bull-Davies had said.

Took a little longer with Shirley. Attaching herself to the curate in Leominster, laundering his vestments, polishing his car, before he'd fled down south. After which, she'd moved to Ledwardine, appointing herself as Merrily's eucharistic handmaiden. Hesitant at first, faintly fawning.

Then the knife going in. Another feature of fundamentalism was the need to cosy up to people perceived as being touched by holiness, and then to demonise them when you moved on.

Shirley stood in silence, hands clenched above her chest now, as if in defiant prayer. Merrily felt guilty. Where was the woman underneath and what had she ever done to reach her? Recalling her faint embarrassment, discomfort at the altar. Maybe all this *was* her fault.

Shirley lowered her head to stare directly into Merrily's eyes.

'The reason I come to your shoddy services and listen to your so-called sermons is to hold up the light so that all may see what you are. It hasn't gone unnoticed, Merrily Watkins, the way you've been dismantling the Christian framework. Reducing the hymns, so that voices are no longer raised in praise. Replacing Evensong with your so-called *quiet time*, when the demonic can enter in.'

'Shirley, who exactly runs your church?'

'All sitting under their candles and opening their hearts to the demonic in the silence that should be full of praise.'

'Who runs the Church of the Lord of the Light, Shirley?'

'The Elders. And I am one of them now. Learning to preach the Word of God.'

And already beginning to master that key technique of making everything, no matter how bonkers, sound like holy writ.

'What about America? Who runs the church's website in America?'

'I don't have to answer *your* questions. Do you think we're stupid?' Shirley began shaking her head very fast like she was trying to present a moving target to incoming demons. 'Your Church ... founded upon lust ... is a nest of maggots! First it was women, now it's homos and perverts. Men who stick their *things* into other men and think they can preach the word of God.'

'So what about the founder of the Church of the Lord of the Light?' Merrily said. 'What about a priest who inserts a crucifix into a woman's vagina?'

She felt sick for a moment. Sick at herself for resorting to this. And what if James had got it wrong about Ellis?

Shirley's mouth had opened like a cavern in a cliff face, air rushing in. Her eyes bulged and her hands grasped the till as if she was about to lift it and hurl it at Merrily across the counter.

'Why don't you ask him about it, Shirley? Send him an email.'

Time to go. This was a wasted exercise. If there'd ever been a chance to get through to Shirley West, she'd missed it.

'Don't think you weren't seen,' Shirley whispered as the shop door opened with a ping of the bell. 'Walking with the Baptist in the place of stones.'

Edna Huws, the organist, came in with two shopping bags.

'Isn't it awful, Merrily? I didn't know until I switched on breakfast television. I'd gone to bed early, thought it was drunks in the street. Trapped in our own village! I don't know what's happening to our world.'

'We were just talking about that,' Merrily said.

'Mr Davies wants me to move out. I won't go. I told him, I've spent the last thirty Christmases in that house, quietly, sometimes with friends, sometimes alone, and leaving it only to play the organ in church, the best service of all the year, and I won't have many more years and I *won't* be evicted on Christmas Eve.' She peered into Merrily's face. 'But it won't happen, will it, Mrs Watkins? It won't come any further up Church Street. Will it?'

'We're all praying it won't, Miss Huws.'

'Thank you. *Thank* you. Oh, good morning, Mrs West. Isn't it terrible?'

'It is indeed, Miss Huws.' Shirley's arms dropping to her sides. 'What can I get you, Mrs Watkins?'

'Just twenty Silk Cut, please, Shirley.'

Shirley smiled.

'I'm afraid we're out of cigarettes today, Mrs Watkins.'

Merrily looked up at the shelves, saw packets of pipe tobacco and Rizla papers.

'Mr Prosser doesn't keep many now, look. Sold the lot last night. Panic buying. You know what people are like. He was expecting a new delivery today. Not gonner happen now, is it? Now we are an island.'

Shirley West, triumphant.

48

History and Fear

THE BLUE STRETCH Land Rover was parked on derelict ground on the edge of the Plascarreg – south of the Wye but not as far south as it had been last night. The Wye was hungry and taking big bites out of Hereford.

Bliss walked back very slowly, past the shell of a black Nissan Micra, twocked and burned out. Without the waxy sky above it and the rainwater pool underneath, you could imagine that Jumbo's blue wagon was an armoured car in the ruins of Baghdad.

For once, even Bliss fitted in. He was wearing what Naomi called *Daddy's SAS kit*: Army-surplus camouflage jacket, cargo trousers, hiking boots, green beanie. He'd climbed down from the Land Rover and walked around the brown concrete fringe of the estate for maybe ten minutes, on his own, trying to get his head round this.

'Feeling better now, is it, Mr B?'

Jumbo Humphries leaning out of the driver's window, offering him a swig of a half-bottle of Bells. Bliss shook his head, went round and got back in on the other side.

Better would not describe how he was feeling.

'Jumbo,' he said. 'Move this heap somewhere else, would you? If I was a cop and I saw a Land Rover on the Plascarreg ...'

If I was a cop? Mother of God, had it come to this?

The back of the Land Rover was like a cell. Vinyl-covered bench seat along one side. No windows. Jason Mebus sharing the seat with Andy Mumford in a donkey jacket.

'You worked it out now, boss?'

Still finding it hard to contain his delight, Mumford looked fondly at Mebus, who was staring down at his hands like they were already locked into cuffs. Didn't look up when Jumbo Humphries started the engine and drove them round the back of the estate, into a field entrance. Jumbo was programmed for fields.

'This all right for you, is it, Mr B?'

'Safer,' Bliss conceded.

Jumbo, a *before* picture for WeightWatchers, got out, squelched through the puddled ground to open the galvanised gate. This way they'd only be disturbed by some farmer, and there weren't many farmers Jumbo didn't know. Bliss sank back, hands behind his head: how to play this ...

Or even *whether* to play it. What any copper with sense would do was get on his mobile and summon the troops. Back off, let them deal with it, hoping a result would save his career.

Two possible reasons for what Andy had done. One, excitement: lower-ranking cops were still being pensioned off at fifty – the new thirty, too young to be thinking the most exciting time of your life was history. Yet Bliss had thought Mumford, who'd looked more than a bit pipe-and-slippers at forty, would've been able to handle it better than most.

Which suggested it was more likely to be the second possible reason.

Charlie Howe.

It was conceivable that Mumford still had a conscience about helping Charlie cover up that death, way back, maybe nursing a feeling that Charlie should go down one day for *something*. Wasn't exactly uncommon, that need to tie up a few ends before you left the service.

And maybe it was actually easier, these days, to come back and tie them: no rules, no stifling paperwork, and you still had all the skills.

Bliss looked over the back of his seat at Jason Mebus. Just a kid. A cold-eyed, corrupted kid, still just about young enough to be at school but with many years of criminal experience. His upper lip was puffed out on one side.

'I really think,' Bliss said, 'that you have to give me a name, Jason. Or, to be more specific, you have to give me *the* name.'

'Don't even know his name.'

'We think you do, Jason,' Mumford said.

Mebus flinched slightly.

'What happened to his mouth, Andy?'

'Resisting a chat.'

Bliss sighed. No paperwork, no rules.

And a strong element of serendipity.

It came down to history. And fear.

It was not a result that Mumford would have obtained if he'd still been in the job and history hadn't cut as deep. Jason Mebus knew too much about the tragic death of Mumford's nephew, Robbie Walsh. Therefore Mebus was afraid of Mumford in a way he wouldn't be afraid of a serving copper.

Mumford had the look of a brooder.

As it turned out, Jason was already in a state of deep unease. What he'd thought would be no more than some drug-trade disposal had turned out to be part of the highest-profile crime in this town in living memory.

'Jittery from the off,' Mumford had whispered. 'I'm talking about cocaine, and his eyes are all over the place and wondering who Jumbo is. I didn't do no introductions.'

'Just fishing at this point?'

'Trying to get you a bigger fish, boss. I know this bastard. He's vicious, but he en't over-ambitious. No way he'd go uptown on his own.'

'Right.'

Good detective, Mumford. Looking across at the Plascarreg's prison-block profile, it had already occurred to Bliss that there was no way Gyles Banks-Jones would come down here on *his* own.

There was someone else in this. A middleman.

'Go on, Andy ...'

'And I'm saying things like, bit out of your league yere, en't you, boy? And I'm tossing names at him.'

'Which names in particular?'

'The names you give me: Gyles Banks-Jones, Steve Furneaux, Charlie Howe. And that was when he ... when he *first* tried to get out of the vehicle.'

And hurt his mouth on the dash, apparently. And other parts you couldn't see, Bliss suspected.

Starting to feel queasy right down to his gut. The information better be solid as a rock because – as Mumford, presumptuously, had already apparently conveyed to Jason Mebus – no way was this going anywhere near Gaol Street.

'I never killed him,' Mebus said. 'You gotter believe me, dad. Why would I? Why would I do an ole feller like that? I en't never even heard of him.'

'Now, that's not true, is it, Jason?' Mumford said. 'You had every reason to wish him no good.'

Bliss could tell that Mumford hated it when Mebus called him *dad*. Even the thought of having a son like this …

'Him being a magistrate and all,' Mumford said. 'You don't remember?'

Bliss smiled, pretty sure that Ayling had come off the bench a good ten years ago, but Mebus wouldn't know that.

It was about pressure.

'Don't tell me you didn't recognise his face?' Mumford said.

'I didn't fucking look at his face.'

'Squeamish?'

'I used to work in a slaughterhouse, dad.'

That was how thick Jason was.

'Who was with you?' Bliss said.

'Justin. My brother. But all he done was drive, yeah?'

'So the bloke you met …'

'Never seen his face. Head to foot in waterproofs, and a black bala-clava with eyeholes.'

'No kidding,' Bliss said.

'Swear to God—'

'Where'd you meet him?'

'In the forest, as arranged.'

'Which forest?'

'Dean. In this … where they been clearing trees?'

'That would be called "a clearing", Jason. And this was arranged by?'

'Birmingham.'

They'd been into this. All controlled substances, including supplies to be delivered to Gyles Banks-Jones's jeweller's shop, came in from 'Birmingham'. Mebus was just a distributor, he didn't know the people he was dealing with. This was normal; if he was nicked, that was where it ended, nobody he could finger to the cops. It was just 'Birmingham'.

At least, Mebus *assumed* it was Birmingham.

'So you'd had a call on the mobile,' Bliss said. 'From Birmingham.'

'I knew the voice.'

'Male or female?'

'Male. Brummy accent.'

'And he asked if you were up for something a bit different. Tell me exactly what he said.'

'He said somebody was gonner to be topped, kind o' thing, and—'

'That was the actual word he used?' Mumford said.

'I didn't know he meant it literally. It was fucking horrible, dad, in the back of that van …'

'White van, right?' Mumford said.

'They said it wasn't hot. False plates and that. We met in the Forest, he gives me the keys and half the money.'

'What build? Short? Tall? Fat? Thin?'

'I dunno – medium? You couldn't tell how fat or thin under all this gear.'

'Voice, how old?'

'He din't say much. I'd had the instructions on the phone. Where to put the … parts. He just hands over the keys and pisses off. He likely had a car somewhere, or a bike? Motorbike?'

'So you looked in the back of the van?'

'Well … yeah.'

'What did you see.'

'There was like a … two parcels? The big one, it was like this roll of black plastic. The … littler one, that was just a bin sack.'

'So you did which one first?'

'The big one. The river.'

'They specify which river?'

'The Wye. We left our wheels in the forest, went off in the van.'

'No problems?'

'Nah, not this time of year, at night. We found this track, rolled it down the bank, went round and dragged it to the water. Just unrolled it from the plastic, straight into the river.'

'What happened to the plastic?'

'Put it back in the van like I was told.'

'All right,' Bliss said. 'Let's talk about the small parcel.'

'Can I have a fag?' Mebus said.

'No. I want to know about the head.'

'I hadn't to open it till we got there. There was a bag to carry it in, like a holdall?'

'Carry it where?'

'Rotherwas Chapel. This old church, back of the council tip? You know the place?'

Bliss nodded. As a matter of fact, he did. Private chapel of the Bodenham family, Catholics. Lovely building. Too lovely to be stuck on the edge of an industrial estate.

'So what went wrong, Jason?'

'Two cop cars is what. Two cops cars parked up near the tip. Nearly shit myself. Like they was waiting for us.'

'Sort of cop cars?'

'Usual sort. Blue and yellow?'

'So what did you do?'

'Turned off, soon's we could without it looking obvious. Drove straight back into town.'

'Didn't you think to try again?' Mumford asked.

'Oh yeah. Like if they was still there they wouldn't notice the same white van? No way, dad. Justin, he wanted to dump the van somewhere, but we had to get back to our own wheels, din' we?'

'You had specific instructions where at Rotherwas Chapel to put the head?'

'In the porch. Somewhere no foxes could get at it, you know? So anyway, we drove around town a bit. I didn't know what to do. I'm thinking it better be a church, right? I was thinking the porch at the

Cathedral, but we got there and there was some service going on or summat, so we was fucked there, too.'

'Nobody you could call and ask for advice?'

'I told you, no.'

'What time was it now?'

'Dunno, seven-ish? Mabbe a bit later. All the churches round town, there was like nowhere to park or people about. And then I remembered this place, the ole monastery down Widemarsh Street. Had, like … reason to go there before and I knew how quiet it was. We was getting a bit desperate by then, look.'

'So you parked up …?'

'Some street round the corner. Takes the bag in there, thinking we could leave him on a wall in the ole monastery?'

'And that's where you left the bag, is it?'

'Nah, we took the bag away with us. Anyhow, we seen this cross thing with the steps. Seemed better than a wall.'

'Whereabouts did you put the head?'

'You telling me you don't know?'

'No, Jason, *I* know. I'm just making sure *you* know. Where exactly did you leave the head?'

'In one of them spaces. There's like these openings, like church windows? Justin found this brick to prop it up.'

'You had to touch it?'

'We had these rubber gloves. They all went back in the van before we poured the petrol all over it and set it alight.'

'And you'd been left petrol for that, had you?'

'Four cans. Had to be a serious fire. We had to hang around, make sure it was well burned out.'

Bliss wondered if Gloucester had found it yet. Wouldn't be much use DNA-wise, anyway.

'You said you didn't look at it much. The head.'

'It was dark, wannit? We took the bin sack out the bag, lifted it up the cross in the bin sack. Then I gets it in position and like … eased the bag away, real slow and careful.'

'So you didn't notice anything odd about it.'

'Only what we'd been … They said to be real careful and not dislodge these bits of stone? In the eyes?'

Clincher.

'Kind of stone?' Bliss said.

'This, like … like you get on graves and stuff? Bit like that.'

'So you left the head in the wrong place, eh?'

'Just done what we thought was best.'

'You had a reaction to that? From Birmingham?'

'Nah. But I en't had the rest of the money neither.'

'How do you normally receive it?'

'Sometimes a bloke on a Harley. Varies.'

Bliss glanced at Mumford, who nodded. Would explain why Jason was jittery. Were Birmingham cross with him? And when people like that were unhappy with your performance, how would they convey their displeasure?

'All right, Jason,' Bliss said. 'Let's go through the highlights again. That first call. Birmingham. They say why they wanted you for this job?'

'Well, we … handled goods for them for a good while, ennit? They knew us.'

'Nothing this big, though, I'm guessing, Jason.'

Jason said nothing.

'Worthwhile, was it?'

'Not bad.'

'So when they called you first, they just said this feller was gonna be topped. They give any indication why?'

'I just thought mabbe somebody they been supplying hadn't paid his bills. Din' reckon on no council big shot, no way.'

'You mean you didn't ask.'

'No.'

'They tell you why they wanted the two bits in different places?'

Mebus shook his head.

'Didn't it even occur to you to ask?'

'It *occurred* to me …'

'Mother of God,' Bliss said. 'You're not the sharpest knife in the drawer, are you, Jason?'

'They said he had to be made an example of. That's why I thought a poor payer.'

'You never said that before.'

'I only just remembered.'

'*Give me strength.* Who sawed Ayling's head off, Jason? Was that you? Deep in the forest, with a chainie that eventually went up in flames with the white van?'

'No! I told you. It was already done.'

'So you never saw his eyes.'

'No.' Mebus suddenly lurched in his seat, his gaze swivelling from Bliss to Mumford and back. 'Hey, none of you's wired, are you?'

Bliss shook his head in weary disdain.

'How about you escort our friend back to his estate, Jumbo?'

49

Sharpest Knife

JUMBO GOT THE message: time for cop talk. Bliss watched him follow Mebus towards the Plascarreg, clap the kid once on the back, then go his own way diagonally across the field. Leather bomber jacket, bouncy walk; he looked like a battered old medicine ball.

'Well,' Bliss said. 'That was a bit of an eye-opener, wasn't it?'

'Thought you'd like it.'

Mumford spread himself on the long back seat, stretched his legs out where Mebus had been sitting.

'Yeh, but what … what am I gonna do with it, Andy? Walk into Annie's sanctum, tell her she's got this case all to cock? Explain exactly how I know she's fallen for what she was supposed to fall for?'

'Rotherwas Chapel. I noticed you liked that.'

'The stones in Ayling's eye sockets were from what the council still prefers to call the Rotherwas Ribbon.'

'Was that on the news?'

'No way, it was what they held back. Served its purpose, too. Told me Mebus wasn't lying.'

'So Rotherwas Chapel …'

'The official ancient monument at the foot of Dinedor Hill. The one they *can't* destroy to put a road through. That was just perfect.'

'If you wanted to fit up the Serpent-lovers?'

'Exactly.'

'Likely Jason done 'em a favour,' Mumford said. 'Takes you a while to put it together, it don't look like you were led there by the nose kind of thing.'

'That's true. So where's this go next? I tell Annie she's a stupid cow, but don't worry about it because I only know the truth on account of I've been working on me own with a private investigator, unethically, on the verge of actual criminality and— *Jesus, Andy.*'

Bliss thumped the top of the seat. Down the field, two seagulls took off like a storm warning.

'Funny thing,' Mumford said. 'I've only realised since I retired how much quicker the process is when you don't have to make out reports.'

'Tell me about it.' Bliss pulled off his beanie, ran a hand through the wasteland of his hair. 'Doesn't help that after I spoke to you last night I went to see Charlie Howe.'

He saw Mumford briefly shut his eyes.

'Boss, you dick.'

'It was indeed a bad, bad move, Andy.'

'What did you think, he was getting old? Lost his teeth?'

'I figured we could have a private chat, agree to keep off each other's backs. Andy, what's the *matter* with me?'

'I figured you wasn't yourself on the phone.'

'Annie'll've heard all about it by now.' Bliss sank his chin into the pillow of his arms on the back of the passenger seat. 'Amazing how fast you can go down. Seen it happen to other fellers but usually it gets a bit of push from the booze or gambling. Never gonna happen to me.'

'All right,' Mumford said. 'You wanner have a think about what you got? Lay it all out?'

Bliss was grateful. Never had a sounding board like Mumford before or since.

'Half of what's left of me brain's turning it over and over as we speak, Andy. How much of Jason can we rely on? I still think the butchering was possibly part of his contract. The killer did a lovely neat job on Ayling – one judicious thrust, one accurate little wound that closed up so fast there wouldn't be much blood.'

'Meaning why would he want to do the messy stuff himself if he could pay an ex-slaughterman?'

'Exactly. I'm guessing there was only one parcel to begin with in the back of that van, and the Mebuses had to haul Ayling down the forest and whizz the head off.'

'Bone could ruin your chain,' Mumford said.

Bliss rolled his eyes.

'Lot of rain to wash the blood away, mind.'

'Now that *is* a good point.'

'Also,' Mumford said, 'if anybody found the signs, they'd think it was just evidence of some poacher having a go at one of these wild boar you keep hearing about in the Forest.'

Bliss nodded.

'And Jason's keeping quiet about that bit,' Mumford said, 'on account of it's got a smell of violence about it. It's a bit more than waste disposal. Leaves you asking the question, did he do the whole thing?'

'What do you think?'

'En't got the balls. En't got the brains.'

'So we're looking for a pro, aren't we?' Bliss hunched himself higher up the greasy passenger seat. 'And a contract killer puts the crime into a whole different arena. It's hard to imagine the Friends of the Serpent having a quick whip round and dispatching their hardest member into the underworld with a bag of unmarked twenties. I think we're firmly back in Jason's world.'

'Drugs?'

'*Fact* – Jason and various members of Jason's family and friends obtain wholesale coke from Birmingham, Bristol, Gloucester, Newport. Comes into the Plascarreg, as we've all known for years, for distribution to the usual suspects, plus the new breed of middle-class party animal supplied by the likes of Gyles Banks-Jones. Which is where I came in.'

'There don't have to be a connection,' Mumford said.

'Yeh, but there *is* a connection, Andy. And it's through a man called Steve Furneaux. Steve is Gyles's next-door neighbour. He was the last person, or – assuming *he* didn't do it – the last but one person to see Clement Ayling alive. And, unless all my instincts are playing me wrong, he's a cokehead. Quite long-term, I'd guess. For a long time, Steve was on the fringe. Suddenly he's looking like a main player.'

'Form?'

'No *way*. All right, let's approach it from the other side. Mebus gets a call from Birmingham. I think we have to assume *Birmingham* is Jason's euphemism for the people he doesn't talk about … whether they're Birmingham or Gloucester or Newport. Whatever, Birmingham calls and discloses to Mebus that a man is going to be topped and an example has to be made of him. Now … if we assume Dinedor is just being used to lay a false trail, who wants Ayling dead? And why?'

'Not a clue, boss.'

'OK … Let's think *out of the box*, as Steve would say. Ayling, Furneaux and Charlie Howe – all members of the same quango. One of these outfits nobody knows what the hell it does but it's obviously above the rules of democracy and public scrutiny.'

'Sounds like Charlie's kind of thing.'

'Yeh. Who's gonna tell us more about Hereforward?'

'Journalists?'

'That's a thought. You know anybody?'

'Bloke at Three Counties News Service? Freelances are always a better bet, my experience.'

'Could you give him a call?'

'I'll try and find him.'

'Thanks, pal.'

Silence. Bliss heard a preliminary patter of rain on the windscreen; probably bring Jumbo back in a minute. It occurred to him he needed to go into Hereford this afternoon, buy some presents for the kids, try and get Karen to wrap them properly ready for the ordeal of taking them over to the in-laws' farm tomorrow. What a bloody desert his life was. He closed his eyes for a moment, shuffled the cards in his head.

'All right,' he said to Mumford. 'Let's cut to the heart of it. What do we know about the killer?'

'Good with a knife?'

'Either good or lucky. Let's assume good. And that in itself … if we assume he's an outsider, brought in to do a quick job, how common is that? Your hit man, almost by definition, uses a firearm. But … there's no basic reason why not a knife. Knife crime's breaking records all over the country.'

'And it's as old as them fellers in skins who built the ole fort on top of Dinedor,' Mumford said.

'Yeh, but the method of dispatch was clearly more scientific than your average slasher, which is why Annie and Brent got a bit excited when they discovered poor old Willy Hawkes might've had commando training.'

'Contract killing en't what it used to be. Any hard kid in need of a few quid … frightening, really.'

'It's what I said to— *Shit.*'

'Wassat, boss?'

Bliss thought, *Sharpest knife in the drawer.*

'It was Annie I said it to. I was trying to wind her up about leaving this Worcester paedophile witness-killing to take command of the Ayling murder, and I made that same point about kids going into the homicide business.'

'*That's* contract?'

'And a stabbing. This feller who was gonna give evidence against his brother-in-law, knifed to death in his garage.'

'Two contract knife-jobs? How often's that happen? You got the PM report on that one? Where the blade went in?'

'Well, *I* haven't, obviously, but it shouldn't be difficult to get me hands on it.'

'Karen?'

Bliss nodded.

'A good girl. And at least she won't have to talk to Howe, who— *bugger me, Andy!*' Bliss threw his beanie at the roof and caught it on the return. 'Listen to this … I said to Annie something like, must be a bit of a problem, you know who ordered the hit but you don't know who actually did it, and she— *frigging hell …*'

The voice like an ice pick in his head: *Actually, it's the other way round, we're fairly sure we know who did it, but we don't know who ordered it.*

'They know him, Andy. They've gorra name for this bastard.'

50

The Heart

As THE COMMUNITY was splitting up, there was a feeling of its coming together. The people, locals and incomers, relying on one another and knowing that they could.

In the chilly, damp air on Christmas Eve.

Merrily and Jane had spent the morning with James Bull-Davies's party of volunteers, helping people on the riverside estate to move furniture upstairs: chairs and TV sets and stereos and computers and phones. Carpets and rugs were rolled up, some of them left on the stairs or on the tops of tables. Items that were too heavy to move or plumbed-in – cookers, washing machines – were covered with plastic sheets or polythene feed sacks cut open.

At the split-level home of one retired couple, thousands of books were packed into boxes to be stored on the upper floor. People who lived on the higher ground were accommodating lawnmowers and bikes and, in one case, tropical fish.

Like the Blitz, someone said, and Merrily supposed comparisons weren't all that misplaced. There *had* been a sense of that old British wartime spirit, which was heartening.

Some families who'd believed it could never happen had been shaken by breakfast-TV pictures of flooded homes in villages no more than a few miles away, like Eardisland and Pembridge. Even though levels in Ledwardine were conspicuously higher than last night, some people only ever believed what they saw on TV.

And on TV they also saw the bridge. Pictures from last night, all blue and orange lights and the floodlit, whitened river blasting between the exploded arches.

Calls were made, families arranging to be picked up by friends and relatives on the other side of Ward Savitch's footbridge. Some of the weekenders, fighting to save Christmas, had grabbed what rooms were available in hotels around Hereford and Leominster.

Merrily borrowed Gomer's jeep to drive over to Savitch's farm in the late morning, following a family of five, off to spend Christmas at the grandparents' farm near Hay, the jeep packed with presents the parents didn't want the kids to see. Helping to carry the stuff across the foot-bridge to where the grandad was waiting with his four-by-four and a small galvanised livestock trailer.

This strange parade of refugees tramping across the field with their cases. There must've been sixty cars behind council and police barriers on the Ledwardine side of the footbridge and several coaches and vans in the free world across the river. And a burger van and a fish-and-chip van, naturally. Lyndon Pierce was there, getting hassled by a guy called Derry Bateman, self-employed electrical contractor.

'You and your bloody bypass. When was that bridge last examined, eh?'

'These en't normal conditions, Derry.'

'And you en't gonner give me a proper answer, are you? You know how many jobs this is gonner cost me? How'm I supposed to get my fucking gear out, Lyndon?'

'Couldn't you hire a van the other side? Carry it across?'

'And leave it overnight in some bloody field to get broke into?'

'We're doing all we can,' Pierce said, Derry Bateman turning away in disgust.

'Tosser.'

Peace on earth: always too good to last. Back on the village square, the Christmas tree was lit up; around it, a cobbled-together choir sang carols from the Christmas service books Merrily had brought from the church and handed round. People making wartime-style jokes as they clustered behind their synthesised smiles.

'Only difference, in wartime, folks was evacuated *to* the countryside,' Jim Prosser said in the shop. 'Have to impose bloody rationing soon.'

Merrily said. 'You're absolutely *sure* you've got no cigarettes?'

Sounding, she was afraid, almost shrill. Jim leaned across the counter, lowering his voice, confidential.

'I'd put sixty Silk Cut away for you, see. Only *somebody* found them, din't they? And sold them.'

The post office hadn't opened, wouldn't be opening, and Shirley West had gone.

'Many you got left, Merrily?'

'Three.'

'Packs?'

'No, Jim, three cigarettes.'

'Oh hell. Best we all keeps away from *you*, then.'

Jim laughing, but nervously. It was two and half cigs, actually. She'd lit one automatically after breakfast and put it out when she'd realised.

By lunchtime, for any number of reasons, she wanted to kill Shirley West.

By two p.m., there were no more people in obvious need of help. It looked like a vacant film set: no cars, no kids playing, no dogs barking. Jane and Mum went back to the vicarage, where Mum went upstairs to make two bedrooms habitable and Jane threw cheese and pickle sandwiches together, putting some into a basket with some fruit and taking it down to the river to find the guys.

Easier to find Gwyneth, the big yellow JCB. All three of them behind her, having a breather. A few metres in front of them, this wall of hardpacked soil, rock and red clay.

'En't much more we can do, Janey.' Gomer, in dark green overalls, leaning up against Gwyneth, rolling a ciggy. 'All down to if it rains again tonight and how hard.'

'And will it?'

Jane looked up into a sky like frogspawn. A holiday caravan was being towed across the field towards higher ground, somebody's emergency home in waiting.

'Count on it,' Gomer said. 'Trouble is – and you don't like to tell 'em – but this could be the best part.'

'You're joking, aren't you?'

Gomer mouthed his ciggy, lit up.

'I done some flood relief once, down South Wales, fifteen, twenny year ago. We come back afterwards, help them clear up. Terrible mess. Get deep water in your house, sometimes it's buggered for a year or more. Folks comes back to find this thick slime on the floor, whole place stinking to hell. Plaster on the walls all ruined. I seen places had to be stripped back to the breeze-blocks.'

'Gomer, what about—?'

'They talks about fire gutting a home, water does it just as well. Sorry, Janey?'

'I was just going to say, what about your bungalow?'

'He'll be all right.'

'Like you can't exactly move stuff upstairs, can you? What I was thinking, why don't we clear out some of your furniture and stuff, store it at the vicarage? We've got masses of—'

'Don't you get fussed, Janey. I got the important stuff out – Minnie's things. Put 'em up the roof space.'

'Yeah, but—'

Minnie had been dead nearly two years.

'You ask me,' Gomer said, 'only place we could have a real problem with – Church Street. En't no earth we can move there. Only sandbags, and sandbags is a poor substitute for a real barrier.'

'It's true,' Lol said. 'You've already got a lake at the bottom. All it needs is for the water to rise another ten feet up the street and it'll be into the first black and whites. Maybe for the first time in history.'

'What about your house, Lol?'

Lol shrugged. There was mud in glistening streaks like snail-trails down the front of his sweatshirt. The square, along with the church, the vicarage, the Black Swan and most of the shops, was at the highest point of the village and therefore considered to be safe, and Lol's house wasn't too far down from the square.

'You're ready for tonight?'

'May not be an audience left, way things are going.'

'You don't get out of it that easily, Lol. All the people who count are going to be there. *You're* coming, aren't you, Gomer?'

'Less there's an emergency, I'll be there, sure to.'

'Aw, Gomer, if there's an emergency, can't you for once let somebody else—? I mean, you've already worked too hard for a—' Jane broke off, Gomer giving her a hard look '—a man who isn't getting paid.'

That was close. Nearly called him an old guy to his face. Jane felt herself blushing, looked away quickly at the new bank Gomer and Lol and Eirion had made, the way the earth was impacted, the way the structure curved, following the line of the swollen river under the bubblewrap sky. Not exactly like the Dinedor Serpent, more like ...

'Oh my God.'

Eirion lifted himself away from the JCB, watching Jane through narrowing eyes.

'I've got talk to Coops.'

'Jane, let the poor guy have a Christmas, huh?'

'It's ... it's just so obvious, Irene. It *has* been staring us in the face.'

Eirion looked doubtful. She knew he believed in her, maybe more than anybody, but he didn't see the pentagram at the heart of the apple.

'It's why it's special. It's the whole key to this place. I'm sorry ...' For a moment Jane couldn't breathe, couldn't find the breath to say it, totally choked up with emotion. 'It's what's behind the whole thing. The Village in the Orchard.'

51

Manic

'YOU DON'T ASK much, do you, boss?' Karen Dowell said.

The cusp of lighting-up time. Bliss was back on the fringe of Phase Two. Still no signs of life in Furneaux's house, but the Christmas tree was twinkling in Gyles Banks-Jones's front window, shadows moving behind it.

Fearful shadows, with any luck.

'And what if he checks *me* out?' Karen said. 'How do I explain my interest? And, more to the point, how do I explain why I haven't just asked Howe?'

Bliss thought about it. Problem was, the DCI babysitting the Lasky case for Howe ... he didn't know this feller at all. Came in from Droitwich a month or two ago. Bliss wasn't sure he'd even been to Droitwich, and a new DCI with Howe to answer to would be wearing belt, braces and two pairs of underpants.

'All right, tell him the truth.'

'Which version of the truth is that?'

'Tell him it's a long shot. Tell him that although we've gorra man well in the frame for Ayling we're covering our arses and we'd like to compare wounds just in case. Tell him you've been trying to get hold of Annie for the last hour, without success. Come on, Karen, *you* know what to say. *Charm him.* And if there's anything approaching a match on the wounds, take it from there.'

'What if Howe—?'

'She won't. It's Christmas. The worst she'll do is make a note to nail you about it when school's back. Trust me, where Howe's concerned you have one big thing going for you here, Karen: you are *not me*.'

Bliss saw a face in Gyles's window, then another face the other side of the Christmas tree. So they'd spotted him. It didn't matter; if Furneaux wasn't available, it would have to be Gyles. Half a story was better than nothing.

'Gorra go, Karen. Keep me informed.'

'What if he's gone home?'

'So ring him at *home*.'

'You sound awful manic, Frannie,' Karen said.

'It's me accent.'

The faces had gone from the window. *Manic? Me?* Bliss got out of the car, and strolled directly across the road, pushed the bell and stood there until a light came on over the door and Gyles opened it.

Unshaven, crumpled shirt, open cuffs hanging loose.

'Well,' Bliss said, 'I can't say this was convenient, to be honest, Gyles, it being Christmas Eve and me off duty, but … here I am.'

'Yes,' Gyles said.

Bliss waited.

'Look, I've been bailed, Inspector. I don't—'

'Why'd you call me, then?'

'What?'

'I gave you me mobile number, Gyles, and you called me.'

'No, I didn't.'

'Hang on …' Bliss got out his mobile, opened it up, held it out towards Gyles. 'Why else would your number be here, under missed calls?'

'I don't know.'

Gyles didn't look at the phone. Bliss gave him a smile that was wry but full of sympathy for the poor bastard's situation, as Mrs Jones's voice elbowed in from the hall behind him.

'Is it that detective?'

Gyles turned, took a step back, telling her it was.

By then, Bliss was inside.

Bliss supposed the reason he hadn't taken much notice of Mrs Jones before was that Gyles had just confessed to everything. They'd given the house a good going-over and found nothing that Gyles hadn't already shown them. He had no form, a cleanie.

His wife had been there all the time, assiduously tidying up after them but hiding nothing, saying nothing.

'We're glad you came,' she said now. 'Aren't we, Gyles?'

Kate Banks-Jones was plumpish, had long brown hair and a mouth that turned down but made her look unhappy rather than petulant. She wore a long grey cardigan over a striped jumper and jeans and no conspicuous jewellery. Maybe she'd binned it all, in fury. The tension had wrapped itself round Bliss as soon as he'd walked in.

'I did *not* phone you,' Gyles said.

'It doesn't matter,' Kate said briskly. Her face was flushed, her eyes full of stored heat. 'We're glad of the opportunity. And I'm glad you're on your own this time.'

'*Kate, for—*'

'I wasn't going to say anything in front of all those other police.' She didn't look at Gyles. 'Or the children.' She spread her arms to show they were alone. 'Thank God for grandparents.'

A downlighter illuminated a white-framed sepia photo of Hereford Cathedral, misty, across the river. Apart from the artificial tree in the window, that was the only light. No other festive decorations. About five coloured globes hanging from the ceiling looked seasonal but probably weren't.

'I've made a full statement,' Gyles said. 'I've admitted everything.'

'And *he* thinks that's an end to it.'

Kate looked up at the ceiling. They were sitting in a triangle, Bliss in a wooden-framed chair that was more comfortable than it looked, the Banks-Joneses at either end of a long settee, a lot of dark blue cushion between them. There was a small plasma telly and a deep bookcase full of books about gems and modern jewellery.

'Well, yes.' Bliss leaned slowly forward, hands clasped between his knees, doing sorrowful. 'It's very far from the end, Mrs Jones.' He looked up, from to face. 'You'll have read, I'd imagine, about the murder of Councillor Ayling?'

Neither of them expecting that. Kate's head and shoulders jerked back. Gyles just went rigid. Good, good, good.

'I'm sorry,' Bliss said, sliding the blade in. 'But if you will mix with criminals, it's no use going into denial about what they might've been getting up to when you're not there.'

'I don't believe you,' Gyles said, and his wife turned on him.

'Don't be *stupid*, Gyles.'

Couple of days' worth of scorn in Kate's eyes.

'I'll be honest with you,' Bliss said. 'I'd been taken off the Ayling case to investigate this trivial shite, and I wasn't best pleased. We do actually prefer working on the big ones. Not well-disposed towards you, Gyles. But I'd forgotten what a small town this was.'

'It said pagans in the paper,' Gyles said. 'I know nothing about any pagans. I don't see how there can possibly be any connection between Ayling's murder and … and …'

'So you have no connections with the local authority? Or anyone who works for it?'

Gyles's eyes were all over the place, but he never once looked at his wife. Bliss let the silence take over the room.

'Look.' Kate Banks-Jones stood up. 'He couldn't possibly have any connection with what happened to Ayling. I mean, *look* at him. Does he look like a drug dealer?'

She bit her lip and sat down, probably realising what a silly question that was.

'And what does a drug dealer look like, Mrs Jones?' Bliss said. 'Have a bit of a think.'

She didn't reply at first, just stared at Gyles until he looked up at her. A little furtively, Bliss thought.

'I don't have to think very hard,' she said.

'No.' Bliss nodded. 'Didn't think you would.'

'Kate, no,' Giles said quietly. 'Don't do this.'

'Oh, the hell with it,' Kate said. 'A *real* drug dealer looks a lot like our next-door neighbour.'

The breath that came out of Gyles creaked at the back of his throat. Kate turned away from him.

'I'm trying to put an end to it.'

'You'll put an end to both of us.' Gyles was rocking on the sofa, gripping his knees, his teeth gritted. 'Think about the kids.'

Bliss sat still, saying nothing, thinking hard. Rapidly turning things over and over and inside out and, whichever way you looked at it, it made perfect sense that Gyles was no more than the frontman, the façade, the patsy.

'… thought Steve was awfully cool at first,' Kate was saying. '*His* idea that Gyles should bring selections of jewellery to parties. Steve went to a lot of parties all over the West Midlands. Whole new world, wasn't it, Gyles?' A sneer, then turning to Bliss. 'Look, I'm not saying we hadn't done any coke before. I mean, when we were first married. We'd been students together. I just didn't want anything to do with it after we had the kids. But Gyles … Gyles, unfortunately, was into his second adolescence. Plus, of course, he was making lots of lovely money.'

'You weren't complaining,' Gyles said. 'You'd been on my back for years about how little we were taking in the shop.'

Bliss said, 'So it was Steve who had the contacts?'

'Steve has contacts *everywhere*,' Kate said. 'He's a planner in every sense of the word.'

'And you are a respectable, long-established family firm.' Bliss looked at Gyles. 'Perhaps not doing as well as you once did. Funny, I was in a place the other week, used to be just a rural garden centre, way out in the sticks, now it's twice the size with a massive jewellery department. Bling up to here. Hard times in the old city, eh, Gyles?'

Gyles said, 'I want to explain—'

'I think he wants to explain, Inspector, that our neighbour can be quite unpleasant. People who use cocaine like Steve uses cocaine can get awfully aggressive.'

'Moderation in all things,' Bliss said. 'That's what my old mam used to say. But they say it doesn't always work with coke.'

'He knows some fairly horrible people,' Kate said. 'People you don't want to … I wanted us to move. Sell up, get out. But we're locked into Hereford. Can't sell the business because Gyles's parents own half of it, and they know nothing of this. We were going to … tell them over Christmas.'

'Didn't you say your kids were with them?'

'With *my* parents. They don't know, either. We've told them we're terribly busy in the shop – that's a laugh – and have to work late. You can see the state we're in. Look at my hands shaking. Some of our older customers are not going to come near us again, are they? And who wants to buy a small shop these days, anyway?'

'It's a problem,' Bliss said. 'And I'm very sorry for you, but … hard to scrap the charges at this stage.'

'Not even if we—'

'We *can't*,' Gyles snapped. 'He … he'll take it very badly.'

'Well, of course he will,' Bliss said. 'But look at it this way, Gyles – I'm gonna nail the twat anyway, with or without your assistance. It's just a question of how long he goes away for. Or if he goes away at all …?'

Bliss crossed his legs, leaned back. Kate started plucking at her cardigan.

Gyles said, 'We'd get protection?'

'Just ask your questions,' Kate said.

At one time there had been an underworld, a criminal community.

Ordinary people had nothing to do with it.

Drugs had changed all that, the ubiquity of drugs. The discovery, by ordinary suburban people who served on the PTA, that snorting a line or two of coke didn't automatically turn you into a denizen of the gutter.

Thus, the suburban snorters became part of the new Greater Underworld.

As Kate had intimated, it was Steve who had the contacts. Steve coming in from Brum to take up his new appointment with the Herefordshire planning department. Very pleasant chap, Kate thought at first. Steve would flirt with her, in an unthreatening, flattering way. At the time, Gyles had been wanting to double the size of his shop window, to allow for a bigger display of his fine jewellery, but the shop was on the edge of a conservation area and the planners had been inclined to refuse permission.

Until Steve had a quiet word in the right place. Steve tapping his nose at Gyles: between you and me, OK, mate?

So Gyles owed Steve a big one, and that was the start of it.

'Who arranged deliveries, Gyles, once the basic structure had been set up?'

'I did. Steve would come round with what he called his shopping list.'

'And *you*'d pay Mebus?'

'Yes. It would come back ... threefold. It didn't seem like crime.'

'Always for parties?'

'And personal use. And sometimes he'd come for a large order.'

'You know what for?'

'We didn't ask,' Gyles said.

'We didn't need to.' Kate sniffed. 'It was usually before he went away somewhere.'

'To where?'

'To something connected with his job. He was on a committee and they went away to thrash out ideas and things.'

'A *blue-sky thinking* weekend.' Bliss smiled. 'So where's Stevie now?'

His phone was throbbing in his hip pocket. He placed a calming hand over it.

'We don't know,' Kate said. 'Birmingham or Gloucester ... or London. I really couldn't say. He has a lot of friends ... and a girlfriend who sometimes lives here. Sometimes he brings her back with him.'

'Not always the same one,' Gyles said wearily.

'You think he'll be back tonight?'

''I think so. He says he likes a traditional Christmas. Talked about going to a service in the Cathedral. A place to be seen, I'd guess. And then he's having a ...'

'Party?' Bliss said.

'Inevitably.'

'Tell me, Mrs Jones, what was his reaction to Gyles getting busted? Sympathy? Some advice about taking it on the chin, pleading guilty and keeping shtum? A gentle warning, perhaps?'

'Not that gentle, really,' Kate said.

Gyles, well out of this conversation now, looked like he was about to be sick. Bliss took out his phone and inspected the screen.

'Right then, guys, I'll leave you to have a think if there's anything else you want to tell me. I'll be just across the road. Someone I need to phone back.'

*

'I'm still shaking,' Karen said. 'I'd rather abseil down the spire of St Peter's than do that again.'

'Good cause, though, Karen.'

'It better be. Thought I was going to have to sleep with him.'

Bliss stood at the bottom of Gyles and Steve's shared drive, away from the only street lamp. He had to smile.

'Karen, I wouldn't've asked—'

'I know. It's just I'm not comfortable lying, never have been.'

'So, cutting to the chase?'

'The answer's yes.'

Something throbbed in Bliss's chest.

'The wounds?'

'One through the aorta, but a few more besides. Maybe after-thoughts?'

'Window dressing.'

'Yeah. Didn't fool their pathologist. His feeling was the bloke was dead almost before the knife went in for a second time.'

'Wooh, wooh, wooh,' Bliss said.

Between the sporadic clumps of housing he could see the lights of the city, flat as a pinball table, and the silver ball was pinging. Ram another coin into the slot before it stopped.

'So you asked him for the name.'

'He said he'd call me back. That was when it got tense. By some incredible good fortune the only guy in the CID room, when he rang to check me out, was Terry Stagg.'

'He called *you* back with the name yet?'

'No.'

'Give him an hour, then call him again and tell him it's important we have it.'

'I *so* do not want to do this.' Karen paused. '*How* important?'

'Well, Karen, I think this might be it.'

'What's that mean?' An edge of panic in her voice. 'What are you doing?'

'Turning over stones.'

'But Frannie, you're *sick*.'

Bliss laughed.

'I mean you're not part of this, are you? How can you do anything when you're out there?'

'I'll think of something.'

'It's Christmas Eve.'

'Yes.'

He looked across at the city with the thick night clouds on top, like a cold compress. When Karen had gone, as it began to rain, he went back to the car, switched on the radio, low. Sagged back in the seat, closing his eyes as a chapel choir sang *Silent night, holy night.*

Another idea came to him. He thought about the options, then switched off the radio and rang Ledwardine Vicarage.

52

Blue Light

WHEN THE RAIN came back, it was so hard and loud it was like the scullery window was being thrashed and thrashed with old-fashioned brooms made of twigs. Jane had to hold the heavy Bakelite phone tight to her ear to make out what Coops was saying.

'… Pure conjecture, Jane, so don't go …'

'No. I won't. Honestly.'

It was like the rain was speeding up with her excitement. She was finding it hard to sit still. Alone in the scullery under the desk lamp, charged up with the importance of this. Could hear the buzz and clink of chat and crockery in the kitchen – Mum in there with Eirion, Lol and Gomer.

'OK, say the orchard's been there since medieval times …'

'Do you actually know that?' Coops said. 'I didn't have much chance to go into the records.'

'Nobody knows. It's just always been there. Can't be the only village in the centre of an orchard.'

'No.'

'And it certainly wouldn't be the only village inside a henge.'

There. She'd said it. *Henge.* A word you could chew. Jane had her modest collection of archaeological textbooks spread out over the desk, cross-referencing.

A kind of circular ritual monument unique to the British Isles with a ditch and a bank …

… May include megaliths, like Stonehenge and Avebury, or timber posts, as at Woodhenge and Durrington Walls.

She also had the fairly rudimentary map of the village in the centre of an old Ledwardine guidebook, produced in the 1930s when the orchard still formed most of a semicircle and neither the hestate nor the housing at the bottom of Old Barn Lane had even been thought of.

And you could see it. When you knew you could *totally see it.*

They were all living in the middle of a henge! The whole village part of a ritual site dating back four thousand years.

There was like a blue light inside Jane's head.

Ledwardine was the pentagram at the heart of the apple.

'This could mean there are more stones, Coops.'

'It's impossible to say. Stones get smashed, taken away, used in buildings.'

'But even if these are the only stones, Coleman's Meadow is only a fragment of the monument.'

'It's all theoretical, Jane.'

'You weren't saying that yesterday. You were totally convinced that Blore had found something, and you were walking all over the orchard in the rain trying to second-guess him. Come on, admit it, you were thinking henge as well.'

'What I was thinking doesn't really matter. It's the purest— There are no obvious signs.'

'That's because they're all under what's left of the *orchard* ... The orchard was actually planted to cover up the henge – maybe the henge was threatened or somebody—'

'That's not something we can ever know,' Coops said.

What was *wrong* with him? Had he had a row with his wife or something, down there in Somerset?

'You'd thought about it before yesterday, too, hadn't you? You'd thought *henge.*'

'Look, all right, it wouldn't be *that* unexpected. A henge is just a circular area with a ditch and a bank. As you probably know, they found a massive one a few years ago not twenty miles from here, in Radnor Forest. But not this side of the English border.'

'What the hell's *that* got to do with it? There wouldn't've *been* a border back then. Why are you being so negative, Coops?'

'I just … just don't go spreading this round, Jane. I mean, obviously *I* can't stop you but …'

'Hey, don't worry, nobody's going to take any notice of me, Coops, I'm just a disgraced applicant to the University of Middle Earth. Look, I just feel this is so *right*. The Village in the Orchard. Encircled by the orchard … concealing *what was encircling it before.*'

'Jane,' Coops said, 'how can I put this? If you start going on about your feelings—'

'If I hadn't had any feelings in the first place, where wouldn't—'

Jane clammed up. He was right. She had to stop claiming credit. That was how she'd fallen into Bill Blore's net, the precocious, big-mouth teen. Yes, she *was* a medium for this – *one* of them, that was all – for something that needed to come out. But if you went round talking like that people would think you were bonkers. That was, the *establishment* would think you were bonkers; Blore was proof that things hadn't changed so much since the leading archaeologists of the day had slagged off Alfred Watkins.

She just couldn't wait for tomorrow, though. Daylight. Christmas Day. Perfect. She'd be out at first light, looking at everything with new eyes. The familiar transformed. Every time she thought about it, something new occurred to her … like where orchard faded into churchyard, she realised that what she'd thought was the remains of a burial mound might actually be part of the bank of the henge.

'The orchard,' she said, 'was preserving it into the Christian era, all through the witch-hunt times. The old pagan spirituality maintained?'

A tradition. From Alfred Watkins to Jane Watkins, via Lucy Devenish.

Miss Devenish would ever wish it so.

Lol was part of this. They were *all* part of it.

There was only one unfortunate aspect.

'Of course, there's Bill Blore.'

Coops said nothing.

'He's going to want to keep this to himself, isn't he?'

Coops still silent.

'How can we get it out first, Coops, just to stuff him? I mean, come on, he doesn't deserve it.'

'No,' Coops said. 'He doesn't deserve anything.'

'So what can we do? I realise I'm not much use here. I'm just a—'

'Jane … you don't understand.'

'So explain it to me.'

'I can't.'

'Coops … what's happened?'

'We'll talk about it when I get back after Christmas.'

'No.' Jane hugged the phone to her ear, the rain blitzing the window. She could feel her heart beating, her blood racing, or something. 'You can't do this to me, Coops.'

'Jane, I know you've had a bad couple of days, and you're right, Blore doesn't deserve … anything. I just think – don't take this the wrong way, please – but I don't think you're mature enough to deal with it, and I don't mean that in any …'

Jane gripped the phone with both hands. She wanted to scream at him, but if she went down that road it would just prove him right about her state of maturity.

'I don't yet know the full details, OK?' Coops said. 'I had a call from my friend in the Chief Exec's office, and it was very risky for her to get the information, so I don't want any comeback on her.'

'All right,' Jane said. 'Listen to me. If you tell me—'

'I can't. Jane, I've got a wife and a baby on the way. I need this job.'

'If you tell me, I promise it won't go outside this house.'

'What does that mean?'

'It means I might tell Mum, because like we're not into secrets these days? But Mum's a vicar and doesn't go shooting her mouth off.'

'That doesn't arise, Jane.'

'But if you *don't* tell me …' Jane kept her voice low, speaking slowly. 'I'll walk up to Blore tonight in front of everybody in the Swan and I'll tell him—'

'Jane, you think anyone will take any notice of what *you*—?'

'I don't *care*, Coops. I don't give a toss what people think of me any more. I'll ask him about the henge. I'll *tell* him about the henge …'

'You'll just make a fool of yourself again. Just stay away from him, OK? Look, give me—' Coops lowered his voice but brought it closer to the phone. 'Listen, I'm in enough trouble with the family. I'm not exactly the life and soul. And I'd need time to explain this. I'll call you back.'

'But I'll be—'

'And when I do, you'd better make sure you're sitting down, Jane, because this is going to ruin your Christmas.'

53

Won't

THE CAR WAS the nearest he had to a home now. At least it didn't have an unplugged Christmas tree and a newly emptied wardrobe – he'd noticed that this morning, along with spaces on the walls, gaps on the shelves; Kirsty must've come back, plundered the place.

Bliss sat there chewing his nails, the rain weeping down the windows, the mobile in his lap.

The Banks-Joneses knew where he was, if they had anything else to tell him. Occasionally one or the other would come to the window, like a kid watching for Santa Claus. It would be too dark to see him now, parked in the foundations of Phase Two.

Tried three times to reach the reverend. Engaged, engaged, engaged. He rolled his forehead against the top of the steering wheel.

Christmas Eve. It was a bad joke. This time next year he could be kipping in frigging doorways. When the phone began to vibrate, he fumbled it to his ear without looking at the screen.

'Karen ...'

'Hate to disappoint, boss.'

'Andy. Sorry. I'm—'

'Talked to my friend Fred Potter. Three Counties News Service?'

'I'd forgot about that.' Bliss straightened up, remembered his chewing gum and reached across the dash. 'You were asking him about Hereforward, right?'

'You likely know this already, boss, it was in the *Hereford Times*. Least, some of it was. Hereford councillor rushed to hospital in the Cotswolds?'

'Can't say I recall it.'

'Heart attack. Councillor suffered a heart attack during a weekend away with other members of the Herefordshire advance-planning group, Hereforward.'

'When was this?'

'Last summer. Potter says Hereforward's one of these names gets mentioned so often on council reports you stop seeing it after a while and folk give up asking what it does. But they have weekends away. They'll go and look at what's happening in some other city. Fact-finding mission. Or else just brainstorming weekends, kind of thing.'

'I like that word *brainstorming*.'

'Well, then, about six months ago – in the summer, anyway – they go for a session at a country-house hotel on the edge of the Cotswolds. Hire the conference suite, as usual, so their intensive deliberations won't be disturbed. Late Saturday night, a member of the committee gets rushed to hospital with this heart attack. Touch and go for a while, but he pulls through.'

'I'm glad to hear it.'

'There were whispers, however, of a toxicology report revealing a high level of cocaine in the blood.'

'Well, well.'

Bliss mouthed a wafer of gum.

'Known for putting a strain on the heart, coke is,' Mumford said. 'They reckon if they keep fit, go jogging and confine the snorting to weekends they can handle it. Big mistake, apparently.'

'My understanding,' Bliss said, 'is that a heart attack is often the result of a novice snorter overdoing it. I did a short course once, very illuminating. Nobody we know, this councillor?'

'Nobody *I* know. Youngish chap. I've mailed you the cutting, but it won't tell you much. Just a heart attack, mercy dash, lucky to be alive, all this stuff.'

'How did they know about the toxicology?'

'Hospitals leak.'

'Oh, they do.'

'But it went no further, anyway. No papers touched the story. Too much trouble, Potter says, too many legal hurdles.'

'Would Ayling have been on this weekend?'

'Potter thinks not. Doesn't think Ayling was co-opted on to Hereforward until a couple of months later.'

'Still.' Bliss chewed slowly. 'Something's definitely coming together here, Andy. I can feel it.'

A weekend of euphoric brainstorming. He could imagine them coming back with pages and pages of brilliant ideas, looking at them on Monday morning, thinking, *what on earth is all this shite?*

'I wonder what else they get up to, apart from coke.'

'You're thinking what's in it for Charlie Howe?'

'Can't help it, Andy. Eats away at me.'

'Quite a liberating experience, cocaine,' Mumford said thoughtfully. 'So I'm told.'

'Plays hell with the inhibitions.'

'Old days,' Mumford said, 'we always thought of councillors and officials as stuffy ole buggers. Fellers in tweeds, retired headmistresses. Times changed, ennit? Plus you got consultants.'

'*Consultants.* I like that word. You reckon they have extra consultants on their blue-sky weekends, Andy?'

'I'm sure they do,' Mumford said. 'But let it go, boss. Don't go making a dick of yourself again. Don't you bloody well go near him.'

'I won't, I won't.'

'You need any help, you give me a call.'

'It's Christmas Eve, Andy.'

'You *seen* the state of Christmas TV?'

Bliss tried Ledwardine Vicarage again. Still engaged. He was reaching for another stick of chewie when his windscreen lit up red.

Tail lights.

Car pulling into Furneaux's drive, just as the phone started trembling.

'Yeh.'

Karen said, 'He won't.'

'He *won't?*'

'He wants to speak to Howe.'

'*Shit*. You told him—?'

'Yeah, yeah, I said I'd been trying to get hold of her. He said when I did I should respectfully ask her to call him. Sounding a bit distant.'

'Didn't you point out to him—?'

'I didn't point out *anything* to him. I don't *like* it when they start sounding distant. When they start calling you sergeant instead of Karen.'

'Jesus.'

Bliss squeezing his eyes shut.

'It didn't exactly surprise me, boss. Would *you* share the name of a suspected killer with some unknown DS from Worcester?'

The tail lights swam in the windscreen, duplicated by brake lights now.

'You think I've lost it, don't you, Karen?'

'I think you've had a very bad few days, boss. I think you should try and relax.'

'Where? In front of the telly in me house, on me own? And if that sounds like self-pity, it is.'

'Oh, Frannie, I'd say you could come round here, but—'

'Your boyfriend wouldn't like it, and quite right, too. All right. No worries. There'll be a way round this. There's always a way.' Bliss watched the red lights go out. 'You have a good Christmas, Karen. I owe yer.'

Who didn't he owe?

'You won't do anything daft, will you, boss?'

'You know me, Sergeant.'

'I do. That's the trouble.'

'Merry Christmas, Karen,' Bliss said. 'I'm blowing you a kiss.'

Option One: he could go back across the road on his own. He could do that.

No warrant, no evidence, but you didn't need any of that for a …

… A cosy chat.

Like the one he'd been ready to have with Steve last night, and what a mistake *that* would've been. Could've blown everything.

Could still.

All right, Option Two. Ring Gaol Street, see who was on tonight: Stagg, Wintle? Tell them he was feeling much better now, invite whoever it was to accompany him. Or pull a little team together. Go in mob-handed. *Ho ho ho. Merry Christmas, Steve, don't mind the reindeer.*

But what was the betting that, in the wake of the busting of Gyles, Steve had absolutely nothing on the premises?

And anyway, how would that tell him who paid the knifeman?

And also he really hated this twat now. That never helped.

Which left Option Three.

Jesus.

The thought of Option Three just made Bliss want to curl up and die.

54

Cold Turkey

STANDING UNDER THE market hall, looking down Church Street, a slow slope, you could see that the centre of Ledwardine really was on fairly high ground. What did that mean? *Could* you have a henge on high ground?

'OK,' Jane said. 'Picture this. If it came around what's now the market square, enclosing the church and the vicarage, the cut-off point would be ...' she pointed through the rain '... about there, just past Lol's house.'

Right on the rim of the henge. Maybe there would be signs of a ditch, or at least a depression, in what was left of the orchard behind Lol's house. That was the first place to check tomorrow.

'I just don't know enough, that's the trouble. Don't have enough basic knowledge. Like, maybe that's how Church Street began, as some kind of processional avenue leading up from the river and into the henge.'

'Cooper told you not to get carried away, Jane,' Eirion said. 'I think he told you that once before?'

'I hear exactly what you're saying, Irene, but I *need* this. I need this so much.'

'You need it, Blore needs it ... Cooper needs it.'

'And Ledwardine needs it. And it just has to be ours. It must *not* be Blore's.'

Jane had told them all about the henge. Eirion and Lol and Gomer and Mum – who was interested but seemed vague tonight, disconnected from everything. The problem was obvious and simple: too much to think about and no cigarettes to help her keep it all under control.

Cold turkey. Poor Mum. Cold turkey for Christmas, and too much pride to go round bumming cigs off other people. She wasn't a *heavy* smoker, compared with some, and if every smoker in the village who had a few to spare would donate just one to Mum … well, that might be better for everybody. It certainly hadn't seemed like a good time to tell her that Coops was hiding something he didn't think her daughter was mature enough to handle.

However, because it was really eating at her she'd dragged Eirion out to the square and laid it on *him*.

They were alone under the market hall. The village Christmas tree had been switched off due to worries about the wiring and all the water swirling around its base, ambered now by the fake gaslamps. Even where there was no flooding the water lay like a skin on the ground, constantly topped up as fast as it was absorbed by the vainly gulping drains. The Eight Till Late was still open, although its food stocks were well down. Emergency service, Jim Prosser said. Eight Till *very* Late.

'OK, listen,' Eirion said. 'If Cooper confirms that a henge is a major possibility, maybe we could get something in the press. They're always desperate for stories just after Christmas. Nothing much happening in politics anywhere in the world. I could call somebody on Boxing Day, email the story about the possible discovery of a new henge surrounding a village … *that* would screw Blore.'

'Yeah, but it might also screw Coops. But … I'll ask him.'

'The other thing is, if Blore actually knew about the henge before he officially started work here …'

'How would he?'

'Looked up your website. Which basically floats the idea of some large-scale prehistoric landscape feature at the bottom of Cole Hill. For which three or four standing stones in a field might just be the tip of the iceberg. I mean *I* don't know. But maybe he came over himself, on the quiet, and poked around. And his experienced eye led him in directions which you, as – sorry Jane – an amateur, would've missed. Identifying the possibility of an original henge, which he's now confirmed. It makes sense. You could even say that's why he stitched you up.'

'He said … that I'd come to the right conclusions for all the wrong reasons.'

Ley lines … God help us.

'Seems ridiculous that a leading archaeologist would want to discredit a schoolgirl,' Eirion said. 'But maybe he also wanted to make sure you'd keep well out of his way for the duration of the dig. And *that*'s worked, hasn't it?'

'You think *that*'s what Coops wasn't telling me?'

'Maybe. He knows what you're like. Tell you one thing, though, Jane. When this comes out, it'll not only mean no development in Coleman's Meadow, it could throw a protection order around the whole village.'

Jane stared at him, blue lights everywhere.

'*What?*'

'Think about it. The excavation alone, something this big could take years, and if there were even just a few more stones buried under the village it could qualify as a Grade One ancient monument. You couldn't build anywhere near it.'

'Holy sh— Irene, that means Lyndon Pierce would be …'

'Stuffed.' Eirion put an arm round her. 'Totally. But just take it slowly, huh?'

'Slowly?' She looked up at him, pulling away. Her face felt flushed, she was trembling. 'Are you crazy? Irene, this is *mega*.'

'Only if it's true.' He put his hands on her arms, like he was fitting a straitjacket. 'Only if there really *is* a henge. Jane, look, time's getting on. We need to get across to the Swan, make sure the visual stuff's all set up for Lol.'

'Yeah. That's part of it, you know? It's all coming together.'

'I'm sure it is.'

'I'm not mad, Irene.'

'I never thought you were.'

'I just need to go to Lucy's grave now. Tell her about this.'

Eirion sighed the long-suffering sigh of a much older guy.

'Of course you do.'

When Merrily came back from the phone, Gomer had left to get himself cleaned up and Lol was looking up at the clock.

'I think I need to be getting over to the Swan.'

'No!' Merrily froze. Pressed him back into the chair. 'You can't go. Not yet.'

'Who was on the phone? Is something wrong?'

'A lot's wrong, but I want to keep the lid on it until after Christmas. That was ... that was Bliss. Wants me to ring Sophie for him. He wants a number for Helen Ayling.'

'Why can't *he* ring her?'

'Because Sophie, like a lot of people, is suspicious of him, and he says he's got no time to deal with that. I've said I'll ring her for him and then ... just give me twenty minutes. Can you do that? It's important.'

He looked at her, his head tilted. He was still wearing the Gomer Parry Plant Hire sweatshirt. He'd insisted he'd be wearing it for the gig, wiping some of the mud off with a damp cloth but not all of it.

Ledwardine red mud. For luck.

She loved him beyond all reason, but sometimes he irritated the hell out of her.

'Stay,' she said, like to a dog.

Back in the scullery, she took her last cigarette out of the pack and sniffed it as she dialled.

Wasn't the same. She'd been across to the shop and bought four packets of extra-strong mints, had already eaten two and a half. She was sure they were making her want to go to the toilet.

'I tried to ring you twice,' Sophie said. 'As soon as I heard about the bridge. You really can't get out of there?'

'Not in a car.'

The past two years she'd gone into Hereford on Christmas Eve, when it was quiet in the late afternoon, and she and Sophie had drunk tea together, reviewed the year, exchanged small gifts.

'What are you going to do?' Sophie said.

'What *can* we do? Sit it out. Almost a third of the population's left the village, to spend Christmas with relatives or at hotels. Some people's furniture's in storage in case the worst happens.'

'What about your meditation service?'

'Still on. I've been over to the church, set up the usual circle of pews and chairs at the top of the nave. Maybe it'll mean more this year. Or maybe people won't have the heart to turn out. Or maybe I should just offer the midnight Eucharist.'

'You sound exhausted.'

'I'm OK. There've been one or two problems which I'll tell you about when we get liberated.'

'They'll put a temporary bridge in?'

'Bailey bridge, yeah. Sophie, listen, do you have a phone number for Helen Ayling that I can pass on to Frannie Bliss?'

'You're using it,' Sophie said. 'However—'

'*She's still there?*'

'In the end, she didn't want to leave until she was allowed to have a funeral. Much calmer now, but I'd very much take exception to her being upset on Christmas Eve by your friend Bliss.'

'He's got problems. Domestic problems.'

'Not, I'm sure, on Helen's scale. What does he want?'

'Well,' Merrily said, 'I do actually *know* what he wants.'

Suspecting something like this, she'd told Bliss she'd be prepared to talk to Helen Ayling herself.

'It relates to drugs. Bliss wants to know about Clement Ayling and drugs.'

Sophie said sharply, 'What about them?'

'Anything.'

Sophie said, 'Are you *serious*?'

Merrily tried to call Bliss back at once, but his mobile was engaged. She brought the Boswell guitar in its case through from the back hallway, laid it on the scullery sofa. Then she went back to Lol.

He was standing by the window. She went over and found herself clinging tightly to him, feeling flimsy as an insect, breathing in the unfamiliar smell of the earth on him, and they were kissing for too long.

'It's only another gig,' Lol whispered.

'No, it's not.'

When they finally separated, she pulled a rusted flake of dried mud from the shoulder of his sweatshirt. He bent and kissed her again, on the side of her mouth.

'Look … if you really want me to change I'll go home and do it. I don't want to—'

'No. Keep the luck. Just … you know … don't take that sweatshirt to America with you. They won't understand the reference.'

'Doesn't arise,' Lol said. 'I hadn't thought it out. I wouldn't even get a visa or whatever you need.'

'Huh?'

'I have a conviction for indecent assault on an underage girl.'

'Oh, for heaven's sake …' She pulled away, stared into his eyes. 'Everybody knows that was a gross miscarriage of—'

'No, they don't. In the eyes of the law, I'm a sex-criminal.'

'Lol, you can get it *waived*.' Merrily was almost shouting. 'If you apply to the American Embassy for a visa and tell them the circumstances, you'll almost *certainly* get it waived.'

'There's no certainty at all, and anyway—'

'Lol … look … What happened twenty years ago … it's now *very* widely known that you were set up. Wrongly convicted. Been in various papers … floating round on the Net. Nobody in their right mind …'

'It doesn't matter.'

'It *does* matter.'

Not going to America because it might not be such a brilliant career move at this stage, that was one thing, but not going because America might refuse him entry as a convicted felon …

'And besides …' God, she needed a cigarette. 'We also know the identity of the real offender.'

'Who's untouchable,' Lol said. 'Who will never be convicted. On account of being dead.'

'Your conviction's discredited. I'm telling you they'll waive it.'

'Mud sticks.' Lol looked down at his sweatshirt. 'You know that. Look, I'll have to go.'

'Wait.' She was backing towards the door. 'There's … I was going to give you this tomorrow, but it's important you should have it tonight. You *need* to have it tonight. Just … stay there. Stay.'

*

The churchyard was bloated and squelchy, like walking on an old mattress, pools of water everywhere, headstones and crosses looking like groynes at the seaside.

Jane ploughed through it in her red wellies, looking up at the church, its steeple edged with amber from the lights on the square. Some churches were floodlit; Mum wouldn't have that. *Has its own light*, she'd said. Floodlighting also wasn't very green, these days, but Jane couldn't help thinking that for special nights ... and compared with total abominations like Las Vegas ...

The lantern over the porch still gilded the cindered path, which had been the old coffin trail, and it was enough.

'Could be some of the neolithic stones are in the church's foundations,' Jane said. 'I *know* – don't get carried away, Jane. But Lucy always used to say the church was built on a pagan site.'

She was back in high spirits, since Eirion's suggestion that what Coops hadn't wanted her to know was the way Blore had manipulated her. And totally energised by the thought of what this could mean for the future of the village. Despite the endless rain, the night seemed incandescent. She looked up into the sky, throwing back her hood, letting it all come racing down on her, washing away the uncertainty.

She was remembering standing on top of Cole Hill, bare-armed in the summer, and seeing the steeple as the gnomon of a great sundial. And she'd been right. She'd been right all along. It didn't matter what the sneering students thought, or the professors of archaeology behind their narrow-minded, self-protective—

'Oh Christ,' Eirion said.

Jane looked down to find him bending over Lucy's grave, water glinting in the moss on the headstone's curve. The moss should never be removed, it said in Lucy's will. Let the stone be a stone.

She ran to Eirion's side, slithering on the slimy grass.

It had been done in white and not too long ago. Despite the rain you could still smell the paint.

DIRTY WITCH

Letters splashed diagonally across the stone, obliterating the lines from Traherne.

Jane looked at it for a long time.

She knelt down in the wet grass, laid her hands either side of the headstone's wet, velvety rim, holding in her fury.

'It's all right,' she said.

She stood up. Eirion had his hands in his pocket. He stamped the ground angrily with a heel.

'Turps,' Jane said. 'That gets it off, doesn't it?'

'There might be something better,' Eirion said. 'I'll go over to the shop—'

'No, you need to help Lol. You get off to the Swan. I'll do it.'

'Jane—'

'It's all right. It's only paint. And she's mentally ill, anyway.'

'You know who …?'

'I'll scrub it off.'

'You should tell the police.'

'What are they going to do, send a helicopter? I don't want anyone to see this. I want it gone by daylight.'

She walked away, face into the rain, back to the church. Eirion drew alongside her.

'You can scream, you know. You don't have anything to prove about maturity. I'd scream, if somebody did that to my friend's grave.'

'Lucy would laugh.' Jane kept on walking, not looking back. 'And I'll do my screaming after Christmas. Through the plate-glass screen at the post office.'

'What are you—?'

'Let's go and see if Jim's got some paint-stripper.'

Her hands felt sticky; she must've touched it. She stopped in revulsion and bent down and swirled them around in the surface water on the cinders outside the church porch. Wouldn't do any good against enamel or whatever this was, but it made her feel …

Oh.

Standing up, under the dusty glow of the wrought-iron lantern above the church porch, she saw that both porch doors had been pulled closed.

And what had been daubed across them.

'Now you'll *have* to tell the police,' Eirion said.

This was also in white, still wet and bubbled with rainwater.

THE ANTICHRIST
IS BORN THIS NIGHT
IN LEDWARDINE

'And we're going to have to tell Mum,' Jane said. 'She doesn't need this.'

Eirion went up the doors. They hadn't been quite closed, and there was a crack of light.

'The lights are on inside. Are they usually kept on?'

'Not any more.'

Eirion grasped both ring handles, pushed the doors open and went in.

55

Option Three

IT WAS PROBABLY Victorian but looked older. Georgian or Queen Anne or something. Bliss wasn't an expert on architecture. It was just a big white house with tall windows converted into flats. Behind it, thousands of lights revealed the spread of the Severn Valley below.

A cool place to live. Classy address, outstanding views and only a short journey to work.

There was the car, the deep green Saab, on the forecourt. He'd been worried that the flat might've been vacated in the fifty-five minutes since he'd rung, number withheld, hanging up when he'd had an answer.

Longer drive than expected. Floods everywhere in Worcestershire. Worse than Herefordshire, according to Traffic, advising him on the safest route to Great Malvern. This was around eight p.m., after the Banks-Joneses had been in – statement from Kate, additional statement from Gyles. He'd rung them from Phase Two so as not to alert Steve, and they'd made their own way to Gaol Street.

Not too bad up here, far above river level. He'd left his car parked by the side of the main road. Thought about phoning to say he was here, request an audience. Might be difficult if he was to walk in on a cosy Christmas Eve with the girlfriend.

Decided against, in the end.

There was a short wall around the forecourt. He climbed over it. The rain was lighter here, and he stood for quite a while outside the white-painted front door. The four bell buttons and the names alongside them, surnames only, were softly lit up.

Option Three. Was he really up for this? Was this any less stupid and short-sighted than driving over to Charlie's place last night?

As he stood with his finger suspended over the second bell push from the top, the one with the shortest name alongside it, the door opened.

Just as smoothly as you'd expect, place like this.

CCTV. Might've guessed.

She was wearing light-coloured jeans and a stripy woollen top, and her hair was down and looked freshly washed. She wasn't smiling, but then it wasn't Christmas yet.

'I don't honestly know what persuaded me to come down, Francis. Must be some kind of warped forensic curiosity.'

She could soften her appearance, but obviously nothing to be done about that drab, vinyl voice.

'I, um …' Bliss coughed. 'I don't where the other bloody carol singers've got to, Annie, but I've gorra tell you I sound terrible on me own. Would it be all right if I just talked?'

The lounge bar was the Black Swan at its most Jacobean. Those deep, leaded mullion windows. Half an oak wood on the walls and ceiling. Beautifully ill-lit.

Lol had never seen it so empty.

'It's early,' Barry said.

He was also, as usual, in black and white. Essex boy, way back, but he'd spent all his adult years in Hereford. An old-style manager. He said people liked that, and they probably did.

'Not going to be quite what I expected, mate, but nothing I can do about that. Act of God. We've been getting calls all day from people who were going to come over for it – one as far away as Chester, ready to book a double room. Asking if there was any way into the village. I said it'd be a two-mile walk across flooded fields, but possible with the right kit.' Barry shrugged. 'Couldn't figure why they lost interest.'

'Probably because, unlike you, they'd never been in the SAS,' Lol said.

Barry nodded, sage-like. Lol saw James Bull-Davies walking through from the public bar with Alison Kinnersley. Alison smiled and waved. It seemed half a lifetime since he'd lived with Alison and written a bitter-sweet song for her including most of the place names in the Golden Valley. He wouldn't play it tonight.

'You'll still get the same fee, of course,' Barry said.

'Barry, forget the fee. Why don't we just call it off?'

'Good God, bunch of local people been really looking forward to it. It's Christmas Eve, mate. The water's rising. There's nothing *else* to look forward to.' Barry wiped his brow with a paper napkin. 'I'm not putting this very well, am I? What I mean is, I think we'll get a few locals who would normally give it a miss. A percentage would've been going into Hereford tonight, or to parties outside. I think the situation makes people want to get together. Kind of security in numbers. Take their mind off it.'

'Social service.'

'*Exactly.*' Barry patted Lol on the shoulder. 'We'll make bugger-all money out of it, but we'll feel better about ourselves in the morning.'

Lol sat down next to his Guild acoustic amplifier and opened the Boswell's case. It shone up at him, like there was a halo around it. Although it had a sophisticated adjustable bridge and an internal pick-up based on the Takamine, something about it seemed older than the Black Swan.

He didn't know what to do. He knew how much Merrily earned, and there was no way she could afford this. He hadn't been able to say half of what he'd wanted to say because she'd almost pushed him out of the door, saying she had an urgent phone call to make.

When he'd gone running home to change into clean jeans and dry socks, he'd found a message on his machine

This is about love, Laurence, Al Boswell said. *The guitar ... well, at least you deserve the guitar.*

Light laughter.

Click.

'Actually,' Annie Howe said, 'I *do* know why I came to the door. I doubt I'd get to sleep tonight if I didn't find out why Karen Dowell had rung Mark Connelly to ask for the name of the man we think did the knifing for Lasky's merry band of kiddy-fiddlers.'

'Ah.'

'And then, when I saw you drowning on the step, something just kind of clicked.'

'Right.'

'My God, Bliss, you really do have to be in some kind of shit to turn up here.'

'Yeh,' Bliss said. 'I think that would more or less encompass the situation. However, Karen ... it's not her fault. She was obeying an instruction I should never've given her. It was an abuse of power. *Mea culpa.*'

He sipped his coffee and looked around. What had surprised him most about Annie Howe's apartment was not its spartan aspects – went without saying – but all the books. Could be a couple of thousand, and not just to fill tastefully fitted shelves, because the shelves weren't tasteful or fitted, some of them no more than planks of new pine separated by bricks – clean bricks, but still ... Bliss could see a lot of law up there – she had a law-degree, he knew that much – and criminology, but also history and geology and a few dozen paperback crime novels. Normal stuff. Human-being stuff.

Maybe she was storing them for a friend.

'I thought you'd be out,' he said. 'It's Christmas. I think.'

'Where?' Howe said. 'On the town? Clubbing? Binge-drinking with my *mates?*'

She was sitting under a blue-shaded brass standard lamp in a rocking chair that was clearly second-hand, a threadbare powder-blue rug underneath it. Bliss was high up on an overstuffed settee, feeling stupid on account of his feet barely touched the stained floorboards.

Also a trifle gobsmacked at discovering a woman who didn't care about decor. Kirsty's lip would be curled double in disgust.

'After the past week,' Howe said, 'I'm more than happy to lock the door, take off my shoes and open a bottle of wine. Perhaps a scented bath with one of my lesbian lovers.'

Bliss tried for the right kind of smile, suspecting there wasn't one.

'Or maybe both of them at once,' Howe said. 'It's quite a generous bath.'

A tiny fibre-optic Christmas tree on the mantelpiece over the blocked-in fireplace changed from mauve to silver.

'Actually,' Howe said, 'if the only men out there were the kind of crass bastards generally found in the police service, I think I might well have gone gratefully down that road.'

'For what it's worth,' Bliss said, 'I didn't actually place a bet.'

'You parsimonious bastard, Francis.'

'Shit,' Bliss said. 'It wasn't for charity, was it?'

Jesus, did Annie nearly laugh then?

'Look,' he said. 'I won't waste your time. I'll just lay this out on the floor and if you don't like it you can kick it down the lift shaft. Essentially, the suburban coke affiliate that was supposed to keep me out of the way until Twelfth Night has turned out to link directly into Ayling.'

Howe was rocking gently. Near-white hair fluffed over her eyes. Glasses – the rimless Gestapo-issue – on the end of her nose. What had happened to the contacts?

'Connection comes through a council planning officer called Steve Furneaux,' Bliss said quickly, 'who turns out to be the main player, while Gyles Banks-Jones ...'

'Frontman.' Howe stopped the movement of the chair with the tip of a trainer. 'Well recompensed, I'd guess, to take all the risks. Idiot, basically.'

'Well ... yeh.'

'Furneaux's a reptile.'

Bliss grew cautious, tilted himself forward so both feet were firmly on the floor.

'Worked in local government and public relations in Birmingham,' Annie Howe said, 'and the Black Country. West Midlands have a slim but meaningful file on him.'

'What's he done?'

'Well, nothing we know about, obviously, or they'd have had him years ago. That house in Hereford, though, he paid cash. He also has a very nice flat in Solihull, which he rents out, and a time-share in Menton. And in case you're wondering about private income, his parents are still alive, both low-grade schoolteachers, so nothing from that end.'

Bliss shuffled uncomfortably to the edge of the sofa.

'And you know all this ... how?'

'Mainly from my dad. They serve together on a quango called ...'

'Hereforward.'

'I believe that's the name. Whenever someone mentions it, I plead ignorance because – you've probably noticed this yourself – no two people ever give the same explanation of what it actually does.'

'And what, uh ...' Bliss hesitated. 'What does County Councillor Howe say it does?'

'You should ask him.'

'I tried. Tried to ask him about a few things.'

'And?'

'He said I was a sick, twisted little Scouser with no friends and no prospects who ought to go home and probably throw himself in the Mersey. But you knew that.'

'Didn't, actually. When was this?'

'Last night.'

'Before you went off sick.'

'I got very wet. Charlie having expressed a wish that I should die of pneumonia.'

Annie smiled, a bit twisted.

'That's my pa.'

'I *was* able though, before I left, to inquire about his new hip, and he said Mr Shah had done an excellent job.'

'I've heard he's the best.'

Bliss stood up.

'What are you doing, Annie? What *are* you *doing*?'

'Sometimes, Francis, I almost think I know.' Howe used a heel to start the chair's momentum, in a slow, meditative rhythm. 'Sit down. Tell me what you hoped to achieve by disrupting my quiet Christmas Eve in.'

'Well ...' Bliss sat. 'There's that information that Mark Connelly wouldn't give to Karen Dowell without your say-so. I think your guy also killed Ayling.'

'It's a possibility. The wounds weren't identical.'

'But you've got Willy Hawkes in the frame.'

'Wilford Hawkes has gone home for Christmas. His chainsaw's clean. We were interested that it had a new chain, and he'd forgotten what he'd done with the old one but we eventually found it. One of the women he lived with had borrowed it to loop over a five-barred gate to hold it to the post. That tells you how blunt it had become, but it wasn't blunted on flesh or bone. Tests yielded sawdust, nothing else. He may be charged in connection with a threatening phone call, but possibly not.'

'Why were you so keen to nail him?'

'Because all the evidence pointed at the Dinedor Serpent.'

'No other reason?'

'Like not wanting to investigate my father?'

'I'm saying nothing, ma'am.'

'Don't call me ma'am again. I know what it means when you use it, and it isn't a term of respect. No, I *didn't* want to investigate my father. All through my career I've been hoping I would *never* have to investigate Charlie Howe … and you breathe a word of this outside this room, Bliss, and you are history.'

'You know I won't,' Bliss said, 'or you wouldn't be telling me. Anyway. I've got no friends, me.'

'Really hasn't lost his touch, has he?'

Annie Howe grinned. A phenomenon like the northern lights and UFOs: you'd heard of *other* people who'd seen them. Bliss blinked, and it had gone.

'Go on,' he said. 'I need to hear it from you. Why you handed me the Gyles case.'

'You'll have a long wait, Francis.'

'Here's my version, then. Sometime in the past, Charlie must've said something to you about Furneaux. Maybe asking you to look into him. Maybe suspicious of Furneaux's affluence. And maybe you made a few inquiries to keep the old guy happy?'

Annie Howe looked up at the cream-washed moulded ceiling, didn't nod, didn't shake her head.

'*Was* he happy? Was he happy to know Furneaux was without form, therefore clever? Therefore …' in for a penny '… safe to have dealings with?'

'Be careful.'

'I bet *you* never forgot Steve's name, did you?'

Maybe she was a better detective than he'd given her credit for. She couldn't possibly have been in the cops for – what, twelve, fourteen years? – without hearing the Charlie stories.

'What happened? You run into Furneaux at some social event?'

'As everyone keeps pointing out,' Annie said, 'it's a small city.'

'Not for very long if the council have anything to do with it. Hear about the toxicology report following a heart attack at that Hereforward weekend spree?'

'I *read* the toxicology report. And I was very relieved that Councillor Howe wasn't there. He was ...' hollow breath '... on holiday in the South of France.'

'Not ...' *oh joy* '... staying at Steve's time-share in Menton?'

'Shut up *now* ...'

'How lovely,' Bliss said.

'It's not a crime.'

'No, no. But when Ayling got topped, I bet you had Charlie on the phone in minutes, assuring you ... well, making certain assurances.'

'It would have been odd if he hadn't phoned me under those circum-stances.'

'Did he, uh ... suggest it might not be a good thing in general for the city of Hereford if a certain nasty little Scouse cop with a chip on his shoulder was in charge of the investigation?'

'That sound like my father?'

'Totally. And did he, by great good fortune, happen to be making a post-op visit to the orthopaedic surgeon who'd done his hip, and ...' Bliss sighed. 'Jesus, Annie that was a sad bloody excuse for a complaint, wasn't it?'

'I've heard better.'

'But I tell you what *would* look bad ... if it subsequently emerged that there *was* a link between Steve Furneaux, Hereforward and Clem Ayling's killing, and Councillor Howe's daughter, leading the investiga-tion, had conspicuously—'

'All right!' Howe stopped rocking. 'Being fast-tracked to the top isn't an *automatic* indication of someone with an honours degree but no basic nous. What've you got?'

'Jesus, you deliberately put me in from the other side to find out if Charlie—?'

'I told you you'd have a long wait and I meant it.'

'You sent me in there with a shitload of grudge against your ole man ...'

'If *you* couldn't involve him then he wasn't involved.'

'And if I *could* involve him?'

'Can you?'

'*You* still think he might actually—'

'You tosser! ' Annie Howe sprang to her feet. 'I've known the bastard for thirty-five years. I know every lie he told my mother, and some even *she* doesn't know about. I know how, despite telling everybody who'll listen how proud he is of my success, that he did *everything in his power* to keep me out of the police. Now what've you *got*?'

Bliss sat with his feet not quite touching the floor. He couldn't remember when he'd last fancied a woman this much. How crass did that make him?

'OK,' he said. 'I know who disposed of Ayling's body. I don't know who actually killed him, but I think I know *why* he was killed. And, for what it's worth, I don't think Charlie was connected to the murder.'

'Furneaux?'

'Furneaux for definite.'

'All right,' Annie said. 'Let's go and spoil his Christmas.'

56

Corrupt

JANE SPRAYED TORCHLIGHT at the church porch door, watching Mum recoil.

Heartsick. That word on her church ...

ANTICHRIST

Mum had been upstairs in the bedroom, dressing for the gig – cashmere and the black velvet skirt, the last cigarette half-smoked and then carefully pinched out. She'd flung on her cape to cover the skirt, but nothing was totally protected in this weather. Pools were already forming around their wellies, and the splashing of the rain made it hard to hear what she was mumbling.

'... come off. Everything comes off, somehow.'

Not easily. It was old wood. Eirion had reckoned they might wind up having to sand it down. She'd sent Eirion to the Swan. Nothing he could do now. It was evidence, anyway.

'I'll ... have a go later if you like,' Jane said.

'... Think I'm inclined to leave it till after Christmas. Let everybody see it. That was the idea, presum—' Mum broke off, her eyes unnaturally wide in the torch beam. 'My God, what did I just say?'

'Makes sense to me. Let everybody see what she's done.'

'And then they can all cross the road when she walks up the street? Use another post office?'

'Saves having to listen to a lot of born-again bollocks.'

'Talk about her behind her back? And maybe some kids will go and spray-paint her front door, thinking they have an excuse for it now?'

'She'd love it. Make her feel like a real martyr.'

Jane played the torch beam through a wall of rain like gilded splinters to the white-sprayed words

BORN THIS NIGHT
IN LEDWARDINE

'What does it mean, anyway?'

'It means exactly what it says. After gradually stripping away traditional Christianity in Ledwardine in favour of a kind of neo-paganism, I'm now going all the way … Jane, its—'

'No, go on …'

'Conspiring with the satanic baptist Mathew Elliot Stooke to celebrate, on the stroke of midnight, not the holy birth but some demonic intrus— I can't even say it.'

'They truly believe that?'

'Who knows? Maybe she thinks this will deter people from coming tonight. Perhaps it will.'

'Somebody has to stop her.'

'I can't do anything.' Mum numbly shaking her head, shoulders slumped. 'In the absence of the police – and they'd be unlikely to come before Christmas anyway – I'm not going to be … judge and jury.'

'Mum …'

'And the truth is, we don't even know it's her, do we?'

'Oh, come *on*—'

'There are supposed to be other members of her … church around. Jane, let's just go home and get— We've got ten minutes before Lol starts, right? So let's just get a bucket, some det—'

'Mum …' *Oh God.* 'You haven't been inside.'

Mum looked at Jane who turned away, tearful. She'd looked so pretty in her best clothes and … kind of glowing. As if tonight at the Swan, with the Boswell and everything, would be the start of a new phase for her and Lol. Maybe even the prospect of …

'Mum, listen, she – whoever it is – is mentally ill. This has nothing to do with religion. Nothing to do with *you*. You've done everything you could possibly—'

'There's more, right?'

'Yeah.'

Jane shone the torch at the ring handles, but Eirion had left the doors slightly ajar anyway. She pushed one open with the end of the rubber torch and followed Mum inside.

To where the chairs and pews arranged for the meditation service had been tipped over, thrown into disarray, a couple of the lighter chairs smashed …

… Along with the bottom left-hand corner of the Eve stained-glass window with its red apple that always caught the sunset. A hole punched in it, glass gone, lead strips twisted, rainwater exploding on to the sill down the wall to spread over the flags.

Mum stood and looked up, past the organ, up towards the chancel and, as if her gaze had been guided, to the rood screen.

Sixteenth century. With those exquisitely carved-out apple shapes at the bottom.

The ancient wood chopped out around them, the delicate tracery of the screen cracked and splintered.

You could still almost feel the frenzy, hear violent echoes from the stone.

It wouldn't have taken long, with a hammer or a hatchet. Nobody came across to the church at this time of day.

Certainly not in this kind of weather, and there weren't that many people left in the village anyway.

And nobody outside would hear the hacking through the noise of the rain.

Lol looked up from his tuning in some surprise. It wasn't so much the noise as …

… The hush, when he played a couple of experimental chords, the Boswell plugged into the old Guild acoustic, a basic E-minor as thrilling and visceral in this crowded, tarted-up Jacobean alehouse as a pipe-organ in an empty church.

He looked around bemused. A swirl of faces. Could be a hundred or more, seated at tables pushed together round the walls, some groups standing in the alcoves. He'd heard them coming in, thought they were just going for drinks. Kept his head down, concentrating on preparing a guitar he'd never played before. No need, really, the tuning was perfect and stayed perfect – in the small accessories compartment in the Boswell case he'd found a note from Al saying the guitar had been strung three days earlier, lightweight strings tuned daily, played once for four minutes, retuned.

Was *ready.*

Like Al had known about this.

The rain hissed and rattled in the leaded windows. He sat in a corner, unobtrusive like a sideshow. Couldn't see Jane, or Merrily or anyone he really knew, but Barry was here, leaning over, whispering.

'Whole bunch of people up from Hereford, did the full two-mile walk across the footbridge, over the fields ... Coach party. Someone said it was like a pilgrimage.'

'For *this?*'

'Bigger than you thought, mate.'

Pilgrimage.

He recalled Jane this morning in deserted Church Street: *Well, I put it up on the Coleman's Meadow website.* It was support for Jane, for the meadow, for the stones; he was just a focus. That made him happier.

'And Merrily says, don't forget, not a word,' Barry murmured. 'Whatever that means.'

It was the last thing she'd said to him before she'd pushed him out of the vicarage, the way Moira Cairns had pushed him on stage that terrible night at the Courtyard in Hereford, the kick-start of his solo career. *Don't dare mention me in connection with the Boswell. Just ... play it.*

Barry grinned.

'We're in profit after all. You ready, mate?'

'Hang on—'

Lol leaned into the amp, gave it a little extra concert-hall depth, the merest hint of reverb, tapped the voice mike – too loud.

'You want an introduction?' Barry said. 'I don't really know how these things are done.'

'I'll just go into it,' Lol said.

'Good boy.'

Lol felt the first shoulder-twinge in days as Barry stepped away, lifting a hand to Eirion, and the lights went down and, on the plasma screen behind him, the first thin red slit of sunrise began to burn between the earthen ramparts on Cole Hill.

Holding the new Boswell close like a woman, he let his fingers find the only riff he figured most of them would know, from *Flicks in the Sticks* showings of 'The Baker's Lament', named after this song. Lol closed his eyes, took a breath. One more time, for propulsion, and ...

'*The shoemaker ... made me some shoes ...*'

The sound low and warm and woody. A rush of applause soaking up the rain.

Merrily pulled off her cape, pushed back her hair.

The oak-panelled reception, lantern-lit heart of the New Cotswolds. No mirrors.

'Look reasonably OK?'

'You look fantastic,' Jane said. 'Now just—'

'Just go *in*, damn you.' James Bull-Davies blocking the door to the square. 'Pair of you. I'll get Parry, *we'*ll deal with this.'

'James, look ...' Merrily clutching his arm. 'I'll cancel it. It'll be simpler.'

'The hell you will. My family kept that church from collapse for four centuries. Damned if I'm going to let some lunatic—'

'We don't *know.*'

'Suspect list pretty damn short.'

Barry came through, rubbing his hands.

'*Two* coachloads. Supporters of the Serpent. Sounds like some sort of secret society. Don't normally allow walking boots in the lounge, but under these conditions, what can you say?'

'Don't let these Watkins women out again, Barry,' James said as the Stookes came in behind him, shaking out an umbrella. 'Find them ringside seats and tie them down.' He stood over Merrily. 'Plan to board the bottom of the window, drape something over the damaged area of the rood screen for tonight. Cover the doors with opaque plastic sheeting rather than risk damaging the wood with paint-stripper. Couple of hours max, OK?'

'James, I'm very grateful but I'm not sure, after that level of violence and ... malevolence, call it what you like ... that the atmosphere's going to be exactly conducive. I think I'd rather put it off.'

James was arching forward, peering at her under half-lowered eyelids.

'Correct me if I'm wrong, vicar, but one rather thought dealing with atmospheres was your *thing*.'

She started to laugh. And maybe he was right. There was time. Maybe.

'James ... have you met, erm, Leonora and Elliot—'

'Stooke,' Elliot Stooke said firmly, the mauve ring around his white smile. He unwound a black scarf. 'We're at Cole Barn.'

Well, well ...

'This is James Bull-Davies, Leonora. You ... met his ancestor.'

'How're you?' James said. 'Talk later, if you don't mind. Work to do.'

'God.' Leonora watched him striding out into the downpour. 'Isn't he so wonderfully *feudal*?'

'Except we don't pay tithes or whatever to the Bulls any more,' Merrily said, 'and he *still* feels responsible for us. I'm sorry, we've had a bit of trouble – nothing you wouldn't understand, so maybe we could have a drink later. If you want to go in ... sounds like he's between numbers.'

Still be hard pushed to say she actually *liked* Leonora Stooke.

Lol was talking into the mike about how Lucy Devenish had introduced him to Thomas Traherne, at a time when his life was turning around and he'd just met a woman who was going to be more important to him than he ever imagined a woman could be.

Jane rolled her eyes, beaming, Merrily shutting hers, aware of a blush coming up. The Stookes went into the passage leading to the lounge and then two men emerged from it.

'... Come in for a quiet drink, and we have to listen to *this* shit.'

Merrily figured County Councillor Lyndon Pierce was at least halfway drunk. He was with his client Gerry Murray, twenty years older, a fair bit heavier, the owner of Coleman's Meadow, inherited. Pierce's gelled black hair was slicked over his forehead. Merrily said nothing, didn't bother smiling, hoped Jane hadn't heard.

As if.

Jane said, 'Why don't you make one of your speeches instead, Mr Pierce, then they'd *really* know what shit sounded like?'

Bugger.

'Jane,' Merrily said, 'I don't think—'

'It's the famous archaeologist, Gerry,' Pierce said. 'I hear Professor Blore was suitably impressed.'

Merrily said, 'Jane—'

The craving for tobacco making her shiver. Couldn't keep a limb still. What would help right now was if Barry came back. She looked across to the doorway to the passage leading to the lounge bar.

Neither Barry nor anyone else emerged. Lol began a song she didn't recognise. Jane restrained herself commendably until Murray was halfway through the main door, Pierce following him, and then she said loudly,

'Mum, wasn't that Lyndon Pierce, the notoriously corrupt councillor?'

Merrily watched Pierce turn, like in slow motion, walk right up to Jane.

'*What* did you say?'

Jane backed up a little. Maybe his breath.

'Nothing you haven't heard before, surely.'

'*You* heard it, didn't you, Gerry?' Pierce said. 'That gives me an independent witness when I take this girl to court.'

'You shouldn't've said that about Lol.' Jane was blinking uncertainly. 'He was asked to play, and a lot of people have come through the floods to see him.'

'Well, that was another good reason to get out of there.'

'And I'm sure they're all glad you did, you ... *uuuh.*'

He'd gripped her arm, hard.

'Cocky little *bitch*—'

'Get your—' Merrily pushed him. He spun round in surprise and stumbled to one knee, and she dragged Jane away. 'You're drunk, Lyndon. Bugger off!'

She was panting in fury, trembling. Her legs felt weak and the yellow light from the lanterns hurt her eyes. She saw Pierce coming slowly to his feet, dusting off his suit trousers, then pointing a finger at Jane.

'You won't be laughing—'

'I'm not laughing now.'

'You won't be laughing when the real truth comes out about Coleman's Meadow.'

He turned and walked out. He didn't look back. Lol sang about honey flowing from rocks.

Jane said, 'What's he talking about? Look, I'm sorry, I just couldn't stop myself after he said that about Lol's music. What did he mean?'

'He's drunk.'

'He *meant* something.'

'Let's go in. Let's just—'

'You go in.' Jane had her mobile out. 'I'm going to call Coops.'

57

Deadwood

ANNIE HOWE HAD noticed the parcels in the back of Bliss's car.

'Your kids?'

'Yeh.'

'How long were you …?'

'Nine years.'

'I'm sorry.'

Sorry? Jesus, last week it had been, *I don't know what your problem is … my information is that it's personal and domestic. But you'd better either keep it under control or seek counselling.*

Could be she was a night person, and when the sun came up the frost would form again.

Bliss drove down into the centre of Malvern. They were going in the one car to discuss strategy. He'd have cleaned the Honda up inside if he'd known she'd be wearing the near-white mac.

'But I still think you could've told me,' he said.

Even ordering him to forget the original Furneaux interview. Like, what if he'd actually done as he was told? He gave her a sideways glance. She'd had a psychological profile done on him, or what?

'What difference would that have made?' she said. 'And no, I couldn't.'

'Or got Brent to look into it.'

'I wanted a result, not a massage.'

'What if I hadn't come looking for you tonight?'

'You had till Boxing Day.'

Bliss finally smiled, waiting for a bunch of kids firing party poppers at one another on a zebra crossing. She was right, of course. If she'd come clean he wouldn't have believed her, he'd've thought it was something she and Charlie had cooked up between them. And no way would he have gone near Andy Mumford.

'But if we *don't* get Furneaux tonight,' Annie said, 'your arrangement with Mebus—'

'Uh-huh. No way, Annie. I'm not saying we shouldn't make every effort to snatch the twat for something else, but I'm not breaking Mumford's word. And, with respect, *ma*— With respect, you also need not to offend Andy Mumford, because if anybody knows the truth about your old man and what happened in the Frome Valley all those years ago … yeh?'

No reply; she was looking out of the side window at the statue of Elgar and the fountain all lit up in the centre of Malvern. Bliss thought Malvern looked good. The floodlit priory and the old hotel in the dip, all mellow. Closest he'd felt to Christmas spirit in … a long time.

Still hadn't got a name out of her, though, for the lad who'd turned his white van over to the Mebus brothers and gone to retrieve his motor bike from the forest. He needed to give her Furneaux.

Giving him this uncertain *Do I know you?* look under the bulkhead light on the wall over his front door. It had a Christmas wreath on it, this door. Buy one, get one free at Sainsburys.

Bliss pulled off his beanie.

'DI Bliss, Mr Furneaux. This is Detective Superintendent Howe.'

'Francis … I'm so *sorry*. How nice to see you again.'

'All right if we come in, Steve?'

'Well, sure, but—'

'Ta. This won't take long.'

Steve's sitting room had a look of second home and IKEA summer sale. Two airport-looking yellow sofas, a fitted TV. Also a surprisingly attractive Asian girl who didn't look at all surprised at strangers walking in on Christmas Eve.

'Get you a drink, Francis and … Anne, isn't it? Think I know your father.'

'Lorra driving to do, thanks, Steve,' Bliss said. Howe just shook her head and Steve glanced at the girl.

'Yasmin likes early nights, so if ...?'

'We certainly do not expect Yasmin to entertain us, Steve,' Bliss said. 'This is strictly about you, cocaine, Clem Ayling, cocaine, Hereforward, cocaine ... Oh, and did I mention cocaine?'

At one stage, Steve actually said it.

At first, he just looked slightly huffed, a touch put-out, saying to Annie, 'I hope you realise, Superintendent, that I'm merely on the edge of this committee. Purely an adviser.'

And then a bit later, so far up against the wall that he just had to come out with it.

'Inevitably, if I go down, a number of people go with me. Including, of course, your father, Anne. An elected representative, a decision-maker. While I ... am a mere adviser.'

Adviser. This was the key word. Consultant. The government spent millions every year on fellers like Steve. Well, maybe not *quite* like Steve, although many of them would look not unlike him tonight, in his violet silk shirt and his Italian jeans.

Bliss turned to Annie, next to him on the flatter of the two sofas.

'I said you'd like him, didn't I, ma'am?'

He'd told Steve that they would, if necessary, search the premises and himself and Yasmin. Pointing out that, from his landing window, he might be able to make out the roof of a police car containing DC Terrence Stagg and two uniforms, one of them female. And the duty spaniel was on call. Even if he'd got rid of all the stuff, the dog would pinpoint where he *used* to stash it. Steve wasn't daft. He knew that one white millicrumb was enough to have him banged up for Christmas and no Waitrose pudding with extra cognac.

'It's good here, though, isn't it, Steve?' Bliss said. 'Some areas of Britain, local government tends to be under less scrutiny than others, and Herefordshire's one of them. Right on the edge of Wales, no daily paper, hardly any local news coverage on the box. And only a bunch of sheep-shaggers to take for a ride. Perfect, eh?'

'I don't know what you mean. And I think you're being rather insulting to a very beautiful part of the country and its people.'

'*I*'m one of its people, Mr Furneaux,' Annie Howe said. 'And what I take offence at is patronising bureaucrats who think we're simple country folk on whom democracy is wasted, so, hey, why bother with it?'

'Ms Howe—'

'Clement Ayling,' Anne Howe said. 'Although I didn't actually know him on a personal level, I do know his *type*. Not averse to short cuts in the interests of putting one over on the opposition or central government. Not incapable of deceit in defence of his local authority or his party. But essentially, *not* the sort to have his drive tarmacked by the highways department. Old school. Rather strait-laced. Especially where … drugs are concerned.'

Annie looked at Bliss, who picked up the story.

'And *not* just a generation thing, Steve. You ever hear about Clem's daughter, Nerys? Not many people know this – he hated to talk about it. Anybody asked why Nerys didn't take over the electrical shop – used to work there, apparently, ran it very well, for a while – oh, she'd left the area. Difficult to run a business from a psychiatric hospital.'

Bliss looked at Steve. Steve didn't react.

'Been in hossie for many years now, Steve. Quite advanced schizophrenia. Never mentioned it, did he?'

'No.'

'Or that it seems to have begun with what we now know as cannabis psychosis. Tragic.'

'Of course Ayling knew that cocaine wasn't the *same* as cannabis,' Annie Howe said. 'It being a Class A drug, compared with Class C.'

'A downgrading which left Clem appalled and disgusted, naturally,' Bliss said. 'But he wasn't a man to go into battle without full ammunition. He did some research on the Internet about the very real perils of cocaine. Or rather, not being too adept with the old dot coms, he got his computer-literate wife Helen to check it out. This would've been some time after the near-fatality during a Hereforward Blue-Sky Thinking Weekend near Stowe-on-the-Wold.'

'Knowing – as I do – Ayling's *type*,' Annie said, 'the very *last* thing he would do would be to make something like this public by raising it at a meeting or going to the police and tarnishing the image of an authority he'd served loyally for many years. What he'd do, having carried out his own discreet investigation and determined the source, would be to confront the perpetrator of this abomination and tell this man he wanted it to stop forthwith. And, naturally, he would want this man to pack his bags, without delay, and remove his shabby arse from God's own county.'

'And that,' Bliss said, 'seems to be how Clement Ayling signed his own death warrant. Doesn't it, Steve?'

'Wildest conjecture.' Steve shook his sandy head. 'I don't believe you have an atom of evidence for any of this.'

'True. All we have at present is more than enough evidence to nick you in connection with the supply of a controlled substance.'

'*What evidence?*' Steve leaning far back into the yellow IKEA stretch sofa, but his face was redder by now than his hair. 'Francis, you're beginning to make me quite angry. I have a number of friends on the police authority who'd be appalled at the idea of Hereford CID behaving as irresponsibly as this.'

'I'm from Off,' Bliss said. 'I don't know any better.' He leaned forward. 'All right, let me put it this way, Steve. Some hard kid – been in more courts than Venus Williams by the time he's twelve – is often difficult to break, I'll admit that. But take a grown man with no form, pop him in the blender, and you don't even have to switch on.'

Bliss let the subtext get fully absorbed and then turned to Annie, like the newsreader quizzing the special correspondent.

'Ma'am, from your local knowledge, why would someone like Steve, with a good job, risk his pension by introducing responsible local administrators to this vile pastime?'

Annie slowly unbelted her mac and undid some buttons, like she was preparing for a long night *chez* Steve. This woman was becoming more admirable by the minute.

'It's about power, I suppose, Francis. Some users like to say cocaine isn't addictive, but of course – while not in heroin's league – it very much *is*. Though perhaps *reliance* is probably a more exact word. And there's a reliance, too, on the supplier. In more ways than one, because you are, of course, partners in crime, and that can be quite a significant bond. *Quite* a significant bond.'

Bliss looked across at the window. The hammering rain could only be increasing the pressure.

'How was it done, Steve? At the end of the day, the only member of that committee who could've participated in the final act would be you. What did you do? Offer to give him a lift because of the rain? Or tell him there was something you wanted to discuss with him privately?'

Annie Howe said, 'But Francis, if Ayling had already warned Mr Furneaux about his behaviour, wouldn't he be a bit alarmed about going with him ... anywhere?'

'With respect, ma'am, I don't think Clem would be in the least worried about being physically damaged by someone like Steve – even if he does go to the gym. Big man, Clem. A very confident man. A man who'd shaken hands with prime ministers, Bill Clinton ... But then, perhaps it wasn't Steve who actually put the knife into him ...'

'How could you even imagine—?' Steve springing from the back of the sofa, clean red hair wafting. 'Superintendent, you have to call a halt to this nonsense.'

Difficult to know how to interpret this. Perhaps Steve thought it was time to start feigning the protestations of an innocent man. Bliss ignored him, the way you ignored a child clamouring for attention.

'I suppose what we're looking at here, ma'am, is the difference between actual murder and conspiracy to murder. Usually many years' difference.'

Annie looked unconvinced, wrinkled her nose.

'We know that the body was taken to the Forest of Dean for butchery. We know that the disposal was handled by other parties with links to the Hereford cocaine trade. Personally, I think it's quite reasonable to presume that the actual killing was done by Mr Furneaux ...'

'Who maintains he's just an adviser.'

Howe did the Ice Maiden's brittle laugh. Bliss turned at last to Furneaux.

'Committee decision, was it, Steve?'

'Don't be ridiculous.'

'I mean, all the aspects of this – particularly the false trail to the Dinedor Serpent – suggest it needed more than one adviser. That it could be on a bigger scale than we imagined.' Bliss turned to Annie Howe. 'I mean, yeh, if we're looking for an easy result, it's Steve getting rid of a man threatening his long and lucrative career. But I'm guessing there'd be quite a few other people who wouldn't be sorry to see Ayling gone. A dinosaur. Deadwood.'

'Far-fetched, Francis. In my experience, the small, squalid solution is usually the correct one.'

'Maybe you're right. And it *is* Christmas. It's all government targets, isn't it, and you don't get extra points any more for being clever.' Bliss stood up, walked over to the other sofa. 'Steven Furneaux, I'm arresting you on suspicion of supplying a controlled substance and also on suspicion of the murder of Clement Ayling. You don't have to say anything, but it may seriously fuck up your defence if you—'

'All right,' Steve said. 'Just ... just give me a minute, will you?'

'Aw, Steve you've made me lose me place. Now I'll have to start all over *again*.'

'Suppose I ... had an idea who'd killed Ayling.'

'He's wasting our time,' Annie Howe said. 'Call Stagg, Francis, and let's get him processed.'

'Suppose there was a ... a contractor.'

'Of course,' Bliss said. 'That's the way local authorities work, isn't it. Maybe you invited *tenders*.'

'*Stop it!*' Steve was on his feet. 'I can help you.'

'You've helped us no end already, pal. All wrapped up for Christmas, and very cheaply, too. Annie's friend the Home Secretary's gonna be—'

'Suppose it isn't finished. The contract ... Suppose there's another one to ... complete.'

Little patch of silence. Bliss glanced at Howe; she made the merest suggestion of a nod.

'Sit down, Steve,' Bliss said.

58

Padded Cell

JANE WAS CLOSE to learning the worst.

'It's unjust,' Coops said, 'it stinks, but we've got a baby on the way and I need this job.'

She was alone in the Black Swan reception, with the mobile.

'You think this isn't more important than anyone's bloody job?'

'Jane—'

'*Jane, Jane*, everybody's— You tell me *right now*, Coops. You tell me right now why I won't be laughing when the truth comes out about Coleman's Meadow. Or I go and ask Blore. Blore's pissed. Blore's pissed and Pierce is pissed and I'm stone-cold sober and I'm getting a feeling of everything falling apart.'

'And you're the last person who's going to be able to hold it together. Or me, come to that. We're little people fighting whole industries and all the tiers of government—'

'*Tell* me.'

'People watching all this crap on TV, they think that's how it is, the whole of Britain's like a big sandpit for archaeologists, strolling along with their trowels like the seven bloody dwarfs. It's not *like* that any more. In fact, you should probably be grateful to Blore for deflecting you from a profession that would only bring you hassle and … heartbreak.'

'All right.' Jane carried the phone down the passage leading to the lavatories. 'I'm taking the phone into the loo. I'm going into the furthest cubicle where nobody can hear me scream.'

'Let it go, Jane, try and enjoy your Chris—'

'I'm pushing the main door open now. I'm completely alone. They're listening to Lol's wonderful concert, where *I* wanted to be but this is more important.'

The toilets in the Black Swan had been massively upgraded in the best New Cotswold tradition; in fact you probably wouldn't find toilets this good in the swishest pub in the *old* Cotswolds. Framed photographs on the walls of Ledwardine at its most luscious, sunrise and sunset. Even the cubicles had thick walls and oak doors, and Jane locked herself in the end one and sat on the closed lid of the seat.

'I'm going to offer you a deal, Coops. I'll seriously aim to say nothing to anyone except Mum and Lol and, OK, maybe Gomer Parry 'cause he's my best mate, but if I *have* to take it further I'll say Lyndon Pierce told me when he was drunk, which he was. He'll never remember he didn't tell me. So just ...'

'Let me sit down,' Coops said. 'If you think this isn't getting to *me* ...'

'It so obviously is. Go on.'

'Stop me if I'm telling you something you already know. When archaeologists are called in to investigate a site proposed for development, everybody thinks it's the council that pays for it. In fact it's the developer. I was trying to tell you this the other night but I'm not sure it sank in.'

'But that's ridiculous. They're like ... they're the very people who don't want anything important to be found.'

'That's why most archaeology is just a matter of record. Establishing *where* something is or used to be. But building still goes ahead on the site, you can't stop progress.'

'But not if it's standing stones, surely.'

'*Probably* not ... but only if those standing stones are found to be in the place were they originally stood, because then the *site itself* is of major importance.'

'And that's my point about Coleman's Meadow. You only have to stand on Cole Hill ...'

'No ... *you* only have to stand on Cole Hill.'

'You're taking Blore's side, suddenly?'

'Jane, I'm on our side, and I still think there's enough evidence of a henge to warrant a number of separate excavations around the centre of

Ledwardine. Coleman's Meadow, however ... the excavation is likely to be closed down in the New Year.'

'What ...?'

Jane stood up. The walls of the cubicle seemed tight around her, like a padded cell.

'Blore's submitted a private preliminary report to the council resulting from his own geophysics and limited excavation of the site. The bottom line is that the report suggests the stones were buried here quite recently and probably from somewhere else.'

'Like ... landfill?'

'Good analogy. He says there used to be a small quarry run by the Bull family in the eighteenth century. Long disused, but—'

'They're standing stones! *You* said they were.'

'Blore's report says there's no evidence that they ever stood. That they were ever prehistoric ritual stones.'

'How ... how can he—?'

'The conclusive proof seems to be the discovery of masonry underneath one of the stones. Masonry dating back no more than a couple of centuries.'

'That's impossible!'

'It isn't impossible. If you'd asked me yesterday I would have said it was extremely unlikely but, no, it's not impossible. The report also says the remains of a tool's been discovered under the same stone, and it's not a flint axe-head. It's a ... pickaxe. Probably early Victorian.'

'He's lying!'

'He encloses photographs.'

'When was all this found?'

'They haven't officially been found at all yet.' Coops sounded close to tears. 'And the chances are they won't be found until next week, when it'll all be filmed for ... *Trench One.*'

'He's going to mock it up?'

'You remember that edition of *Time Team*, when they discovered a collection of authentic Celtic swords and things on a site in South Wales, and it turned out to be someone's private collection that had been buried? Still made a good programme, didn't it? And so will this, probably starting off with that interview with you, showing how a young girl's fantasy—'

'Don't! I can't— It's—'

'It's wrong and it's disgusting, but if you say a word about it now there'll be a big investigation about how it got out, and I'll lose my job and the nice woman who read the letter to me will lose *her* job and probably her pension, and she's a widow and—'

'All *right!*'

'Leave it till I get back, and I'll find a way of hearing about it officially, and then I'll protest and see what happens. You can tell your mum, but please, nobody else.'

'OK.'

'Jane, I'm so desperately sorry. I'd love to think he's faked the evidence, but he's a powerful and respected figure. Look, I've got to go, all right?'

'Coops—'

'Try to have a good Christmas, Jane.'

'Neither of us is going to, are we?'

He'd gone.

Jane leaned against the cubicle wall, holding the phone in front of her, tears in freeflow now.

59

Charming Myth

Periodically, in a break between songs, while Lol was retuning, someone who recognised Merrily would lean across and whisper *Where's Jane?* Usually, one of the Serpent people from Hereford. How did they know whose mother she was, out of uniform? Hoped to God she wasn't on the CM website like Lol and Lucy.

'We're Coleman's Meadow activists now.' A guy in his sixties, completely bald, white beard, an earring with a red stone in it. 'We lost on the Serpent, but those bastards won't take the Meadow.' He looked angry. 'I'll strap myself to one of the stones before I'll let them take it away. Go on hunger strike – that always gets results if it en't a terrorist.'

'It's important,' Merrily said, 'but it's not worth a life.'

Wondering where she'd heard that. *Blore.* On the radio before he demoralised Jane. She could see him over by the bar, his dense hair tied back, presumably so it wouldn't dangle in his beer. He seemed to be drinking a lot of beer and laughing a lot.

Unlike the Stookes, who weren't talking to anyone, not even one another. Life, for the Stookes, must be tense and formless. What happened after you'd taken on the biggest target possible and would never know if you'd won until you died ... and only then if you'd lost.

Merrily smiled. Stupid – she was looking at their lives from *her* perspective. Better go and talk to them afterwards.

Lol said, 'I'm going to kind of hum, but if you imagine it as a cello, OK? Now. If you know Elgar's Cello Concerto, the main bit goes like ...'

She was proud of him. Totally in control, as if, performing, he was possessed by the spirit of an extrovert. Mouth close to the mike, he hummed the rolling-hill melody that would always take her back to Whiteleafed Oak on the edge of the Malverns and would always be tinged with tragedy. Melancholy enough, already.

'If you all want to hum along we can maybe cover up the fact that we don't have a cello. Try it ...'

They didn't need asking twice. No need for the old hand behind the ear, *I can't hear you* routine. Merrily thinking how she gigged every Sunday, and never captured this much attention. Maybe she needed to learn to play something.

Barry had found her a seat by the door. She drank a spritzer, finding it didn't go too well with extra-strong mints. Nothing went with extra-strong mints except more mints.

But she knew this song and its origins, had been there at its birth. It was about how, close to the end, Elgar seemed to have lost his faith, his lifelong Catholicism. But all he really wanted, in Lol's view, was to side-step the complicated spiritual bureaucracy of Catholic death, the Catholic afterlife, have his spirit absorbed into the landscape that had given him his music ... specifically, this music.

After a couple of minutes, Lol let the audience do the humming and began to build a guitar structure under it, finally picking up Elgar's tune with his own words, the percussive rain behind it like he was singing from the eye of some inner storm.

> *Save me from the Angel of*
> *The Agony. I want*
> *No pomp*
> *Or circumstance*
> *I'll take my chance.*

Lol's voice dipping into a valley on *agony*. Then rising to welcome a dawning euphoria. He held up a hand to fade the humming. Merrily saw Eirion messing with the two amps and then, with the flat screen full of bubbling water, Lol's voice rose up clear but distant, with a faint echo, as if from distant hills.

Where the Severn joins the Teme
I'll drift downstream
And feel release
And sing the trees
Their own song …

Lol and the lights went blurred. Merrily wiped her eyes discreetly, one at a time.

'Didn't think he'd mind too much,' Lol said afterwards into the dying applause. 'He was all right, Ed.'

'That was amazing, but I didn't fully get what it was about,' the bald guy with the ruby said. 'Dunno much about Elgar. What's the Angel of the …?'

'Agony.'

Lol, clearly loving this interplay with his audience, explained about Elgar's attempt to glimpse his God in the choral masterpiece *The Dream of Gerontius*, from Newman's epic poem about the progress of a soul through the various tiers of the Catholic afterlife.

'So the Angel of the Agony is this mournful combination of sin eater and celestial advocate, pleading for the soul's admission into Heaven. But close to the end Elgar's Catholicism had kind of lost its grip, and when he was dying he told a friend that if he was ever walking in the Malvern Hills and he heard the tune you've just been humming … Ed said, *Don't be afraid. It'll just be me.* He'd told everybody he wanted to be cremated and have his ashes scattered at the confluence of the River Severn and the River Teme, but he was talked out of it.'

'I've been to his grave,' a woman said. 'Little Malvern? It's interesting the way his wife's name is at the *top* of the stone, as if Elgar is bowing to the female principle in nature.'

'Not sure about that,' Lol said. 'All I feel is he wanted to be part of the landscape, for all eternity, and … I think he probably is.'

'In the end, that's paganism …' The long straight hair identified Sara, the Dinedor witch from the *Sunday Telegraph*. 'Or at least pantheism. And that line about singing the trees' songs, that's from what it says under the Elgar statue in Hereford? Hearing the trees singing his music … or is he singing theirs? Hey, why not?'

'Actually,' Elliot Stooke said, 'the biography I read suggested very strongly that Elgar had lost his faith completely. The idea that he reverted to some sort of paganism is ... a bit of speculation?'

'Probably is,' Lol said.

'And he was using the idea of his ghost haunting the Malverns as a metaphor, surely?'

'Metaphors on his deathbed?' Lol said. 'I don't know.'

'If you believe he was channelling the spirit of the landscape,' Sara the witch called out, 'the whole thing makes—'

'Another charming myth,' Stooke said.

'All I know ...' the bald guy stood up '... is that I came out of a very bad experience today with the clear conviction that if we lose our spiritual bond with the land there'll be nothing left of us as a nation.'

'Part of the earth. I'll go with that.' Bill Blore was on his feet, tankard clamped to his chest. 'Bury me in a Bronze Age fucking longbarrow with a flint axe in my hand, that'll do me.'

When the laughter died, Lol said, 'Well, Elgar was here, we know that ... and there's even evidence that he visited Coleman's Meadow when Alfred Watkins ...' he smiled at Bill Blore '... found the ley running through it.'

Merrily couldn't make out Blore's reaction. She spotted a few local people, including Brenda Prosser and her daughter, Ann Marie – Jim still working in the shop.

'But if anyone really inhabits *this* landscape ...' Lol stroked a chord '... we're probably looking at a woman.'

The lights dipped and the room went quiet as the only known image of Lucy Devenish took form on the screen.

Merrily was startled.

It was the lack of definition that produced the effect, and the way the brown tones of the picture faded into the shadows of the crooked old room. And Eirion had rephotographed it, so it was digital now.

Pixels. It was pixels.

Lucy middle-distant in her poncho, the blur of her face as she tried to avoid the camera, the amplified grain on the blown-up photo converted into pixels ... fragments of the essence of Lucy separating and re-forming, suggestive of movement, creating new splinters of some old wildness in those falcon's eyes.

'Christ,' someone said, 'the old girl just turned her head.'

Someone pushed urgently past Merrily's table and she looked up in the dimness and saw, in Mathew Elliot Stooke's face, the confusion of expressions she'd seen and been unable to work out just before she left Cole Barn last night, after Stooke had said:

Some kind of Stone Age warrior. Short cloak or a skin …

Merrily rose abruptly and followed him out.

60

New Void

THEY WERE SITTING in Bliss's car, watching the diminishing tail lights of the police car containing Terry Stagg, two uniforms and Steve Furneaux on his way to Gaol Street to be processed.

Now they were alone, Bliss dared to breathe. Let it come out in one big spasm of relief, his body arching over the wheel and then falling back into the seat.

'We did well,' Annie Howe said.

She was staring through the windscreen like somebody interested in rain.

'He can still get away with this, mind,' Bliss said. 'He hasn't killed anybody *personally*. He's merely given his professional advice, and a committee decision's been made. We're contemplating the dark underbelly of democracy, Annie.'

It was the way things were going. People realising how little time they had left to get rich before the planet melted.

'Let's go over it,' Howe said, 'and then make a decision. Two men to talk to. We either bring them in or we go to them.'

'If they're where I think they are neither of those options is gonna be exactly a walkover ... Or in fact a frigging walkover might be *exactly* what we're looking at.'

What had finally smashed Steve's defences was dropping those names. Experimental, taking a chance, but he'd been fairly confident.

'Where did you *get* those names?' Annie said.

'Got Blore from Steve himself at that first meeting in Gilbies. He was their consultant on the Serpent. I remember him saying Blore didn't help an awful lot ... *considering we were paying him.*'

'Hereforward were paying him?'

'And then, while still acting as consultant to Hereforward, he publicly slags off the council for its attitude towards the Dinedor Serpent. Lunacy … they're never going to employ him again, are they? All right, he's making a bomb from telly, but it still didn't feel right to me. Didn't seem too significant at the time, mind.'

Annie Howe looked at him. She was snuggled into a corner under the seat-belt hook, her face in shadow.

'Why did Hereforward *need* a consultant on the Dinedor Serpent?'

'In case the city might be missing out on a massive tourist attraction. Fortunately for the council, the *idea* of the Serpent is more exciting than what you can see.'

'All right,' she said. 'So William Blore was publicly *pro*-Serpent while secretly advising Hereforward that it was unlikely to make the county much money. What does that *tell* us?'

'Shows he's capable of double-dealing. But, more to the point, think of the technical advice he'd be able to offer anyone planning to take out Ayling and direct the blame towards the Serpent supporters. The quartz glittering in the head? The body in the river?'

'It's not enough. You could get all that from the Internet.'

'It rebounded nicely on Steve, though, Annie. Soon as we throw him the word *Blore*, he starts to roll over.'

'True.'

Howe patted her wet, ash-blonde hair, Bliss finding himself wondering for the first time if it was natural.

'So there's something else,' he said. 'Something we're missing.'

'Something we don't know but perhaps he thinks we do. Connected with the second name you dropped on him?'

'Lyndon Pierce. Blore's in charge of the dig at Ledwardine, where Pierce is the local councillor. When I first talked to Steve in Gilbies he said, the *local councillor wanted us to intervene*. I thought he meant Pierce wanted them to stop Blore getting the Ledwardine contract, maybe because he'd attract too much publicity … to an excavation Pierce was hoping would be inconclusive.'

'You've lost me.'

'Pierce is backing a plan to put expensive housing on that site. He doesn't want there to be anything exciting under there that might spell conservation. Furneaux told me he'd asked Hereforward for help, but they weren't overfussed because it was just a housing scheme, not like a major new road. However, if what I was told is right, this housing scheme is the key to this massive redevelopment and expansion of Ledwardine.'

'This is from Mrs Watkins, is it?'

'I don't know what you've got against that woman.'

'Ask her what she's got against me.'

Bliss smiled. Women were weird. Like when the WPC, Sammy Nadel, went up to tell Yasmin it looked like Steve would be spending the night in town, Yasmin apparently just acknowledged it and went back to sleep. No big deal. Merry Christmas.

'All right,' Bliss said. 'Officially Hereforward isn't helping Lyndon. But you've gorra bunch of mates here. Coke-buddies. One of whom is the archaeologist in charge of the Ledwardine dig.'

'*Coke-buddies*. God.'

'Only buddies until the shit hits the fan. Furneaux is pretty sure in his mind that if we're talking to Blore and Pierce, both of them are going to try and hang the whole deal on him.'

'Probably quite rightly. He's the ideas man, the guy who's turned Hereforward into a dirty-tricks department. He's ... what do they call it? An *enabler*?'

'He thinks *out of the box*. But this time the lid's coming down too fast and he takes a wild leap. He's probably regretting he told us about the second contract, because I really *don't* think he knows who it is or why. And if he's already too late, that's gonna make it a whole lot worse for him than if he'd kept his mouth shut.'

I swear I've told you all I know ...

Then how do you know there's going to be another, Steve?

Because, Steve had said, sweating now, *I know how much he charges, and I know much he got.*

The man called Glyn Buckland.

Annie said, 'Francis, I need a coffee. My head's ...'

'You planning to interview Steve tonight?'

'I'm inclined to let him stew. A night in a cell works wonders with someone who's never been in one before. Especially Christmas Eve. And the good thing about tomorrow is that we get a holiday from the press. What's the time?'

'Half ten, thereabouts. A pub? Bar?'

'Yeah, why not? But we need to make it quick.'

Nobody else in the packed, shiny bar in Broad Street was drinking coffee. Nobody else seemed to be over thirty, but it hadn't been hard to find a table; the only ones who were sitting down were the ones who looked like they were about to be sick.

'He was born in London,' Annie said. 'Brought up in Worcester.'

'Any particular reason you've been sitting on that for so long?'

'Only because we weren't completely sure. It's the new generation, Francis. I'm thirty-five and I can't connect with it. You said it yourself. Kids who'll do it for a few hundred pounds – couple of thousand, anyway – knowing the worse they'll get is eight or nine years.'

'And a degree in sociology. Don't forget that. What's this lad's history?'

'We learned about him from his older sister, as a result of the BBC *Crimewatch* programme. That something you'd ever consent to watch, Francis?'

'Not often. I hate to see old mates behaving like complete tits. *We need to get this man, Kirsty, before he strikes again.*'

The presenter being called Kirsty, that didn't help. What a weird, weird night this was turning out to be. If you'd told him he'd be sharing an intimate pot of coffee with the Ice Maiden, surrounded by binge-drinkers on Christmas Eve …

'*Crimewatch* can be useful,' she said, 'often in unexpected ways. We got a piece on, a year or so ago, about a fatal stabbing up in Evesham, and this woman rang in convinced it was her brother. Been fascinated with knives since he could crawl. Once stabbed their mother in the thigh when he was about ten – they'd covered that up, as parents are inclined to, telling the hospital she'd done it herself. Slicing an onion while sitting down or something.'

'As you do.'

'Anyway, he wasn't our guy, as it turned out. We got someone else within a couple of days, DNA and all. But what Buckland's sister had to say was fairly alarming. Things like he'd ask for books on anatomy for his birthday?'

'Don't tell me – the parents thought he wanted to be a hospital consultant when he grew up.'

'You know more about parenting than I do.' Howe coughed. 'Sorry.'

'You kept an eye on him, then.'

'Oh, sure, we had a round-the-clock obbo on his flat.'

'Yeh, yeh, insufficient manpower and no brownie points for prevention. How you can be mates with that frigging dim—'

'Leave it out, Francis. We'll talk about the Home Secretary when we've nothing more urgent— Oh *shit* ...'

Some kid had backed into their table. Howe mopped up spilled coffee with a paper napkin.

'Where's Buckland now?' Bliss said.

'We don't know.'

'Yeh, that's helpful.'

'He's entirely respectable. Twenty-seven years old, probably looks younger. No form.'

'At *all*?'

'No record except as a victim. He was badly beaten up in a pub when he was seventeen.' Annie released a brittle laugh. 'Main guy responsible was found stabbed to death in a car park. Killer never found.'

'Presumably CID talked to him about that?'

'It was four and a half years after the pub incident. And several years before we learned about Glyn's lifelong fascination with blades. And no DNA traces, no basis for reopening the inquiry.'

'Dish best served cold?'

'Cold's the word. In the current moral climate, you no longer have to be a psycho to kill without remorse. When did *you* last encounter a knifeboy with a conscience?'

'Or even one who could spell it.'

'Conscience?'

'I was thinking knife.'

Howe laughed.

'Actually, Buckland's intelligent enough. And in full-time employment. Self-employment. Moves around, which is why he's difficult to track. Also been known to use different names – for security reasons, allegedly. He's in the security business.'

'What kind?'

'Any kind. Driving factory wages to advising on burglar alarms. My guess is that's how he meets people who are feeling threatened enough to want to take extreme measures. Just … another kind of security.'

'How sure are you that he did the Lasky job?'

'Circumstantial, but good circumstantial. He worked for Lasky fairly regularly. Lasky recommended him to his clients. Just not quite enough to bring him in for a chat. But I'd be reluctant to, anyway.'

'Because he doesn't know about the sister coming to you. He has no reason to think you're onto him.'

'That's the situation. Leave him alone until we're sure of him.'

'All right,' Bliss said. 'If we're looking at a Hereforward subcommittee, does that include Bill Blore, maybe Lyndon Pierce in a consultative capacity?'

'Anyone else?'

'You're wondering about Charlie?'

'If I have to, I have to.'

Her narrow face was flushed, her hair flung over to one side of it in white waves. There was a little coffee stain, like a birthmark, on the side of her mouth. She didn't look like Charlie.

Bliss said, 'I think Charlie was fixed up with totty to keep him sweet, and maybe that's where it ends. I think we're looking at Ledwardine here, but I'm buggered if I know why.'

'It's not a big place.'

'Not yet, no. But unless Traffic knows otherwise, it's not a place you can get a car into tonight. It's got a moat round it.'

'Blore's there?'

'I'm sure Pierce is. How do we play it?'

Howe tapped the table slowly with a sugar spoon.

'This feller …' Bliss said. 'You've gorra have a fairly low moral threshold to whack a bloke to get a bunch of paedos off the hook.'

'He's a child of the new void,' Annie Howe said.

Still tapping.

61

See You Shine

MERRILY WATCHED STOOKE throw open the front door of the Swan and walk out into the rain. She stood for a moment, undecided, looking behind her. Nobody had followed her out of the lounge bar.

Lol was beginning a song she hadn't heard before, Lucy rearing over him like a guardian bird of prey.

Guardian?

Oh God, it was late. It had been a long, long day. The church had been desecrated. She was full of the jitters of nicotine-deprivation. She stood looking down at her hands. It was pixels. Pixels right?

Behind her, behind two oak doors, Lol sang softly,

'*... and then you feel your heart can't let it go*
Miss Devenish would ever wish it so ...'

Sod it.

She straightened up and walked out into the night.

Jane sat hunched for a long time, elbows on her knees, head in her hands. Was this it? Was this the final severance? Could she even bear to go on living here? Perhaps she'd form a mild attachment to whichever college town she ended up in. Maybe Cardiff, to be near Eirion, if he still wanted a manic-depressive. Somewhere too big and chaotic to feel a responsibility for.

Mum would be left on her own, of course. No good. She should marry Lol and move away. A perfect time now Lol was on a roll. Only she'd feel she had to stay out of some misplaced, masochistic sense of mission. Nothing left here, though, nobody worth saving … well, except Gomer, Jim at the shop, a few other people.

And Lucy. Lucy would always be here, a forlorn, broken ghost around her besmirched grave.

God, God, God. Jane stood up, furious. *No justice, anywhere. Scum rises, bastards rule.* She unlocked the cubicle door and walked out to the wash basins. Didn't look in the mirror; perhaps people would think she'd been moved to tears by Lol's songs. Only hoped that Blore had gone back to his caravan to bed one of his students, because if she saw him again tonight, doing his booming laugh, she'd smash his beer glass into his …

At the door of the Ladies, she stopped, the water gargling in the pipes, and someone …

… someone sobbing in one of the cubicles?

Merrily found Mathew Elliot Stooke alone between the two oak pillars at the end of the market hall, looking down Church Street to the end of the world.

'You're not wearing a coat,' he said.

The rain was slower now, but the water was deep enough on the cobbles to reflect the inner globes of the fake gaslamps. You were walking on light.

'I'm guessing this isn't the first time,' Merrily said.

'Merrily …' Stooke didn't look at her '… while you're not *quite* the last person I'd want to talk to at the moment …'

'It's actually not that uncommon – I mean denial. Even religious people often go that way because they don't think it's—'

'No.'

'No what?'

'No basis for discussion here.'

'You were keen enough to question *me* the other day.'

'Because I'm a journalist, and you're … someone with an axe to grind.'

Merrily peered down Church Street. Couldn't see the water at the bottom, not from here at night, but you could sense it somehow, and you knew it would be higher again tonight. She tried again.

'*Not Lenni*, you said. You didn't think Lenni had seen it, just you.'

'I don't know what you're talking about. Go back and listen to your boyfriend.'

'You do, though, Elliot. You do know what I'm talking about.'

'Look.' He turned at last to face her, the Devil's spin doctor haloed in amber. 'I made it up. My wife wanted you to get that woman off our backs. Didn't bother me, personally. And you … you have to keep on fooling yourself to justify the absurdity of your job.'

'The other night, you described a warrior-figure with a short cloak that you'd seen in the field, near the orchard. As if it was somebody from Shirley's church, but I don't think anybody from Shirley's church has been here, ever. I think she's keeping you for herself. Whether she's been in contact with Ellis in America and he's manipulating her, the way he always could with women …'

She thought about it. It was the way Ellis would work, grooming Shirley by email, making her feel important, *chosen*. Getting inside her mind, the way he used to use a crucifix … and she *must* keep it to herself.

'Lucy Devenish,' Merrily said. 'When the picture of Lucy faded up on the screen … Lucy, in her poncho, always reminded me of an old Red Indian warrior.'

'You're mad, Merrily. You're as mad as any of them. I find that very disappointing.'

'Lucy's face, whether or not it moved, as some people seemed to think … Well, the important thing for me was *your* face. That look of shocked recognition followed by this … not quite *hunted*, more something … catching up with you. Again.'

He hissed in contempt and half turned away, a stocky, irritated man in a black fleece. Merrily closed her eyes for a moment.

'I don't think that was the first time. Dreams, premonitions, figures in the bedroom when you were a kid? Unpleasant? Scary? And always the fear of madness. Then, when you're grown up and it's still happening, you think, sod this, I'm going to turn and fight it, I'm going to *kill* it. Stamp it into the ground.'

He said nothing, didn't move.

'And then, just when you think you've kicked it to death, there it is again, right in front of you and you're out of there. Out … here.'

'I walked out,' Stooke said, 'because I'd had a row with my wife, who'd dragged me here knowing I'm not a particular lover of this kind of music. I walked out because I couldn't bear to spend any more time in the middle of all those wispy New Age clowns with their oh-so-serious drivel about *the female principle in nature*. I told my wife I'd walk home and she could come back when she liked. Now go back into the pub, you'll catch cold.'

'If you'd come out with the intention of walking over half a mile home, you'd have brought a coat, an umbrella ...'

'I was going back to get them.'

'Your wife ... as good as told me you were a hack, in it for the money. I think it's much more complex than that. Sure, you were in a business full of cynics, which must've helped, not as if you were sailing against a tide ...'

'How can I get rid of you, Merrily?'

'You can tell me the truth.'

From somewhere came ribbons of laughter. There were lights in most of the houses, a splash of fluorescent white from the glass door of the Eight Till Late.

'These things,' Stooke said. 'Anomalous phenomena. All down to brain-chemicals.'

'Sure. To an extent.'

'Let's say a glimpse of an old woman did cause some aberration. False memory, déjà vu. Where part of your brain thinks you've seen something before but in fact you haven't.'

Merrily laughed.

'But above all ...' Stooke spun at her, throwing out a sudden white smile. 'Above all, it in no way suggests a god. Above *all*, it does *not* imply *that*.'

Merrily caught a squeal from the bottom of the street.

'*You* know that,' Stooke said. 'You spend time – waste your life, some of us might say – ministering to people who ... their bulbs blow, ornaments fall off their shelves. It doesn't mean *anything*. What does that say about divine purpose? It's random. It's anomalies ... blips. Pointless. It means *nothing*, Merrily.'

'You're right.' She watched the amber lights bobbing in the waterlogged cobbles below the steps of the market hall. 'In the end, we all still face the chasm. No matter what we've seen or think we've seen, that leap of faith is still required. The admission of helplessness which, in the end, makes us all equal … you and me and Einstein and Dawkins. Charles Darwin, Lucy Devenish …'

'Bullshit.'

Stooke was shaking his head as another cry came echoing up Church Street. A cry conveying outrage, disgust. More lights were coming on in houses on both sides of the street, upstairs and downstairs, outshining the sprinkling of coloured Christmas lights, like they were sending signals to each other. Signals of distress.

'I think someone's in trouble, Elliot.'

'Not me,' Stooke said.

'No, I mean—'

'The flood.' He sighed. 'I'm tired of the very word.'

'Could be into the houses. We'd better get help.'

'All right,' Stooke said. 'You go back to the pub and fetch some people. I'll go down there and see what I can do.'

'Be careful, it's going to be very deep now.'

'I won't do anything stupid.' He walked out of the market hall, turning to face her with another glowing smile. 'Doesn't mean we're selfish, you know. Doesn't mean we don't care. All this talk of Christian charity, as if you've cornered the market. That *really* makes me sick.'

'I'll catch up with you,' Merrily said.

Jane burst back into the lounge in the slipstream of her fury. Had to get this out, now: the hypocrisy, the treachery.

She stood in the doorway, laughter blossoming around her in an atmosphere mellow with lamplight and the haze of beer and spirits.

Needed Mum, and there was no sign of her. Lol would know what to do, but Lol was busy. Busy winning. No space any more between him and his audience. No divide either between the locals and the Serpent people who'd come in the coach from Hereford.

Ken Williams, the farmer who'd let Gomer build the new riverbank on his land, stood up in the middle of the floor, pint glass in one hand.

'Tell you what, boy,' he said seriously to Lol, 'you're wasted on plant hire.'

Even Jane smiled for a moment. Somebody was asking Lol why he hadn't written a song about the Dinedor Serpent. Jane spotted Eirion, with his sound mixer and his remote control for the video and began to squeeze through the crowd. She saw Lol pausing to think for a moment before pulling the new Boswell on to his knee and hitting a couple of chords.

'Actually, I can only remember the chorus, which ... Anyway, you can sing along just as soon as you pick it up.'

Lol looked around, eyes glittering between his little brass-rimmed glasses, high on the energy. Singing lightly.

> *'Dinedor Serpent*
> *'I'd do anything*
> *To see you shine.'*

Jane stopped, recognising the tune: 'Sidewalk Surfer' by Super Furry Animals. Perfect fit.

'That's it?' a guy said.

'That's it,' Lol said.

He did it again. He smiled.

'Altogether now, *Dinedor Serpent* ...'

If this had been a summer festival, they'd all have lit matches, held them up. River of light. Jane spotted Eirion rocking back in glee.

'*Eirion!*'

His grin fading as she stepped over wires and collapsed next to him at his card-table under the deepset window. She hadn't called him *Irene*.

'Listen ...'

He couldn't hear her, with the whole audience going,

'*We'd do anything ... to see you shine.*'

Everybody loving it. Everybody loving it so much they wouldn't notice Mum come in with her hair all soaked and her make-up running. Jane leapt up, but the crowd had closed between them.

62

En't Good

You could smell him now. Smelled foul. It was almost sexual, Jane thought. Swollen, invasive, obscene, the river engorged.

Bastard hadn't listened to a word she'd said. Rapists never did.

Jane, in her rain-darkened parka – she lived in the thing now – skipping back in disgust as he licked at her wellies. Eirion steadying her as she backed up against someone's wall, clutching her mini Maglite torch like a votive candle.

Too late for prayers. You could tell why flood was such a powerful biblical device: fire consumed, flood just degraded everything, turned it into sludge.

God's verdict on the vanity of the New Cotswolds.

Somebody had driven a car, a Mercedes four by four, halfway down the street and left it in the middle of the road with the engine running and the headlights on full, turning the churning water caramel, finding the roof and blind windows of another car, this one drowned. Parked on what used to be the street.

Jane and Eirion were standing just above the Ox. It had been evacuated; you could see tables piled on top of tables under the sallow bulbs of the public bar, its pool-table covered with heavy plastic, its gaming machines unplugged. The water, knee deep on the floor, looked like bad, gassy beer and smelled worse, and the road outside was full of people, like extras discarded by Hieronymus Bosch. Glistening like slugs as they struggled into waterproofs, joining the trickle down Church Street to the banks of the new lake.

The river was already a quarter way up the walls of the lowest two houses either side of the street, swirling like dark oil here, out of the headlights, and rising, rising, rising; if you tried to reach one of the door-knockers, the water would be to your chest.

'Oh God,' Jane said. 'Poor Miss Huws.'

The last evacuee. You could see bits of her life washed into the street, a wooden stool, the floating lid of a breadbin, a loaf of sliced bread.

'I can't,' she was sobbing. 'Not in that!'

Gomer's Matbro, this yellow hydraulic lift. The extended metal platform closing in on an opened upstairs window, its frame banging back against the wall. Someone was standing up in the platform, holding on to the metal guard rail, leaning across to the window.

'Coming in, Miss Huws.'

James Bull-Davies.

'Probably the first time a man's ever been inside that bedroom,' Jane murmured to Eirion.

It wasn't funny, though. Edna Huws, a frail moth in her parchment-coloured clothes, shrilling at James in front of a crowd of sympathetic voyeurs.

'I can't! Where will I go?'

'Rooms at the Swan,' James shouted. 'Barry's attending to it now. Just leave the window—'

'What can I wear? My clothes, my night-things—'

'Worry about that when we get you out, old girl.'

'This should not have happened, Mr Davies!'

'Well, I'm afraid it bloody well has.'

'Jane.'

Hand on her arm. Jane turned to find Mum at last.

'God, you're soaked to the skin.' Horrifying reversal of usual roles. 'You've got to go back, Mum, and get out of those clothes.'

'Is Miss Huws OK?'

'James Bull-Davies is in there, trying to persuade her to come out through the window. They've got all the people out of the other houses. And two labradors. Mum, listen—'

'Good. You can't believe it, can you? How quickly it happens.'

'The point is there's nothing you can do here. Come back to the vic, *please*. Look at you, your skirt's all covered with—'

'Where's Lol?'

'Putting his gear away. Barry was saying they should lock it in. He's worried about looters.'

'In Ledwardine?'

'Yeah, well … Look, Mum, please? Something I have to tell you.'

James was helping Edna Huws out of the window and into the Matbro, putting a small suitcase in after her. Miss Huws had a long raincoat round her shoulders; she was making kind of chicken noises as the platform came down to ridiculous cheers. All this crazy goodwill that came with communal adversity and Christmas.

'Mum! Vicarage!'

'I seem to have lost a heel.'

Mum reached down and pulled something from a shoe, hobbling back up the street against the flow of water coming down from the square.

All the same, the rain was easing off and the sky was actually clearing, disclosing a fragment of moon now, like one edge of a silver ring in a crumpled grey tissue of cloud.

But it was no better on the ground. Reaching the entrance to Old Barn Lane, Jane saw another, smaller crowd assembling halfway down where there was a dip in the road – like a reservoir now. Front gardens were underwater, all the lights were on in all the houses and there were people with plastic buckets and washing-up bowls vainly trying to send it back.

'Oh Christ!'

A man's voice, falsetto with shock. He came stumbling out of the water, shaven head, earring like a coiled spring. Derry Bateman, the electrician.

'Anybody know about artificial respiration?'

'A bit …'

Mum started limping over to the crowd making a semicircle on the edge of the flood.

'I thought it was a sandbag, I did.' Derry Bateman looking shattered. 'Oh, bloody hell. Everybody get back, this en't good.'

'I think it's too late, anyway,' a woman said.

The water almost thigh-high on two men dragging a body. Torchbeams converging.

A woman screaming, 'Please God, no.'

'Here ...' Derry guiding Mum to the waterside. Jane didn't even know she could do artificial respiration. 'Turn him over.'

The woman said, 'I think he's dead.'

Someone else howling, 'Who is it? *Who is it?*'

'I'm *telling* you ...' A quavery, elderly voice. 'Someone was sitting—'

'I don't know him,' Derry shouted. 'I've never seen him before.'

'You don't know *what* you saw, Reg.'

'I tell you I saw someone ... I thought they was sitting on a sack, but they was sitting on *him* ...'

'Who was?'

'He went that way. All in black, look. I en't making this up.'

'Everybody looks black in this—'

Jane ran down after Mum, but Eirion was holding on to her arm.

'*You* don't know artificial respiration, do you Jane?'

'Well, no, but—'

'I saw a boy once who'd drowned,' Eirion said. 'Believe me, you don't want to see this.'

Derry Bateman and a couple of neighbours had carried him out of the flood and laid him in the back of Derry's van, surrounded by compartments of tools and electrical supplies. Nobody could think of anywhere better. Nobody was volunteering to accommodate a drowned man in a sitting room all decked out for Christmas.

Derry had covered him with blue plastic sheeting, like the stuff draped over cookers and washing machines on the riverside estate.

Merrily was wiping her dripping hands on her sodden skirt. She felt heartsick.

'You say you know who he is, vicar?'

'Yes.'

'I'm sorry,' Derry said. 'There really was nothing we could do.'

'Nobody see what happened?'

'Nobody seen a thing, else we'd've gone to help him. I still don't see how he could've gone in that far, less he was drunk.'

'Derry, who's Reg?'

'Reg Sutton? David Sutton's old man. I think he's Reg, en't he, Peter? He only come to live yere a couple of weeks ago. He's pretty old, you can't really rely on too much he says.'

'Where's he live?'

'He's … one, two … five houses down, end of the terrace. White gate.'

'Thanks.'

Derry nodded uncomfortably at the body.

'Who is he, vicar?'

'He's the guy who rents Cole Barn.'

She could still hear him, the exasperated voice of reason: *anomalies … blips … means nothing.* Saw his fluorescent white smile.

Merrily flattened her back against a gatepost, gazed up at the moon, coddled in smoky cloud.

Above all, it in no way suggests a god. Above all, it does not imply that.

And now he knew. Or not. She looked down at the plastic bundle, fogged and glistening and it was very hard to believe in a life after *that.* And, oh, this was not right. There was *nothing* right about this, and certainly nothing to be salvaged from the Book of bloody Daniel.

'What's he doing down yere then, vicar?'

'I don't know.'

Maybe somebody had called out to him. Maybe there were too many lights at the bottom of Church Street. *Christ.*

'We better call the police,' Derry said. 'Though how they're gonner get here tonight, less they can get a helicopter.'

'I'll call them,' Merrily said.

'Only, if there's any way of … I mean, I don't really want …'

'No, you're right. He can't stay here. Why don't you drive him up to the church? We've got a long table in the vestry. Do you mind carrying him again?'

'En't got no choice, do we?'

'I need to find his wife.'

And the old man had said: *I saw someone … thought they was sitting on a sack.*

Someone. Man or a woman?

She saw Jane and Eirion standing near the top of the lane, hand in hand, like children. All she could think of, as she walked up towards them, was Shirley West. She hadn't seen Shirley anywhere tonight, only the marks of her madness.

63

Do the Dying

WHEN SHE CALLED Bliss on his mobile, from the vicarage, he answered in seconds, sounding wide-awake, focused. Excited, even.

'Merrily, touch *nothing*.'

'Too late. They had to bring him out of the water, he might've been alive. And we couldn't leave him in the van.'

'So where is he?'

'In the church. Vestry.'

She'd managed to find James Bull-Davies, give him the keys and he was over there supervising it. Well, where else could Stooke's body have gone, where *else*?

Bliss sighed.

'So what are you saying, Frannie, I should've got out one of my many rolls of police tape? Cordoned off the area?'

'Well, don't let anybody in the frigging vestry.'

'Damn,' she said bitterly, 'and I was planning to charge admission.'

'You all right, Merrily? You don't sound well.'

'I'm fine.'

Could hardly keep her voice steady. Jane was standing in the doorway with arms full of a bath towel and dry clothes. She'd plugged in the electric fire, all three bars.

Bliss said, 'Tell me why you think he's been killed.'

'I ... I just think it can't be ruled out, that's all.'

Signalling to Jane to put the clothes on the sofa, telling Bliss quickly about Shirley West, the Church of the Lord of the Light, the damage, the graffiti. He didn't say anything. He got her to go over a couple of points again. He asked her if Stooke had had any other obvious injuries. Twice he said, *drowned isn't right*. Clearly he was not impressed.

'Is there ...' shaking now '... something I don't know?'

'A lot. Listen, gorra get things organised this end, then I'll call you back from the car. We're coming over. Only problem is how we get into the village.'

'You'll have to leave your vehicles the other side of the footbridge at Caple End, and I'll have to persuade people to pick you up. How many?'

'Say half a dozen, initially. More later if we agree with you. Or if ...'

'What?'

'Keep your mobile on, I'll see you at Caple End.'

'It won't be me. I have a service to do.'

'Oh, Merrily!'

'It's Christmas Eve. It's what I *do*. How long before you get here?'

'Thirty, forty minutes. I can call you back in five from the car.'

'All right, I'll wait.'

Despite dry clothes and the electric fire, she was still shivering. The rain was no more than a peppering now and, through the scullery window, you could see the grey-blue froth of night clouds.

Gomer was going to Caple End with his big Jeep, Jane and Eirion to the church to tell people the service would be a little delayed. But first ...

Jane came into the scullery alone, shut the door behind her.

'It won't wait, will it?' Merrily said. 'Only—'

'No,' Jane said, 'I don't think it will.'

Jane told her about Professor Blore's private report to the Council. His alleged discovery of comparatively modern masonry and artefacts under one of the stones.

'What does Neil Cooper say?'

'He thinks Blore's lying. Really he's scared to say *what* he thinks. Scared of losing his job. Looks like Blore could've been got at by ... I don't know.'

'A combination, probably. Landowner, developers ... maybe several of them already getting in line for a stake in Ledwardine New Town.' Merrily instinctively reaching for a cigarette, letting her hand fall empty to the desk. 'Would take a lot, mind, to make it worthwhile for Blore to virtually destroy everything. The henge? How sure *are* you and Neil about the henge?'

'It's got to be more than wishful thinking. It's just—'

A tapping on the window. Lol's face. Thank God.

'I'll let him in,' Jane said.

'No, I'll do it. You go to the church with Eirion. Tell whoever's there, if anybody, that I'm sorry and I'll be with them in ten minutes, soon as I've spoken to Bliss again.'

'Mum, you don't have to do this. We're in the middle of a crisis here. Even the church has been—'

'That's *why* I have to do it.'

'And I haven't finished,' Jane said.

But Merrily was already into the passage, and the phone was ringing behind her.

You could only see the ghost of the last word now. *Witch.*

James Bull-Davies had been as good as his word. *The Bull,* Lucy used to call him, always having difficulty separating him from his more unsavoury ancestors. Maybe she would now, having seen him scrubbing at her gravestone.

He was in the church, making sure nobody went near the vestry. His old car wouldn't start, and Eirion had gone in his place to Caple End to ferry cops to Ledwardine. Jane put her hands on the shoulders of Lucy's stone. It was becoming a natural thing to do, made her feel stronger and less confused. In theory.

'That your gran, is it?'

She looked up, mildly startled; hadn't noticed him coming over.

'What are *you* doing here? I thought you'd gone home for Christmas. Thought you'd be legless in High Town by now.'

'Bleeding bridge. Should've left earlier. The fucking sticks, eh?'

'You could've gone on one of the coaches.'

'Prefer me own wheels, sweetheart,' Gregory said. 'Anyway, I don't live in Hereford. Not enough happening for me. Figured in the end might as well stay here as go there.'

'You went to Lol's gig?'

'Who?'

'Lol Robinson? The gig at the Swan?'

'Didn't you see me?'

'I didn't get to see much of it in the end.'

'It was good,' Gregory said.

The night was lighter now. Not much, but enough to make out his thin features. He looked starved. He was wearing a short leather jacket and tight black trousers that looked like they were fused to his legs.

'You're soaked.'

Really soaked. He even smelled wet.

'Where's your bloke, Jane?'

'He's ... gone to help bring some people from Caple End.'

'Coppers?'

'Maybe.'

'They've even closed the footbridge now. Nobody can get across the river without having to walk about ten miles to the next bridge. That's what people's saying. What's that about?'

'Somebody got drowned.'

'That a fact.'

'Guy who lived near your site, actually. Cole Barn?'

'Don't know it.'

'You never walked over there?'

'What for?'

'Just ... a walk.'

'A *walk*,' Gregory said. 'You people kill me.'

'What people?'

'People who can live in a shithole like this and go for ... walks.'

'Hey, it's not my fault you got wet.'

'Never said it was.' He seemed on edge. Angry. 'Not seen Blore, have you?'

'Not for a while.'

'He's got the keys to my bleedin' caravan. Give him the keys when I thought I was leaving.'

'If I see him, I'll ... get somebody to tell him you're looking for him.'

'Thanks.'

Jane said, 'Gregory ... you know all that stuff you were giving us about Blore having sex with his students?'

'So?"

'Anybody special?'

'When?'

'Currently?'

'Nah. He don't separate them out much when he's pissed. It's all fires and mantelpieces with Blore.' Gregory nodded at the people filing into church. 'Wass all this?'

'Midnight service ... delayed. They're waiting for my mum. She's the vicar.'

'Must be popular, night like this.'

'I think people are a bit ... spooked. The flood. The drowning. Want a bit of reassurance. And – I keep forgetting – it's Christmas. Come in if you want.'

'What happens?'

'Well, it won't be an ordinary midnight mass. In view of everything, I think she'll be playing it by ear.'

'I wouldn't know. I've never been to one. I mean ... you know ...' Gregory shrugged awkwardly '... why?'

'You don't believe in anything?'

'Never thought about it. Wassa point? It don't get you anywhere, do it?'

'You don't think it's, like ... interesting to think there might be something, somewhere, bigger than all this?'

'Like what?'

'Like, you know, a life beyond this life? Somewhere you go after you die?'

'Best thing is not to die. Let other people do it.'

'Huh?'

'The dying,' Gregory said roughly. 'The trick is to let other people do the dying.'

CHRISTMAS DAY

Shall dumpish melancholy spoil my joys …

Thomas Traherne
'On Christmas Day'

64

Sickness

'WE HAVE TO try and hold this together,' Merrily said.

Standing on the chancel steps, in jeans, a black woollen top, her heaviest pectoral cross.

No mass, no meditation, but the church was full. It was almost eerily full, as if there'd been a timeslip back to medieval days, when the timbers of Ledwardine were young. When life was simpler and faith, out of a kind of necessity, was strong.

And when, as each new comet was sighted, they'd still talked about the Endtime.

She saw Jim Prosser and Brenda sitting with Brian Clee. In the Bull pew, James Bull-Davies with Alison. Maybe fifty local people and as many strangers. She saw the man with the ruby earring. She saw the witch from Dinedor who'd had visions of the Druids along the Serpent.

Something was holding them together.

Edna Huws was at the organ. A good thing for her, perhaps, and for all of them. There would be carols. There would have to be carols, voices raised against the dark.

There was no sign of Shirley West.

'No point in dressing this up,' Merrily said. 'A man's been found drowned at the bottom of the pitch in Old Barn Lane. A man I'd got to know ... if not well.'

Or not well enough soon enough.

'The police are on their way. And, erm ... they may need to come in here. Which limits us a bit.'

Murmurs. Merrily looked down and saw she was still wearing wellies. She wanted to get them to pray in silence for what remained of the spirit of Christmas, some small, still light, to come into this place. But there wasn't much silence in her head.

She'd called Bliss back on her mobile. Listening, while walking over to the church with Lol, to his theory that Clem Ayling had been murdered by contract. A connection with the non-democratic focus group Hereforward, to which Ayling had been co-opted by the county council. Ayling discovering that his colleagues on Hereforward had been indulging themselves, on weekends away, with cocaine supplied by a man called Steven Furneaux.

It's about control, Bliss had said. *About binding people together. If they've been mutually involved in one level of criminal activity they'll keep quiet about others.*

Merrily hadn't needed reminding why Ayling would have found the drug element particularly repugnant. Unfortunately, he'd thought he could deal with it himself, underestimating what other interests were at stake.

A little coterie of unscrupulous bastards, operating under and around the democratic process ... and making themselves a lot of money on the side.

Sensing a connection, she'd told him about Blore's report on the stones.

If Bliss was right, Ayling's death was not directly connected with the Dinedor Serpent but meant to deflect the investigation in that direction. Discrediting opponents of the development of Dinedor and Rotherwas, as well, presumably, as the Coleman's Meadow Preservation Society. Making it look like Herefordshire was home to some obsessive semi-pagan underculture.

Well represented, it seemed, in this congregation.

'This was going to be a meditation,' Merrily said. 'That was when I was only expecting about a third as many people and no police. We were going to sit around in a circle and think about what it means – Christmas. Birth and rebirth. The coming of the light.'

Aware of the green curtain behind her, which had been hung over the smashed area of the rood screen, and the roughly-sawn square of hard-board fitted into the stonework over the bottom quarter of the broken stained-glass window.

It was making her think about Clem Ayling's head, the pieces of quartz, the body in the Wye.

'I've been realising that sometimes we have to fight for the light. Whether it's the midsummer sun rising over Cole Hill or the moonlight shining in the Dinedor Serpent.'

Somebody cheered and got shushed. Merrily smiled.

'And it's not paganism in the heathen sense, it's paganism in the original sense. Ruralism. It's an understanding that people living here thousands of years ago had different ways of perceiving God, but it always came back to light. We have the advantage because, thanks to what happened on this day over two thousand years ago, we also know about the higher levels of love.'

She looked up, heard the latch lifting on the church doors and saw five people heading towards the vestry. All of them, except Bliss, were women. One was Jane, who'd been waiting in the porch, one a uniformed policewoman. The third woman was Leonora Stooke and the fourth – oh hell – Annie Howe? The Ice Maiden?

They stood either side of the vestry door, waiting.

They didn't have the key.

'I'd like us to pray for that light and that love. And then – with the help of the unstoppable, heroic Miss Edna Huws, whose home, as most of you know, was flooded tonight, we'll have some carols. During which I may have to pop out.'

It was a difficult situation. She couldn't prolong the agony for Leonora Stooke, waiting to identify her drowned husband.

She abbreviated the prayer, busking it. Leaving fifteen seconds of silence before giving Edna the nod.

The vestry was sometimes a gift shop now. Money-raising scheme of Uncle Ted's. Displays of postcards and booklets, notelets and framed prints had been pushed back against the walls. Elliot Stooke's body lay on the trestle table under the dark, leaded window. It was still covered with the blue plastic, a big, shiny cocoon. The room smelled dank and sour.

Annie Howe was wearing a long off-white mac and a scarf. She'd nodded briefly at Merrily.

'Take your time, Mrs Stooke. Tell me when you're ready.'

Leonora was wearing her turquoise Gore Tex jacket. She was pale and somehow beautiful in her distress.

'I can't. I just—' She looked across at Merrily, her red hair tumbled, her eyes glassy. 'Why can't *you*? You know him. *I* don't want to remember him like this. Why should I have to?'

'Mrs Stooke,' Howe said. 'I know how terribly hard this is, but it's something *we* have to ...'

'I can't believe it. I cannot believe how this could happen. How it could be *allowed* to happen.'

Merrily saw Jane in the doorway. Signalled with her eyes for her to go back into the nave. Couldn't believe Jane would want to see this. But Jane wasn't looking at the body, and she didn't move.

Merrily saw Leonora nod.

The policewoman went over to the table and peeled back the blue plastic. Leonora looked once and jerked back, as if a bolt of electricity was going through her, shut her eyes, nodding hard.

Shuddering. Howe steadying her, guiding her out. The policewoman drew the plastic back over Elliot Stooke's face. They came back out into the nave, and Merrily closed the vestry door. Some people in the pews glanced over their shoulders, still only halfway through 'Once in Royal David's City'.

As quick as that. Bliss followed them into the porch, where Lol was standing, with Eirion, and Merrily finally got to speak to Leonora.

'Look ... you're not going to want to go back to the barn tonight. Why don't you stay with Jane and me?'

'I'm staying at the Swan.' Leonora looked away, as if Merrily had let her down badly by refusing to identify her husband's body. 'I'll be leaving tomorrow anyway.'

Merrily nodded.

'And he shouldn't have been brought here. It's a fucking gratuitous insult.' Merrily collecting a hard glance. 'I suppose *that* was you.'

Merrily said nothing. Leonora turned her back on her.

'There's an underlying sickness in this place,' she said to Annie Howe. 'We were both aware of it.'

'Mrs Stooke, if there's anything you want to tell me, perhaps we should go somewhere else.'

'There's nothing I really want to say to anyone.' Leonora's fists tightening inside leather gloves which squeaked. 'Mrs Watkins invited us tonight to meet some local people, but the local people ignored us and the others – it was like it was calculated to offend, the shit they were coming out with. Elliot just … I don't suppose he even knew where he was going or cared, as long as it was away from *them*. All that on top of the religious mania. Said he just wanted some fresh air.' She looked down at the flags. 'I should've gone with him. Let him down.'

'All the way,' Jane murmured.

She was standing with her back to the double doors into the church, pale yellow light in the crack. Merrily looked at her, appalled. Jane had her hands rammed down into the pockets of her parka, held her shoulders rigid.

'By my reckoning …' She looked up slowly. 'And I'm, like, I'm only guessing here … but I reckon that when Mr Stooke was dying in the flood, that would probably be around the time Lensi was in a cubicle in the Ladies' at the Swan.' Stared defiantly at Leonora. 'Shagging Bill Blore.'

65

Off the Wall

THEY WENT THROUGH the inevitable. The whole *lying little bitch* routine, Lensi's face full of twisting shadows, before Merrily was pulling Jane back into the church, steering her into the corner behind the font.

Jane's face was flushed, and she was panting.

Bliss had followed them, standing with his back to the doors.

'Yes,' he was saying almost lightly. '*That's* it.'

The organ pipes were sounding the exultant opening chords of 'Hark the Herald Angels Sing'. The congregation, perhaps excited now, sensing something happening, staying with it. Behind the font, Merrily held Jane by both shoulders.

'I hope to God you're—'

'I was trying to tell you!'

'Tell *me*, Jane,' Bliss said.

'I was in the toilet at the other end. After I talked to Coops.'

'After he told you about Blore?'

'I've told Frannie about that,' Merrily said to Jane. 'And the significance.'

Bliss had his hands together, like in prayer, the tips of the fingers tentatively tapping together.

'You *are* absolutely sure about this, aren't you, Jane? Because if there's any doubt at all, you need to tell me now.'

Jane looked at the doors. Bliss went and pulled them open. Merrily heard Lol telling him that Howe had taken Leonora back to the Swan.

'For a long and meaningful discussion, I hope,' Bliss said. 'All right, let's all go back out where we don't have to whisper.'

'I thought she was sobbing.' Jane said. 'At first.'

'Sobbing,' Bliss said.

'It's … quite a similar sound, when you think about it. See, I'd just been sitting there on the loo. For a long time. Not ready to face anybody, you know? And like the toilets, they're all refurbished now, padded walls, very plush. They obviously didn't know I was there, they were at the other end. I didn't know what to do. I just stood there. I couldn't identify her voice, but there was, like, no mistaking his. He was going, *Better, now? That better?* With every … thrust. Like a dad talking to a little girl. Which was so sick. And then she started to, like, giggle, in this slightly hysterical way? I just felt … *yuk.*'

'But not yuk enough to walk away, I hope,' Bliss said.

'Hung around outside … well, just inside reception, at the end of the passage. And then he came out. He didn't see me. Just went through to the public bar. And then, a few minutes later, *she* came out – obviously taken some time to, like, clean herself up? And she did see me. And I go, Hello, Lensi, and she just smiles at me, briefly, like to somebody she just vaguely knew, and didn't say anything, and went through into the passage.'

'So now she knows,' Bliss said. 'She knows *you* know. Let's hope Annie's doing the right thing here.'

'What's the right thing?' Merrily asked him.

'I don't really know. I don't know whether I want her to let this woman go off so she can rush back to Blore, or take her away and talk to her, so I can have Blore to meself. I don't know if this is something new – Mrs Stooke and Bill Blore – or if they've been an item for a while. Any thoughts?'

'*She* wanted to come here,' Merrily said. 'She wanted to rent that house, and for no obvious reason. Elliot didn't. He didn't like it here.'

'Maybe knowing Blore had his eye on Coleman's Meadow? That he'd be here? But that would pre-suppose Blore had known about it for quite a while. And that he'd get the contract. Which is interesting in itself. It seem like a happy marriage to you, Merrily?'

'It seemed like a slightly tense marriage, but I put that down to living with death threats and getting this abusive mail from … God, you see, nobody knew they were here, except for me. And Shirley.'

'I've got people out looking for Shirley,' Bliss said, 'as we speak.'

'And Shirley only knew because Leonora went into the post office and wrote out a cheque for an electricity bill, with the name Stooke on it. Very apologetic about that. Stupid mistake.'

'Except it wasn't?'

'She's not a stupid woman. And then they – allegedly – get all the hate mail from Shirley's church. Which didn't surprise me because I know the provenance of this church, and it's not healthy. And I *think* that was genuine, the mail – they showed me an example. I mean the odd thing is that she came to tell me about it, ask if I could do anything about Shirley. Which struck me as strange because she didn't know then that I knew they were the Stookes, not the Wintersons.'

'Looks like she *wanted* you to know, Merrily. Know who they were and know about the threats. No better witness than the vicar, if anything was to happen to Stooke.'

'You actually …' Merrily pressing one hand over the other to stop both of them shaking. 'You think that's why they came here? For Stooke to be killed?'

'I don't know. We may never know, unless one of them talks. Whether it was long-term planning or whether she just wanted to come here to snatch some precious moments with the current love of her life …'

Jane said, 'Blore has a caravan on the site. Gregory told us about all the students he—'

'That's another thing,' Merrily said. 'He still has a room at the Swan, doesn't he? Why didn't they just go up there if they couldn't wait? One flight of stairs? I mean, *the ladies loo?*'

Bliss had a little smile forming.

'Think about it. Let's go from the premise that they know Stooke's going to be done tonight. I'm thinking aloud here, Merrily, I'm thinking Stooke's gone out there, into the flooded village … and our man's out there already. Primed and paid. Glyn, his name is. We know who he is, we know his history. Glyn is out there.'

'Now?'

'Oh yeh. Somewhere. So here they are in Laurence's gig, and Mrs Stooke's suddenly realising Mr Stooke may not be coming back. Gorra be a sobering moment. This is *it*. Mr Stooke may soon be no more. Whatever kind of cold bitch she is, Blore sees that Mrs Stooke is rapidly turning into someone who people might soon be staring at. What's the lighting like in there?'

'Well, it's not an auditorium, Frannie, it's a pub. Yes, you could see everybody quite well.'

'He needs to get her out of there, calm her down, make her laugh, take her mind off it. Do something a little outrageous, a little … dare I say off the wall?'

Jane laughed, but it was a shocked laugh, a frightened laugh. The pipes expelled the lowering, slightly sinister opening chords of 'While Shepherds Watched'.

Bliss said, 'Jane, who's Gregory?'

'He's the security guy.'

'Where?'

'The security man on the site. He's done other jobs with Blore. They're kind of mates.'

'The *security* man. How old?'

'I don't know. Early twenties?'

'Gregory,' Bliss said diffidently. 'And his last name is …?'

Jane thought for a couple of seconds then shook her head.

'Don't know. Why don't you …?'

'Ask him? How could I do that, Jane?'

'I saw him earlier. I was at … in the churchyard. He came over. He was pretty well … Oh God …'

'What?'

'Wet,' Jane said. 'Like really wet? Head to toe?'

Merrily moved closer to Jane. She was aware of Lol standing with Eirion in the entrance to the porch, under the lantern. The congregation sang, '*Fear not, said he, for mighty dread …*'

'Where did he go, Jane?' Bliss said.

'I don't know. He was pretty hacked off. Not like the last couple of times I saw him – cocky, Jack-the-lad, you know? He was really angry.

Going on about how he hated it here, and the countryside generally. He was asking where Blore was – he said Blore had the keys to his caravan. I assumed he wanted to get some dry clothes?'

'Angry at Blore?'

'Yeah. That's the impression I got.'

'Coleman's Meadow, this caravan? Thanks, Jane,' Bliss said. 'I've said a few uncomplimentary things about you. Just occasionally. I take them back. You're not a bad kid.'

'I'm not a kid.'

'Sorry, eighteen, I forgot. Welcome to the shit end of life.'

Bliss went out into the graveyard, full of moving shadows.

'Terry, I need foot soldiers!'

Then he came back, pressed something into Merrily's hands.

'Wow,' she said, 'you remembered.'

From a pocket of his camouflage jacket, Bliss also brought out a book of matches.

'Do us a favour, Merrily. Explain to your congregation why we're not letting anyone over the footbridge just yet. Tell them it's for their own safety, yeh?'

She nodded, and he moved away into the shadows of graves and men, and Merrily walked out into the damp night, tearing off the cellophane with her teeth, shaking out a Silk Cut, igniting a match and cupping a hand around the flame. Jane was sticking close to her, Lol on the other side, Eirion following.

'Gregory?' Jane said. 'I don't understand? What's Gregory *done*?'

'Apart from cover up for Blore,' Eirion said. 'He was telling us about all the women students Blore took into his caravan.'

'Perhaps just one woman and not a stud—' Merrily took in too much smoke, gave in to the coughing, hugged a stone cross until it was over. 'It was very convenient, wasn't it. *Just popping out for a walk, darling. Get a few pictures.*'

'She was taking Blore's picture on Saturday,' Jane said. 'And I was just thinking ... that first morning I met her ... when she said she'd been out with her camera? It would explain her ... the way she *was*. Like she'd just ... I don't know.'

'I'm going back now, guys.' Merrily squeezed out her cigarette, half-smoked, slipped it into a pocket of her jeans; it was enough. 'Stay together.'

She patted her hair, took a deep breath of cold night air and walked back through the porch into the nave.

The carols were over, the congregation had fragmented and conversations had broken out like small bush fires, people leaning over to talk to friends in the pews behind. Nobody in a hurry to leave.

Edna Huws was waiting by the lectern with Uncle Ted, senior church-warden.

'Is it settled?' Miss Huws said, stiff-backed.

'It's ... no, it isn't really.'

Ted said, 'Have you any idea what time it is?' Gesturing into the nave. 'What are you going to do about all this?'

'Finish the service.' She smiled weakly. 'Happy Christmas, Uncle Ted.'

Ted scowled. The nave was untidy with noise, like an airport lounge. No alternative but to become a real priest. She walked down to where the still-unlit Christmas tree stood forlorn, in front of the chancel, a couple of paces from the pulpit.

Bent and plugged it in. It came instantly alive, all the lights working. A small, determined glow at the centre of the orb.

The chat faded as she started to walk back to her old spot on the chancel steps, then she changed her mind and crossed to the pulpit, the big old play fort, and went up the wooden steps and placed her hands either side, too low down as usual.

'I'm really sorry,' she said. 'This has been ...'

Feeling around with her feet for something to stand on, encountering something that shouldn't be there and looking down to find Shirley West smiling up at her from the dark oaken well of the pulpit, eyes wide open to the Endtime.

66

Endtime

THE SMALLER CARAVAN was all black, but in the windows of the big one there was a steamy grey-white glow, weaker than the muffled moon.

Terry Stagg held up the open padlock, the metal gate already hanging loose. Bliss nodded, went through the opening into Coleman's Meadow. The night was still and cold and unfriendly as an unlit cellar.

Three uniforms behind them. They'd all come in Gomer Parry's jeep, the old bugger still at the wheel, having refused to hand over the keys on the grounds none of them was insured. All too often this job was close to dark comedy.

'We'll knock, I think,' Bliss whispered.

It wasn't necessary. The metal door was hanging open, a big man standing at the top of the two steps, with the mean light behind him. He was wearing a rugby shirt and he had a beer bottle in his right hand. He took in Bliss from boots to beanie.

'The fuck are you? Know what time this is?'

'It's almost one a.m., Mr Blore.' Bliss could no more call him *Professor* than he could call Iain Brent *Doctor*. He flashed his ID. 'And I'm here to wish you a very merry Christmas on behalf of West Mercia CID. Just something we like to do periodically.'

Felt his blood racing. Hadn't expected this. Not Blore himself, forsaking his nice comfy room back at the Swan for a wet Christmas dawn in Coleman's Meadow. Only one possible reason for this. He was either not alone or not expecting to be alone for long.

'If you're here about the flooding,' Blore said, 'we've been spared. Which is just as well 'cause I'm back on the job on Boxing Day.'

Bliss beamed.

'My information is you were on the job this very evening, sir.'

'Well, your information is wrong.'

Blore didn't get it. Perhaps just as well. Bliss jerked a thumb at his companion with the ancient anorak and the greying moustache.

'My colleague DC Stagg. Have you seen your security officer tonight, sir?'

'No. But then I wouldn't expect to. He's gone home for Christmas.'

'You don't need security over Christmas?'

'Why I'm here … Inspector, was it?'

'That not a bit of a risk, personal-safety wise, Mr Blore?'

'Self-employed,' Blore said. 'Means I can give the nanny state the finger.'

'Sure about that, are we, Mr Blore?' Bliss hated cops who called people *we*; hoped Blore did, too. 'Sure we haven't seen Glyn?'

'Who's Glyn?'

'Did I say Glyn? I meant Gregory.'

'No.'

'It's not a nice night, Mr Blore. Would you mind if we came in?'

'Yes, I would, actually. You arrive at my excavation in the early hours of Christmas morning, you ask me inane questions without giving me a good reason and now you want to invade my limited fucking *space*.'

'Mr Blore …' Bliss sighed. 'I won't pretend I've gorra warrant, but if you don't invite me in, my lads will just camp outside until I get one brought to Caple End, by which time I'll've become *horribly* suspicious and just a mite less friendly than I've been so far.'

Blore sniffed and stood to one side.

'Be my guest, then.'

When the church was empty, Merrily unplugged the Christmas tree, switched out the lights and stood alone, watching deep Gothic windows coming silently to a grey and ghostly half life.

At the door, she said a prayer for Shirley's soul, followed by the Lord's Prayer and a precautionary St Patrick's Breastplate. Then she grabbed her coat from the peg over the prayer book rack, went out and locked up, and in the porch her breath came out very like a long-suppressed sob.

She'd made herself stand there in the pulpit, her foot inside a wellington touching one of dead Shirley's hands. Standing there, slowly becoming aware of the smell, very calmly apologising to the bemused, restive, overtired and disappointed congregation, explaining that the village was now at the centre of a murder investigation and that nobody was being allowed to leave for the present. Suggesting that those who couldn't go home should go across to the Swan for the time being.

And that those villagers who could go home should not go alone.

She hadn't told Uncle Ted what was inside the pulpit, certainly not Edna Huws. Outside, she found Lol and Jane and Eirion waiting under the lych-gate, like some kind of dysfunctional family.

'Home?' Jane said.

'Swan, I'm afraid, flower.'

At the Black Swan, Barry took them in his office, explained that Superintendent Howe and the other policewoman had borrowed his car to take Mrs Winterson to Caple End.

Sounded like Leonora had been arrested, was going to be handed over at the bridge to cops from Hereford.

'Howe'll be back?'

'That's what she said.' Barry spread his hands, someone outside shouting for him. 'You'll have to excuse me—'

'Sure ... OK.' Merrily handed the bunch of church keys on a rusting ring, like gaoler's keys, to Eirion. 'Could you give those to Annie Howe when she gets back? Needs to be Eirion,' she said to Jane. 'You and Howe have too much history.'

'Mum ...?'

'OK ...'

Merrily told them and watched Jane go instantly pale. Throwing an arm around the kid in a way she hadn't done for years. Not since Jane had become that little taller than her mother.

Both of them aware, at this moment, of how close ...

'Don't give the keys to anyone else. Don't, of course, go in. Under any circumstances.'

'*He* killed her. Gregory?'

'It's ... likely.'

A puncture in the coat, a little blood like a cluster of holly berries. Maybe Shirley disturbed him smashing the stained-glass window or the rood screen, scattering the chairs. *Him* smashing things? *That* way round?

Jane said distantly, 'He said the trick was to let other people do the dying.' She looked up at Merrily. 'Why are you leaving the keys with—? Where are you going?'

'We have to go and find Bliss. We have to tell him about this.'

'We?'

'Me and Lol, I think.'

'But, like … why don't you just ring him on his mobile?'

'Because I've tried, and Coleman's Meadow seems to be one of those blank spots. If he's talking to Blore, he needs this.'

'We'll all go,' Jane said.

'No, we won't.'

The caravan had three rooms and Gregory wasn't in any of them.

On a table in the very plush living room, heated by Calor gas, there were two beer bottles, but that didn't mean anything.

What had probably happened, Bliss figured, was that they'd heard the jeep approaching and Blore had simply opened the door and let him out and stayed in the doorway drinking his beer. Arrogant twat.

'Well, thank you, Mr Blore. Everything seems in order.'

'You going to tell me what this is all about, Inspector?'

'Of course. We're investigating the death of Mathew Elliot Stooke. You did *know* about that?'

'You mean Winterson? Thought the poor guy was drowned. Why's that need further investigation, including a search of my fucking caravan?'

'Because we think he was murdered.'

'Homicide by drowning?' Blore shrugged, let out a small burp, pushed stubby fingers through his dense hair. 'Suppose these things happen, don't they? Western world's reverting to some kind of neo-neolithic barbarity, Inspector. Suicide bombers, kids shooting other kids on the streets, torturing old ladies …'

'Godless,' Bliss said.

Part of him wanting to hang that toilet scene on the bastard, but without a signed statement yet from Jane it was unsafe. At the door, as Terry Stagg was stepping down into the mud, Bliss turned quickly.

'Oh— We were only talking about you earlier on. With Steve Furneaux?'

'I'm sorry?' Blore squinted at him. 'Oh … yeah, *I* know who you mean. Guy from the Council. Smooth sort of bastard.'

'That's right. He *was* smooth. He's spending the night with us.'

'Drink-driving?'

Bliss smiled.

'God, Mr Blore … You're a clever twat, aren't you?'

'I like to think so,' Blore said.

Merrily drove out on to the square. With Old Barn Lane blocked, the only way now was up past the church. Past the entrance to Blackberry Lane, a circuitous route bordering the orchard and eventually coming out, through the new housing, to the bypass.

There was a single track road from here, leading directly to Coleman's Meadow.

'Jane's right,' Lol said. 'You don't get out. If we don't see Bliss we blow the horn.'

'Right.'

'We don't tempt fate,' Lol said.

'No.'

They emerged on to the bypass near the place where Lucy Devenish had died next to her moped. Merrily could tell Lol was thinking about it too. You just did, whenever you passed this way.

'So *he* wrecked the church,' Lol said. 'This guy.'

'The Endtime.' Merrily brought the Volvo down to second gear in the mud-track to Coleman's Meadow. 'The flood, the Antichrist. The whole madness of it. The insane idea that Elliot Stooke and I were working together towards the birth of the Antichrist on Christmas Eve. Leonora could've put all that together from the Lord of the Light website. All the crap you find on the Net. They had this Gregory on the payroll. Told him exactly what to do.'

The damage reinforcing the idea of a dangerously unbalanced

fundamentalist with a fear and hatred of Stooke. If Stooke's drowning was, in the end, not considered accidental, the police would have had Shirley in the frame, and Shirley's attitude would have convinced them they were on the money.

'She'd probably have been judged unfit to plead,' Lol said. 'Case closed.'

Merrily reached out for his hand, knowing he was thinking of his own case, the tunnel-vision of policemen chasing a result.

'Only, the poor woman was mad enough to be in the church,' she said. 'Maybe hiding – we'll never know, will we, how she and this psycho came face to face.'

'She'd been stabbed?'

'Yes.' The car bucked and shuddered over a deep rut in the track. 'Lol, I … I bloody demonised her. As soon as I heard Nick Ellis might have some connection with the Church of the Lord of the Light, that was enough. We don't *know* if Ellis poisoned Shirley's mind from wherever he is, and it doesn't matter really. I should've tried to get through to her. I should've tried. I demonised her just as much as she demonised me.'

The hedges rose up in the headlights, yellow and dripping on either side.

'You did your best,' Lol said. 'You always do your best.'

She tried to smile. It would mend, the church. It would cost, but it would mend. It always had, always would, even if it ended up as a local museum in a secular state where Christianity was just a vaguely tolerated eccentricity.

When they reached the parking area short of the meadow, the clouds had cleared from round the moon. A soiled potato of a moon. You could see Cole Hill, like something dumped on the horizon.

And Gomer's jeep.

Gomer leaning on it, still in his overalls, smoking a ciggy, blinking through his bottle glasses at their headlights. Then he raised a hand and ambled over, grinning his old familiar grin, and Merrily quickly opened one of the back doors for him, and he got in.

'Merry Christmas, vicar. Lol, boy.'

'Gomer …' Merrily switched off the engine. 'You shouldn't be doing this sort of—' She gave up. Pointless. 'Where's Bliss?'

'Went through the gate, him and the other coppers. He'll be all right. This boy en't gonner pick a fight with the whole bunch of 'em, is he?'

Gomer stretched his legs out behind Merrily's seat, ciggy in his mouth, hands across his stomach.

'Been a funny ole couple days, ennit, vicar?'

'Could put it that way,' Lol said.

Merrily thought about a cigarette and something else. Denied herself the cig and leaned over the back of her seat.

'Gomer, you know you said they were using Gerry Murray's JCB on the site – the excavation?'

'Ar.'

'What was Gerry Murray actually doing?'

'Strip the grass off, kind o' thing. I dunno. Bit of a bent deal how he got hisself hired, sure to be.'

'Mmm.' Merrily turned to Lol. 'Would explain how Blore managed to plant modern masonry under one of the stones, wouldn't it? Who could you trust to do it and keep quiet more than the landowner?'

'Blore directing him,' Lol said. 'Then the earth goes back. And all the rain ... all the mud. Couldn't have better conditions. And who's going to challenge his findings? One of the students?'

'We need to make sure Bliss deals with this as well. If we can get it out in court, that's going to turn it all around, and maybe Jane gets her henge. We can win this yet.'

Gomer sat up, listening. A car door slamming. Gomer furiously leaning on the door handle.

'That's my jeep, vicar! Some bugger's in my bloody jeep!'

Hit the door, lurched out of the car and he was off into the dark, like a young, angry man, Merrily crying out,

'No ...'

Turning, in fear, to Lol, but Lol had already gone after Gomer.

God, God, God, God, God ...

She fumbled at the key, started the car, threw on the headlights. Saw the figure coming out of the jeep, one arm raised up. A glinting.

Saw them all for an unending moment in the whitewashed night.

All four of them, three in motion, one still.

CHRISTMAS NIGHT

'Twas strange that people there should walk
And yet I could not hear them talk.

Thomas Traherne
'Shadows in the Water'

'No such thing,' Bliss said. 'Not yet.'

'No?'

'Well, all right, we're getting killers who are *close* to inhuman. When they become *totally* inhuman, detectives will be redundant. Nothing to go on. Nothing to get hold of. I don't wanna be doing this job when that happens.'

Seven o'clock Christmas night.

'It wasn't even rage that did for him,' Bliss said. 'Nothing so over-the-top. It was much smaller, a much more human thing – he was *aggrieved*. He'd been taken advantage of. Exploited. Even *wairse* ...' Bliss could feel his accent dipping into the Mersey. 'He'd been asked to do something *beneath him*. He'd been *dissed*. He was being treated like the odd job man – oh, and on your way, Gregory, if you could just pop into the church. And buy a spray can, would you, there's a good boy.'

'Spends years refining a technique,' Annie Howe said. 'Has this image of himself as a well-oiled killing machine. And he's made a lot of money – an increasing amount of money. And he's realised that the further up-market his clients are – like Lasky – the less chance he has of being nicked.'

'Yeh, but what he may've taken a while to realise is that his clients don't see him as a fellow businessman. They don't respect him – not like he, in some way, respects *them* – you heard the way he talked about Blore. Admiring. This big, confident git with a professorship and a world-class reputation and his own TV show. But when you hear Blore talk about Glyn ...'

'Not that he has yet,' Annie said.

'He will. Sooner or later, he will. He won't be able to hold it in. Not with Glyn running off at the mouth. Some of what Glyn's been saying

– when we tell him – will offend Blore deeply. Hit him right in the intellect.'

'All right,' Annie said. 'So they used him to mess up the church.'

'Daft idea. Overkill. They always went that bit too far, like with Ayling. Glyn's feeling put-on, demeaned, and when this mad woman comes out of the shadows, calling him satanic, demonic, screaming the place down … what's he gonna do? What *can* he do?'

'Stooke was to have been knifed, too, I take it?' Annie said. 'Until someone thought, why not take advantage of the conditions? Blore, I'd guess?'

'Merrily tells me there's a quote from the Bible about the Antichrist being drowned before the Endtime … it's not perfect but it'll do. But Glyn's a knifie. He doesn't like this idea. But because of his respect for Blore, a famous man who still likes a beer with the lads, he'll do it. Waiting out there. Gives Stooke a shout. *Here, mate, giss a hand.* But although he's stronger and fitter it's bloody hard work. Put the blade in, the target's disabled immediately. This way, the target's fighting back, fighting for his life, and you get pissed wet through. Plus, you've gorra hit him and stuff. I'll be interested to see the PM report, what other damage has been done.'

'The worst aspect of this,' Annie said, 'is that Glyn is not, by any normal definition, a psycho. He is – and, ironically, Frederick West was another example – a man doing a job, to the best of his fairly considerable abilities.'

'We're having to move the goalposts,' Bliss said. 'In the old days no remorse was the primary symptom of a psychopath. Nowadays, it's almost the norm in the criminal classes. Conscience is an anachronism. Now whether you could put that down to … what Merrily Watkins, say, would put it down to … I don't know.'

'I'm not sure what *I* know any more.'

Annie rolled over on to her back. Her breasts were quite a bit smaller than Kirsty's and her body was more angular. Her face – most of the time – was more than a touch severe. You could see her bones. Feel her bones. Bliss put a hand on Annie's bare stomach. He could feel the gym in her.

Well, that was OK. It was all OK, really.

And what he really loved – hold on, back off, Frannie – what he *was loving* was the cop pillow talk. You got home after a result, you were high on it, and Kirsty never wanted to know. You did not bring felons into the bedroom.

At some stage, he'd start to hate himself again, about Kirsty and the kids. It was his fault. No question. He hadn't even tried to save it this time. Hell, he'd put a wedge into the split.

He'd nipped over with the presents mid morning, left them in the porch at the farm, buggered off quick. Too soon to discuss visiting rights. Then back to his house in Marden, where she was waiting. She'd even cleaned the place up a bit. Well … changed the duvet cover. Would've been safer to go to Malvern, but they both needed to get back to Gaol Street later. So much to do. So many long hours of interrogation on the schedule. Frigging sublime.

'Something's just struck me,' he said. 'Do you reckon it's conceivable that some small portion of our council tax will have helped pay for the murders of Clement Ayling and Mathew Elliot Stooke?'

'Francis – do not even ponder the question.'

'Hmm. Leonora? Much more to come from her?'

'Thought it was going to be downhill all the way, Francis, but she's quite clever. She's realising that there might be a way of putting Blore firmly into the driving seat. Yes, she'd known him a while. Which she knew could be proved, because she did the pictures for a Sunday magazine feature on him about a year ago. It may well have started there. It was clearly a very strong physical attraction. And the way she talks about Stooke, it's as if he'd served his purpose, time to move on. And, for some reason, he was becoming irritating. Starting to lose it – she said that twice. Lose what?'

'I've talked to Mrs Watkins about this, and I'm definitely not going *there*, and nor will the CPS. Let's just say there's a lorra money to come from Stooke's royalties. Most she'd get would be half if it was divorce. And Blore – not as rich as you might think. Three kids from a defunct marriage to maintain, apparently, down in Surrey. *That's* what the CPS understand.'

Bliss kissed Annie's neck. She put a slim hand over his hand on her stomach.

Charlie's daughter.

Woooh.

They hadn't talked much about Charlie, and he could tell she was in two minds, one of them thinking if it came out through Furneaux, well, at least it would be over. Probably no more than a minor sex-scandal, the procurement of women by Steve in the same way he procured drugs. Control. Except you could only control Charlie when he found it useful to *seem* to be under control.

Bliss had tentatively mentioned it to Annie about an hour ago. Annie who'd become like she was because of Charlie. Because she'd needed to put a big, big space between what she was and what Charlie Howe had been.

'Whatever,' she'd said, hand on the inside of Bliss's thigh. '*This* will hurt him far more profoundly, if he ever finds out.'

'And will he?'

'Might do.' And then she'd said, 'I saw a picture of you and your wife on the sideboard downstairs. She's rather beautiful, isn't she?'

Bliss had raised himself up and looked down at the severe, angular face. He could've told her about the *no felons in the bedroom* rule and a lot of other stuff besides.

'Annie,' he said. 'I've gorra tell you, this is one thing you just don't understand.'

Later he woke up in the dark, the Acting Detective Superintendent still asleep, the curtains open, a scuzzy moon over the chimneys. It hadn't rained for nearly a day. It could even be over.

Bliss and Annie had decided to go for it and nick Blore on suspicion of conspiracy to murder. While they were still waiting for the CPS, Blore had wandered into Gaol Street himself, mid morning. Casually bumptious. Thought he ought to drop in and make a statement about Gregory. He didn't get to walk out. It would be hard going for a while, but when Blore worked out the depth of shite he was in, he might start off by giving them Lyndon Pierce to dilute the mix. And that would rebound.

And they had Gregory. Straightforward, open. Comparatively. Be a star in the slammer – not only could he make a serviceable shiv out of a plastic teaspoon or whatever, but he knew where to put it and he'd have nothing at all to lose.

When you thought about it, he'd had nothing to lose last night on the edge of Coleman's Meadow.

It was clear that Gregory – finally betrayed by Blore's amateurism in the craft of killing – had figured his last hope was to nick Gomer's Jeep and take off across the fields, smashing through barriers, negotiating floods until he was clear.

Bliss had been nauseously sure that one of them – Gomer or Lol Robinson – was going to get the blade.

What had sapped the lad's resolve was hard to figure. According to Terry Stagg, first through the gate, he'd done one precise, calculated downward sweep of the knife through the empty air, at nothing, and the momentum of it had brought him to his knees, the knife burying itself in the earth.

When they'd cuffed him and bagged up the blade, Bliss administering the caution, Gregory had been gazing out over the empty field towards the derelict orchard, and he'd been going, 'Just keep that ole woman away from me, all right? I don't like her.'

And then twice more, 'I don't *like* her.'

Credits, plus ...

They are covering the snake, they are covering the snake,
covering it over. But don't worry. The people that know
will know that it's there, the people that know will know.

Amanda Attfield, 2007

The Dinedor Serpent/Rotherwas Ribbon was discovered by archaeologists just a few months after publication of *The Remains of an Altar*, which described the events leading up to the Cole Hill/Coleman's Meadow revelations. And, as you've just been reading, it led to a similar furious row. Eight protesters were arrested, some detained in cells as far away as Worcester before the charges of aggravated trespass were dropped.

The coincidence was inescapable: same situation, same council. There was no way I could avoid finding out how the serpent might wriggle into the *Dream of the Dead* scenario. The new road, by the way, is now open, although the controversy goes on.

It should be emphasised, however, that none of the councillors or officials in this book is in any way connected with existing or past members of the Herefordshire Council.

And no members of the current Herefordshire Council have ever served on any quango called Hereforward. (Good name though, ennit?)

Many thanks to the archaeologist Jodie Lewis for crucial background on the way digs are organised and financed these days and checking certain chapters. Also to Tracy Thursfield, who knows about these things. However, any damage caused to the archaeological profession and its traditions are entirely down to me. I particularly made a point of not approaching any archaeologists working for Herefordshire Council, so the opinions of Neil Cooper are entirely his own.

Thanks to the people in and around local government in this area who, for obvious reasons, would rather not be named.

In roughly the same period, the Border area was affected by widespread flooding – not as severe as nearby Tewkesbury and Upton-upon-Severn, but still fairly devastating. Many people didn't get home on several nights. Thanks to Mike Eatock for exhaustive technical background on bridge collapses, and his wife, Yvonne, for processing it.

Thanks to Chris Hinsley re. Dinedor and for helping with suggestions for the cover picture which, in the end, was pushed out by the Wern Derys standing stone. This cover was problematic for a long time, and the excellent (and flexible) John Mason spent many long days exploring possibilities.

Disturbances connected with ancient sites: thanks to John Moss, of the British Society of Dowsers, and Clare Dewhurst, who told me about her experience at Avebury.

Thanks to Hereford journalist Sally Boyce. Fiona Hopes, of the Gatekeeper Trust; Maggy Anthony, for inspirational thoughts on the origins of a complex kind of atheism; Peter Bell for a Hereford trader's viewpoint.

To Peter Brooks for parish affairs, guardians, Endtime and other problems. Michael Nicholson for artistic considerations.

Melvyn Pritchard, for letting me have a quick go on his JCB.

Allan Watson for the citrine and giving me the Elbow.

Karen Dowell, who donated her name a few years ago, probably never suspecting that the then DC Dowell, who she does *not* resemble, would get promoted into regular service.

Bernard Knight for an eleventh-hour advice re stabbing people accurately.

Gabrielle Drake and Cally for oiling wheels, re Nick Drake, and Kobalt Music Publishing Limited, 4 Valentine Place London SE1 4QH for permission to quote the lines from Nick's 'River Man'.

Bev Craven for his brilliant designs for the Ledwardine Leisurewear collection, available exclusively from the tireless Terry Smith – details on the website www.philrickman.co.uk, designed and maintained by Krys and Geoff Boswell and Jack.

Jonathan Black's *The Secret History of the World* (Quercus) planted some seeds.

On the editorial side, endless, heartfelt thanks to Carol, who slaved for so many weeks and always thought of ways out. And, in the Endtime, to long-suffering copy-editor Nick Austin and my agent, Andrew Hewson, who read the MS twice in two days, as we ran out of injury time and into penalty shootouts. Finally to Nic Cheetham, Georgina Difford, Laura Palmer and Lucy Ramsey at Quercus, for ultimate patience and unfazeability.

The saying, *To dream of the dead is a sign of rain*, was told to Ella Mary Leather, author of *The Folklore of Herefordshire* by a Mrs Powell, of Dorstone.

Thank you, Mrs Powell.